The
SECRET LIFE
of
JOSEPHINE

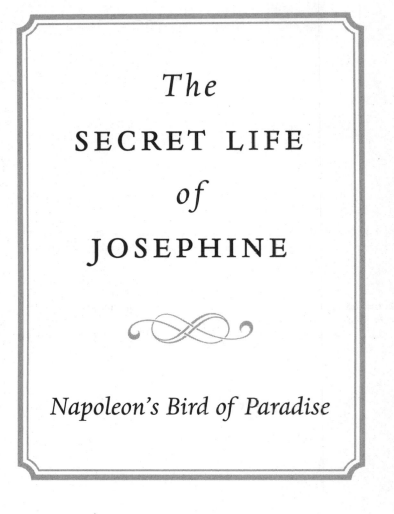

The
SECRET LIFE
of
JOSEPHINE

Napoleon's Bird of Paradise

CAROLLY ERICKSON

ST. MARTIN'S PRESS 〽 NEW YORK

This is a work of fiction. All of the characters, organizations, and events portrayed in this novel are either products of the author's imagination or are used fictitiously.

www.stmartins.com

Design by Sara Gabkin

LIBRARY OF CONGRESS CATALOGING-IN-PUBLICATION DATA

Erickson, Carolly, 1943–
    The secret life of Josephine : Napoleon's bird of paradise / Carolly Erickson. —
1st ed.
        p. cm.
    ISBN-13: 978-0-312-36735-0
    ISBN-10: 0-312-36735-X
1. Josephine, Empress, consort of Napoleon I, Emperor of the French, 1763–1814—Fiction.
2. Napoleon I, Emperor of the French, 1769–1821—Fiction. 3. France—Kings and rulers—
        Fiction. 4. Empresses—France—Fiction. I. Title.

PS3605.R53S43 2007
813'.6—dc22
2007021013

First Edition: September 2007

10   9   8   7   6   5   4   3   2   1

To the memory of my dear mother Louise Kiger Bliss

(1912–2006)

Malmaison, March 1814

MY EYES ARE WEAKER NOW, I seem to live in a perpetual twilight. I cannot do needlework any more, the stitches are too small for me to see, so I sit beside the window in the long afternoons, looking out at the red and pink blur of my roses, while Christian—dear man!—reads to me from a box of old love letters I cherish.

I have great plans, but they have come to a temporary halt, and it is frustrating to me, sitting here, my eyes dimming, tears sometimes coming unbidden to wet my lined cheeks, cheeks that were once plump and pink but now are wrinkled and reddened from the rouge-pot.

I may not be able to see my reflection very clearly any longer, but I am more careful than ever to maintain my good looks. I have a skilled hairdresser who comes every day to arrange my hair and when she threads bands of silver through the dark dyed strands it looks quite charming and youthful—or so the flatterers from Paris tell me.

They come in their hundreds, the visitors from Paris, even though the spring is chilly, and my gardens are not yet in full bloom.

"Is she still beautiful?" I hear them say to one another as they pass below my window. "Or has she shriveled and withered, now that she no longer wears a crown? Now that the former emperor no longer loves her? She must be fifty years old now! She must have lost her looks."

They make me smile, the envious Parisians. I was never truly one of them, always an outsider, even in the days of my greatest exaltation, when the Emperor Napoleon Bonaparte himself put the crown on my head. They sneered at me, though they always feared me for the power I had over Bonaparte. He ruled them, and I ruled him.

I can still look beautiful, or so I am told. And I am more of a celebrity now than ever, because I was once Bonaparte's wife and because I am wealthy and have an infamous past.

Let the Parisians sneer! I am what most of them will never be. I am—myself. No one owns me. I live as I choose, even if my eyes are growing dim and my throat hurts and my migraines have returned, despite the leeches the doctors put on my neck and arms and feet to draw out the poisons.

I don't allow others to watch that, only Euphemia, from whom I have no secrets. The doctors rub my forehead and apply compresses to my sore eyes and wash me and cover me with toilet water to disguise the stinks of age. Not until the doctors have left and I am fresh and sweet-smelling do I allow Christian in, to read to me from my casque of letters preserved from long ago.

I sit back against my pink satin pillows and close my eyes and listen, the dear words of love still fresh after so long.

"My rose of Roses, my beautiful Mademoiselle Tascher, the memory of you enchants me," Christian reads. "I cannot wait to hold you in my arms again. Until we meet once again, I kiss your hands, your eyes, your lips, your everything."

My first love note from Scipion du Roure, the officer I fell in love with on a May night in Martinique, when the moon was full. I was fifteen, he was nineteen. He was promised to a woman in France, as I later found out. But that did not matter. Nothing mattered that night but the cool, soft moonlight, and the sound of the waves breaking on the white sand below the veranda where we danced, and the intoxicating scent of jasmine in the air.

As I listen to Christian read the letters I am carried back to that night, to the music of the violins and flutes and guitars playing the Ronde Sentimentale, while the crickets chirp in the tamarisks and hibiscus. Scipion, blond, beautiful Scipion takes my gloved hand and raises it to his lips . . .

I

THAT NIGHT, the night I first met Scipion du Roure, all I could think of was the ball and my gown of pale yellow silk and the garland of fragrant white flowering jasmine Euphemia had woven into my hair. I hummed as I dressed, practicing walking in the wide skirt on its stiff wire frame and glancing at my reflection in the pier glass that stood in the middle of my bedroom.

My eyes were bright, my skin warm and glowing in the candlelight. I remember thinking, I am beautiful. Every man at the ball will want to dance with me.

I was living with my parents in Martinique on the plantation known as Les Trois-Ilets, the Three Little Islands. The year was 1778. My poor harassed father Joseph Tascher was drinking far too much and going deeper and deeper into debt, and my mother and grandmother were hounding him relentlessly. I tried to ignore their arguing—they argued a lot—and keep my thoughts on the ball to come. But the raised voices were hard to ignore.

"You must ask your brother for another loan," my mother was insisting. "Do not wait. Ride to Fort-Royal tonight."

"Gladly, my dear," was my father's wry response. "Only I know what his answer will be. No more loans. Not until I agree to make him co-owner of Les Trois-Ilets, and name his son as my sole heir."

"Your sole heir, indeed," sniffed my grandmother. "If you were man enough you'd have sons instead of daughters."

My grandmother Catherine des Sannois, who was born plain Catherine Brown on a farm in Dundreary, had the fiery temper of her Irish ancestors and never lost a chance to criticize my highborn father.

"And if my wife did her duty she would give me sons. The fault is hers."

"How dare you speak to me in that way when I nearly died giving birth to the last one?" My mother rose from her chair and approached my father accusingly. "And how dare you show such disrespect for poor Catherine, and her in her grave these past two months!" My sister Catherine, who had been frail and sickly most of her life, had finally succumbed to a fever and was buried in the little church on our plantation.

"I wish to heaven you were in your graves too," I heard my father mutter as he turned aside. "Then we could all have some peace."

"Peace? peace? You talk of peace, when everything you do upsets the rest of us?" My grandmother continued her harangue. "You neglect your daughters. Neither of them is betrothed. You neglect your wife. How many mistresses do you have there in Fort-Royal? Three? Six? And with how many octoroon bastards who look like you? Worst of all you neglect this plantation, which my husband and I gave you, worthless idler that you are, so that your family would not starve. Look at it! Where are the cane fields? Returned to the wild. Where are the slaves? Run away, most of them. What do you have to show for seventeen years of ownership? A fine plantation in ruins! That's what! And a family on the brink of starvation!"

Father took out his silver flask and drank from it, his lined face weary and his thin, greying hair coming loose from his untidily tied bag wig. In that moment, while there was a pause in the combat, I came forward to show off my gown.

I walked slowly past father, mother and Grandma Sannois. I saw a light come into my father's eyes as he watched me, and knew it for a gleam of admiration. My grandmother nodded. "It's time she was betrothed," she said curtly. "Past time." My mother looked me over critically, from the top of my garlanded head to the gleaming bows on my yellow satin slippers.

"Watch out for the men," was all she said.

THE NARROW, twisting torchlit streets of Fort-Royal shone yellow under the moon as our carriage—really a cart, with a makeshift canvas top tied on to shield us from rain—climbed the hillside toward my uncle's imposing house above Fort-Royal Bay. My Uncle Robert Tascher was commandant of the harbor, and he and his family lived well. Some five hundred guests, drawn from the best society—the Grands Blancs, as we were known, the Great Whites, or Europeans—were to attend the ball on this night, and I was among those fortunate enough to be invited.

I was chaperoned by my Aunt Rosette, my father and Uncle Robert's tremulous, withdrawn spinster sister. She was the perfect companion, all but silent and extremely unprepossessing in her old green gown with the faded crimson rosettes—the same one she wore to every party and ball. She never interfered with my good times. I knew she admired and envied me, for she had never been good-looking and indeed she seemed to fade into the wallpaper in any room she entered.

The air was humid, and my yellow silk gown was already damp with perspiration when we arrived at the imposing front gate of Uncle Robert's mansion. The curls my maid Euphemia had arranged across my broad forehead with such care clung wetly to my skin.

Once inside, I drank thirstily from the cup of rum punch a tall African servant handed to me, and asked for another. I sat down by an open window and let the music of the orchestra, the murmur of voices, the susurration of the bright swaying gowns and the welcome play of the wind off the bay wash over me.

I did not sit there long. Soon a young man came up to me and asked me to dance, and then another and another. I danced every dance, I remember, and as the evening wore on I began to feel dizzy when I turned and twirled in the steps of the quadrille and minuet. I was glad when there came a lull in the music and some of the guests began to leave.

Then, before I knew it, a man in a smart uniform was bending down toward me, and extending his hand. I looked up, and saw his fine grey eyes fixed on me, a mischievous smile on his full lips.

"Lieutenant Scipion du Roure, mademoiselle. Will you do me the honor of dancing with me?"

I floated, I walked on air, I melted into his arms—and all too soon our dance was at an end.

"Come for a walk with me," he whispered as he kissed my gloved hand in parting. "Meet me by the mango tree in half an hour." There was a huge old mango beside the veranda of Uncle Robert's mansion. I had no doubt that was the tree he meant. I felt a tingle of anticipation, for it never occurred to me not to meet him.

"Watch out for the men," my mother had cautioned me, but in that moment I forgot her warning. My only thought was, how will I slip away? My Aunt Rosette, my self-effacing chaperone, had been watching me dance all evening long while eating from a plate of vanilla custards. As I went up to her I saw that she had eaten too many, and looked ill. As I approached she hastily put her plate down and wiped her mouth with the back of one ungloved hand.

"You look tired, Aunt Rosette. I'm sure Uncle Robert could find you somewhere to lie down."

She gave me a sharp look. "You know I cannot leave as long as you are here. You cannot be abandoned without a relative to watch over you."

"But I won't be abandoned. Aunt Louise is here." As hostess of the ball my aunt was, of course, present in the large room, though hundreds of guests milled about between her and me.

A look of pain crossed Aunt Rosette's face, and she put her hand over her stomach.

"You need some oil of wintergreen, Aunt Rosette—and now, without delay." I reached for her free hand and she let me lead her down a corridor to where a clutch of servants stood, out of sight of the dancers in the ballroom, watching the festivities through a partially open door. Among the servants I recognized Denise, the housekeeper.

Over Aunt Rosette's increasingly feeble protests Denise and I persuaded her to rest in a darkened room and to drink an infusion of oil of wintergreen. Leaving her in Denise's care I hurried back to the ballroom and out along the veranda toward the garden. The huge mass of the great mango tree, heavy with green fruit, its wide branches gleaming in the silvery moonlight, stood out from the tall palms and flowering tamarisks around it. At the foot of the tree stood Scipion du Roure in his smart blue naval uniform, leaning nonchalantly against the trunk, arms folded. He smiled as he watched me approach. As I came up to him he held out his hand.

"There you are, my lovely Bird of Paradise."

I stripped off my gloves and took his outstretched hand. His smile was languid, seductive—though I did not know those words at the age of fifteen. I knew only that I was excited to be meeting him, and that our meeting was all the more exciting to me because it was forbidden. For us to be alone together in the dark garden, with only the sleepy birds and croaking frogs for company, was outside the rules of conduct for Grands Blancs. I liked breaking the rules. And I liked the name he called me. Bird of Paradise.

We walked hand in hand along a stonework path that led to the shore of the wide bay. As a child I had walked that path many times before, with my cousins, on our way to the beach to swim. But we had always gone in the daytime, never at night. I had never before seen the silver path made by the moon's reflection in the waters of the broad bay, or felt the balm of the cool night air on my fevered cheeks. And I had never before inhaled such a powerful scent from the night-blooming jasmine that lined the path on either side, a scent that put the fragrance of my own jasmine garland to shame.

In response to my eager questions Scipion told me that he was nineteen years old, and a lieutenant aboard the frigate *Intrepid*. He had served for three years and had been wounded twice. My eyes widened as he described a skirmish between his ship and the British vessel *Orkney* only a few miles from where we stood, how his vessel had come alongside the *Orkney* and he and his men had boarded her, swords in hand. He lifted his hair up to show me his right ear, which bore a long red scar.

"English musket fire," he said. "I was lucky. It only grazed my ear. It could have taken my head off."

"But we are not at war with the British. I heard my father tell our steward that we are not."

Scipion looked grim. "We will be, before long. That's why they spy on us from their lookout posts on St. Lucia. They know it is only a matter of time before war comes."

All my life, it seemed, we had been fighting the British. They coveted our islands, the Windward Islands. Above all they wanted our island of Martinique.

"My father worries that they will invade Martinique and take our plantation."

"Then we must hope that if they come, I and my brother officers will defend you." He smiled. "And in any event, I do not think they will come tonight."

I took off my slippers and stockings and we walked along the beach, in the smooth white sand, avoiding the scuttling crabs and staying out of the way of the incoming waves that flung themselves up onto the shore in a froth of white. Scipion held my hand tightly, and I gripped his in return. He bent down and brushed my cheek with his lips.

"How old are you, Rose?"

"Fifteen."

He drew back in surprise.

"You look eighteen at least. But then, if you were eighteen, you would probably be married. Girls marry early here, I understand."

"I have no dowry."

"Ah. Good breeding but no money. A familiar situation. Still, you have beauty."

I warmed to his words, suddenly wishing my father wasn't poor. Would Scipion want to marry me, I wondered, if I had a dowry of twenty thousand livres like my cousin Julie, Uncle Robert's daughter?

We walked on a ways in silence. Presently we came to a rocky outcrop that marked the end of the beach.

"Behind these rocks there's a cave," I told Scipion. "The old Carib chiefs used to hold their ceremonies there. They sacrificed animals to their gods, and prayed for rain, and healed people of their diseases."

"The priests say that's just heathen nonsense. Only the Christian God has such powers."

"A Carib chief healed our priest at Les Trois-Ilets when he nearly died of fever."

"It was your prayers, Bird of Paradise, that cured him."

I didn't argue. I knew that many outsiders to our island did not believe in the power of the Carib gods, or the African gods the slaves worshipped. But then, there were many who no longer believed in the Christian god either, especially in France. Or so I had heard my father's friends say.

The last part of our walk was the best. I will never forget how I felt as Scipion escorted me back along the beach and through the garden to Uncle Robert's mansion. We hardly spoke at all, but our feelings spoke for us. How my heart pounded when he kissed me under the mango tree! And how sad was our parting as he left me there, promising to visit me at Les Trois-Ilets as soon as he could.

I cried, I rejoiced, I danced, I despaired. I was not the same from one moment to the next. How could I be, when I was so giddy from the lateness of the hour, the exertion, the lingering effect of the rum punch—and most of all, the touch of his hand and the feel of his lips there in the dark garden, under the spreading mango tree.

2

THE FOLLOWING AFTERNOON I SET OUT, all on my own, to climb the tall volcanic mountain called Morne Granthéaume in search of Orgulon, the most feared of all the quimboiseurs, our island sorcerers. It was a hot afternoon, but as soon as I entered the dim green rain forest that cloaked the hillside I felt cool under its shady canopy. Slippery wet leaves beneath my feet made walking difficult, and the farther I went into the greenish depths of the forest the more I had to push my way past liana vines and creepers that caught in my hair and clutched at my gown.

No one except my maid Euphemia knew where I was. Had they known, my parents would have sent some of the slaves after me and punished me by locking me in my room or forbidding me to ride my mare for a month. Euphemia had tried to dissuade me from going to look for Orgulon, calling me a ninny and a lovesick fool.

"Now I ask you," she said to me as I was preparing to leave, "how stupid can one girl be? Don't you know Orgulon can kill you with one look? Haven't I told you about those bad quimboiseurs from the time you were a little girl, afraid of the dark and clinging to me while I sang you to sleep?"

Euphemia had been there all my life, taking care of me, warning me about the things that come in the night to do harm. She seemed very old and wise and I had always heeded what she said. She wasn't like the other

African slaves on our plantation, for she had very light café-au-lait skin and she spoke the creole French of the Grands Blancs with hardly a trace of an African accent. It was understood that she was my half-sister, the daughter of one of my father's African mistresses. She was clearly worried about me now, and when she worried, she scolded.

"I heard a story in the marketplace about Orgulon," she went on. "He made a man's heart shrivel up inside his body, just because he didn't like the way the man was whistling!"

"That's just another idle tale from the marketplace. Most of what you hear there isn't true, Euphemia, and you know it."

"Oh, I believe this. This really happened."

"I've heard frightening stories too. But now I need Orgulon's help. I must have a charm to make Scipion du Roure love me. I must know my future. Will I marry him?"

"This man you just met last night, at the ball. This Scipion. This is the one you want to risk your life over."

"Yes."

"Even though you may never see him again."

"My heart tells me I will see him—and that he will love me. But I must be sure. I must have a charm! And Orgulon has the best ones. The strongest ones. Everybody says so."

Euphemia threw up her hands and said something in her mother's language, the Ibo tongue, and turned away from me. She said nothing further until I was going out the door.

"Don't go blaming me if you get killed up there on Morne Panthéaume. I tried to tell you not to go."

"If I get killed, I can't very well blame anybody, can I?"

As I made my way along beneath the green canopy, my feet slipping on the rotting leaves, I began to feel uneasy. I had heard that Orgulon lived in a cave high up on the mountain, at a place called the Sacred Crossroads, a place of ceremonies, but I had never been there and only knew of it from hearing the slaves gossip as they went about their work. I trusted that all paths going up the mountainside would lead to the Sacred Crossroads. But as the path turned upward and became steep, and the going got much harder, I began to wonder whether my assumption was correct.

The path twisted and turned, winding upward out of the jungle and around sharp jutting boulders, past shallow caves where water dripped and formed pools. Birds called in the thick underbrush and on the higher slopes above I could glimpse mountain goats with tall horns. Here and there a rockslide obscured the path and made the climb so difficult that I almost turned back. But just then I caught sight of something strange: a cairn of rocks with the bodies of many small birds, their entrails spilling out, arranged in a circle.

It must be a sign, I thought. A sign that I am on the path to the Sacred Crossroads.

My slippers had become clumps of mud and my toes squelched with each step. My gown too was muddy, and my long hair, which was full of twigs, had come free of its fastenings and spilled down my back and over my cheeks. I longed for a cool drink and a bath, but I kept on, climbing higher, heartened by fresh discoveries of cairns with the bodies of slain toucans and macaws.

Clouds covered the top of Morne Canthéaume and it was beginning to rain, a hard rain that pelted down on the rotting leaves, when I first heard the drumming. It was a low, distant sound, hardly more than a whisper at first, but as I climbed higher the noise became louder and more distinct. I had often heard the slaves drumming at night at Les Trois-Ilets, I knew the sound well. I moved toward it now, confident that I was close to finding Orgulon.

The sound of the drums grew louder, and I could discern singing and clapping. There was an electricity in the air, I sensed the presence of others though I could not yet see them.

Suddenly the growth on either side of the path gave way and I found myself at the edge of a large clearing. There must have been a hundred slaves, the men in nothing but loincloths, the women in thin shifts, some with babies in their arms, all moving to the rhythm of the drums. At the center of the clearing was a thick tree trunk, the tree having been severed, and standing on the trunk was a tall, thin old man wearing a red cloak and with red feathers in his scraggly grey hair. Though clearly elderly he was powerful, with his necklace of shark's teeth and bits of what looked like shriveled flesh, his skin a rich glowing black and his long, thin arms outstretched, his head flung back as if in rapturous expectation.

I was so awestruck at the sight of the clearing, the dancing people and above all the red-cloaked man that I forgot to consider what effect I myself might have. A dishevelled young girl in a muddy linen gown and dirty slippers, a girl of the Grand Blancs, entering the ceremonies at the

Sacred Crossroads—for that is what I assumed the place to be—was bound to evoke a reaction.

But to my amazement, the dancers appeared to take no notice of me whatsoever. So intent were they on their dancing and singing, so caught up in the rhythm of the drums, that I was not even a momentary distraction. Hurriedly I retreated to the safety of the path, and hid in the thick wet undergrowth.

How long I stayed there I do not remember. Quite possibly I too was caught up in the sounds and rhythms around me, and lost track of time. The afternoon sun was already below the top of Morne Ganthéaume and the sky was beginning to glow with the fiery reds and pinks of sunset when the drumming stopped and Orgulon (I had no doubt it was the great quimboiseur Orgulon himself) began to speak. In a loud voice he half-talked, half-chanted in an African language, while a fire was lit and scented herbs were thrown into it to suffuse the air with pungent odors.

A huge sow was led in, squealing and protesting, and Orgulon took a cane knife and slit her throat. Immediately the celebrants rushed forward to catch the blood of the dying animal in hollow coconut shells and drink it, anointing themselves with what remained until the entire clearing, or so it seemed from my vantage point, was red with gore.

I had had nothing to eat or drink since leaving home hours earlier, and I was beginning to feel queasy and ill. The metallic smell of the sow's blood turned my stomach. I longed to run down the mountain and return home, but I was far too tired. I lay flat on the sodden earth and closed my eyes, willing my nausea to pass.

3

I MUST HAVE SLEPT, for when I again became aware of my surroundings it was dark, I was very cold and the sky was full of stars—the brilliant stars of Martinique, which are not like white diamonds in the sky but come in many colors: flashing red, bright yellow, brilliant blue. I raised myself up on one elbow and saw that the clearing was empty, the fire gone to glowing embers. I had an urge to go nearer to the fire, to draw whatever warmth I could from it. I began to stand up, feeling my limbs stiff and sore, when a voice stopped me.

"Don't move!"

I recognized the voice. It was Orgulon, and the words he spoke were French. But I could not see him.

"Stay where you are, girl!"

Shivering with cold and fear, I obeyed as best I could.

I heard a loud thump, then another and another. I shut my eyes tightly and gritted my teeth.

"There. It is all right now. It's dead."

I opened my eyes. Orgulon, in his red cloak, stood before me, holding a long dangling thing by its tail.

"The fer-de-lance. It came for you. I felt it coming. I knew you must not die. So I killed it." He turned and walked into the clearing, and as he passed the dying fire he threw the carcass of the snake into it.

My heart was beating very fast and I was panting for breath. Orgulon had killed the snake that was going to kill me—for the bite of the dreaded fer-de-lance is always deadly. Orgulon saved my life. The great quimboiseur who might have killed me with a glance had used his power to preserve me.

I scrambled to my feet and followed him to the opposite end of the clearing, where an open-fronted tent had been erected and a blanket spread out on the wet earth. A calabash full of water, a plate of fried plantains and a flagon of rum were laid on the blanket. Orgulon stretched himself out and began to eat and drink.

I approached the tent slowly. With a rough, impatient gesture he beckoned me to come closer. I saw that his hands were clawlike, with long cracked yellow nails. I wondered how old he was. Quimboiseurs were said to live for centuries, and to have no fear of death.

"Revered Monsieur Orgulon, I thank you for saving my life." I heard my voice tremble as I spoke, and realized that I was still recovering from the terror I had felt only moments earlier.

He looked up from his plate of plantains. I saw that he was grotesquely ugly, blind in one eye and with few remaining teeth. An odor of rot emanated from him, a stink so strong it made me want to draw back.

"You think you are here to see me. No. I will tell you what you need to know. You have a life across the great water. I saved you so you could live that life. A demon sent the snake. Beware of that demon! I killed the creature, but not the one that sent him."

Impulsively I interrupted Orgulon. "Will I marry Scipion du Roure?"

The old man waved his hand dismissively. "He does not matter. You do. You have been saved for a purpose." He went back to his food and drink, and though I asked him several more questions, he ignored me. I stood waiting, wrapping my arms around myself for warmth, unsure what I should do. At length he ate the last of the plantains and drank deeply from the flagon, wiping his mouth with the back of his clawlike hand.

As if at a signal two men with lit torches came toward the tent and removed the plate and brought Orgulon a long pipe, which he began to smoke. He spoke a few words to the men in a language I did not understand. They went back into the bush and reemerged with a sort of hammock slung between two poles. They motioned to me to lie down in the hammock and, exhausted as I was, I gladly did as they indicated. I felt no fear, only weariness as, hoisting the sling onto their shoulders so that I was suspended between them, the two men set off along the path that led down the mountain, under the brilliant stars.

4

I HAD EXPECTED to find Les Trois-Ilets in turmoil on my return from
Morne Ganthéaume. My father, I thought, would be out looking for me
with search parties of slaves and members of the local militia, which he
commanded. My mother and grandmother would be frantic with worry,
Euphemia would be weeping hysterically and even my sister Manette,
young as she was at only eleven, would be awake and wondering where
I had gone and why I had stayed there so long.

But in fact, all was quiet when I was set down on the veranda by the
two men who had carried me down the mountain. The plantation
buildings were in darkness. I made my way inside the converted sugar
mill where we lived and along the hallway to my bedroom where
Euphemia, wrapped in a voluminous pink nightgown, sat quietly reading
by candlelight.

"So you're back," she said. "At last. Now I can go to sleep."

Instead of being relieved and thankful that I had gotten away with my
dangerous escapade I was a little annoyed. No one had missed me,
apparently. Was I of such little consequence?

Euphemia was chuckling to herself.

"I told them you couldn't come down to dinner because you ate some
bad crabs and you were throwing up all over everything. That kept them
away, I can tell you!"

"Didn't father come to look in on me after dinner?"

Euphemia sniffed. "Your father is in Fort-Royal. With his quatroon mistress. Your mother was very upset. She said she had a headache and went to bed early."

I yawned and lay on my bed without even turning down the covers, suddenly aware of how exhausted I was.

"I assume you did not find Orgulon."

"Oh, I found him," I answered sleepily. "And he talked to me."

Euphemia got up from her chair, suddenly alert, and came over to my bed.

"Yes? What did he say? Did he frighten you?"

"A snake frightened me. A fer-de-lance."

She gasped, crossed herself and murmured a prayer in her mother's speech.

"It's all right. Orgulon killed it. He saved my life."

Euphemia would not let me sleep. She demanded to know all about my journey up Morne Granthéaume and every detail of my encounter with the quimboiseur at the Sacred Crossroads. Her eyes were wide as I told her what Orgulon had said about Scipion du Roure and about my being an important person, saved for a purpose. And about the demon, and the life I would have across the great water.

As I told the story it sounded almost too farfetched to be believed, yet she believed me. Was I imagining it, or was she a bit in awe of me from that time on, because of what Orgulon had said? She took off my muddy slippers and ruined stockings and brought a quilt to cover me, sitting beside my bed in her rocking chair and watching over me until I fell asleep.

I slept until well past noon the next day, and when I awoke I sat in the big metal bathing tub for what seemed like hours, while Euphemia poured scalding water over me again and again, washing away the grime and mud from my scratched legs and arms. Finally I felt clean, and put on a fresh gown of lilac-colored linen for the evening meal.

"Ah, Yeyette," my father greeted me when I came to the table, "we've just been talking about you. Are you recovered?"

"Yes, father."

"Good." I sensed tension in the room, and noticed that neither my mother nor my grandmother was looking directly at me; they kept their eyes on the floor, looked out the windows, glanced at each other—but did not look in my direction.

My father cleared his throat and took a drink from his cup of rum. "Yeyette, we have had another letter from your Aunt Edmée in Paris."

Aunt Edmée, my father's lovely blond sister, wrote to us often, always urging that my sisters and I be sent to France to stay with her so that we could go to a good convent school and acquire a pure Parisian accent to replace our provincial creole speech. We must be turned into Frenchwomen, my aunt said in all her letters, so that we could marry well and enter good society. Aunt Edmée always spoke of us in her letters as "the three sisters," though of course we were now only two. My father replied to most of Edmée's letters, and always said the same thing: that he could not afford to send us to France. I regretted our lack of money deeply. Nothing would have delighted me more than to make the journey to Paris.

"Let me read her letter to you," he went on, putting on his glasses and unfolding the thick sheet.

> "My dear Joseph,
> I am writing in haste to tell you excellent news which I am sure will benefit our entire family. Our dear Alexandre, who is now seventeen years old and a junior officer in the Sarre regiment, desires to marry one of your daughters. Once he is married he will begin to receive his inheritance, which is an annual income of forty thousand livres. Please obtain passage on the next ship for yourself and one of your daughters. I will order her trousseau once she arrives in Paris. No time must be lost.
>
> Ever your affectionate
> Edmée Renaudin"

"Can I go please, father? I never liked Alexandre much, but I'm sure I will love Paris." I hugged myself and held my breath, watching my father's face.

"I am not convinced that we should send either of you girls to Paris," my mother said. "I don't trust Edmée. She's a schemer."

"The scheme," said my father icily, "is quite transparent, my dear. The boy wants his money. For that he needs a wife. If we provide one, he will overlook her lack of dowry and reward us by saving us from bankruptcy."

"And what of Edmée's profit in this scheme?"

"Ha! That's easy enough to guess," said my plain-featured, iron-grey-haired grandmother, who had a low opinion of the beautiful Edmée. "Her old lover Beauharnais is dying. How old is he now? Sixty? Sixty-five? And gouty and feeble, from what I hear from my acquaintances in the capital. Edmée won't get any of his fortune when he dies—she's only his mistress, after all—so she wants to marry his son Alexandre to her niece. That way she knows she will get her share, in time."

"How accurately you put it, mother-in-law. And how discreetly. But you overlook the obvious. We too will be part of the scheme. We will profit more than Edmée will. Yeyette will go to France, marry a well-to-do officer, and live a life of comfort, sending money to us every month here in Martinique. Won't you, Yeyette?" I nodded vigorously, afraid to speak. "We can sell Les Trois-Ilets and move to Fort-Royal—"

"Never!" Father was interrupted by mother, whose loud utterance made my ears ring.

Father sighed, grandmother snorted.

"If you send me to Paris, I will give you every sou Alexandre lets me have. Enough to buy you a new plantation if you like."

"Thank you, Yeyette, but I don't believe your husband will be quite that rich."

I thought of Alexandre, blond and fair like Scipion but superior in his manner and fastidious and snobbish. I had not seen Alexandre in eight years, not since he had left Martinique when he was nine years old and I was six. I remembered him very well indeed. He had lived with us all my life and most of his, tormenting me and my sister Catherine and being tormented in turn by bigger and tougher boys who called him a sissy. Adults liked Alexandre because he was polite to them, and highly intelligent. We children hated him because he was mean and arrogant.

But what did any of that matter? I would be going to Paris—if only my mother would agree. But of course she would agree, she had to. Hadn't Orgulon told me that I would go across the water and live my important life there? Here was my opportunity.

After three days of arguments, during which Euphemia and I quietly packed my trunks—for we both felt certain that I would go to France—my mother relented and my father had his way. He inquired at Fort-Royal and found a ship bound for the harbor of Brest. I said my tearful goodbyes to Scipion and, full of excitement, prepared to embark.

But on the day we were to go, we suddenly heard the booming of cannon across the bay in Fort-Royal. The English navy, we learned, had seized the nearby island of St. Lucia and were attempting to invade Martinique. My father, ordinarily so indolent, rode swiftly to summon the militia. Our family barricaded ourselves in the sugar mill. Our navy fought the English, as I prayed for Scipion's safety.

There was no way I could go to France to be married. I was trapped on our island, and no one, not even Orgulon, could release me.

5

FOR MONTHS WE WERE AT WAR, and it was during those months that I had a series of strange experiences that I have never spoken of to anyone. Experiences that revealed to me something vital about who I am.

There was a boy who came around the plantation at dusk, and watched for me. Sometimes I saw him lurking in the shadows, or hiding in the bushes near the mill. Once I thought I saw him in a long line of convicts chained together, walking along a path beside one of our fallow fields. Often he came to the beach at Les Trois-Ilets, that loveliest of white sand beaches where Euphemia took Manette and me to swim in the clear aquamarine water and watch the dolphins leap and dive farther out toward the islands in the bay.

The boy never quite revealed himself fully, he stayed mostly out of sight but he made sure I caught tantalizing glimpses of him and he seemed to sense that I welcomed his presence—how, I don't know.

He wasn't like anyone else. That is, he wasn't a laborer or a member of the Grands Blancs (though he dressed in the ragged remains of a nobleman's embroidered waistcoat and breeches) and he did not have the look of a townsman from Fort-Royal. I wondered whether he might be a renegade from a titled family in France (we had a number of these on the island, exiles from all that was familiar to them, strangers in our midst and nearly all of them wretchedly unhappy) or a runaway soldier or even a pirate or smuggler. But a pirate would be away at sea for long periods of time, I reasoned, while this boy was nearly always there at Les Trois-Ilets, at dusk, and smugglers were rich, far too rich to dress the way he did, in castoff finery.

He was an enigma, and that made him all the more interesting to me. And, of course, I liked the way he looked. His long dark straight hair was tied back loosely off his neck, with one brown lock hanging down over one eye. His face, deeply tanned from the tropical sun, was lean, his lips full, his eyes a deep brown. His torn shirt was open at the neck, showing his muscular chest. He was lithe, like a panther, when he moved.

Had Euphemia seen the boy, she would surely have yelled at him and shooed him away, for he didn't belong on our land and for all I knew he might have been planning to break into the mill and steal the money (very little money, in actuality) my father kept in a chest in his bedroom. But he was clever; he didn't let Euphemia see him. I had the feeling that he only revealed himself to me.

I found myself watching for him each evening at dusk, finding excuses to sit near a window with my embroidery frame or even, when I was feeling bold, to sit out on our veranda and pretend to be watching the sunset—when in fact I was watching for the intriguing boy.

I was of course greatly preoccupied with Scipion during those months, though he was on duty most of the time, on his ship guarding the harbor and occasionally engaged in a skirmish with the English fleet. He came ashore from time to time and visited me, and between visits he sent me love letters and keepsakes wrapped in squares of silk and tied in wide satin ribbons. His visits were intense, and passionate. We went riding on the grounds of the estate, or we met at my uncle's house and walked in the gardens or, every month or so, Scipion took me to a dinner or ball given in Fort-Royal by one of his senior officers. We were often alone, and then he took me in his arms and kissed me.

Scipion was in anguish over the fact that I would be leaving Martinique as soon as peace was restored and going to France.

"How can you think of marrying that fop Alexandre de Beauharnais when you could stay right here and marry another Grand Blanc?" Scipion knew Alexandre slightly, his squadron was based in Brest as was Alexandre's regiment.

"It is all arranged within our families," I said. "I have nothing to say about it. Besides, you will not be in Martinique forever. You and I can meet in Paris." I moved closer to him and smiled up at him in a way that always made his face go soft with longing. By this time, Scipion had told me that he was engaged, to the daughter of a marquis, an engagement that had been in place since they were children.

"Besides," I said, "you would object to any man I married, whether here in Martinique or elsewhere."

"I will be jealous, yes. Perhaps I shall challenge your Alexandre to a duel, and shoot him."

"I warn you, he is a very good shot. Or so my aunt tells me."

We both laughed at this, and kissed, and I felt a pang, knowing that our meetings could not go on forever. Yet there was a part of me, even when I was near Scipion, that was mindful of the boy who waited for me each evening at dusk, and who I knew would be there again that night.

There came an evening when I looked for the dark boy in vain. I went to the window of my bedroom, and looked out, and he was not there. I went out on the veranda and peered into the shadowy foliage, through the palm trees and out toward the beach. But his familiar figure was absent. I waited, minute after minute, the minutes stretching into half an hour, then an hour. He did not come into view.

Where was he? What had become of him? Did he have an accident? Had he been waylaid and attacked? I knew that there were gangs of renegade slaves on the island, and thieves and pickpockets in abundance in Fort-Royal. Had he been the victim of criminals?

I worried over him, and resumed my watch after supper though it was too dark to see anything, only the broken turf that ringed the mill. I waited until moonrise, but still saw nothing other than the silvery light reflecting off the broad plantains and palm fronds, a light that seemed to me nothing more than a silvery emptiness without the outline of the boy.

The following morning Euphemia and I went by cart to Fort-Royal to buy a length of lawn for undergarments for my mother and Manette. My mother did not like to go to town for fear she would encounter one of my father's mistresses, and she did not trust any of the servants to know her taste. So she sent us in her place.

I loved going to Fort-Royal. The town hummed with activity, and I was drawn in to its color and the life of its dusty unpaved streets, full of deep ruts and holes which no one ever bothered to fill. The cries of the street vendors, the braying of donkeys and squawking of chickens filled the humid, still air and every so often a cluster of drunken men would burst into song as they reeled past. Sharp smells lingered among the rickety stalls where live chickens and rabbits, ducks and barrels of crabs, rum and flowers, baskets and cheap crockery were displayed for sale. As everywhere on the island the scent of sugar was strong, along with the pungent odors of pig manure and leather, unwashed bodies and roses and cinnamon and garlic.

I left Euphemia to select the lawn and shop for herself (she had a weakness for liquorice) while I went off by myself toward the street of the charm-sellers. African women in loose cotton blousons cut low on the bosom and skirts tight across the hips strolled along, sampling the food and feeling the goods offered for sale. I had always admired the frank sensuality of their swaying walk, the way they balanced their purchases on their hips and held their heads proudly, wide bandanas covering their black hair. The street of the charm-sellers was full of such women, stopping to listen as the vendors pointed to their bottles and baskets and described each of their wares.

"This potion will bring him back to you!" "Put this charm under your pillow, and you will dream of your lover." "Here is a tea to mend your broken heart!" "Love-juice to make you a mother!"

There were cures for head colds and upset stomachs, fetishes to restore virility and remedies for the English disease, the bane of soldiers and sailors who slept with women of the streets. (Fort-Royal had plenty of these, many of them beautiful exotic women of mixed race who took pride in their ancestry.)

I bought a charm for headaches for my mother and one to bring prosperity for my father, intending to put it under his bed when I got home. I bought a love potion, and tucked it into my bag. I was turning to leave the small shop to rejoin Euphemia, when I saw him.

He was quite close to me, leaning against the side of a low building, his arms folded and his gaze fixed on me with such intensity that I almost reeled at the sight of him. I was in no doubt, he was the dark boy I had seen so often at Les Trois-Ilets. His hair fell untidily across his forehead in the same way, he wore the same breeches and torn waistcoat, and he aroused the same mixture of excitement and fear in me as he had at the plantation.

I reacted quickly, turning away from him and walking as rapidly as I could along the rutted unpaved street in the opposite direction. I walked on, tripping, my slippers snagging on objects in the roadway. Was he following me? I felt that he was, though I didn't dare turn to look. Up one narrow, twisting street and down another I half-walked, half-ran until I turned into an alley where a cart had overturned and a crowd had gathered. All was confusion as some people sought to right the cart and others rushed in to gather the limes and plantains and barrels of meal that had fallen from it.

Trapped within the widening crowd, I was unable to go forward or back. Just then I felt an arm encircle my waist. The touch was like fire, like no touch I had ever felt. I drew in my breath, and in the next instant his mouth was against my ear. I felt his warm breath, and the tingling along my spine overwhelmed me. Then, just as quickly as the touch had begun, it was withdrawn. I saw his back as he adroitly slipped through the unruly crowd and disappeared from view.

It was the boy, of course. He was teasing me, tormenting me. I thought about what had happened the night before and imagined that he had been watching me, keeping just out of sight, enjoying my distress as the night grew later and later and I had no sight of him. Like it or not, I was engaged in an erotic game of hide and seek with this boy, a game he controlled but I enjoyed.

All the way back to Les Trois-Ilets, riding along, chatting with Euphemia who shared her liquorice with me, I watched the lush roadside foliage for a stirring of the leaves, a glimpse of shirt or a quick movement of a hand. Once or twice I looked back along the way we had come, thinking that he might be following us on horseback. But the road was clear, save for an occasional donkey-cart like ours, or a swift rider on a costly mount, galloping toward Morne Mirande or one of the forts on the north part of the island. There was no further sign of the boy, only the marks of his hand on my pale pink sash, and the lingering memory of his warm breath in my ear, a memory that continued to make me tingle with desire.

6

EUPHEMIA TOOK ME AND MANETTE to the beach most afternoons, when it was not raining. We would go for a long swim and then lie in the shade of the palm trees, drowsing and napping. I loved these long lazy afternoons, the swim in the warm clear water, watching the yellow and blue and green fish dart and hover around and under me, the sun dazzle on the water, like a splash of gold across its aquamarine surface, the heat of the fine soft white sand between my toes, and the delicious tiredness that came over me and made my eyelids droop.

The first time I saw the boy at the beach I was startled. Euphemia and Manette were in their hammocks, asleep, and I was lying on a blanket under a palm tree. There was no one else on the beach. Euphemia was snoring gently and Manette did not stir. I awoke suddenly, and saw the boy walking purposefully toward the gentle surf. Ignoring me, he was nearly at the water's edge when he flung off his clothes and jumped onto a rock. He stood there, in his slim nakedness, as if poised to dive in.

I had seen naked slaves before, but never a naked white man—or boy my own age. He was beautiful, I thought, as he stood there, his muscles taut, his shoulders well molded, his stomach flat and his penis and scrotum like those I had seen on the copies of Greek statues my uncle Robert had in his gardens in Fort-Royal.

He let me admire him for several minutes before plunging into the bay and swimming to one of the islands, where he disappeared, not to be seen again for the rest of the afternoon. With the image of his body strongly in my mind I napped once again. Yet the image lingered, and came back to me in dreams over the next several days.

Just then many things preoccupied my family's attention and kept our household in a stir. The fighting between our fleet and the British, the news from Scipion (who was wounded in a skirmish off St. Lucia at about this time), his urgent messages to me and occasional visits, plus my father's absence with the militia all kept us in a state of uncertainty. More letters arrived from Aunt Edmée saying how eager Alexandre was for our marriage to take place and how vital it was that father and I come to Paris on the next available ship.

I answered my aunt's letters as best I could, explaining that we could not sail as long as the fighting continued and that our island might be captured by the British. I realized as I wrote this that Alexandre might decide to give up on me and choose another bride. My chance to go to Paris might well be slipping away—and with it, my father's chance to salvage his finances and keep Les Trois-Ilets.

Restless in mind about these things, I thought of attempting to return to the Sacred Crossroads to consult Orgulon. But the days passed, and I did not climb Morne Canthéaume. Instead I went to the beach with Euphemia and Manette, and forgot my worries as I swam and rested and napped—and watched for the boy.

One warm afternoon, as I lay napping, I was awakened by the soft touch of his lips on mine. I felt no fear, my body yielded to his and our kiss became an embrace. I wore only a light shift and could feel his strong, muscular flesh close to mine. I lost myself in his arms, forgetting the others, forgetting everything but the feel of him beside me, on top of me, surrounding me. His mouth tasted of fermented cane beer and spices and he smelled of salt water and sweat.

When he took me he was gentle, without roughness or force. Our bodies merged naturally, as if made for this moment of union. All that I had ever heard about the coupling of man and woman passed into oblivion then, replaced by the pleasures of his touch and the ease with which we changed from strangers to lovers.

We lay thus under the hot sun, with no sound other than our own breathing and the lapping of the waves against the sand, until Euphemia turned in her hammock and the boy raised his head to listen. Then, abruptly and without a word, he got to his feet and was gone. He did not look back. I was alone. I began to shiver. Eventually I slept.

Later, I heard Euphemia and Manette stirring and talking to each other. I sat up, feeling dizzy, and wrapped a light quilt around my shoulders as I customarily did when returning home from the beach. Euphemia, who was gathering her hammock, looked over at me.

"Some rats made a nest in your hair while you were asleep, Yeyette." I did my best to smooth my long dark hair back from my face and comb out the worst tangles with my fingers. Did I look different, I wondered? Had I changed? My mouth was swollen from kissing and my muscles ached from the strain of lovemaking. I would never be the same inside, no matter what my outer appearance might be.

For what I discovered, on that long-ago afternoon, was that I was made for love. I thirsted to be caressed, kissed, touched. To be loved physically as well as emotionally. I loved Scipion with all my heart, but I had loved this boy, this stranger, with my body. And of the two kinds of love, this love of the body was far stronger and richer and more desirable. I knew then that I would always yield to it, no matter how hard I might try to resist.

7

I WORRIED, of course, that I might find that I was pregnant. But my monthly flow arrived, and I felt enormous relief. And just at that time there was widespread relief all across the island of Martinique, for the English fleet moved off toward St. Lucia and for the first time in months French ships were able to enter and leave Fort-Royal harbor. My father took advantage of the opportunity to book passage for us on the small ship *Ile-de-France*, part of a convoy bound for Brest.

It happened quickly, and we lost no time in going on board the ship, despite my father's weakness (he had been ill all spring) and my mother's last-minute pleas that we change our plans and stay home. Our trunks had been packed for a long time, so it was only a matter of putting on our traveling cloaks and filling our hampers with food and making the trip from the plantation to the harbor. Scipion met us at the quayside, wearing the uniform of a lieutenant commander. I congratulated him on his promotion.

"Lieutenant Commander du Roure, at your service," he said with a deep bow. "I have been assigned to the *Ile-de-France*."

As soon as he learned that we were to make the journey to France he made certain that he would be assigned to our ship. He told me that he wanted to be near me during the long trip, to protect me.

"You may come under attack, you know. It will be very dangerous at sea. The convoy is carrying an immense treasure in jewels and gold, all the valuables the colonists want to ship to their relatives in France for safekeeping. But try not to worry. I won't let you come to harm."

He led us to our cabin, a tiny space with a ceiling so low I could barely stand and my father had to stoop. How we could all fit in the cramped space I couldn't imagine, for there were four of us, father and I and Euphemia and Aunt Rosette, and our trunks and boxes as well. I had never been on shipboard before—in fact I had never left the island—and had no idea what to expect. It was clear we would have to learn to adapt—but how?

We had not been at sea more than a couple of days when the first storm struck. The rocking and pitching of the ship made our stomachs lurch. Nauseated and in pain, we huddled in our shared cabin, wretched and throwing up, unable to eat or sleep. I had never been so miserable. The ship's surgeon came to examine us but said he could do nothing; it was seasickness, he told us, and nearly everyone on the ship was affected by it. We would feel better when the storm passed.

But the storm lasted three days, and more storms followed, with hardly an interval of calm weather between them. I clutched the pouch of herbs and chicken bones I wore around my neck—a talisman against death by drowning—and tried to swallow the warm broth Euphemia brought me several times a day. Even as I drank, however, the ship lurched violently to the side, and the broth spilled out onto the floor where it mixed with the seawater that constantly sloshed there. It was no use: I could eat little, and what I did manage to eat, I could not keep down. I grew thin. I dared not try to look in a mirror for fear of what I might see.

In the fourth week of our journey an English frigate bore down on the frigate that guarded our convoy, the *Po-nona*. We were in the rear of the long line of French vessels, many miles behind the flagship. Still, we could hear the booming of cannon and see the dark yellow smoke on the horizon ahead of us. The English frigate sailed off, but as Scipion explained to me, our convoy had to alter its course to avoid another encounter with English vessels. The course change brought us into latitudes where the likelihood of storms was even greater than before. Rain and wind lashed at the ship, and my father, who had needed constant care from the start of the voyage, began to look deathly ill.

I put my fetish around his neck as Euphemia muttered a prayer in her mother's African tongue.

"Take that vile thing off me!" he protested weakly, clawing at the fetish dangling from its cord. "And stop that voodoo praying! If I'm going to die, let me die in peace, without any mumbo-jumbo." The St. Christopher medal he wore gleamed on his chest, and his eyes were bright with fever.

I wanted to help him but most of the time it was all I could do to cling to my own narrow hard plank bed, shivering under my wet blanket, and try to endure my own nausea and pain.

Finally there came a day of calm seas and clear skies, when the ship was steadier and a few of the hardiest passengers came up on deck for fresh air. Stumbling up out of the hold, grasping the railing along the stairwell, I felt as though I had been dead and shut away in a dark tomb and was only now coming back to life and emerging into the light.

Scipion was at his post on the foredeck, wearing his freshly pressed uniform, looking handsome and fit. He was scanning the horizon with a spyglass.

"With luck, we should be in Brest in another six weeks," he told me. "Unless we encounter more storms and are blown off course. Tell me, what will you do once you disembark?"

"Alexandre and Aunt Edmée are going to meet us, I suppose. My father wrote to tell them that we were about to sail."

"And then you will get married."

"Yes."

Scipion sighed. "He'll be giving up a lot, becoming a married man, your Alexandre. He's known for keeping company with many women."

"Aren't all you young officers alike in that way?"

"Alexandre de Beauharnais surpasses us all."

"Then why did he have to send all the way to Martinique for a bride?"

"Because, my dear Yeyette, he wanted a young virginal girl for his wife. Most of his conquests are married ladies. Besides, it is usually best for a young man with a title to marry within his family, a distant cousin or niece. It is expected."

Our conversation was interrupted by the delighted cries of passengers who had caught sight of dolphins leaping and playing alongside the ship. We watched them for a long time, exulting in the fresh sea air and dazzling sunlight, walking back and forth along the deck to exercise our long-unused legs. I had not worn any but wet clothes for weeks; merely to be dry was a great comfort.

We had more days of sun, but before long the rain and wind returned, and we were once more confined to our small cabin. Our seasickness returned as well, though it was not quite as severe as before. We grew irritated with one another almost past endurance. Our civility wore thin, we fought and jostled each other and reverted to acting like spiteful children. We were constantly hungry, for we were living on rancid meat and ship's biscuits crawling with worms. All the fresh food on the ship had long since been eaten or spoiled. From being constantly wet the walls of our cabin became coated with green slime, which dropped on us whenever the ship rocked and worsened the stench that enveloped us.

At last, after four months at sea, we came in sight of the French coast. The harbor was shrouded in fog. A lighthouse sent out a bright beam across the water, but it gleamed only fitfully, and the waves were high— too dangerously high for us to disembark on small rowboats and go ashore. We decided to wait until morning to leave the ship.

That night, lying in the fetid, dark cabin, uncomfortable on my narrow bed, I swore I would never, ever spend another night at sea.

In the morning, however, I could not help but feel excitement. I would soon be in Paris! With Euphemia's help I dressed in my least rumpled, least waterstained gown and let her dress my hair as best she could, using only a damp comb. The gown was too large for me, I had lost so much weight. And when I looked in the small mirror Aunt Rosette handed me I was shocked. My complexion was ashen, my once plump pink cheeks sallow and thin. Dark circles ringed my eyes and my bosom no longer swelled enticingly.

"You look like the survivor of a shipwreck," Aunt Rosette said with a sly smile.

"Well, I practically am. We all are."

Aunt Edmée and Alexandre were waiting on the dock to meet us. Aunt Edmée, looking lovely and rested, her shining blond hair piled into an elaborate coiffure with fruit and flowers interwoven among the tresses, her lilac silk gown stretched over wide paniers, was smiling a warm welcome. But Alexandre, stiff and correct in his immaculate white uniform and dark tricorn hat, a long saber at his waist, looked irritated.

"Joseph! Rose—or shall I call you Yeyette? You are here at last. How very glad we are to see you!" Edmée stepped forward and embraced us warmly, graciously endeavoring to overcome her natural reaction to the foul smells that clung to us—smells her rich perfume was not strong enough to cover up. "And you too Rosette. I see you are still wearing that familiar gown. Well dear, we'll have to find you a different one. I have dressmakers waiting in Paris to sew Yeyette's trousseau. They can make a gown for you too."

Edmée acknowledged Euphemia with the barest of nods, reluctant to show any connection to her though Euphemia, being my father's bastard daughter, was in fact her niece. In Martinique, such relationships between Grands Blancs and people of mixed blood, being very common, were taken for granted and freely acknowledged. Evidently in France they were not.

I returned Aunt Edmée's embrace and turned toward Alexandre, who was looking at me fixedly.

"Where is your hat?"

"My hat?"

"No lady goes out in the sun without a hat. The sun ruins the complexion. Yours has already suffered."

I looked at Aunt Edmée, who was nonplussed. Among the decorations in her complicated coiffure was a small but unmistakable straw hat decorated with artificial lilacs.

"Alexandre, I have just spend four months in the dark hold of a ship, being sick. I assure you, the last thing I needed was a hat."

"Perhaps what you needed even more, mademoiselle, were some manners. I am not accustomed to being addressed so outspokenly, and in such an insolent tone."

I glared at him. This was the Alexandre I remembered, the cold, haughty boy who criticized other children and was so disliked by us all. But there was a major difference: this Alexandre was tall, and very good-looking. His disdain only enhanced his manly appeal. Indeed it was difficult to believe that he was only nineteen.

"Nonetheless," he added, taking my ungloved hand and lifting it toward his lips without actually touching his mouth to it, "since you are my betrothed I shall do my best to overlook your lapse, and hope it will soon be mended, along with your chapped skin."

Alexandre summoned a cabriolet and took us all to an inn, where, as I recall, I spent a blissful hour in a copper tub of hot soapy water and ate a meal of fresh chicken and soft white loaves with not a worm in sight! Ah, comfort! Refreshed, fed and clean, I received Alexandre in the room I shared with Aunt Rosette. Immediately on entering the room he began pacing back and forth, his hands behind his back, his tricorn hat under his arm.

"The ceremony will be held at ten o'clock tomorrow morning. All the documents have been prepared. We will take our first meal as man and wife in the *mairie,* and then we leave for Paris. The bankers there are awaiting us."

"I doubt if father will be able to travel. He is very ill."

"Then we can leave him here with your maid to attend him. He can join us in Paris when he is better."

"I'm not leaving him."

"You will do as I say."

"I'm not your wife yet, Alexandre. Don't try to give me orders."

Aunt Rosette, who was sitting beside me on the sofa, coughed and poked me in the ribs with her elbow.

"In a day or two, I'm sure, my brother will be recovered," she said in an effort to make peace between the increasingly vehement Alexandre and myself.

"Yes? And what if he dies?" He glared at poor Rosette, who shrank beneath his harsh gaze.

"How can you speak so? He is my beloved father, and the man who took you in when you were a child in Martinique! You owe him a great debt, and now he is ill and needs your help. Have you no feelings?"

"Pardon me, Rose, if I remind you that it was your father who was eager for us to marry. He knows as well as I do how important it is that we settle the legal arrangements as quickly as possible! He is deeply in debt, and I have agreed to lend him ten thousand francs to satisfy his creditors. But I cannot do that unless we marry, and take the proof of our marriage to the bankers in Paris!"

The long uncomfortable silence that followed this outburst was broken by Rosette.

"Alexandre, try some of this excellent brandy the innkeeper brought up for us. It will calm you and fortify you."

He held up one hand in a gesture of refusal, and strode to the door. Before leaving he turned toward me.

"Ten o'clock. St.-Luc-sur-Mer. I'll send the cabriolet to get you."

8

HAD MY FATHER NOT INSISTED that I follow Alexandre's order I might never have gone to the church of St.-Luc-sur-Mer and married Alexandre Beauharnais, and I might have spared myself much anguish.

But my father did insist, and told me frankly that without Alexandre's loan our family would surely be ruined. His eyes were full of suffering, and I could not resist doing what he asked. It was, after all, the sole reason we had come to France: so that I could marry Alexandre.

And so I put on the simple white gown Aunt Edmée had brought from Paris for me to wear on my wedding day, and the white lace veil my grandmother had given me before we left Martinique—the veil she had worn many years earlier when she had been plain Catherine Brown of Dundreary, marrying the French aristocrat who became my grandfather. Alexandre had a bouquet of greenhouse roses sent to me at the inn, so that I would have flowers to carry when I stood before the altar.

One thing I did on my own, however, and it surprised everyone. I sent a note by the innkeeper's son to the *Ile-de-France,* to Scipion, asking him please to come to the wedding. When I got to the church I was much comforted to see him standing there, the only guest apart from Aunt Edmée and Aunt Rosette (father was far too ill to attend) and a few of Alexandre's brother officers.

I got through the brief wedding ceremony by keeping my mind

focussed on my absent father, and how greatly it would distress him if the financial arrangements he had made with Alexandre were to fall through. I stumbled over the words of my vows, and could not look at Alexandre when he spoke his. Afterwards, Aunt Edmée told me that I looked beautiful and that the sound of my voice repeating my vows was so low and sweet and girlish that it made her cry.

"Listening to you, I couldn't help but think of your poor sister Catherine," she said. "Dying so young the way she did. She was our first choice as Alexandre's bride, you know. A much better age for him than you. A man should be at least five years older than his wife, I always say, and you are only three years younger than he is. Yes! It should have been Catherine standing here today. But then, if it had to be anyone else, dear Yeyette, I'm glad it is you. Such a dear, innocent bride. Such a lovely face. You and Alexandre will have many beautiful children, I'm sure."

I stood beside Alexandre while his fellow officers came up to offer their congratulations. One was gallant enough to call me "a breath of the islands" and kiss my cheek, but the others made bawdy remarks and looked me up and down in frank appraisal.

"I hope she's worth it," I heard one of them say. "She looks a little pinched and peaked."

"For forty thousand a year, I'd have married the coachman's daughter!" another retorted, without bothering to lower his voice.

"She's a treasure beyond price." It was Scipion, coming forward to defend me. "I can assure you of that. And she is a wellborn lady who deserves the utmost politeness in address." He came to stand at my side, and looked at each of the officers in turn, his gaze coming at last to rest on the unsmiling Alexandre.

"How do you know that my wife is such a treasure?" Alexandre asked Scipion in a loud, challenging tone. "Have you had experience of her yourself?"

I heard Aunt Rosette give a little cry at this offensive remark. Aunt Edmée began to walk toward us.

"Sir, you forget who and where you are," Scipion said.

"There is nothing wrong with my memory."

"Only your behavior."

"I ask you again. Have you had experience of my wife?"

Aunt Edmée reached us. "Alexandre, calm yourself. You know full well that your wife is a virginal young girl."

"I have had the honor of Mlle Tascher's acquaintance in Martinique," Scipion said. "And the privilege of offering myself to her as a protector during her long voyage."

"Lieutenant du Roure has given us a great deal of help," I put in. "We are in his debt."

"Indeed so," Edmée added. "Had it not been for the lieutenant's assistance, they would have had a much more difficult voyage."

Alexandre looked at each of us in turn, shaking his head in disgust.

"Colonials!" he said. "Provincials! What a blunder I've made!" And he turned on his elegant heel and walked out of the church, leaving me standing with Aunt Edmée, Aunt Rosette and Scipion, the bunch of roses I carried wilting in my hands.

9

ALEXANDRE DID NOT RETURN TO US THAT DAY, or the next, or the day after that.

"He is often petulant," Aunt Edmée told me. "Men of sensitivity and high intelligence are like that. He will come back eventually, when he recovers his temper."

On the fourth day Alexandre strode purposefully through the door of our room at the inn, taking us by surprise.

"I've made arrangements for our journey to Paris," he said curtly. "The coach will come for us at noon." He kissed Aunt Edmée on both cheeks but avoided looking at me. "I trust that officer—du Roure was it?—has gone back to his ship and will not trouble us further."

"Scipion escorted us here after you left us," I said. "I was grateful to him. I did not expect to be abandoned on my wedding day."

"And I did not expect such an appalling bride," was my husband's icy retort, delivered to the empty air as he moved about the room, picking up objects and tossing them into Aunt Edmée's open trunk.

"Leave that, Alexandre, the maid will do it," Aunt Edmée said.

"The maid is going back to Martinique. I don't want any half-breeds in my household."

"What?" My loud question rang in the small room. "Euphemia is not some half-breed, as you put it, she's my sister!"

"Half sister," Edmée corrected me in an undertone. "And it's not something we talk about, here in France, not in polite society."

"I know full well who she is, and she is going back where she belongs."

"Then I'm going with her," I heard myself say.

"Nothing would please me more, I assure you, but I need you to remain here, at least until all the legal matters concerning my inheritance are settled, once and for all, by the Paris attorneys. After that you may go to the devil."

"I will not go to Paris, I will not sign any papers, and I will have nothing further to do with you if you send Euphemia away."

Alexandre looked at me for the first time, and for a moment his mouth curved upward in a slight smile. Then he shrugged and left the room.

As the hour of noon approached we got ready to leave. Aunt Edmée assured me that Alexandre would not deprive me of Euphemia's companionship.

"I know him," she said. "He spoke rashly. He will think it over. He won't take your beloved Euphemia from you—partly because he can see what trouble you would make for him if he did, and partly out of sympathy. Besides, his roots are in Martinique, like yours. For most of his childhood he had a mulatto nursemaid, whom he loved. He keeps a miniature portrait of her hidden in his jewelry-case, along with a portrait of his mother."

No further threats were made to send Euphemia back across the ocean to Martinique, and so I tentatively prepared myself for the long coach journey to Paris. The harbor town of Brest was many miles from the French capital, and I knew it would take us a long time to get there. The weather was turning colder each day, with frost on the grass in the mornings and a bitter wind sweeping down from the mountains in the afternoon. I worried about my father. Would he be strong enough to withstand the constant bumping and jolting of the coach during the long journey, the indifferent food and hard beds of wayside inns? He had not gotten out of bed since the day of my wedding, and lay listless, slow to respond to the herbal tea Euphemia brewed for him to reduce his fever.

I went to sit by his bedside. He was asleep, his face turned away from me, his thin cheek with its grey stubble giving him the ravaged look of one who has been ill a long time. I longed to take him back home to Martinique, where he would be well cared for, until he recovered. But the sea journey would probably kill him, I knew. And besides, my fantasy was in truth a selfish one; I wanted to go back to Martinique for my own sake, to be free of this cold, disdainful man I had married, free to go back to the life I had known.

When the hour of our departure came we climbed into the big hired coach with its eight strong, sleek horses, their muscles rippling under their shining coats, their feet stamping on the cold cobblestones. I watched as Alexandre motioned to Euphemia, indicating that she was not to ride inside with us, but up on top of the vehicle with the trunks and Alexandre's dour, broad-shouldered Turkish manservant Balthazar. She glowered at Alexandre but heaved her considerable bulk up on top, making the coach sway dangerously.

Aunt Edmée, Aunt Rosette and my trembling father took their places on the upholstered seats and we started off. We took the road for Morlaix but had not traveled more than an hour or two before my father fainted and fell from his seat and Alexandre shouted to the coachman to stop. A few sips of brandy appeared to revive him, but he soon vomited all he had drunk, and with it, a good deal of blood.

"We must turn back," I said. "We must get him to a doctor."

"Milizac," Alexandre said. "It is very near."

"No!" I was surprised at the vehemence of Aunt Edmée's outcry.

I looked questioningly at Alexandre. "It is an estate nearby," he said. "I know there is a physician there. He has been in attendance on—on someone I know."

"Do not do this, Alexandre!" Again Aunt Edmee was very forceful in her words, far more forceful than I had ever seen her.

Alexandre looked at my father, whose blood was staining the yellow velvet of the seat. He lowered the window of the coach and leaned out, calling up to the driver.

"Let the maid come down! Then take us to Milizac, as quickly as you can. One of our party is ill. Hurry!"

I felt the coach lean to the side as Euphemia climbed down and got into the interior of the vehicle with us, sitting beside my father in order to give him whatever help she could. I saw the tears spill down her cheeks at the sight of his misery, and my own tears flowed afresh.

The coach lurched forward then, the pull of the strong horses pressing me back against the seat. I reached for the protective fetish I wore around my neck, under my gown, and clasped it. "Please, don't let father die," I whispered. I saw Aunt Rosette's lips moving, her head bowed and her eyes closed, and knew that she too was praying. Euphemia held my father's head and put his lace handkerchief to his bloodstained lips. Aunt Edmée continued to glare at Alexandre, frowning, and he turned away.

I had no idea why my aunt was so set against our going to this place, Milizac, when Alexandre had insisted there would be a physician there. Surely that was what my father needed most.

We turned off the highroad onto a country lane and the horses could no longer maintain their fast pace. The coach swayed suddenly and I had to hold on to the seat to keep myself from falling onto the floor. We were all shaken. The road narrowed and passed through a wood. Tree branches scraped the sides of the vehicle and we splashed through a stream. My father coughed, then was silent. His eyes were shut, and I could detect no fluttering of his eyelids. For one horrible moment I thought he might be dead.

"His heart beats," Euphemia murmured to me in creole French. "His strong heart beats."

We must have ridden for at least another half hour, though it seemed far longer than that, through the gathering darkness. At last we came out of the wood and approached a large, stone-fronted manor house whose windows glowed with yellow light. When we reached the courtyard, Alexandre opened the door of the coach and, nimbly jumping down, called for help. Grooms came forward to carry my father into the house. They appeared to follow Alexandre's orders without question; clearly they knew him and were accustomed to obeying him.

We were led inside and treated with courtesy by a liveried servant, who showed us to a suite of rooms and told us to make ourselves comfortable.

"Milady has retired," he said, "as the hour is late and she has been indisposed for the past few days. But she asks me to tell you that you are welcome to stay the night, of course, while Monsieur Tascher is being treated. I will ask the physician to speak to you after he has seen the patient."

We saw nothing further of Alexandre or my father, and presently we settled ourselves by the fire in the warm room and ate and drank from the trays of food brought up to us. Aunt Rosette fell asleep in her chair. I fretted, worried about father and uncomfortable in this strange house. I was full of curiosity and wanted to ask Aunt Edmée just where we were and who milady was, but something in her nervous, highly unsettled manner kept me from it. Besides, I was eager to hear how father was and what the physician would have to say.

Eventually he knocked at our door, and told us that father was suffering from a consumption of the lung and would need a long rest.

"No disturbances, plenty of nourishing food and an untroubled mind, that's what the old man needs," he said.

"But father isn't an old man. He's only forty-six."

"Is he indeed? I would have thought him a man of fifty-five, at least. Perhaps a few years older."

We spent a few moments talking of my father's life in Martinique, how he had been burdened with financial and family worries and how he drank a great deal of rum to console himself. When I described the long sea journey the physician nodded.

"Ah, I see now. He has weakened his lungs with sea-damp and the rum has corroded his stomach. Well, the damage may be able to be repaired— in time. Meanwhile you ladies look very tired. You must rest." We thanked him and he said good night.

Where, I wondered, was Alexandre? This was the first night he and I had spent under the same roof, as husband and wife. Yet he had abandoned me again, just as he had on our wedding day. Confused and worn out, I did not know what to think or what to expect. The suite we occupied had a sitting room and several bedchambers. I chose one and prepared for bed. But when I lay down under the soft coverlet and closed my eyes, sleep would not come. The crackling of the dying fire, the sound of the wind outside, above all my unsettled feelings nagged at me. Aunt Edmée had not wanted Alexandre to bring us here, even though it meant help for the brother she loved. Why? And where had Alexandre gone? Why wasn't he with me?

Where was my father? How was he? If I could find him, I could sit beside him in case he needed anything during the night.

At last, unable to doze off and driven by the questions that tugged at my mind, I got out of bed and, taking the bedside candle, went quietly out through the sitting room into the corridor outside.

It was cold and still in the dark corridor. The candles had burned low in the wall sconces, and gave little light. I saw not a single servant as I walked along past the old, wood-panelled walls, the floor uneven under my feet. Everything about the house was new to me, and very unlike the houses I had known in Martinique. No breeze from out-of-doors swept aside the stale air. No bright colors relieved the darkness of the wainscotting. There were no scurrying lizards climbing the walls, no scuttling bugs crawling across the carpet. Only the silent dimness.

And then I heard, very faintly, a baby's cry.

I followed the sound, which grew louder as I approached a door beneath which a spill of golden light shone onto the floor. It must be a nursery, I thought. There would be a nurserymaid inside, taking care of the child. Perhaps she could tell me where I could find my father.

I opened the door—and to my amazement, saw Alexandre, in his nightshirt, lying in a large bed next to a whimpering infant and a blond woman in a lace nightgown.

"Rose. What are you doing here?"

For a moment I could not speak. "Looking for my father," I said at last.

"He is not with us. He is in the next room."

I swallowed. "Who is that woman? Why are you in her bed?" My voice sounded faint in my ears.

"It is my bed, Rose. This is Laure de Girardin, the woman I love. She has just presented me with our son." He reached over and took the fussing child in his arms.

"Here he is. You may as well get to know him. He is named for me. Alexandre. Only three days old today. Tell me, Rose, have you ever seen a finer child?"

10

I RAN BACK ALONG THE DARK CORRIDORS to my room and, once safely inside, I threw up into the washbasin.

My stomach lurched and my head ached. I lay down on the rug in front of the fire and waited for the pain and nausea to pass.

Anger surged through me. I wanted to find a knife, a big long cane knife, and chop Alexandre and the hateful woman Laure to gory pieces. I wanted to kill them with a glance like a quimboiseur. I wanted to put poison into their food, the food they no doubt shared from a single plate, while lounging naked in their big bed.

Murderous images flashed through my mind as I lay there on the rug, hot tears running down my cheeks. They had humiliated me, my husband and his mistress. They had no regard for me whatever. They were content to ruin my life, just so Alexandre could have his inheritance.

The thought that, for most of the past year this blond woman had been carrying Alexandre's child made me furious. He loved her, she was bearing his son—and all the while he was cynically bargaining with my father to make me his wife. Did my father know all about Alexandre and his mistress? Clearly Aunt Edmée knew. That was why she protested when Alexandre told the coachman to take us to Milizac. Who else knew? My mother? My grandmother?

My nausea passed but the anger I felt persisted. When Alexandre

came into my room the following morning, before I had completed my
toilette, I unleashed my fury.

"How dare you deceive me about that woman? How dare you marry
me, in church, in front of God and all his saints, when you already have a
wife in all but name? Wait till I tell my father! And Scipion! They will
avenge me!"

I wrapped my thin dressing-gown tightly around my waist, suddenly
aware of my state of undress. Alexandre had never before seen me
without a gown, or with my hair as it was now, loose and falling in waves
down my back. I felt my face grow hot as I spoke, and knew that my
cheeks were pink and flushed.

Alexandre leaned against a table, his grey eyes appraising me coolly.

"I blame Edmée," he said at length. "She should have prepared you."

"Prepared me for what? For being an unwanted legal wife when you
already had a family with your mistress? For being humiliated?"

"For your role as Vicomtesse de Beauharnais."

I had never before heard my new name pronounced. It startled me.

"Let me instruct you, as no one else seems to have thought it
necessary to do so. Lesson one, Madame la Vicomtesse is always
agreeable, good-tempered, with a sweet disposition."

He raised himself up and began slowly circling the room, arms folded
as if in thought, speaking to me in measured tones as he paced.

"Lesson two, Madame la Vicomtesse does nothing to create discord.
She never complains. She never criticizes. She is gracious to everyone,
especially her husband, whom she admires and to whom she is grateful
for giving her his exalted rank."

I swore then, repeating a foul curse I had often heard in the
marketplace in Fort-Royal.

Alexandre went on, unperturbed. "Lesson three, Madame la Vicomtesse
never soils her lips with vulgar language. And lesson four—" he came
over to me and reached for the ties of my dressing gown, slowly pulling
on them until the gown fell open. I wore very little underneath. I felt
mesmerized, unable to resist. Even as he was doing this I thought, why
am I permitting this intimacy? Why don't I scream at him to stop?

He appraised my body coolly, then pulled the gown back into place.

"Despite your uncouth manners, you are not without appeal. There
are times when I must be apart from Laure. And much as I am attached
to the son I have with her, he cannot inherit my future title or my estate.

I must have another son, and you must be his mother. All this," he concluded, "Edmée should have explained to you." He paused, and raised one eyebrow inquiringly, as if seeking confirmation that I had understood what he said.

I was still seething with anger, but it was no longer a hot, blind fury. While I listened to Alexandre it had congealed into an icy fury.

"What I now see," I began quietly, "is that the arrogant, hateful boy I knew in Martinique has grown into a selfish, callous man. A man I can never love or honor. I have pledged myself to you, but I regret it. Oh, how I regret it! And if I should, one day, bear you a son, I will pray every hour that he grows up to be nothing like you!"

He shrugged and left the room. I was shaking, and felt a chill. I called Euphemia, who warmed my sheets and put me to bed with a bladder of hot water. I told her what had happened, and she listened, rolling her eyes and clucking her tongue.

"Men think they rule the earth," she said, shaking her head, when I finished. "Especially Grands Blancs." She thought for a moment. "Why couldn't you have married that good Monsieur du Roure, the one that was so kind to us on the ship? Maybe you should have gotten a love potion from Orgulon after all. What do you think?"

"I think, Euphemia, that I should never have left Martinique." And with that I cried, my anger having at last given way to pain.

I I

I WISHED WITH ALL MY HEART, on that terrible morning in Milizac, that I had never left Martinique. But a few weeks later, when at last we reached Paris, and I found myself in the midst of the vibrant, noisy, crowded streets of that city I had dreamed of for so long, I could not help but feel elated.

There we were, driving down the rue Saint-Martin and the rue Pontchartrain, past grand mansions and along dim alleyways, with Edmée and my father (whose health improved once we came in sight of the capital) pointing out the city's landmarks with great pride. It was very cold, I remember. Rain dripped down from the roofs, the water running along the centers of the narrow streets, and Edmée remarked that we would probably have snow before long. I had never seen snow, having lived all my life on a warm tropical island. But I knew what it looked like, from pictures in books.

We drove along the Seine, past the Pont Neuf and the Pont-au-Change. Dozens of small boats crowded the river, some heaped with coal and grain and wine, others filled with laundry baskets and red-faced women vigorously slapping wet clothes against the sides. There were rain-drenched markets where old clothes and scrap-iron and flowers were for sale, and streets of fine shops where elegantly dressed men and women stepped out of their gilded carriages to browse and buy.

Paris was a vast, sprawling place, far larger than Fort-Royal. Its streets led on and on in endless serpentine windings, past lodging-houses and taverns, all-night bath houses and workshops, churches and monasteries and gambling-halls. Often we had to stop while angry carters confronted one another, or to permit accidents to be cleared from the roadway. Soldiers of the royal guard marched past, very wet from all the rain, the feathers in their hats quite sodden. At the Place de Grève an execution was under way, and a crowd had formed to watch a man being broken on the wheel. The poor wretch hung limply from his instrument of torture, while from the pavement nearby a street singer chanted a mournful tune.

"This is the rue Thevenot," Edmée announced as we turned into a street lined with run-down large houses. "The marquis de Beauharnais rents an establishment here."

"What's that smell?" I asked. The air reeked of animal ordure and rot, and some other overpowering stench that I had never smelled before. So strong was the odor that I could not smell the stink of the open sewer that ran down the middle of the street, or the reek of the garbage piled in adjacent alleyways.

"It comes from the tanneries," Alexandre said. "And from the tripe factory not far from here. Don't worry. You can only smell it when the wind comes up from the river—which is most of the time."

Holding my scented handkerchief in front of my nose, I entered the house where my aunt and Alexandre lived, along with the ailing marquis. A dimly lit foyer led to a marble staircase which had once been grand but now was discolored, the marble chipped and the chandelier that hung above it choked with candlewax and in need of cleaning. A dozen dour servants stood in line to receive us, the women curtseying, the men bowing. It seemed strange to me to see white servants, I could not get used to the idea that in France, all the servants were as pale as the Grands Blancs. Back home in Martinique, of course, all the servants were African. And there was another difference. French servants did not smile, while in Martinique the African house servants were warm and pleasant, even mirthful.

Edmée took me upstairs into the salon to meet the marquis. He sat on a pile of cushions in a deep armchair, one leg extended, resting on a footstool. His body was grotesquely stout, his round head nearly bald, with a few wisps of whitish hair around his ears. His eyes, when they rested on me, were penetrating, eyes one could not hide from. He reached for his spectacles and put them on.

"So young, so young," he murmured. "Come here, girl."

"She is sixteen, François. Nearly seventeen."

He nodded. "And what do you think of our city, Rose? Is it not a grand and imposing place?"

"I think it goes on and on and never stops. I think it is amazing."

I wanted to appear positive, yet I confess that the marquis's gloomy house dispirited me, and reminded me that my life as Alexandre's wife was likely to be an unhappy one. My low spirits must have registered on my face, because the marquis peered at me for a long moment, and then said, "Come, sit by me." He pointed to a low chair. "Edmée! Go and help your brother and sister settle in while I get to know my daughter-in-law."

The kindliness in the marquis's voice, and his evident interest in me broke my composure entirely. I looked over at the old man, willing to open my heart to him.

"I can see you are unhappy, child. Tell me why."

"It is Alexandre. He humiliates me, my lord marquis. He is always criticizing me, saying how ignorant and provincial I am."

"These shortcomings can be corrected, my dear, with patient tutoring and exposure to the world of higher culture. I fear my son's arrogance and unkindness are incurable, however. They are so deeply ingrained in him. But then, you knew Alexandre as a boy. You knew what he was like."

I nodded, hanging my head. "But no one told me, when I agreed to marry him, about Laure de Girardin—or her child."

"A young man's folly. Nothing more."

"He says Laure is the love of his life."

The marquis snorted. "Ha! The love of his life! He barely knows what love is—yet. If he is like me he will have many loves, but only one wife. One affectionate, steady presence to give him a home. To give him children. You will be that valued wife."

He took my hand. "Come and tell me if Alexandre is unkind to you. Tell me, not Edmée. She indulges him."

"I will, my lord marquis."

"Call me father, my dear. I want to be a second father to you."

"Thank you—father. I'm grateful."

He smiled. "Thank you, my dear, for joining our family. And as for your education, you must meet my sister-in-law Fanny. She scribbles. Verse, novels, songs. She holds a salon every Thursday evening at her house in the rue Montmartre. I can't stand to go there myself. Too many preening versifiers, always looking at themselves in mirrors. But you should go. You will learn a lot."

"I will."

Alexandre lost no time, once he was back in his father's house, in claiming his inheritance. Now that he was married he was entitled to receive his money, which was to be paid to him in large installments every year. It made him a wealthy man—and he set about spending his newfound wealth lavishly. New uniforms, a fine sword of Toledo steel, a set of duelling pistols decorated in etched silver, and breeches and waistcoats of heavy silk with ruby buttons were among his first acquisitions, along with a becoming new bag wig. He looked very handsome as he set off each night in the marquis's carriage for balls and receptions at the mansions of his titled friends.

He never included me in these excursions.

"You are far too young, Rose," he said in his most condescending manner when I asked if I could go with him. "Too unworldly. I may take you when you are older and have more understanding, more to contribute."

"Does Laure de Girardin come to these balls?"

Alexandre's lip curled. "That is nothing to you."

"On the contrary, it concerns me very directly, if you and Laure are seen together. It is an insult to me."

"As I said, you are too unworldly for Paris society." He turned to go, then faced me again. "Not that it matters, but Laure is in Milizac. She does not like to come to Paris in the winter. Having been raised in the tropics like you and me, she finds it too cold."

That Laure did not accompany my husband on his nightly excursions gave me some comfort, but I was nonetheless alone each night, my only diversion endless games of cards with Aunt Rosette and Edmée. During the day, however, I found a delightful new pastime.

One afternoon Alexandre surprised me by giving me a sum of money to buy a trousseau. I tried to pretend that I was accustomed to receiving large amounts of money but in fact I was quite thrilled and excited by the sight of so many gold coins. I had never possessed so much wealth. When I was alone I laughed aloud and amused myself throwing the coins up into the air and catching them and making them clink in my hands.

I asked Edmée to take me to the bank and arranged to send some of the money to my mother and grandmother in Martinique. With the rest I went shopping.

The establishments along the rue Desjardins near the marquis's house soon became familiar to me. At the corset-makers I bought chemises, expertly fitted to my body and beautifully trimmed in lace and with tiny pink roses embroidered on the bodice. I had never owned such fine stockings as those I bought from the hosiers next door, soft, sheer things that clung to my shapely legs in the most flattering way. Abandoning any thought of economy or prudence I bought shoes with high heels—the kind the queen wore, I was assured—and fur muffs to warm my freezing fingers (it was very cold that winter) and woven shawls from the Far East in pale colors of green and beige and creamy yellow.

"Madame la Vicomtesse has very good taste," the clerks murmured as I made my selections. "It is a pleasure to serve Madame la Vicomtesse." Some of the proprietors who served me were humble and gracious, others stole predatory glances at me, no doubt calculating how much profit they were making from my purchases. I was spending recklessly, thoughtlessly, and I knew it; carried away by the gold coins in my purse, I bought and bought, disregarding the mounting expense. When all the gold coins were gone I went on buying, asking that the bills be sent to my husband.

I deserved all the beautiful things I was buying, I told myself. I deserved more than these, as compensation for my unhappy marriage. Alexandre spurned me and insulted me, therefore he ought to be made to pay. Was I not giving up my youth and my freedom? Was I not sacrificing my hope of a happy life for his benefit? I was! Therefore he owed me— everything.

I can say nothing in my defense except that I was angry, and I was not yet seventeen years old. I liked to make a drama of things.

One morning I took Aunt Rosette to a dressmaker and together we chose three new gowns for her, one in cream silk with a billowing skirt and a blue satin sash, one in gossamer-thin lilac muslin with a low neckline and ruching on the sleeves, and one in pale blue.

"No green," she said firmly. "I don't want to wear green ever again."

For myself I ordered a dozen gowns, though I already had a good many new ones. Then I took Aunt Rosette to the milliner's where we each bought a new hat. Aunt Rosette chose the style called "the dragon," a round hat with golden acorns and peacock feathers. I had been wanting a Turkish bonnet, of the kind I was told the queen liked to wear, a fanciful thing made like a military helmet with three long reddish plumes. I bought one and wore it home, drawing many a quizzical glance on the way.

Pleased with myself and my new bonnet, I wore it to supper. As soon as Alexandre saw me he reacted strongly.

"Take off that hideous thing immediately. Have you no taste?"

"I like it. I want to wear it."

"It makes you look like a gargoyle, with your goggle eyes and thick nose. Take it off!"

I looked over at the marquis, sitting at the head of the table, hoping he would come to my defense. But he was nodding. He had fallen asleep. Aunt Edmée looked uncomfortable and shifted in her seat. Aunt Rosette stared down at the tablecloth and did not take her eyes from it.

"Such a to-do, over a silly hat!" my father murmured.

"The queen wears a bonnet just like this one," I said, challenging Alexandre. "Do you think she has poor taste?"

"Everyone knows that the queen throws money away on foolish trifles. She is bankrupting France—just as you are bankrupting me! I have your dressmakers' bills and your drapers' bills and all your other bills sitting on my desk, unpaid! I want no further reminders of your extravagance. Take off that ridiculous hat at once!"

I got up from the table. "I'll have supper in my sitting-room," I said and walked toward the wide double doors of the dining room, my feathered plumes waving. The last thing I heard, before I left the room, was Alexandre's angry voice saying "I hope you choke on it!"

12

∞

THE FOLLOWING THURSDAY NIGHT I went to visit the marquis's sister-in-law Fanny de Beauharnais at her home on the rue Montmartre. It was a large, imposing house, with a columned portico, three stories and a sloping roof. A footman in red livery opened the door to me, and I was shown into a spacious salon so lavishly decorated that it almost made me dizzy.

Red velvet lined the walls and draped the windows. The sofas and footstools were upholstered in rich red brocade and the immense Turkish carpet that covered the floor was patterned in vivid reds and golds. Carved and gilded cupids adorned the doorways and ceiling, and from every table and cabinet more cupids, vases, statues and jeweled boxes shone forth. A large golden harp filled one corner of the room.

So lavish and so colorful was the display of red and gold that I almost felt out of place in my gown of delicate shell pink, until a tall, broad, portly woman swathed in crimson gauze approached me.

"Little Rose, is it not? How charming you look! Come in, come in, let me introduce you."

Fanny de Beauharnais was dressed fantastically in a sort of harem costume, with a wide tunic and long full trousers that were gathered in at her ankles. A deep burgundy-colored vest trimmed in tiny gold bells that jangled as she walked completed her toilette. She had dyed black hair, a broad, mannish face with full features and an infectious grin.

"Rose, this is Seraphin Lamblin, who is going to read to us tonight from his epic *Le Coeur Sauvage*." The tall, slight Seraphin bowed politely to me but looked distracted, his pale, wispy hair in disarray and his watery blue eyes anxious.

"I have misplaced a quarto," he murmured to Fanny. "I am quite distraught."

"Improvise, improvise!" she exclaimed heartily, taking my arm and pulling me in another direction. Two men, dressed identically in waistcoats and trousers of green cloth of silver, held their lorgnettes up to their eyes and regarded me.

"Henri and Bernard," Fanny said. "We call them the Inseparables. Both poets, can you imagine? Underappreciated, I'm sorry to say."

"I wouldn't say that, Fanny," said one of the two men in a tone of wounded dignity. "We have had notices in the *Revue des Inconnus*."

"Unflattering notices, as I recall," said Fanny bluntly. "But perhaps the next ones will be kinder."

She continued to lead me around the room, which was growing more and more crowded, introducing me here and there, pointing out critics and academicians, novelists and an occasional musician. There were far more men than women, I noticed, most of them shabbily dressed though a few noblemen among them stood out for their costly coats, jeweled buttons and fashionably styled wigs, fresh from the wigmakers' shops.

I joined a circle where a discussion of the theater was under way.

"Did anyone see Vestris the other night?" asked a woman in a dramatically plain white gown, a circle of laurel leaves in her hair. A white angora cat was draped around her neck. "He fell right through the stage! Everybody was shocked, of course. I saw a woman faint. She had to be carried out. He recovered, of course. But someone had to take his place for the rest of that performance. Never let it be said that Paris theater lacks drama!"

"I prefer Talma to Vestris," drawled a man whom Fanny had pointed out to me as a prominent critic. "Have any of you seen his Brutus? Quite the finest portrayal of the season."

They went on, discussing this performer and that, mentioning names that were unfamiliar to me. All seemed to be in agreement that the current crop of stage productions was mediocre.

"What does any of that matter," asked a newcomer to the circle, "when so many are freezing this winter? The hospitals can't hold all the sick, even though they cram them in, six to a bed. And if they do survive the cold and illness, they starve. There is famine in Paris this winter."

"Thank heavens that the arts endure, no matter how harsh life becomes," said the woman with the cat.

"That's easy for you to say," retorted a man whose torn waistcoat and well-worn breeches made his own poverty evident. "You have enough firewood to last the winter, and a full pantry. I could probably live all winter on what you feed your cat. But there are thousands with nowhere to turn. What good are the arts to them?"

"Beauty fortifies the spirit," said someone else.

"Beauty is worthless, as long as a corrupt government and a do-nothing king stifle all attempts at reform."

Listening to this conversation, which was growing more and more heated, I waited for a chance to join in. My opportunity came when one of the men changed the subject, saying that he was attempting to publish a novel, *Souls in Torment*.

"I wish I knew if it had the least chance," he said wistfully.

"The tarot cards can tell you," I said, reaching into the pocket of my gown and bringing out the deck of cards I always carried. "Would you like me to read them for you?"

He hesitated. The others fell silent, surprised and intrigued.

"Yes. All right," the novelist said.

We sat at a card table and I began to lay out the cards. A small crowd gathered around to watch. I had been telling fortunes for years. Euphemia had taught me to read the cards when I was a child and I had often watched the fortunetellers in the marketplace in Fort-Royal.

"This is the card of new beginnings," I said. "You are beginning your search for a publisher. You have strong opposition, however. A rival author, perhaps. Yes. I see a jealous rival, someone who is working behind your back to destroy your chances. I see another figure, here," I went on. "Someone with great influence. A woman, perhaps. Do you know anyone like that?"

"I have met the king's sister-in-law. She is a lover of novels."

"Could she help you?"

"Perhaps."

"And I see money. Quite a lot of money. Flowing around you. I can't tell whether it is coming to you or whether you are paying a lot of money."

"Could it be," came a sardonic voice from among the onlookers, "that you see a large sum paid to you for reading the cards?" This comment provoked general laughter, in which I joined.

"My readings are free. This one is over. Good luck, monsieur. Who else would like a reading?"

My offer was quickly taken up. One by one the guests sat down at the table, asking me to find out answers to their questions. Will my play be produced? Will my lover return to me? Will I come into my inheritance soon? As in Martinique, the cards were expected to produce answers about love, money and success.

I read on until Fanny announced that it was time for Seraphin Lamblin to read from his epic. Then I put my deck back in my pocket and sat down to listen. The room grew quiet as the wan Seraphin, in a voice that trembled with emotion, read his alexandrines. I was no judge of poetry then—indeed I am not a particularly acute judge now—but I feel certain, looking back, that *Le Coeur Sauvage* was not a very distinguished piece of work. The guests seated around me were politely stifling their yawns, and looking at one another with ill-disguised expressions of boredom. After half an hour Fanny stood, interrupting Seraphin, and began clapping. Others joined in, clapping as much from relief as approbation.

By this time it was late in the evening and the guests began to leave, thanking Fanny for the evening and promising to return the following Thursday night. I decided that I ought to leave as well. But as I put on my cape and gloves and prepared to go, many of those whose fortunes I had told came up to me and, thanking me, slipped coins into my hands.

"Not payment—just a token of thanks," one whispered. "Please accept this small gratuity," said another. Each had a polite phrase ready when the money was exchanged. At first I wanted to give the gifts back, for I had never before dreamed of charging anyone for my readings. But then I thought, why not accept it? I can send this money to my family in Martinique, or give it to my father to pay his debts. So I thanked the givers with a gracious smile, and slipped the coins into the pocket of my gown, along with my deck of cards.

"You were a great success this evening," Fanny told me as she said goodbye to me at the door. "When François told me about you, he didn't mention that you had hidden talents."

"He doesn't know. I have not read the tarot for anyone in Alexandre's family. I know Alexandre would scoff and criticize me if he saw me telling fortunes."

"We wives have a lot to put up with," Fanny said. Her tone was light, but her eyes hinted at pain. "I for one decided years ago not to put up with it any more. I separated from my husband. I've been much happier since."

I didn't know what to say to this, so I was quiet. I had heard about so many separated couples since coming to Paris. The marquis was separated from his wife, Aunt Edmée was separated from her husband, many of Edmée's friends were either separated or obtaining separations. The list was long.

"I hope we will see you next Thursday evening," Fanny was saying. "Will you come?"

"With pleasure," I told her. "I will look forward to it."

The following week I was at the house on the rue Montmartre at the appointed time. I wore my most colorful gown, an elaborate design in rose-colored brocade with gold embroidery, the bodice cut very low, and with it a pair of earrings Aunt Edmée lent me, with large yellow diamonds that flashed and sparkled when I moved.

Many heads turned to look at me when I entered Fanny's salon, and I was gratified by the attention. Acquaintances from the previous week came forward to greet me, and to ask, somewhat shyly, whether I had brought my deck of tarot cards. I produced the deck from my pocket and heard sighs of relief. After spending some time in conversation, I went to the card table where I had sat the week before and asked, "Now, who would like a reading?"

Once again I was in demand. For an hour and more I laid out the cards and answered questions, made suggestions and commented on what I saw in the future for one person after another. The circle of onlookers widened. Here and there a skeptical voice was heard, but on the whole I was treated as an oracle, a favored being with special powers. When I let it be known that I had learned my skills in Martinique the respect I was accorded grew.

"Martinique!" someone said. "Where everyone is rich!" "Why, they're all Africans there, aren't they? Don't they have the second sight? Isn't that where the demons walk at night?"

A mystique certainly surrounded my childhood home, I discovered; I had only to speak the name of Martinique and an awed look came over people's faces. The French colonials who lived there were assumed to be fabulously wealthy, and the island itself was supposed to be a place of magic and marvels.

I had just completed a reading when I heard a familiar voice.

"Can it be my little Bird of Paradise?"

I looked up—into Scipion's grey eyes!

I jumped up from the table and embraced him. It seemed like an age since we had last seen each other, on the day of my wedding, though in fact only a few months had passed. Abandoning my tarot readings I found a quiet corner where Scipion and I could talk undisturbed.

I had so much to tell him, about Alexandre and Laure de Girardin, my dull life in the house on the rue Thevenot and my regret at having married Alexandre. He in turn told me of his forthcoming marriage and of his recent promotion—and about a place he knew, by the Pont Neuf where, he said, one could meet real Parisians and observe the genuine life of the capital at first hand.

"Come on, Yeyette, let me take you there. How long has it been since you had a good time?"

It had been far too long. I agreed to go with Scipion. Grinning like wayward children, we got into Scipion's waiting carriage and told the driver to take us to the river.

13

"NIGHT, O CHARMING NIGHT, be kind to lovers all," Scipion sang as we drove along, through the old dark streets and torchlit alleyways of the capital, toward the low-lying banks of the Seine. The song was a popular one that year, I heard it sung by the ballad-singers on the street and even the marquis's grooms hummed it. When we came to the Old Bridge we got out of the carriage and Scipion led me down an ancient stair to a small café at the water's edge.

Inside all was noise and revelry. Men in fishermen's smocks and laborers from the docks sat at long tables drinking. Musicians played a lively country tune and a few men and women were dancing. The room was dimly lit, and the air was full of smoke, so that I could not see clearly. I stumbled against something as we made our way to a bench and sat down. Turning to look behind me, I realized that my foot had struck the oustretched leg of a drunken man, lying face-down under a table.

There was a commotion at a nearby table, where a man stood, holding a flagon. He shouted something in a language I didn't understand, and others at his table greeted his shouting with a loud cheer and a waving of their own flagons.

I looked over at Scipion. "What are they saying?"

"I don't know. I don't understand Flemish. They are bargemen from Flanders, who go back and forth between Paris and the lowlands to the north. Their boats are tied up right below us. As soon as the river rises, they'll be gone."

"Calvados!" Scipion called out to the waiter who approached us. "You'll like it," he said to me. "It's apple brandy. Very sweet. Very potent."

All around us, tables and chairs were being pushed back to make room for more dancing. A bottle of golden-brown liquid was brought to us and we drank a toast "to night, to charming night."

"The Cossacks are coming!" someone exclaimed, and in a moment half a dozen blond, burly men in gleaming white shirts, wide red sashes and black top boots entered the café. There were whoops and yells of recognition. "Sing for us! Dance for us!" the patrons called out and the Russians, after helping themselves to liquor, stood in the center of the cleared space and began to sing and clap.

The musicians in the café fell silent as the Russians began a slow, dirgelike melody. Their voices were strong and plaintive, with an edge of yearning. Gradually the tempo of the song quickened, the clapping grew louder. Soon everyone in the room was clapping along with the men, who linked arms and began to dance, their black boots rising and falling in unison. I had never before seen such feats of whirling and kicking, bending and leaping. They contorted their bodies in impossible ways, keeping their balance while crouching on their heels, flinging out their legs wildly in time to the music. Finally, after one last frenzied burst of acrobatic dancing, they gave a loud shout and the dance ended.

The clapping was so thunderous that I thought I could feel the room swaying, though it might have been the effect of the strong apple brandy. I looked over at Scipion, who was grinning.

"It's like this every night," he said, struggling to make himself heard over the din of voices and applause. "Always something exciting. Actors come here, and even singers from the opera. They perform if the crowd demands it. Vestris was in here one night, and danced for the bargemen and carriage drivers."

"What is this place called?"

"Café Lestrigal. The name is painted in big blue letters outside, only you can't see it very well in the dark."

We lingered at the Café Lestrigal, Scipion and I, far into the night. It was exciting, this world of high spirits and noisy camaraderie. A fight broke out and one of the men had to be taken outside, his head and hand bleeding. Streetwalkers in gaudy cheap gowns paraded in front of the entrance, though they did not come inside. The proprietor forbade it, Scipion said. Amid the drunken singing and laughter and exchanges of insults there was much conversation. I heard several men debating the state of the world.

"Everything's coming to grief," one of them said. "The end is near."

"Don't be foolish. There is no end. That's just some nonsense in the Bible."

"When Mercury trines Jupiter, and Saturn turns direct in Leo, that is a sure sign of the end of things. Just look around you! Are things getting better, or worse?"

"For me, better. I have a new lover, as ripe as a juicy pear."

Scipion and I both laughed at this talk, and drank some more of the delicious Calvados.

"I can't imagine Alexandre enjoying a place like this," I said at length. "He would be far too fastidious. These rough men would repel him."

"Alexandre is much more comfortable in the company of women than men, as I think I once told you."

"You were right." I had a sudden thought. "Scipion, could you smuggle me aboard one of your ships and take me back to Martinique? Alexandre often says he doesn't care what I do or where I go. He says I can go to the devil. Surely I can go to Martinique."

"And what would you do once you got there? I can't imagine Alexandre would send you an allowance every month. You'd be married, but you would have nothing to live on from your husband. And he would surely demand that your father return all the money he lent him. He would probably seize your father's plantation. Then where would you live?"

I shook my head. "If only I could live in a shack on the beach, and eat fish and crabs and jungle fruits."

"And tell fortunes."

"Yes."

"No, dear, you are far too pretty a girl to go back to Martinique and waste away on the beach. Think of the hurricanes!" I knew he was teasing me. But then a more serious look came into his eyes. "I wonder, Yeyette, if you realize how very alluring you looked tonight, there in Fanny de Beauharnais's salon. You were a breath of fresh air among all those jaded poseurs and faded poets. You have something of value to offer, here in Paris. Something rare. You are genuine. You carry the bracing winds of the islands with you. Trust me, you will be a great success."

"That's what Fanny said to me." It was also, I recalled, what Orgulon had told me. That my future lay across the water. That I would be an important person one day.

"Listen to Fanny. She is very observant. Nothing escapes her."

It was nearly dawn when Scipion delivered me to the marquis's house in the rue Thevenot. No birds were yet astir, but the earliest of the carts full of timber and coal were trundling along the streets.

"Good night, dear Yeyette. Think about what I have said."

"Good night, Scipion."

He kissed me briefly on the lips, then escorted me to the door which was opened by a sleepy groom.

I had not considered that there might be consequences to my staying out most of the night. The marquis and Aunt Edmée knew that I had gone to Fanny's salon, and approved of my going. Alexandre never asked where I was or what I did, and as he himself was usually out all night it did not occur to me that he might be home, waiting for me, when I arrived at five o'clock in the morning.

But I had no sooner stepped inside the foyer than there he was, my wrathful husband, still in his evening clothes, leaning against the jamb of the door that led into the reception room.

"Are you aware of the time, madame?"

"As it happens, I am not." I heard myself speak, and was aware that I was slurring my words.

"I can tell you've drunk too much wine."

"It was Calvados, actually. It was delicious." I began to go up the stairs, intending to go to my bedroom, but Alexandre stopped me.

"Come in here," he said, indicating the reception room. "I have not finished speaking to you."

"I am tired. You can speak to me in the morning."

He strode up to me and seized my arm. "You will listen now." He spoke through clenched teeth. With a sigh I followed him into the large room where the remains of a fire glowed.

"Sit down."

I sat, suddenly very weary.

"Where have you been?"

"At the Café Lestrigal, near the New Bridge."

"A bargeman's café?"

"You could call it that. There were a lot of bargemen there."

Alexandre narrowed his eyes. "And were you alone?"

"I had an escort. Someone you have met. Scipion du Roure."

"Your lover."

"Scipion and I have never been lovers."

"You are never to see him again. And you are never again to disgrace this family by going to places of low amusement."

"As you do."

"Where I go is none of your concern."

"I'm going to bed." I rose to leave, but once again Alexandre caught me by my arm. I could smell the wine he had evidently been drinking. His eyes were bloodshot, and he was breathing with effort.

"We'll go to bed together. It's time I made you my wife. If your lover du Roure is enjoying you, then why not take my turn?" He spoke of love, but his tone was savage.

Still holding my arm, he took me up the stairs to his bedroom. I had never been in that room before. High bookcases framed the hearth, full of leatherbound books whose spines gleamed with gilt-embossed patterns. An old-fashioned panoply hung on another wall—a sword, breastplate, gauntlets and helmet, inlaid with silver and bronze. On a third wall was a portrait of a young blond woman, whom I assumed to be Laure de Girardin, holding a baby.

Alexandre pulled me into the room, slammed the heavy door shut and locked it. Then, quickly throwing off his jacket, waistcoat and shirt, and pulling off his boots, grunting and straining as they were very tight, he began tugging at my clothing. In a moment my lovely red gown lay in shreds at my feet, the torn petticoat hanging loose around my waist, my chemise agape. He pushed me down onto the bed and restrained my arms—for I was fighting to get free of him—while he finished undressing me.

This was nothing like my beautiful, natural coupling with the dark boy in Martinique. This was conquest—angry conquest. Alexandre parted my legs and thrust himself into me until I cried out in pain. Closing his eyes, intent only on his own pleasure, he quickly consummated his barbarity. With an animal grunt he heaved himself off me and collapsed onto the bed, exhausted by his effort.

Weeping and in pain, so furious I wanted to rip the ancient sword off the wall and run Alexandre through, I got down from the high bed and ran to the door. But it was locked. Alexandre had locked me in. But he had been careless with his keys. I found them where they lay on the carpet near his discarded boots, their metal gleaming in the firelight. I snatched them up, then tugged at the coverlet on the bed until it came free. Wrapping the coverlet around me, I unlocked the door as swiftly as I could and ran down the corridor, passing a startled maid who was brushing the stairs on her hands and knees.

I found my room and gratefully took refuge inside. Panting, frightened and hurting badly, I went to the washbasin and filled it with clear cold water from the pitcher. I wanted a bath. I wanted to rid myself of every reminder of Alexandre, even the wine smell that clung to me. But I dared not wake Euphemia to bring out the iron tub and fetch the steaming hot water from the kitchens. I did not want to have to tell Euphemia what had happened. Not yet. I needed time to recover, and to plan my revenge.

Revenge was all I could think of just then. How to punish Alexandre for his cruel ravishing of me, and for his contempt, and for crushing my dream of love. For he had shown me, in a few horrible moments, how the precious union of two bodies could be an ugly thing, and how the sweetness of lovemaking could be turned, through force and terror, into a fearsome hell.

14

I COULD NOT IMAGINE facing Alexandre after what he had done. I lingered in my room all morning, napping and soaking in a tub of soapy water. Then I read until the middle of the afternoon, and finally, when I could postpone it no longer, I went downstairs, hoping I would not see my husband. When Aunt Edmée told me that Alexandre had left to rejoin his regiment in Brest I was greatly relieved, especially when she added that he would not be back for at least a month, perhaps longer.

By the time a month had passed I felt certain that I was carrying Alexandre's child. Euphemia had no doubt of it. She suspended a thimble from a string and held it over my belly.

"If it turns to the left it will be a boy, to the right it will be a girl," she told me. Fascinated, I watched the silver thimble twist and turn in the air, as if uncertain which sign to give. At last it began to turn in a wide arc—to the left.

"A boy then," Euphemia said. "Good. If you give Alexandre a son, he will probably leave you alone."

I told Euphemia about the brutal way Alexandre had treated me. She shook her head.

"It's the way men are, especially when they've had too much to drink. They think we are their playthings. They can use us any way they like. They don't care about us, really."

But I knew that what she said was not true of all men. It had not been true of the dark boy—or had it? He had toyed with me, made me long for him. And then he had taken my virginity.

"I don't want to see him ever again, Euphemia."

"Do you want him dead? I know a charm for that."

"I don't want to murder him, I just don't want to ever see him again."

"Well, you won't be seeing him for awhile anyway. I heard your aunt say he might go far away, to a place called Italy."

Alexandre did in fact leave for Italy soon after this, and was gone for many months. He did not even return in time to be present at the birth of our son. I named the baby Eugene-Rose, and rejoiced in his strength and health. He was a sturdy, active baby with round red cheeks and bright eyes. He seemed to welcome the world, and to be at home in it. I loved him with all my heart, and was very relieved to see that he resembled me and not Alexandre.

My father and Aunt Rosette were delighted at baby Eugene's arrival, and seemed to feel that, now that I had had a child, they had fulfilled their responsibility. They could go home to Martinique. I embraced them both on the day they left for the coast, to wait for the ship that would take them on their long sea journey. I felt that I was losing something very precious, and my heart ached. Though none of us said what was on our minds, we all knew that we might not meet again.

"Try to please Alexandre, Rose," my father said to me. "Be what he wants. When he sees what a devoted mother you are, he may think more highly of you."

Aunt Rosette wept and patted my cheek. "Send me some modes, dear," was all she said. "I want to know what is being worn in Paris." I assured her that I would send the latest styles. Then she climbed into the carriage beside my father and they drove off.

Alexandre had been gone so long I began to wonder whether he would ever return. The marquis rented a house in a better neighborhood, near the church of Saint-Philippe du Roule, and we all settled in there, relieved that we no longer had to live day and night with the stink of the tanneries. As it happened, the new house was not far from where Scipion lived, and he called on me from time to time. He became a favorite with the old marquis and Edmée too liked him.

Life went on comfortably enough, in Alexandre's absence. In the mornings the nursemaid brought Eugene to me and I took him out in the garden, wrapped up warmly against the chill weather. In the afternoon I went out shopping or called on Fanny, who had become an enjoyable companion and who often had interesting people at her house, even when it was not her night to host her salon. Sometimes I went out driving. The marquis let me use his carriage. I liked to dress up and drive in the fashionable parks where people of consequence in Parisian society gathered in the afternoons. I was very bold, riding out alone with no chaperone or escort, and Edmée did not approve. I merely laughed and said that if my husband abandoned me to go off to Italy, he ought to expect me to adapt to living on my own.

Eugene was nearly a year old when Alexandre finally returned. His manner to me was frosty but he was genuinely pleased with the baby, who crowed and gurgled and was already beginning to say his first few words.

Alexandre swept Eugene up in his arms and walked him all around the house, announcing what a fine boy he was and how like himself he looked. (In this he was wrong, but I did not correct him.) Watching him with our son, I could not help but wonder about that other boy, the one Laure de Girardin had borne. Where was he now? Would he and our Eugene ever meet?

Alexandre had brought with him several wagonloads of artworks from Italy. There were marble statues of fauns and nymphs for the garden, an antique bust of Pompey that had been dug up at a place called Herculaneum, and a mosaic of leaping dolphins recovered from a Roman villa. With these were a number of old paintings, much darkened by time and in need of restoration. And there was one more thing, the prize of them all: a very old leather cuirass that, Alexandre insisted, had been worn by Julius Caesar himself.

"How do you know it was worn by Caesar?"

"Because the antiquities dealer assured me that it was, and he has an impeccable reputation. He has sold valuable artworks from ancient times to several prominent collectors, including the Duc de La Rochefoucauld."

The duke was Alexandre's sponsor in the Sarre regiment and had often given him hospitality on his estate. In Alexandre's eyes, the Duc de La Rochefoucauld was a sort of deity, a man to be emulated in every way.

"I assume you paid a lot for this," I said, indicating the strips of greyish leather.

"I don't mind telling you, it cost me nearly five thousand livres."

My eyes widened. I had no idea such relics from Roman times were worth that much. Of course, it was the name of Caesar that was valuable, and his lingering aura of greatness, not the old leather harness itself.

"That much! For five thousand livres we could have bought a home of our own."

"I am perfectly content living with my father and Edmée."

But it was clear to me, when Alexandre had only been back a short while, that he was far from being perfectly content. He was restless, pacing the rooms of the suite we shared, waking often at night and keeping me awake with his wakefulness, sitting brooding in front of the fire until dawn and then dashing off to go riding. He wrote many letters, but when I asked him who he was writing to he refused to say. Through the Duc de La Rochefoucauld's influence Alexandre had been promoted to the rank of major, and I supposed that this carried certain new responsibilities with it, and perhaps the need to write letters to his fellow officers. When I asked, however, he was very curt with me and would say nothing.

In one respect our marriage was different now—and, as I thought, better. Alexandre and I shared a bed, and he showed no more of the brute savagery he had demonstrated on the night Eugene was conceived. He was not a tender lover, and no endearments passed his thin lips. But at least he did not force himself on me, and I took some pleasure from our coupling.

I thought it was pleasure—though perhaps it was no more than relief. After he had been so very rough with me, the fact that he could now be less brutal seemed a boon.

And there was another, far greater benefit. I conceived another child.

I thought Alexandre would be pleased to learn that I was once again expecting, but the news seemed to have the opposite result. He was irritable, and his restlessness increased. Hardly had I begun to accustom myself to the idea of being the mother of two children than I awoke one morning to find Alexandre gone, and most of his possessions gone with him.

Fastening my dressing gown around me I sought out Edmée, who always knew what was happening in our household. When I found her she looked distracted.

"Where is Alexandre, Aunt Edmée? Why are all his things missing?"

She shook her head. "His goings and comings are a mystery to me. But I know he has not been happy here. He says he dislikes this house, that it makes him melancholy."

"Perhaps he misses the stink of the tanneries."

She did not smile at this, but instead handed me a letter.

"I found this under my door when I awoke. It is addressed to you."

I ripped open Alexandre's letter.

"Rose," it began—not "My dear Rose," or "My dear wife"—"I take my leave of you today. It is not possible for us to live together contentedly. I have been appointed to the staff of General Burel, who is in command of our forces on the island of Martinique. Laure and I and our son Alexandre will soon sail together aboard the frigate *Venus*, bound for the Windward Isles."

15

I WILL NOT DWELL on the sordid aftermath of Alexandre's abandonment of me, except to say that, once he got to Martinique, he attempted to defame me before the world. He called me faithless, and claimed that my beloved Hortense, our second child, was not his. He spread lies about my behavior in the years before our marriage, saying that I had had dozens of lovers and that I was a disgrace to my own family and his. He told everyone who would listen that he would never live another day under the same roof with me. And, in the end, he sent me a letter ordering me to leave the house on the rue Neuve-Saint-Charles without delay, or face his wrath.

Even before I received his poisonous letter I had made up my mind to leave. I had had more than enough of Alexandre and his moods and caprices. The venom he was now unleashing against me surpassed all his previous criticisms. Fortunately, according to the letter I received from Aunt Rosette at Les Trois-Ilets, most of what he said about me was not believed.

I had long envied Fanny de Beauharnais the freedom she enjoyed being separated from her husband; now I decided to take that freedom myself.

I went to the public prosecutor and asked him for a legal separation from Alexandre. In time, it was granted.

Now I had what I wanted. I was still the Viscountess Beauharnais, but was unencumbered by a husband who mistreated and slandered me. I was much gratified to discover that Alexandre, when he returned from Martinique, was alone; Laure de Girardin had left him for another man. I had news of him from time to time. I learned that he had fathered another illegitimate child, that he was deeply in debt, having squandered his annuity, and that he had been promoted in rank once again. I was very glad to be rid of him.

Aunt Edmée and my father-in-law the marquis rented a house in Fontainebleau, where King Louis and Queen Marie Antoinette and their court were in residence for the fall hunting season. As I was very short of money I moved in with them, excited at the prospect of being so near the king and queen and eager to be so close to the royal court.

I sold the last of my jewelry for enough money to be able to have two gowns made by M. Leroy, the fashionable dressmaker. One was of silver tissue with a rose-colored satin petticoat beneath it and the other was of the palest blue, with the bodice edged in gold lace.

With these gowns, and a few letters of introduction Fanny had given me, written to her acquaintances at court, I was ready to make my entrance into the realm of the royals.

Euphemia and I went each day to wait at the outermost gate of Fontainebleau Palace for the queen's coach to pass. I was eager to see her, having heard so much about her—most of it very negative.

But when one morning her glittering gilded coach came into view, its panels painted with scenes of plump winged cupids, its doors elaborately carved, the postilions in waistcoats and breeches of lavender velvet, I caught my breath at the sight. Through the window of the coach I glimpsed Queen Marie Antoinette, her lovely face in profile, wearing no jewels but only a simple gown of red and white brocade. Her fair hair was lightly powdered and becomingly arranged, and when she turned to look through the carriage window at those of us who were waiting to see her I could tell that her brow was white and unlined and her eyes were a light porcelain blue. I thought she looked much younger than her thirty years.

"Isn't she beautiful, Euphemia!" I exclaimed. "I think she's one of the most beautiful women I've ever seen."

"Beautiful or not, she's a bad woman," Euphemia muttered. "You know what they say—she spends all the king's money. She's ruining the country. And she has lots of lovers, both men and women."

"I can't believe that someone with such an angelic face could be wicked. The people who say such bad things about her must be jealous."

I saw the queen again at a ball given by Countess de Rancy. I wore my silver gown and Euphemia arranged my hair simply, like the queen's, and added a cream-colored feather. The ball opened at nine-thirty and at about ten o'clock there was a stir of anticipation in the crowded ballroom. I heard the usher tap his stave on the parquet floor and announce the queen's name.

She billowed into the room, floating on a cloud of pale pink silk. Her skirts flowed in soft folds to the floor, her ample bosom was encased in a silken bodice entwined with white flowers. Once again I was struck by the sweetness of her expression, and by the delicate molding of her hands and arms. She moved through the room with exquisite grace. The king was not with her. He had worn himself out galloping through the forest in pursuit of game, it was said. After eating a huge meal he had gone to sleep.

I could not take my eyes off the queen—until I heard a voice at my elbow.

"Viscountess Beauharnais, may I have the honor of this dance?"

I looked down. A very short, very ugly man stood beside me, his thick black hair escaping untidily from under his ash-white wig. He had large darting black eyes, a broad nose and very full lips. His embroidered coat was of pale green, the wide ruffles of lace at his wrists fell across his small hands and he wore many costly rings. I am barely five feet tall myself and this man was a good deal shorter than I. Still, the orchestra was playing the Monaco, a dance I liked very much at that time, and I had been tapping my foot in time to the music.

I said yes and took the little man's hand.

While we danced he introduced himself as Henri, Baron Rossignol, a Picard and an acquaintance of the queen's chief steward.

"I lend him money," he confided to me on tiptoe, putting his thick lips as close to my ear as possible. "He says the money is for his own use, but I know it is really for someone else. Someone very important."

"Do you mean the queen?" I asked.

"Hush! Do you want the whole court to hear?" The baron looked at me accusingly, then winked. I knew that I had guessed the truth.

"Tell me, Viscountess, are you in need of a loan?"

The boldness of the question astonished me. Money was something one gossiped about with friends, but did not discuss with strangers.

"I may be one of the few people in Paris who isn't in need of a loan," I said, untruthfully. "If I am in need, I simply tell fortunes. People give me generous gifts in return."

The baron paused in midstep.

"These people whose fortunes you tell, they must trust you."

"Yes. I am good at reading the cards."

"Perhaps we could assist one another. If you will permit me, I would like to call on you in a few days." The Monaco ended, and the short little baron led me back to my place. "Until then," he said, kissing my hand.

I danced until I was weary that night, until long after most of the guests had left, and then went home and told Euphemia that I had seen the queen and danced nearly every dance. For days afterwards I practiced imitating the queen's graceful movements and gestures, the slow, easy way she sat and stood, even her benign facial expression. I am not like her, she was a very large woman with a long face while I am quite petite and my face is round, my cheeks full. Yet I tried, in those days in Fontainebleau, to make myself as much like her as I could, so strong was the impression she had made on me.

Baron Rossignol came calling a few days later as he had said he would and when he sat down on the sofa in the reception room of the marquis's rented house I was once again struck by how short and how ugly he was. Aunt Edmée, who was in the room with me, did not conceal her distaste at the sight of him. I asked my aunt if I could speak with the baron alone, and she left us—with an audible sniff of disapproval.

The baron laughed at her scorn, then turned his bright darting eyes on me.

"Viscountess," he began, after I invited him to sit down, "I sense that we are—how shall I put it?—we are two men of business, only one of us is a woman. You are avid to advance yourself, and I may be able to aid that advancement, while at the same time benefiting myself.

"Let me tell you about who I am. My lineage is exalted. I am descended from Hugh Capet, the first Capetian king of France." At this he drew himself up to his full height, adding perhaps an inch to his stature. "My family has held estates in Picardy for many centuries. But my father was unfortunate. A cousin claimed all the lands my father held, and went to the law courts. He took everything. We were not able to save anything. We had nothing to fall back on, for my mother's family had been impoverished for several generations. They had their rank and titles but little else. I was destined from birth for a military career, but as you can see, my physical endowments prevent this. I had no desire to enter the church. So I found another avenue of employment: I became a moneylender."

All the moneylenders I had ever heard of were Italians or Jews. That a titled nobleman could be a moneylender seemed strange to me. I listened with increasing interest as the baron went on.

"Of course I have no money of my own to lend. My source of funds is a rich Englishman. He transfers large sums into my bank account and I draw it out to make the loans.

"But, my dear viscountess, the borrowers are becoming frightened. They fear that the government will collapse, and all the banks will close. Everything of value they possess will become forfeit."

I shivered at his words, for I had often had these fears.

"What I need you to do, viscountess, is reassure them. When you read the cards, say, 'You are in difficulty about money, but a stranger will soon come to your aid.' I will be that stranger. They will think my arrival is providential. They will trust me and do business with me."

"And if I offer this reassurance, what do I get in return?"

"One hundred livres for every thousand that they borrow."

I thought for a moment. My father had always told me that moneylenders were dishonest scoundrels. "Nothing but thieves, every last one," he had said. Well then, I thought, if they are thieves, I will take as much as I can from them.

"Two hundred," I said.

"One-fifty."

"One seventy-five."

"Done."

The little man beamed at me. "Ah, viscountess, you are a better man of business than I am. You bargain like a fishwife haggling over a basket of eels. And I fear you are as slippery as an eel, no matter how elegant you look and how sweetly you smile. I will have to watch you."

"And I you. In the meanwhile, I have no doubt there is money to be made."

16

WE PROSPERED, the baron and I. I continued to tell fortunes, and to persuade desperate men and women to be on the alert for a helpful stranger who would lend them money. The baron made the loans, and rewarded me with what seemed to me large sums in cash. I stored the coins in a chest in the marquis's wine cellar, hidden behind dusty furniture and piles of lumber.

Month by month our enterprise grew. I sent some of my newfound wealth to my father in Martinique and some to Aunt Rosette. With the rest I invested, along with the baron, in land and buildings. So many people were building mansions in the wealthiest district of Paris—and so many found themselves unable to afford the great houses once they were completed. Baron Rossignol and I bought these abandoned mansions at low prices and resold them to new speculators who then, as often as not, found themselves in financial difficulties and abandoned the great houses once again.

We prospered, but many others failed. An uncle of Alexandre's, Etienne de Beauharnais, drank a heavy dose of laudanum and died, leaving a letter to the marquis in which he confessed that he faced bankruptcy and could not endure the shame.

I attended the funeral, which was held at the church of the Ursuline Sisters in Fontainebleau. Eugene and Hortense were with me, Eugene a handsome boy in his school uniform which resembled that of the palace guards, Hortense quiet and subdued in her little gown of black velvet. After the funeral mass ended Alexandre came up to us and kissed the children, who were glad to see him. I was relieved to notice that he was as warm to Hortense as he was to Eugene. I hoped that meant that he no longer doubted her paternity.

"I've been seeing your name in the newspapers," I said to Alexandre. "They say you speak out often on the issue of political reform. That you are a persuasive orator."

He looked proud and self-important, hearing my words. "I hold strong views. I express them openly. France must change if she is to survive, and the change cannot come from our timid king. The people must create their own future."

"How?"

"By coming together, as they did centuries ago, when their parliament, the Estates-General, met and consulted. Only the Estates-General can prevent the king from becoming a bankrupt like my Uncle Etienne." Alexandre seemed like a man possessed, so passionately did he speak of the need for reform. It was as if all the passion he once had for carousing and womanizing was now being redirected into politics—with the result that he was a changed man. Perhaps even a nobler man. I was gratified to see that he had found a worthwhile outlet for his intensity of purpose. At least, some considered the cause of political reform worthwhile. Others condemned it and called it treasonous.

"I've had a letter from Martinique," Alexandre told me toward the end of our conversation. "From a colonel who knows your father well."

"Oh? And how is father?"

"Ill and weak—and growing weaker. He has had a fever. The colonel says he is determined to rescue Les Trois-Ilets from ruin despite his ill health. He works in the fields alongside the slaves, with his shirt off, in the fierce hot sun."

"Poor father. He won't last long, doing that. Mother must be browbeating him, forcing him to work. She has never forgiven him for his lazy ways and his vices."

My conversation with Alexandre increased my concern for my father, and made me homesick for Martinique. When a letter arrived from Aunt Rosette, telling me that my grandmother Catherine had died I knew I had to return home.

I found a ship that was due to sail within a few weeks and made hasty preparations to be on it. Eugene remained at his boarding school but Hortense came with me—and Euphemia of course. I took gifts for everyone, a new gold-topped walking stick for father, a large gilded birdcage for Aunt Rosette, to keep her parrots in, a necklace of topaz and a harp for my mother, a leather-bound edition of the works of Montesquieu for my Uncle Robert and various other small gifts for my cousins and friends.

I did not relish the idea of another ocean crossing and dreaded the prospect of sharing a tiny cramped cabin with Hortense and Euphemia— and my mother's harp. Because we were the last of the passengers to make our arrangements we were given the smallest and most uncomfortable cabin.

"By all that's holy!" Euphemia blurted out when she saw it. "It's barely big enough for two roaches to fight in!"

The damp, rotting walls of our tiny cabin seemed to close in around us as the days passed and the weather grew hotter and more humid. Green blooms of mold appeared on the ceiling and dropped on us as we slept. Hortense was very ill right from the start of the voyage and could keep nothing in her stomach; her piteous retching woke us often during the long nights. No sooner had she recovered than Euphemia turned pale and began vomiting in her turn. Eventually, after a week of bad storms, I too succumbed.

We were a fine sight, we Parisians in our stained, limp gowns that reeked of sea-damp, our hair disheveled and our faces pinched and thin. Still, when we were fit enough we went up on deck, eager for fresh air and company, and I quickly made the acquaintance of two planters who were returning to Martinique after a long sojourn in Paris.

"I tell you, I'm selling up," said the older of the two, who introduced himself as Felix Houlier. His weathered face was creased by years in the sun, and his eyes, sunk deep in their sockets, were full of discouragement. "Just as soon as the next crop of fourteen-month cane is in, I'm off for France again. I've built myself a house near Chambord. I'll sell this crop and pay off the bankers. With luck I'll have enough left over to live on."

"I can't afford to sell," said his companion, Barthélemy Ariès, a dapper, sharp-featured man who I judged to be in his thirties. "I go deeper into debt every year. If only my father would die and leave me his money! But he won't. He's a crusty old bird, still strong and mean at sixty."

Both men knew my father—most Grands Blancs knew one another, as our island of Martinique is small. They spoke of him with respect, which surprised me as I had always assumed he was a failure. I had heard my mother and grandmother say this so often that the idea was deeply implanted in me.

"Tascher is sound enough," Houlier said, wiping his sweaty brow. "He's not had an easy time of it, after all. I heard that half his slaves ran off to join that ragtag army in the hills."

"What ragtag army?"

"The ones who call themselves Friends of Liberty," spat out Ariès. "Friends indeed!! What they really want is to kill all the Grands Blancs. They tried to poison us all last summer, by putting rancid meat out in the marketplace for us to buy. They steal our cattle and kidnap our children. They threaten our women and terrify the house slaves. They want us all dead and gone, so they can take over the island and rule it themselves."

I was shocked at what I was hearing. Aunt Rosette, in her letters to me, never mentioned any slave army or threats against the Grands Blancs. Yet she was an exceptionally nervous and timid person. If she were frightened, wouldn't she have told me?

When we finally disembarked in Martinique I could feel the tension in the air. Passengers hurried off the ship, and the friends and relations waiting on the dock to meet them gave them the swiftest of greetings before hurrying them into waiting vehicles and speeding away.

I was relieved to see that Uncle Robert was there to meet us, his tall, portly figure a comforting sight. He embraced me and Euphemia, then held out his arms to Hortense, who ran to him willingly.

"Look, Uncle Robert, I've learned the hornpipe." She danced and twirled there on the dock, repeating the steps the sailors had taught her after she recovered from her seasickness.

"Brava, little one," he cried out. "What a fine little performer you are!"

"Perhaps she can dance for pennies in the marketplace," I said jokingly. Instead of smiling Uncle Robert's face became stern. "Not in the marketplace," he said firmly, hoisting Hortense up in his arms and holding onto her tightly. "Not these days at least. Now then, Yeyette, you can all ride in my carriage. Joseph wanted to come and meet you but your mother forbade it. You will understand why when we reach Les Trois-Ilets."

Driving through the marketplace, I began to see what my uncle meant. The once lively, bustling square was all but deserted, the few pathetic-looking stalls that now clustered in one corner offered few goods for sale and the few shoppers appeared to be clutching their marketbaskets tightly, as if in fear. Armed guardsmen patrolled the margins of the square, swinging thick truncheons, cane knives stuck into their belts.

"We had an incident here last Wednesday," my uncle whispered to me. "A Grand Blanc was found hanging upside down, butchered like a hog. His guts and blood were all over the cobblestones. Part of his skin was flayed off. I tell you, Yeyette, it was the most horrible thing I have ever seen."

"But who did it?"

"He had a sign hanging from his feet. It said 'Friends of Liberty.' "

I shuddered, imagining the ghastly scene.

"Every night since then we have patrolled the streets here in Fort-Royal, rounding up runaways and rebels. They have paid a heavy price for what they did, I assure you. Look!"

I followed Uncle Robert's pointing finger and saw, hanging from a lamppost, the crumpled form of an African, naked except for a loincloth, a thick rope around his neck. Quickly I covered Hortense's eyes. I did not want her to see the dead man's frightening face, the lolling tongue and staring eyes.

"There—and there—" Uncle Robert pointed out more dead bodies, most of them very black, a few lighter, like Euphemia.

"We even had to hang the police," Uncle Robert went on. "They were no good. They joined the rebels!"

"Surely not all of them!"

"Many. The rest ran off to the caves in the mountains."

All the way to my father's plantation of Les Trois-Ilets I held Hortense's hand and tried to distract her from looking out the carriage window. Every African face I saw on the road looked menacing, every group of slaves working in the cane fields seemed a threat. The thick plantings of cane, the clumps of broad-leaved banana trees and plantains, no longer appeared beautiful to me. Now they seemed like hiding places for rebels, camouflage behind which an army of angry blacks lurked, waiting to kill us all.

I tried to tell myself that I was not thinking clearly, that in my tired state, worn down by the hardships of the long sea journey, I was allowing my fears to run away with me. I had grown up among Africans, I had loved them as playmates, beloved servants, friends. My half-sister Euphemia was closer to me than anyone, except perhaps my father. How could these familiar companions threaten harm?

When we reached Les Trois-Ilets and Uncle Robert left us, hurrying off in his carriage, I sensed at once a pronounced chill in the atmosphere, a tension that told me my father and mother were in conflict. Sadness overcame me as everything I saw in the converted sugar mill where my family lived reminded me of my grandmother. We would not see one another again. My dearest grandmother! If only she were here, with her clear-eyed understanding of things and her tart tongue, I would not feel so sad, confused and frightened.

My father, showing a vigor that quite surprised me, given all that I had heard about his weakened state, came into the room that served as a front hallway and greeted us. There was a light in his eyes and a confidence in his speech that I had not heard since I was a young child.

"Yeyette! You have become a true Parisienne!" He gazed in admiration at my costly gown, overlooking the salt stains on its fine fabric, and also noted my jeweled rings and dangling earrings. "You will no doubt find Martinique tedious, after the pleasures of the capital. And your lovely little Hortense, dear child, come and kiss your old grandpapa." She went to him, smiling, and kissed him on the cheek. "And where is Eugene, the young warrior?"

"Still at school, papa, preparing to enter the military academy."

"Yes, of course. He is a dedicated boy, isn't he? And a handsome one, to judge from the miniature portrait you sent me."

My father chattered on, his energetic flow of talk seemingly unceasing. Finally I interrupted him.

"Papa! Where is mother? Where is Aunt Rosette?"

"They have chosen to move into the wind-house."

"The wind-house? But that's nothing more than a cave in the rocks!"

He shrugged. "It was their choice."

"No, father. I cannot believe that. Something has happened. Does it have anything to do with the savage attack Uncle Robert told us about, the killing of that poor man in the marketplace?"

"Let us not speak of that in front of the child. Euphemia, take Hortense upstairs and put her to bed."

After a moment's hesitation, Euphemia looked over at me. I nodded to her. "Yes, Euphemia, please take Hortense to my room and let her lie down."

"Now, father," I said when they had gone, "tell me what is going on."

But there was no need for him to say anything more. A woman came into the room and walked over to him, her walk sinuous, a wide smile on her dark brown face. She wore a red and gold gown that clung tightly to her shapely thighs and barely covered her full round breasts, a gown no respectable woman, Grand Blanc or African, would wear. Golden earrings hung from her earlobes, and her coppery brown skin shone as if oiled. She approached my father with an unmistakable seductiveness, and he drew her to him with an embrace so intimate that it left no doubt that they were lovers.

So brazen was their revelation of intimacy that I almost felt embarrassed, as if I were witnessing something too private to be viewed. I turned away, suddenly angry on my mother's behalf. I began to gather my things, intending to leave the room. But before I could do so, the woman spoke, her language a heavily accented creole French, her husky voice rich and full.

"Yeyette! Don't you recognize me?"

I turned to face her. "I am addressed as Madame la Vicomtesse by slaves."

"Selene is not a slave, Yeyette. I gave her her freedom long ago. I thought it a shame that such a lovely body should be wasted, working in the fields." He passed one hand down the curvaceous length of the woman, from her bare shoulder across one breast, inward to her slim waist and outward again along the thrust of her hips and on down her leg.

"When I was very young, and just off the boat from Africa, I served you," the woman said to me. "I sat on the floor while you slept, and pulled on the rope that turned your fan. I kept you cool. You never spoke to me. Not once. You never said, 'Selene, are you hot too? Are you thirsty?' You never looked at me. To you, I was not even there. I was a ghost, a wraith. A phantom raised by a quimboiseur."

I looked at the woman, offended by the brazenness of her speech— and offended far more by the way her hand rested possessively on my father's shoulder.

"No. I did not speak to you. You were a slave child performing a necessary task. There was no need for us to talk to one another. Just as there is no need for us to talk now."

"Oh, I think there is, Yeyette. You see, we are family, you and I— and Euphemia too. We are all related through Joseph, we all carry his blood. You and Euphemia are his daughters. The child inside me will be his son."

17

A THIEF HAD BEEN CAUGHT, accused of stealing and hoarding sweet potatoes from the garden, then running away.

All the slaves from Les Trois-Ilets were summoned by the tolling of the great bell that rang out over the cane fields. They had to watch the thief be punished, a warning to them, in those times of deepening conflict and unrest, that they too would face punishment if they did not obey the master.

I stood beside my father on the veranda of the converted mill, waiting for the thief to receive his due.

"It looks well to have the family with me at times such as these," my father said. "As a reminder that we Grands Blancs are in charge, and will be for generations to come."

For once Selene was not clinging to my father's arm—indeed she was nowhere to be seen. Her belly was becoming larger and larger. My father confided to me that the African midwife in Fort-Royal thought Selene might have twins.

"How would that be, Yeyette?" father said proudly. "Imagine that. Twin boys. And at my age!"

"You can hardly expect me to welcome Selene's children into our family. Not while mother is shut away in the wind-house, humiliated and robbed of her rights." I had said as much as I could on that subject, and had gotten nowhere.

The slaves were slowly filing into the open space below the veranda. I watched their faces. Some were impassive, some resentful, many openly hostile. It was impossible not to notice, watching the slaves assemble, the scars they bore. Scars of their captivity: marks of the whip on their broad backs, raw weals from recent beatings, hands and fingers cut off, eyes and noses missing.

"With the money you've sent me I bought fifty new Africans," my father said. "And I've hired a new overseer. There'll be no more runaways now."

A tall, lithe man was walking in front of the assembled slaves, his walk neither fast nor slow, his step confident. He wore the leather breeches, linen shirt and dark vest of a planter. His dark hair, worn long, was tied back off his neck. His lean, tanned face was handsome, his expression unreadable.

He motioned for the thief to be led in, and briefly—ever so briefly—he looked up onto the veranda, and into my eyes. The intensity of that furtive glance was unmistakable. It was the dark boy!

I knew him at once—and felt my body respond.

The dark boy had become a dark man, the power of his gaze intensified tenfold by his maturity. Seeing him, and feeling my desire for him sweep over me as it had so many years earlier, I had to reach out for the railing of the veranda to steady myself.

"Who is he?" I asked my father as I began to regain my customary control. I indicated that I meant the overseer, who was tying the thief's hands with a length of rope.

"That's Donovan. Donovan de Gautier. Used to be a soldier, so he says. Has no family—or none that he admits to having. He's the best overseer I've ever had."

So the dark boy had a name. Donovan. Not a creole name. An English name. Or was it Irish, like my grandmother?

I could not take my eyes from him. I remembered the look of his slim, muscular naked body the day he dove into the sea when I was a girl. I remembered all of him. The look, the smell, the feel of him. The sheer joy of our lovemaking.

I realized that I was smiling, and forced my mouth into a solemn line. The overseer was pointing to a pile of wood over which a metal grate was being placed. On his orders the thief—a terrified young man, cringing and weeping—was lifted roughly and placed face-down on the metal grate. Lighted torches were brought and held close to the wood.

A murmuring began in the crowd of slaves.

"Yes, you all can tell what will happen to this thief," Donovan was saying. "He will be burned alive. He will be roasted, until his skin peels from his body like the skin of a chicken is peeled from its flesh. From now on this is to be the punishment for theft: to be roasted alive."

The murmuring grew louder. It was a sound of protest.

"And anyone who objects," Donovan went on, "will be roasted alongside the thief."

"My God," I heard my father mutter. "My God, this is too much."

I saw that the overseer was cruel. But that realization barely registered in my mind. I realized with shock that the horror of the present moment paled beside its promise—the promise that Donovan, the dark man, might be mine once again.

The torches were held closer to the wood. Any second now the fire would blaze up and consume the shaking, sobbing boy. Once again I was dizzy and overwhelmed. I thought that I might faint.

Donovan lifted his arm. The horror was upon us.

Then, suddenly, he shouted. "Wait!"

The pause seemed to last forever.

"Wait," Donovan said again. "I think this thief will live. The next thief to be caught will be roasted alive. This I swear. Who will be the next thief? You? Or you? Or you?" He stepped closer to the group of slaves and pointed an accusing finger at several of them in turn. Each one stepped back, lowered his head and said, "No, sir."

I heard my father chuckling. "He's frightened them half to death."

Donovan ordered the thief to be whipped and sent him away. But the boy broke free of the two men who were holding him and knelt at the overseer's feet. To my astonishment, the boy kissed the dusty toes of Donovan's black boots.

"Now, that's the way to make them behave," my father said. "Treat them like naughty children. Scare them. Then be lenient with them. The man's a genius."

The slaves were sent away to return to their labors. Donovan moved off toward the stables. I watched him go, unable to take my eyes from his broad back and long legs. Just before he turned the corner of the mill he glanced back in my direction, his mouth turned slightly upward in the merest ghost of a smile.

18

WHEN WOULD WE MEET? When would I see him again? How should I behave when we were together? Questions whirled through my eager, worried mind. Was he married? Was there a woman in his life? A Selene, perhaps? What did he know of me? Of my years in France, and my difficulties and disappointments? Did he care?

I slept that night, but Donovan's face and lithe body wove themselves through my troubled dreams. And when the following day dawned I swore that I would seek him out. I would place myself in his path somehow, to give him the chance to approach me.

But I did not see him that day, or the next. Protecting my complexion with a large umbrella, I strolled along the margins of the cane fields, watching for his tall figure amid the stalks of ripening cane. In the past he had been elusive, playful. We had been involved in an ongoing game of hide and seek. Now that we were adults, would that game continue? Or was I foolish to imagine that the pleasures of the past might go on?

When three days had gone by and I had seen nothing of the dark man I asked my father about him.

"I've sent Donovan to Les Plages. It's a small estate on the slopes of Morne des Larmes. Your Uncle Robert bought it last year. He'll be back in a week or two."

"Why has he gone there? What have you sent him to do?"

My father sighed. "I may as well tell you, Rose, that we believe a slave insurrection is being planned. All the Grands Blancs are taking what measures we can to protect ourselves and our properties. The Grands Blancs are at war. Donovan is organizing a militia at Les Plages, and gathering firearms, and making certain everyone knows what to do and where to go when the emergency comes."

"Surely you mean if an emergency comes."

"Oh, it will come, Rose. And before long. But we can endure it, just as we endure the great wind storms and the terrible floods. We are creoles. We are made of strong stuff."

One night my Uncle Robert and a number of other plantation owners came to Les Trois-Ilets and assembled in the largest room of the converted mill. Donovan was among them, as were several militia officers and the head of the police force in Fort-Royal. Rum and coffee were served, and there were plates full of sweet cakes and ripe fruit. But the food, I noticed, was barely tasted. The men were intent on the business at hand.

"The *Vengeur* is due to arrive this week, from Brest," my uncle told the others. "She brings another hundred muskets, plus powder and spare stocks."

"If only it were five hundred," another man said. "Nothing but massive firepower will stop them, if they come in force."

An assessment was made of each militia on the island, how many men it had enrolled, how many weapons were in its cache.

"All the women and children must share a single dormitory, heavily guarded at night, and the men must take turns at the watch, sleeping in shifts."

"When you hear your neighbor's alarm bell ringing, ring your own at once."

"Listen for any change in the sound of the drums. We know the drums are a code. But it is constantly changing. Only the rebels can understand it."

"Why not just lock up all the slaves until the army can come from France and deal with them?" one plantation owner asked.

"Because there are far too many of them," came the curt reply. "For every Grand Blanc there are a hundred Africans. And France, as you may have noticed, is not overly concerned with the fate of her colonies."

"She will be concerned when no more cane is shipped. When no more taxes are paid."

The men wrangled and argued, and I sat listening, my presence largely overlooked except by Donovan, whose eyes sought my face and body several times.

"There is one thing we must always keep in mind," my Uncle Robert was saying. "This is no ordinary warfare we face. Potent African forces are being set loose. Orgulon, the mighty quimboiseur, is said to be prophesying a bloodbath."

Dismissive remarks greeted this pronouncement.

"Scoff if you like, but he commands obedience from many of our own Africans. He has been holding meetings at the Sacred Crossroads on Morne Ganthéaume. Our people go there to pay tribute. Unspeakable things go on there, I am told. Human sacrifices. Dead bodies reanimated. Orgies with spirits of the dead."

Yes, I wanted to say. Powerful things go on where Orgulon is. I have seen them. And he saved my life, when the fer-de-lance was about to strike.

"Orgulon is coming down from Morne Ganthéaume," said Uncle Robert, "and we all had better watch for him. One word from him and our plantations will go up in smoke."

"We are not children," Donovan said, standing as he spoke. "We do not fear the bogeyman. We know that this Orgulon is nothing more than flesh and blood, an old man with a weak old man's body and a wily brain. What we must respect, I suggest, is the fear Orgulon creates in others."

Grunts of assent greeted this statement.

"Orgulon has convinced his weak, foolish followers that he can kill a man with a glance, or stop the wind from blowing, or converse with the old gods of Africa through some pagan rituals. It is belief we must be concerned about. Belief in magic. Belief in the occult."

"Yes, that's the real enemy. Pagan belief. False belief," said another of the planters, and there were murmurs of assent.

Or was the real enemy the force of change, I wondered. The power of an idea—the idea that the day of the Grands Blancs is over.

The following morning I went to the wind-house where my mother and Aunt Rosette spent their lonely days. I needed to tell them about the emergency plans being made, about the insurrection that was expected and the safety precautions they needed to take.

"It would be best if you came back to the mill for awhile, maman," I told my mother. "You and Aunt Rosette can be protected there."

"There is nothing for me in that place but humiliation," she replied angrily. "Until that woman is gone, I will not set foot in the mill."

I soon saw that my mother had grown more stubborn. Living in her self-imposed exile had become the rock on which she built her pride, her self-respect. To leave the wind-house, I knew, would mean abandoning the most precious part of herself and acknowledging defeat.

"He always used to keep his whores in Fort-Royal, you know," she remarked after a time. "He kept them in their place." Hearing my mother allude to my father's perennial infidelity so casually was painful; she had never discussed it before in my presence. "I hated them all," she went on, "but I couldn't touch them there. So I let them have their town, and my husband, and I kept order here at Les Trois-Ilets."

She smoothed her skirt, running her thumbnail down a crease along one seam. She had never been a pretty woman, but there had always been an abundance of youthful color in her cheeks, and her eyes were an attractive shade of blue, lighter than my own. Now, however, she looked washed-out and pale, her hair a faded shade of grey, her skin ashen, her eyes ice-blue and ringed with dark circles. She would never admit her true age but I guessed that she was past forty-five.

"I kept order here," she repeated, "until six months ago. Then your father chose this girl to be his next mistress—this girl who had been our own house slave!—and began living with her, right alongside the rest of us. I tried to turn her out but he defended her.

"'I'm dying, old woman,' he said to me. 'Can't you see I'm dying? Can't you let me enjoy my last months?'"

She made a scornful sound, and brushed her hand across her skirt as if to clear away an offending bug or bit of lint.

"Of course he's no more dying than I am, or you are, Yeyette. He'll live for years, just to spite me."

"But you can't go on staying out here in the wind-house, mother. It's miles away from everything. You must come back to the mill, where you can be protected. What if you should get sick, or have an accident?"

"I have Rosette, and three of the slave girls, and Jules-sans-nez who brings us food from the mill kitchen nearly every day." Jules-sans-nez, or Noseless Jules, had been a cart driver at Les Trois-Ilets for many years. He was a mellow old African man with long grey hair worn in thin braids and a sunburned skull, always singing as he drove, his voice with an odd whistle to it because of his disfigurement. It was said his nose had been cut off when he was only a child, by a cruel overseer. I had known Jules all my life.

My Aunt Rosette had been sitting in a corner of the cavelike room, eyes downcast, hands folded in her lap. I now saw that her cheeks were wet with tears. She looked over at me.

"Can't you see, Yeyette, that we cannot go back while Selene is there?"

"I will not have that girl's name spoken in my presence!" my mother barked.

Aunt Rosette went on, unfazed by my mother's reproach. "Moving here to the wind-house is the only protest we can make against what Joseph is doing. But you, Yeyette, you can make him get rid of Selene."

"Quiet, I say! Not that name again!" My mother glared at Rosette, trembling with rage.

"Joseph respects you," Rosette was saying. "You stood up to Alexandre. You had the strength to leave your marriage. He could never admit to you that he admired you for it, but I know he does. And he admires you for being able to make money, which he cannot. Make Joseph see reason and move that girl to Fort-Royal!"

Seeing the two of them, my mother and aunt, there in the wind-house on the side of the hill filled me with sorrow and vexation. My mother's pride, and Aunt Rosette's loyalty to her, kept them in their isolation. But in their stubbornness they could not appreciate the danger they were in. Somehow they had to be made to realize, in the days ahead, that they must come home.

19

HE CAME FOR ME, as I sensed he would, on a warm, fragrant night when the air was full of the scent of jasmine blossoms. He knocked at my window, standing on the veranda, and when I went to the door to let him in he gently took my hand and pulled me outside. My feet were bare and I wore only a thin white linen nightgown. My hair was long and loose, tumbling down my back in dark waves.

He led me to a bare room where newly cut cane was sometimes stored. The sugary scent of the cane was overpowering. He had piled blankets under an open window and together we sank down into their softness.

As he began stroking my cheek I felt all the tightness in my chest and stomach unravel, and my worried mind let itself relax. I was safe, time was suspended and all was forgotten—all but the pleasure we took in one another.

We lay together all night. Our passion rose and fell, rose and fell, its heights indescribable, its depths a seductive invitation to begin anew. I lost myself in him, my longing for him deepening even as our bodies merged. It was a longing beyond longing, a craving of the flesh, as urgent as hunger or thirst. He had been a beautiful boy, but his manly beauty was far greater and I responded to it with all my senses, opening up to him like a flower opening itself to the sun.

He gave himself to me, fully and completely. And then, at dawn, he rose from the tumble of blankets, put on his clothes, leaned over to kiss me one last time—and was gone.

He left me breathing in the pungent, lingering scent of him, and the strong scent of sugar, and the rich musky odor of our lovemaking, an odor that was ours alone. I had nothing else from him, beyond my memories, and my hope of our meeting again.

But something had changed. In the past he had been the dark boy. Now he was my father's overseer, a man among other men. And he had a name: Donovan de Gautier.

20

IT WAS IN THE FALL OF MY TWENTY-SIXTH YEAR, the year 1789, that the astounding news began to arrive from France. Every ship that docked at Fort-Royal brought fresh stories, word of surprising events.

First we heard that the king had sent thousands of troops into Paris, frightening everyone. Then we heard that a huge armed crowd of unemployed workers and angry radicals had marched to the old fortress of the Bastille and broken in, killing the soldiers inside. And that all the Parisians were wild with joy over this and went to tear down the walls of the old place, as if it were a strong castle and not a forgotten and disused antique of no importance.

For years there had been talk of reform. Now, it seemed, reform had arrived—and no one was in charge of it, to prevent it from going too far. We heard the remarkable news that all the nobles had given up their titles, and that Alexandre had been among the first to renounce his! I was no longer Vicomtesse de Beauharnais, but plain Rose Tascher, Citizeness Beauharnais. All male citizens were now equal in France. Throughout Paris the watchwords were "Liberty, Equality, Fraternity."

It sounded fine and noble—until one thought about where such a philosophy might lead. Not everyone was highminded. Not everyone was altruistic. It did not surprise me when we learned that throughout

France, thieves were ransacking the mansions of the rich, demanding equality of wealth.

News of the sudden social changes in France made the existing conflict between slaves and masters on Martinique much worse. There were many freedmen in Fort-Royal, former slaves who had received their freedom, and from among their ranks orators now arose who spoke eloquently of the rights of all slaves to be equal with their masters. There should be no more servitude, they proclaimed. No more bondage. All men ought to be free.

The immediate result was turmoil, on a scale never previously known in Martinique. (Or so Jules-sans-nez assured me, and he was said to be over ninety years old.) Field hands ran off, house slaves refused to work. The cane stood uncut, ready for harvest, rotting where it stood. Fishing-boats were idle, market stalls empty. Cattle lowed in their pens, waiting in vain to be fed and watered.

Slave riots broke out, we heard rumors of Grands Blancs being castrated and hanged, of their wives being raped and garroted. Runaway slaves were seen in the streets of Fort-Royal wearing necklaces made from the pale white ears of Grands Blancs. All across the island, slave drums could be heard, passing messages. And we had no doubt the messages meant us harm.

Day after day, night after night the tension grew until on one moonlit night the savage pounding intensified to a new level of threat. Euphemia, frowning, went to the latticed window to listen.

"They are coming," I heard her mutter. She added more words in the Ibo tongue that I felt certain were prayers and incantations. Then she kissed the small statue of the Ibo Red Goddess that she wore around her neck and acted quickly. She picked up Hortense and, calling to me to follow, hurried with her down into the root cellar, a big, dim, cool room full of bins of sweet potatoes and tubers and casks of rum.

A half-dozen others followed us, among them Jules-sans-nez and Selene, her eyes wide with fear, her grossly swollen belly making it hard for her to descend the stairs.

"Stay down here," Euphemia said to the rest of us, taking charge. "No matter what. Bolt the door when I go. I am going to warn the master."

Euphemia never used the name "father," nor did our father call her "daughter." The social gulf between them was too great, I supposed. Though I had heard it said that my father had loved Euphemia's mother more than any of his other mistresses—until now, that is. Until Selene.

Euphemia mounted the stairs and we bolted the door as she had told us to.

We waited, as the sounds of drumming grew more insistent and with it, a clamor of voices. Men's voices.

Where was Donovan? I wondered. He was often away at Les Plages. Had he gone there tonight, to gather the militia?

We waited, in the dimness, tight with fear and dread. Euphemia did not return. Had she been captured? I was afraid for her.

We heard a sudden pounding on the heavy door. No one moved. The pounding grew louder.

"Let us in! Let us in!" It was a woman's voice. A voice I recognized. It was Aunt Rosette!

Swiftly I let go of Hortense, who had been sitting on my lap.

"Aunt Rosette!" I called as I ran up the stairs. "I'm coming, Aunt Rosette!" I unbolted the door and there stood my aunt, her face smoke-blackened, her gown torn and her bare feet muddy. Beside her was my mother, equally bedraggled.

"Do you have any food?" were my mother's only words. She was weak and hollow-eyed.

"We have eaten nothing for three days," Aunt Rosette told me matter-of-factly. "They kept us shut in the wind-house, behind those big heavy doors. There were thousands of them, singing and clapping. It was horrible! We thought we were going to die."

My mother had come down the stairs and was rooting in a bin of sweet potatoes. She began eating one, as ravenous as a starved dog. Rosette too came down and began to feast on the raw potatoes, both women heedless of decorum.

Through the high barred windows of the root cellar I could glimpse a lurid red light. Torches, I thought. They're burning the cane fields! In a moment I could smell the smoke and hear the crackling of the burning cane.

A piercing shriek tore through the clamor from outside. It was Selene. She leaned against the stone wall, clutching her belly, her eyes rolling wildly. Fear had brought on her labor.

"We must get her away from here." I said. "She can't have her baby here."

"Her babies, you mean," Aunt Rosette corrected me. "Jules-sans-nez told us the midwife said she is carrying twins."

My mother looked up from chewing on her sweet potato long enough to say, "Let her die."

We broke open a cask of rum and tried to give some to Selene, to calm her. But she flung the wooden cup away, the dark liquid spilling out over the stone floor in a widening circle.

"The midwife," I said. "We must get her to the African midwife in Fort-Royal."

My mother looked up at me, her cheeks bulging.

"Rose! I forbid you to risk your safety for the sake of that slut! Who knows what mayhem there may be in Fort-Royal?"

"For her children's sake as well, mother." I did not need to add, "For the sake of the boys your husband has always wanted."

"She will not need to risk her safety." It was Euphemia's voice. She stood at the dim and shadowy far end of the room, in an open doorway, one that I had not noticed until now. As we watched, the strong barred door swung wider, opening into a void of blackness. Euphemia was looking over at Jules-sans-nez, who nodded to her.

"The Grands Blancs know nothing of this tunnel," she was saying. "It leads to the church in the village, to an opening under the crypt. The priest helps runaways."

"Father Herault helps slaves to run away?"

Euphemia nodded. "He believes in the changes going on in Paris. Liberty, Equality, Fraternity. He helped build the tunnel. It was only finished last month."

She spoke rapidly, her voice loud, straining to be heard above the increasing noisy tumult from the outside that reached us through the small high windows.

Listening to Euphemia, I shook my head in amazement. Father Herault, stout and aging, who became red-faced from the slightest exertion, had helped to dig a tunnel through the earth so that our slaves could escape. Surely an astounding transformation was under way, if the priest from our village was abetting runaways. The church had always supported and defended the Grands Blancs in their mastership of slaves. Everything we had on Martinique, our whole way of life, depended on this partnership of slave owners and the church that taught slaves to obey their masters. What would father say, I wondered, when he found out about the tunnel?

Selene's scream brought me back from these thoughts to the immediacy of the moment.

I looked over at her, her features contorted in pain, her eyes clenched shut, her hands gripping her distended belly. I knew well how intense, how agonizing and above all, how frightening the pains of labor could be. I had struggled for many hours before giving birth to each of my children, especially my dear Eugene, who seemed to hold back, unwilling to be born. And Selene was undergoing all the pain and fear in the midst of the greater terror we all felt as the flames from the cane fields cast their brilliant red light on the walls of the root cellar and the shouting outside grew louder.

I went to kneel beside her.

"Can you walk?" I asked Selene, realizing that these were the first kindly meant words I had ever addressed to her.

She nodded and Euphemia and I helped her to her feet. She did not look at us, she merely grasped our hands. We started for the open doorway, Euphemia, Selene and I, with Hortense trotting along after us.

"I want to help too, maman," Hortense said, and I hugged her and told her she was a good and brave girl and that we would be going on an adventure.

I heard my mother and Aunt Rosette protest but did not pause to respond. Seizing the burning torch Jules-sans-nez took from the wall and handed to me, and taking a last gulp of the damp, stale air of the root cellar I plunged, fearful but daring, into the darkness of the tunnel.

2 1

THE FIRST THING to assail us was the heat.

As soon as we entered the narrow tunnel, its ceiling barely high enough to permit us to walk without stooping, the temperature rose, and continued to rise the further we went. Sweat coursed down my face and my hand, holding Selene's, was soon slippery.

We were underneath the burning cane fields. I imagined that the very ground over our heads was burning, the heat penetrating into the soil and parching it until it crackled. I tried not to think about what would happen should the ceiling of the tunnel give way, trapping us. Or of what would happen if smoke choked the tunnel, suffocating us.

Selene walked slowly, dragging her feet, head down, moaning, her moans rising to loud cries when pains clenched her belly and she had to stop. At times we seemed barely to crawl along at a snail's pace, making my heart race from fear. To calm myself I tried to calculate how far it was to the church in the village, but though I had walked the distance many times above ground and knew every twist and turn of the path through the fields, I could not calculate how far it actually was, or how long the tunnel must be.

We had not gone far before I smelled the smoke. Sweet, cloying cane-smoke, the scent so strong it distracted me and made me nearly drop the sputtering torch.

The choking smoke drove Selene to the edge of hysteria. Coughing, crying, she tossed her head violently from side to side and shouted that she could not go on.

I did the only thing I could think of, to make her go on.

"Snakes!" I yelled. "There are snakes in this tunnel!"

With a pitiful shriek Selene stumbled forward, her refusal to move forgotten.

The smell remained overpowering, but the air did not thicken further and we breathed, panting, as we continued along, our eyes on the uneven ground, watching for slithering forms and hissing tongues.

Selene was pausing more and more frequently and crying out in pain.

"She's coming near her time," Euphemia whispered to me. "Those babies are going to be born long before we get to Fort-Royal."

By the time we reached the last length of tunnel, and could glimpse a door in the wall ahead of us, we knew that Selene's hour had arrived. She slumped down, exhausted, while we pounded on the door.

We heard footsteps, then a voice. Father Herault's voice.

"Who knocks?"

"Rose Tascher, father," I said, using the name by which he had known me most of my life. "I have my daughter and two others with me. One of my companions is in labor."

We heard the heavy lock slide back and the door swung open. The scent of incense replaced the lingering odor of burning cane. We were in the dark crypt of the church, where my grandfather des Sannois was buried, and my dear grandmother Catherine, and my two sisters, and a host of other Grands Blancs. The cold stone coffins gleamed softly in the torchlight.

"What of the others at Les Trois-Ilets?" Father Herault asked. "Is anyone injured?"

"We left mother and Aunt Rosette safe in the root cellar of the mill. I don't know where father is. As for the slaves—" I could not finish the sentence. I simply did not know.

"Your father and his overseer were here. They have gone to gather the militias. Your uncle has been captured by the rebels. They hold Fort-Royal."

Father Herault brought embroidered kneeling cushions from the sanctuary and we laid Selene down on these. She had begun to make animal sounds, low curdled cries that stuck in her throat, then burst forth in explosions of agony.

Euphemia put her small statue of the Red Goddess in Selene's hand and she clutched it. I told Hortense to wait in the sanctuary and say her prayers for Selene.

"Ibo women drop their babies right where they are working, between the rows of cane, don't they?" I asked Euphemia after Hortense had gone. "They don't always need a midwife."

"And many of them die," was her blunt retort.

I remembered my own childbirths, how the accoucheur kept a fastidious distance from the bed while I, lying prone but writhing and contorting my body with each fresh pain, longed for him to do something—anything—that would shorten my labor. It seemed to me that the African way was better.

"Let's try to get her up," I said to Euphemia. "Let her crouch."

After many protests from the wailing Selene we helped her into a crouching position, putting the pillows below her.

Her pains were coming rapidly now, succeeding each other in prolonged waves of agony. Euphemia was muttering an African prayer. Father Herault, whether out of decency or squeamishness I couldn't have said, had left the room.

"Now, Selene, you must press down hard when you feel the next pain. Yes, I know how much it hurts. I have had two babies myself. Yes, I know you want to die. Every woman thinks that way when she is in labor."

I went on talking to Selene in an encouraging way, hoping to distract her from the acuteness of her suffering.

"Press down, press down," I urged, and from the tight clenching of her teeth I could tell she was doing her best, weak though she was, to obey me. Water spewed out from between her legs, warm water that smelled faintly of brine.

She gasped, sobbed and screamed—but as she screamed a small dark head emerged.

"Press again, harder, harder," I yelled, as much from excitement as urgency.

Euphemia caught the falling child and dipped it in the basin of holy water—the only water available—to bathe it.

"You have a daughter, Selene," I told her. "She is the color of cocoa."

In a few moments the pains resumed, and this time, after the exhausted Selene had given the last of her effort, a baby boy was born.

But unlike the baby girl, the boy did not cry or move his tiny legs. His lips were blue, his eyes closed.

Neither Euphemia nor I had the courage to tell Selene that her little son was dead. But it did not matter. Nothing mattered any more, for Selene's exertions had cost her her life. She slid to the floor, gave a last pathetic gasp, and died.

FEELING UTTERLY SPENT, bereft, as if hollowed out inside, I stared down at Selene's lifeless body, then at her little daughter. Euphemia had rinsed her off in the basin and was wrapping her in a length of linen torn from her own petticoat. Like Euphemia herself, this little girl was my half-sister. My own flesh and blood. Yet she was motherless, and I knew my father would not want her. He had always said he was cursed with daughters. My mother, I knew equally well, would do everything in her power to prevent Selene's child from being raised in her house.

I reached out and took the infant from Euphemia.

"Coco," I said aloud, almost without thinking, "I baptize thee in the name of the Father, and of the Son, and of the Holy Spirit." I had heard the familiar formula repeated so often, I knew it by heart. Now if this child dies, I thought, she will at least avoid the pains of hell.

There was a deafening crash in the sanctuary above us. I heard a child scream.

"Hortense!" I thought, and started for the stairs that led upward to the sanctuary, the infant Coco in my arms.

But before I had taken more than a step or two I heard the savage, gleeful whoops and cries of men on a rampage. Thumps and crashes, the sound of glass shattering and furnishings being thrown down. And the sickening scream of a man in pain.

The invaders swept down into the crypt, driving Father Herault before them with the sharp points of their knives. He was injured. He had been struck on the head. Blood dripped down his forehead and on his full cheeks, and stained his worn black cassock.

"Maman, maman!" Hortense came running down the steps, past the bleeding priest, and dove into the folds of my skirts. Holding the baby in the crook of my arm, I pressed my trembling daughter against my legs with my free hand, in a vain effort to shield her from the fearsome scene.

Euphemia and I backed up against the wall of the crypt, ignoring Selene's body which lay neglected nearby.

I thought, they are going to kill us all. Then dread blotted out all thought.

Father Herault stumbled and fell. Almost as soon as he struck the stone floor the mob of crazed men was on him. Knives pierced his body again and again, his blood gushing forth in a dozen thin streams. With an inhuman cry one of the madmen severed his head, and held it aloft with a gleaming smile of triumph.

My stomach heaved, my senses disordered by the horror I was witness to. I saw knives, I smelled blood, I was aware of cruel hands reaching toward me—yet before the hands could touch me a shot rang out, clear and sharp.

A musket shot. Then another.

More men were rushing down into the crypt. Grands Blancs this time. There was fighting, shouting. I clutched the children. I could hardly draw breath, I was so frightened.

All around me, men were yelling and cursing. There were groans and cries of anguish, blows being struck and the commotion of a brawl.

I felt someone seize my arm.

"Come at once, madame. I will take you and the children to safety."

The voice was that of a Grand Blanc, speaking the creole tongue. Speaking firmly, with authority. I had to trust that voice.

"Gerard de Sévigné at your service, madame. From the Les Plages militia. Please come quickly."

I was led through the crowd of brawling men to the upper part of the church and then outside, where dozens of horsemen and many carts and wagons were assembled.

Dawn was breaking. In the early morning light I saw many Africans, manacled, being led away. I supposed that they were the rebels that had come to Les Trois-Ilets and set the fields of cane on fire.

I asked my rescuer, Gerard de Sévigné, where my father was, and was told that he had gone to Fort-Royal with the local militia.

"Those of us from Les Plages have been given the task of finding the remaining marauders and rounding them up. We have no way of knowing how many of them there are, or where they are. So we have been searching every plantation and settlement. It's lucky we came across you when we did."

He beckoned to another militiaman and asked him to bring one of the trophies seized from the rebels the previous evening.

It was a long wooden pole surmounted by a bright yellow banner. In the center of the banner was a crude painted depiction of a white-skinned infant skewered on the point of a sword.

I clutched Coco, who began to cry—the shrill, high-pitched cry of a newborn.

But Coco is brown, I thought. Not white. Surely she is safe, even in the arms of a white woman like me.

"Yeyette!" Euphemia was brought up from the crypt by another militiaman, and embraced me and the children.

Seeing her, I was quite overcome. All of a sudden the strains and exertions of the long fearsome night rolled over me and left me limp. I remember being led to a hard cot and given food and drink. Then I fell into a troubled, dream-filled sleep.

22

IT WAS DONOVAN WHO WOKE ME. He put his lips close to my ear and spoke tenderly, softly, as he did when we were alone.

"Come, you can't stay here," he said. "You've got to get off the island. There is a ship in the harbor. The *Sensible*. You have a friend aboard, from what I hear. Commander Scipion du Roure. He is taking many Grands Blancs to France."

Donovan had ridden to the village with others in the Les Plages militia. Gerard de Sévigné had told him about my escape from Les Trois-Ilets and the fighting in the church crypt. Hearing Scipion's name I felt a pang of nostalgia.

"I cannot go without Hortense. And Euphemia."

"There will be room for them as well. I will insist on it."

"And—" I started to say, "And Coco," then stopped. Selene's baby was not my child, yet I felt an attachment to her. I could not leave her.

Donovan read my thoughts.

"While you were sleeping Euphemia found a wetnurse for the little girl. A young girl with a baby of her own. She is going on board the *Sensible*."

"And you, Donovan?"

He kissed me.

"I must stay on here, to do what I can to prevent more bloodshed." His jaw tightened. "We cannot give in to chaos."

I clung to him. "But I don't want you to be hurt. And I don't want to leave you."

He is flesh of my flesh, I thought. He and I are joined. Fused. I need the closeness of him.

He hugged me fiercely. "Quickly. Gather your things."

Fort-Royal was under bombardment and as Donovan drove us along the narrow streets of the town toward the waterfront we were surrounded by the continual pop and crack of musketfire and the booming of guns. The forts on the heights above the town had been seized by the rebels and were being commanded by the Friends of Liberty. My Uncle Robert had been kidnapped. I knew nothing about my aunt or my cousins.

The wagon in which we rode swayed dangerously from side to side, the terrified horses that pulled it neighing and plunging, as Donovan struggled to veer away from burning buildings and the sound of explosions. Hortense put her hands over her ears and shut her eyes. Euphemia, the Ibo Red Goddess dangling from a cord around her neck, held the sleeping Coco.

Finally we reached the crowded dock and hurried aboard the *Sensible*, the sailors reaching out to help us scramble up the improvised gangplank. Donovan and I had time only for the briefest of embraces.

"Remember me," he whispered. Then I ran along the uneven boards, pulling Hortense along, and up onto the heaving deck of the ship. When I turned back toward the rail I could no longer distinguish Donovan's wagon from the mass of vehicles and horses and clamoring people, the air was so thick with dust and smoke from the pounding guns.

Then we were launched on the outgoing tide, the sails of the *Sensible* belling outward, her prow plunging and rearing in the hilly seas.

WE WERE EIGHT WEEKS ON THE VOYAGE back to France, and during those long weeks I took comfort from Scipion.

He had put on weight since I last saw him in Paris, his strong, compact body not as lean as it once was, his grey eyes less keen and a large blond moustache decorating his upper lip. When he came to greet me he was warm and kind, anxious to hear what had happened at Les Trois-Ilets and to confirm the story he had heard about my dangerous adventure on the night the cane fields burned.

"You are a heroine, you know," he said as he hugged me. "It's all over Fort-Royal how brave you were, going down the escape tunnel and saving that slave girl and her baby." He was grinning, but his eyes were filled with concern. "I'm just glad no harm came to you, Rose."

His solicitude meant much to me. He invited me to dine at his table (and thoughtfully sent extra food to my cabin for Euphemia and Hortense). When the weather was fair, he took me for leisurely strolls around the deck of the small ship, and sometimes, in the evenings, we played cards with other passengers.

Gradually our warm comfortable friendship led to lovemaking, but it was the affectionate, nurturing lovemaking of devoted friends, not the all-consuming, fiery passion I knew with Donovan. I sought shelter in Scipion's arms. That was understood, just as it was understood that when our ship docked at Brest, I would go ashore with my family and Scipion would take on another command. When the time came, we parted lovingly.

Nothing could have prepared me for the startling change that had come over Paris in the years that I had been away. The old Bastille was gone, of course, its ruin a shrine to liberty. Gone too were the fine carriages and costly clothes and gems of the nobility, the well-kept mansions and immense households of servants, the expensive shops where I had once spent money so extravagantly and incurred Alexandre's wrath.

Paris had always been dirty, but now it was much dirtier, with huge mounds of reeking sewage and refuse from kitchens and stables heaped in the center of every street and each alley full of trash and teeming with rats. There were still crowds in the streets, but the faces we saw were hollow-cheeked and anxiety-ridden, not jubilant or carefree. I had not been in the capital long before I realized that everyone was feeling the burden of rising prices and shortages of food. My own wealth, I discovered, had been confiscated by the Constituent Assembly, the current ruling government. As Viscountess Beauharnais I had been affluent; now that I was plain Citizeness Beauharnais I was in want.

Monuments to the Revolution were everywhere: statues of the goddess of Liberty, altars to the Citizen, posters praising an end to tyranny and the dawning of a new age. But everyone was on edge, as if the enthronement of the new ideals unnerved them and made them frightened. Shoppers in the marketplace hurried from stall to stall, counting out their assignats (the new paper money issued by the government) in haste and furtively hiding their purchases in their pockets or under their coats. No one seemed to trust anyone—or to trust the future.

I rented a modest room in a lodging-house for myself, Euphemia and the children, but the rent took the last of my money. I went to find my former business partner, the moneylender Baron Rossignol—Citizen Rossignol now—and was told that he had been arrested by the Committee of Public Security and taken away.

When I heard this I felt a shiver go up my spine—a shiver of dread. Who were these new rulers, who took it upon themselves to confiscate the money of citizens and arrest people at will?

When I went to visit my oldest friend in Paris, Fanny de Beauharnais, I found that her salon was nothing like it had been before the fall of the Bastille and the supremacy of the new government. Her red velvet salon was now decorated in the revolutionary tricolor, with walls, carpets and furnishings covered in patriotic stripes of red, white and blue cloth. Fanny herself was liberty personified in her simple togalike gown with revolutionary cockades in her hair.

"I only compose hymns to the Revolution now," she told me on the first night I visited her. "You never know who might be listening." It was a common topic of whispered conversation that the Constituent Assembly had spies everywhere, reporting on what people said and did.

Fanny's literary colleagues were equally careful about what they wrote. Seraphin Lamblin, the tall, thin, wispy-haired poet I had met at Fanny's house several times before, told me that he was at work on a new epic poem, "The Bastille," and the two men Fanny always called the Inseparables, Henri and Bernard, had joined forces to write an angry sonnet called "Aristocrats Must Die."

"But you are both highborn," I protested. "You have renounced your titles. We all have. Who is left to die?"

Henri raised his eyebrows. "Those who oppose us. Those who rebel. And those who are gathering on our borders, preparing to invade France, to try to destroy the Revolution."

I had heard that there were regions in the west of France that were holding onto the old ways, resisting the changes brought by the Revolution. They were fighting against the revolutionary armies. And I knew that many nobles had fled France for Austria, Italy, the Swiss cantons. They were collecting arms and hiring soldiers and forming themselves into armies, planning to invade France and force a return to the pre-revolutionary state of things.

People spoke of these uprisings and dangers in whispers, glancing around furtively; heaven forbid that they should be overheard, or that it should be thought that they were sympathetic to the rebels or the émigré armies.

No matter what our fears or misgivings, we all had to act as if we would defend the Revolution to the death. We wore our tricolor cockades and gave up every jeweled button and silver shoe buckle we owned. We denounced the king and queen, cursed the church and the priests (the revolutionary government had turned against religion), swore loyalty to the people of France and called each other Citizen and Citizeness. We tried to be brave—but in truth we were cowards.

We did not stand up and say, Enough!

We did not protest when the violence increased.

We did not defend France against herself.

One hot August night I was awakened by a loud clangor of bells coming from every part of the city. There was shouting in the streets, and the sound of running feet and galloping horses. Soon I could hear an angry murmur and, looking out the window of my rented apartment, I saw hundreds of people, milling about in noisy clusters, waving torches and singing revolutionary songs. Hortense and Coco slept through all the commotion—Eugene was not with us, he was away at his military boarding school—but Euphemia came to stand beside me at the window, shaking her head and talking to herself in the Ibo tongue.

We could not sleep at all that night, and when we tried to nap the following day our sleep was interrupted by neighbors and street criers announcing terrible news. The rampaging crowd had invaded the royal palace of the Tuileries, killing and mutilating the guardsmen and servants who were attempting to protect the king and queen. Gruesome stories spread, stories of crazed Parisians cutting off heads, hacking at arms and legs, slicing off women's breasts—sparing no one. We were afraid to go out, or even to send our single servant girl or Coco's wetnurse, who lived with us, to the bakery or the marketplace for food.

But those dark days were only the beginning. I tremble as I write this, for I am now coming to the part of my story that sent me into such a state of fear I thought I might be losing my mind. My Nightmare Days were about to come upon me.

From out of nowhere savage men in blood-red caps, wearing butcher's aprons, began running through the streets, killing every priest they met. There were still many priests in Paris in those days, and they were murdered, one by one, until the very gutters in the streets ran red with their blood. The red-capped assassins were not satisfied with killing all the priests they could find; shouting that Paris was under attack, they assaulted the prisons and dragged out the poor prisoners, stabbing and bludgeoning them and hacking off their quivering limbs.

We lived very near the Abbaye jail and I could hear the prisoners screaming and begging for mercy. Five poor men were carried out into the courtyard and hacked to pieces practically before our eyes and the blood spurted over the low wall into our garden.

Oh, the stench of it! With every breath of that blood-reek I remembered the screams of the men as they died, and the grim, merciless assassins who killed them. For a week I tried to wash the gore from the wall, pouring buckets of vinegar over it and brushing it as hard as I could. But the red stain remained, no matter what I did. There are many red walls in Paris to this day.

Wearing my most garish red-, white- and blue-striped gown, and hoping I looked patriotic, I went in search of Alexandre. He was a member of the new government, the Convention, that had just declared that France no longer had a king and queen and was a republic. I could not help feeling sorry for poor King Louis and his beautiful wife Queen Marie Antoinette. People said such terrible things about them but I thought, they are just a family, they have children and want to keep them safe, just as I do.

I found Alexandre in the great hall where the Convention met, arguing with other delegates over the new republican army. He still looked handsome but his face was thinner and more lined than when I had last seen him. He wore the long loose-fitting black trousers of a laborer, with a laborer's rough clogs on his feet and a cheap red vest and stained blue neckcloth. A black beret with a cockade covered his blond hair, which had begun to be streaked with grey.

The transformation in his appearance startled me at first. All trace of the arrogant, well-to-do young nobleman he had been was gone, and in its place was the earnest, well-spoken man of the people, Citizen Beauharnais.

"Citizen," I called out to him, trying to ignore the stares of the other men, "I wonder if I might have a word with you. It is about our children."

For a brief instant he looked alarmed, then resumed his impassive demeanor and detached himself from those he was debating with.

"What is it? As you can see, I have urgent business here. The people's business."

"I want to send Hortense and Eugene away, to safety," I told him. "An old friend, the Prince de Salm, has offered to take them to Coblentz with him. He leaves in two days."

Alexandre's eyes darkened. He pulled me aside, as far as possible from the milling delegates. He spoke through clenched teeth.

"Have you no common sense! Never mention the name of an aristocrat in this chamber! Especially not that of a traitorous Austrian!"

"This traitorous Austrian, as you call him, may be our only hope to get our children out of Paris!"

"And how would that look, Rose? A delegate to the Convention like myself, a man who took the lead in abolishing the monarchy and declaring the French Republic, sending his children out of the country like a coward!"

"You would look like a good father. Now, do I have your cooperation in this, or will I have to make what arrangements I can, on my own?"

"You will find it difficult." His tone was detached, his words brusque. "The gates of Paris are going to be closed. No one will be allowed in or out. We expect an invading army within weeks. I am to take command of the Army of the Rhine"—his chest puffed with pride as he spoke these words—"and Eugene will come with me, as a junior aide-de-camp."

"But he is only twelve years old!"

"I am well aware of my son's age, Citizeness. And of his patriotism, and his desire to serve France."

"What of Hortense?"

Alexandre's shrug was eloquent. "France has need of all her children. She can sew. She can grow vegetables. She can make bullets. Little hands are always useful."

I saw that there was no point in arguing with him. I prepared to take my leave, drawing on my red, blue and white gloves. But I had one more thing to say.

"Do you imagine, Alexandre, that you will command your Army of the Rhine against your brother François, with his Austrian Army of True Patriots?"

His eyes blazing, Alexandre quickly moved toward me and roughly put his hand over my mouth.

Under his breath, he called me a string of obscene names.

By mentioning Alexandre's brother François de Beauharnais I meant to touch a nerve, but the violence of Alexandre's response, and the evident fear that lay behind it, surprised me. The Revolutionary Commune that now governed all that the Convention said and did had begun singling out for punishment all those who had émigré relatives. Alexandre's brother—my brother-in-law—was not only an émigré, and a strong supporter of the deposed King Louis, but he had been given a prominent command in the Austrian army.

"If you ever speak that name again I'll make you sorry we ever met," Alexandre whispered. "You and your stupidity will get us all killed!"

2 3

JUST AS THE SOLDIERS began their sharp crackling rat-tat-tat on the drums I felt the cruel weight of a hard wooden heel on my toe. I cried out, pulling my foot back, but no one heard me. I could not tell who it was that had trodden on my toe. I stood amid hundreds of others in Revolution Square, crowded in tightly, hardly able to move. Like the others I was watching the tall scaffold where the guardsmen in their blue jackets, swords out and bayonets at the ready, stood to attention around the dreaded guillotine.

It was Aunt Edmée who warned me that I had to attend the terrible spectacle—or risk coming under suspicion as an enemy of the Republic. I had to join the enthusiastic, noisy, milling crowd that gathered in the square each morning to watch the executions, she said. I had to show to the world—and especially to the many spies that reported all our movements to the revolutionary tribunal—that I was an ardent patriot who loved to see justice being done.

There were so many, many spies. They kept their eyes on all of us, it was said, but especially those, like me, who had once been titled ladies.

A fat bare arm shoved up against me, nearly knocking me off balance. It was a woman's arm, and she was clapping and chanting, heedless of those around her. A seamstress, I thought. Or a flower-vendor, or a laundress. She was well along in years, her face painted with

thick powder and rouge, her lips a bright crimson, her brassy blond hair
threaded with gray.

> *"Red lady, red lady*
> *Kill kill kill!*
> *Red blood red blood*
> *Spill spill spill!"*

The chant was taken up, many voices rose above the clatter of the
drumming.

"Here they come!" someone shouted, and in a moment I felt squeezed
even more tightly by the bodies around me as the crowd parted.

A plain wooden cart with slatted sides was being dragged through the
mob, toward the waiting scaffold. Inside were a half-dozen of the most
wretched-looking people I had ever seen. Not even the slaves on
Martinique, after they had been whipped and deprived of food as
punishment, were as dejected and pathetic as these three women and
three men, thin and dirty and glassy-eyed, their hands bound, the
women's soiled mobcaps askew.

One of the women, I noticed, was hardly more than a girl. She was
delicate, slight, with a face that had once been pretty. Who was she, I
wondered. An aristocrat's daughter, like me? Or a girl of the streets? She
wore a wisp of lace at her neck, a keepsake, I imagined. A small reminder
of her former life. She looked around her at the eagerly chanting,
clapping spectators with such fear in her eyes, fear like that of a doe in
desperate flight from the hunters.

The chanting died away, giving way to a murmur of acclaim. The
executioner, an enormous man with a wrestler's muscular physique,
wearing a blood-stained purple apron, was taking his place beside the tall
mechanical killing machine whose gleaming, razor-sharp blade hung
suspended, as if in midair. His face was hidden beneath a black mask, so
that he appeared expressionless, inhuman. The crowd was greeting him.

The drumming ceased. A hush fell. The first victim was brought out
of the cart. A mature woman. She was spat upon and jeered. She
stumbled as she was being pulled up the steps toward the guillotine,
and appeared to faint.

"Coward!" someone yelled.

"Damned aristo!"

"Traitor!"

She was hastily lifted up and laid face-down on a rough plank beneath the gleaming blade. The drum roll began again. The executioner lowered the wooden neckpiece in place and pulled the lever that loosed the heavy slicing knife.

With an audible thwack! the head was severed and a fountain of red blood spurted forth, drenching the wooden platform and splashing onto those in the forefront of the cheering onlookers.

The dead woman's headless corpse had hardly been thrown onto the ground when the next victim, a man, was brought forward, shouting and protesting.

"It is the clockmaker, Citizen Carteret!" came a voice from the crowd. "It's too late for you, Carteret. Better look at your clock! There's no time left!" More jokes followed, and laughter mingled with the frisson of excited horror that passed through the gathered spectators when the clockmaker's head was severed and his body flung over the edge of the scaffold.

I was feeling ill. Waves of nausea rose to my throat and I struggled, swallowing, to prevent myself from vomiting. The stench of blood, combined with the overpowering odor of the unwashed bodies all around me, hemming me in and making me feel trapped, was having a strong effect.

I saw that others were staring at me, observing my strong physical reaction. Would they doubt my patriotism? I swallowed very hard.

"Vive la Sainte Guillotine!" I yelled—and was gratified to see those around me grin, and clap, and take up the cry. I was one of them again.

But when the delicate young girl was brought up from the cart and handed over to the black-hooded executioner I could hardly bear to watch. I forced myself to keep my eyes on the girl, though my sight was blurred by tears as she begged for mercy, on her knees, imploring the implacable butcher in his stained apron to spare her life.

There was no pity to be had, no pity and no mercy. The girl was thrown down head first upon the plank, amid catcalls and rude noises and obscene suggestions. Swiftly the blade fell, swiftly the spurt of blood sprayed outward, staining the red apron afresh. With a quick heave the slim red carcass was discarded.

Now the scaffold was drenched in blood, blood dripped off the reddened planks and onto the thirsty brown earth, turning it the color of rust. I seemed to see blood everywhere I looked, on the faces of the people around me, on the stone façade of the Tuileries Palace facing the square, on my own hands.

"Red lady, red lady," I chanted, with the others, "Kill kill kill."

Could that really be my voice? Was I no different from the others, with their grotesque eagerness for death, their blood lust?

They were still eager, but as the morning went on their eagerness was losing its edge. They had begun to shout at the executioner to hurry, to chop off two victims' heads at once. They were stripping the discarded carcasses of their meager blood-drenched garments and tossing the garments back and forth, whooping when each shirt or smock was caught and hissing when one was dropped. My nausea had been replaced by a burning thirst. Near me, a man was talking.

"A bigger guillotine is coming soon," he was saying. "One with four blades. Think how fast it can work! Chop, chop, chop, chop!" He sliced the air with his hand.

The last of the victims was being brought out of the cart. A short, black-haired man with fleshy lips and a broad nose. A familiar man.

"Baron Rossignol!" I started to say, then quickly checked myself. "Citizen Rossignol! The moneylender! He lent money to the Widow Capet!" (The former Queen Marie Antoinette was known by the humbling title of "Widow Capet," her husband having been executed by the Red Lady several months earlier.)

The baron shook off his guards as he climbed the steps to the scaffold. He lost his footing and slipped, then recovered. I saw now that his hands were not tied, as those of the other prisoners had been. Had he bribed the guards to free his hands? He was clever—though not clever enough to avoid the fate he now faced. Or was he?

He opened his shirt and collar and then, to the surprise of the onlookers, stepped rapidly to the edge of the scaffold and began to speak.

"I am Henri de Rossignol, descendant of Hugh Capet, France's first king. Royal blood runs through my veins. To kill me is regicide! Regicide!"

At a signal from the officer in command the guardsmen began their loud drumming, drowning out the baron's urgent words. Two soldiers reached for him, but he was nimble. He began shinnying up the side of the tall guillotine, his short legs remaining just out of reach of his pursuers as he climbed.

Avoiding the sharp blade, which hung suspended near the top of the wooden structure, he scrambled up onto the heavy horizontal plank that crowned the device and stood there, shouting, though the drums muffled his words.

Now the crowd was intrigued. A few people yelled encouragement to the baron, admiring his daring. But the majority, inflamed by his mention of the monarchy and of his royal blood, wanted him dead.

"Get him! Catch him! Don't let the aristo escape!"

One of the soldiers tried in vain to climb the guillotine but stopped halfway up, daunted by the hanging blade. A cavalryman urged his horse up the scaffold steps and slashed at the baron with his saber, but it was not long enough to reach him. The little man was too high. He laughed at his pursuers.

Watching the drama, I could not help thinking, this is his moment of glory. Despite my discomfort, and the renewed jostling of the restless crowd, I could not help but smile.

Then one of the officers was handed a musket. He took aim and fired. The baron paused, convulsed, and fell heavily, landing at the executioner's feet. His corpse was tossed onto the ground.

A huge shout arose from the crowd, there was clapping and cheering and sporadic singing.

"Long live the nation!"

"Power to the sansculottes!"

"Blessed Sainte Guillotine, pray for us!"

I noticed, though, that as the crowd began to disperse, quite a few of those who had come to watch the spectacle, to savor the punishing of the traitors to the Revolution, made their way to where Baron Rossignol's small body lay sprawled on the ground, and furtively dipped their handkerchiefs in the blood of the last of the Capetians.

24

THEY CAME FOR ME on an April morning in the year 1794, Citizen Lacombe and Citizen George, knocking on my door and holding a warrant for my arrest.

"Citizeness Beauharnais," the tall, owlish Citizen George announced, "by your conduct, and your connections, you have shown yourself to be a partisan of tyranny. You are an enemy of the Revolution. You are to be detained, by order of the Committee of General Security."

I fainted then, and Euphemia had to revive me with smelling-salts before they could take me away.

"The children—" I said to her as she bent over me.

"Don't worry. We know where to go."

We had often talked of what Euphemia would do if I was arrested. We agreed that she would take Eugene and Hortense and Coco to the house where my Aunt Edmée and the marquis had lived before they immigrated to Italy. The landlady there promised that she would find room for them.

For several months, ever since the former queen was executed and the Law of Suspects was passed, I had been more and more afraid that I would be arrested. I carried my certificate of citizenship with me, and was careful of where I went and what I said, lest I be reported on negatively by spies, but every day more and more former aristocrats like myself were taken off to prison, to await execution, and I felt increasing dread that I would be arrested too.

Only a few weeks earlier Alexandre had been taken to the Carmelite prison, despite his service to the Revolution. His émigré brother François was winning battles against the French armies, while Alexandre, when given command of the Army of the Rhine, lost every battle he waged. He was accused of treason, and taken away. When I heard that that had happened I sensed that my time was running out.

I thought of trying to escape, of fleeing into the countryside in disguise, even of stowing away on a ship bound for the Windward Isles. It could be no worse there, I reasoned, than in Paris. I would take my chances among the people I knew best, the Africans and Grands Blancs of Martinique.

But of course I could not run away, for the same reason I had not left France months earlier: because of the children. Alexandre had refused to give his permission for Eugene and Hortense to leave France, and without their father's written permission they could not get past the border guards. I could not bear to go on my own, without them. So I waited, hoping and dreading at the same time. In the end, that which I dreaded most came with a knock at my door.

From the first, I had no doubt that I would die—and soon. The pace of killings by the fearsome Red Lady, the cruel guillotine, was accelerating. The prisons of Paris were nothing more than waiting rooms, holding pens for cattle waiting for the slaughter.

Along with dozens of others arrested that April day I was herded into the former Carmelite monastery, where I knew Alexandre was, a place notorious for the massacre of monks that had happened there only a few months earlier. Bloodstains were splashed along the dull grey stone walls, the once crimson blood turned dark magenta. We were led along dim narrow corridors and assigned to small, low-ceilinged rooms that had been the monks' cells. There were six of us in the room assigned to me, six people sharing one thin, stinking straw-filled mattress alive with bugs, six people sharing a common waste-bucket.

"Don't worry," the guards said when they brought us our one daily meal, a bowl of gruel and a small coarse loaf of black bread apiece, "it won't be for long. Soon you'll be leaving here." They smiled as they said it, for of course what they meant was, "Soon you'll be sent to your deaths."

How soon? It was the question that haunted us all, day and night.

Each evening a roll call of names was read out. The names of those who were to die the following day. As each name was read there came a scream, a gasp, a shout—some response from the condemned. When the list had been read, those of us who had not heard our names felt enormous relief. Another day of life! But another day, too, of dread, for our name might well be on the list the following night.

Anxious, sleepless, half-starved, we paced like uneasy specters along the corridors—and were pulled into the arms of strangers.

For since we all faced death, we felt an overpowering urge to affirm life, and to express love. Or rather, to express lust. We reached out for one another blindly, instinctively, craving the solace of the flesh. I do not know how many lovers I had in the Carmelite prison, only that I was not alone, and that I gave as much pleasure and comfort as I received. Lovemaking, not revolution, was the true leveler in those senseless, blood-mad days; lovemaking brought aristo and commoner together, rich and poor, former master and former servant.

I found Alexandre along a dark corridor one night, and forgetting all that had gone before, we lay together on a filthy blanket, with water dripping down the wall beside us. Having been in the prison longer than I, he had suffered more; when I held his naked body I could feel his ribs, he had grown so thin. His cheeks were covered with a matted beard, his hair was long and dirty and he smelled of sweat and slime.

There was no violence in him that night, no sense of possession. The last ounce of arrogance seemed to have leached out of him, in the face of death.

"I am for the Red Lady soon, Rose," he said to me as we lay together. "Promise me that you will not be sad, when my hour comes. I am glad to be giving my life for my country, for the Republic."

"But this is senseless! All this slaughter, the sacrifice of so many good lives, for what!"

"For purity. To cleanse the nation of traitors."

"But you are no traitor! Nor am I."

"In purging the genuine traitors, some loyal citizens must be sacrificed."

"Absurd nonsense. The old Alexandre, the Alexandre I married, would have laughed at such foolish logic."

"I have learned much since then."

I laid my head on his bony chest and he stroked my hair. I wept, partly from exhaustion, partly from sorrow. There was no truth any more, no sense. Only cravings, and pain, and a world from which all the humanity had been taken away.

Amid the madness I clung to one hope: that I might become pregnant. Pregnant prisoners were not executed, but moved to another prison to await their deliveries. If I conceived a child I would be spared execution for nine months—and by then, I hoped, France might come to her senses. Or she might be invaded by a foreign army, and the monarchy might be restored. King Louis was dead but his little son, it was rumored, survived in a prison somewhere. He could reign over us. All could be as it was before.

My monthly flow had stopped and I hoped I was indeed carrying a child. I told the surly guard who watched the six of us in my cell that I felt ill, clutching my stomach and pretending to be on the verge of throwing up. He stared at me suspiciously at first, then disappeared down the corridor. Much later he returned with a young, blond curly-headed physician who listened to my heart and examined me and looked at me sympathetically.

"I wish I could send you to join the mothers-to-be," he said. "But I cannot be certain of your condition. When a woman doesn't eat much, her monthly flow ceases. It happens quite often here. I will come and see you again in a few days."

"If I live that long," I snapped.

He did come back, and I learned that his name was Karel Osnolenko, and that he came from Cracow. He was very kind to me, even attentive, with a well-bred courtesy that I found to be very sweet and touching. He held my hand and stroked it as he talked to me, a fatherly gesture. It soothed my jangled nerves.

I confided in Karel. Feeling that death was very near, I told him the story of my life, and he listened with interest and concern, stopping me when I recounted painful things and making me pause until my heart stopped pounding.

I lost track of time. One day was like another in the prison. We were in constant darkness, save for the torches on the walls; day and night meant nothing to us, except that the terrible roll call came with our evening meal. I felt myself growing weaker, losing vitality. Two of the women in my cell got sick and died before they could be executed. All along the corridors we could hear sounds of coughing and spewing and feverish voices calling out for water.

I now come to the worst night of my life, the night I very nearly gave in to despair.

I had fallen ill, and though Dr. Osnolenko did what he could for me, I felt myself sinking lower and lower. The summer was very hot and we sweated in our airless cells. How I longed for cold clean water to bathe my face! I lay on the straw mattress allotted to us, in a stupor of pain and weakness, my mind disordered, imagining at times that I was in Martinique, and that I saw my dead sisters walking toward me on the veranda of the sugar mill, or that I was in Fontainebleau and the queen was riding past in her carriage. All was a blur, a jumble of images and sounds.

One sound I heard distinctly: the voice of the head jailer, that dismal night, reading from the dreaded roll call.

"Citizen Beauharnais," he read. And then, "Citizeness Beauharnais."

I am told that my scream filled the prison and reached the street outside.

I remember calling out, crying out in protest, though my voice soon grew hoarse and I coughed uncontrollably. I sank into a terrible despair— a despair so profound and so painful that I wanted to die, just to be relieved of its crushing weight. Oh, the blackness of that night! The sorrow, the loss, the tears I shed for my dear children.

As if in sympathy with my dark emotions a storm broke over Paris and for hours high winds whistled around the corners of the old monastery and rain beat down on the roof like the ominous drumming of the soldiers on guard around the scaffold.

I must have slept, finally, for I was shaken awake by the guards tipping over my mattress and rolling me roughly onto the stone floor of my cell. It was one of the indignities that preceded execution; when a prisoner was due to be killed the mattress was removed from his or her cell.

But to my amazement, a new mattress was soon brought in and I was laid upon it, with a clean blanket over me. I was speechless. What was happening?

Dr. Osnolenko came in, the head jailer accompanying him.

"She cannot last more than a day or two," I heard the doctor saying. "She has the prison fever. You might as well let her die here. You can hasten another traitor's death by giving him her place. Save the Republic some time and expense."

"Yes, that always pleases the Committee of General Security." There was a pause, and then the jailer added, "Who was she—not that I care, but I will have to strike her name from today's list."

"Citizeness Beauharnais."

"What was her crime?"

"I believe she had an in-law who was an émigré. She herself is quite blameless. Of that I'm certain."

"None of us is blameless, doctor. For all have sinned against the Republic, and come short of the glory of Robespierre."

His ironic words made me smile, for the first time in many hours. My smile broadened when the jailer left and Dr. Osnolenko sat down on the mattress and took my hand.

"Don't be frightened. You are not really dying, and you are not going to be executed today."

I thought of Alexandre with a pang of sorrow.

"My husband?"

The doctor shook his head. "I cannot save him. He must be left to his fate. You, on the other hand, have a reprieve of sorts. You only have to do one thing: look as though you are dying, for as many days as possible."

I did my best to look fatally ill. The guards ignored me. Dr. Osnolenko brought me food, and I ate in secret, when everyone else was asleep. And after a week of this subterfuge, I learned, much to my amazement, that the terrible reign of the Red Lady, the time they now call the Terror, was over. A new group of revolutionaries had come to power. The killings had stopped—for the time being at least.

I was free to go home.

Never have I felt such joy as on the morning of my release from the Carmelite prison. I was still quite weak, and had to lean on Dr. Osnolenko's strong arm as I made my way out of the dark corridor and into the light of freedom.

At first, the light outside was too bright for me, unaccustomed as I was to seeing the sun or feeling its warmth on my upturned face. I blinked, then closed my eyes, then blinked again. Gradually my vision began to clear, and I saw the most welcome sight anyone can ever see— the smiling faces of my beloved children, holding out their arms to me in welcome and homecoming, their eyes brimming with tears.

25

OH, HOW WE REJOICED THAT SUMMER, after the Great Terror ended and those of us lucky enough to have survived were set free! So many had died—we had to live twice as intensely, for their sakes. And in truth, we did not know what the future would bring; perhaps there were more terrors to come. So we went wild, enjoying a surfeit of pleasure each day and making each night a feast for all the senses, a banquet to be savored until we were replete.

What good times we had, going to the Café Lestrigal (now refurbished and enlarged, with a stage and a Russian band) and the Elysée National to hear Black Julien's Band, dancing on the tombstones at the Zephyr's Ball in the cemetery of Saint-Sulpice, paying our compliments to the Altar of Love at Wenzell's where the subscription parties were so crowded we had to dance out in the street. The theaters full, and the tickets exorbitant, though most of the theaters, it must be said, were little more than brothels then because the foyers were full of bare-breasted prostitutes and all the balcony seats were bought by expensive courtesans soliciting rich clients. At the Variétés, it was rumored, a man could hire a different woman every night for a year, there were so many inviting companions for sale.

We indulged in fads and went mad over silly things like wearing green wigs and purple wigs, men's trousers, and coachman's hats. We invented foolish ways of talking, leaving the r's out of our words or babbling like babies. We called each other extravagant names: I was Puff Pastry because of my ample breasts, my friend Therese Tallien was Eclair, Julie Récamier was Profiterole. We were often seen in the park driving herds of goats, or riding ponies, or feeding the tame gazelle Scipion brought me from Africa.

It was in those days, right after my release from prison, that I learned to drive a phaeton and often rode through the park in the afternoon, stopping to call on friends or visit my dressmaker and milliner and corsetier. I bought lavishly and ran up huge debts. Beyond the cost of my rented house and Eugene's military school tuition, Hortense's school fees and little Coco's governess, there were servants to pay and food and fuel to buy. Everything was expensive, but like many other survivors I felt that nothing was too good for me. I deserved it all.

And besides, I had someone to pay for it. I had Paul Barras.

"You know what they say about him," Scipion commented to me on the night we met at the Carmelite Dance Hall (the former Carmelite prison, where I had been so wretched and ill and had thought of ending my life). "They say he is the richest man in Paris."

"The richest in France," I corrected him. "You should see his mansion. He lives as grandly as a prince." Barras not only lived like a prince, he looked like one, with his dark, somewhat overripe handsomeness, his charm and easy grace of manner, his unruffled demeanor, his abundance of magnificent rings and subtly elegant dress. In actuality he was a minor Gascon nobleman. I guessed his age at forty-eight or nine.

"He was in the army, you know," Scipion was saying. "Long before the Revolution. They threw him out for perversion. No scandal, just a quiet exit."

"What sort of perversion?"

"It seems he enjoys both men and women in bed."

"At the same time?"

Scipion laughed. "I don't know. You'll have to ask him."

Paul and I had become lovers late one night after a ball given by the former Duc de Lorgne, an old acquaintance of mine from my days at Fontainebleau, in the rue Saint-Germain. I had been introduced to Paul earlier in the evening and we had danced together—the new fashionable dance, the German waltz. At the end of the evening we found ourselves going out the door at the same time, and he offered to drive me home in his large carriage.

The carriage, I soon discovered, was a vehicle made for seduction. The seats folded out to make a soft bed, there were scented pillows and a blanket in a small cabinet next to the door. The driver, who had undoubtedly been given instructions beforehand, knew to go slowly and the horses clip-clopped at a walking pace. I yielded eagerly to Paul's searching hands, accustomed as I was, after my time in prison, to lovemaking with strangers. I was not disappointed.

Paul was generous. From his extravagantly large fortune, made from selling sour wine and rotting grain and rusty muskets as a provisioner to the army, he sent me large bank drafts and bought me my charming phaeton decorated in gold leaf, and the two black Hungarian horses that pulled it. In a short time I became part of his inner circle, the inner circle of a powerful man. For Paul Barras was not only my protector and defender, he was the leading figure in the current government.

"You should be wary of him," Scipion said brusquely. "He's corrupt. And cynical."

"Aren't we all corrupt and cynical these days?" I was goading Scipion, who I knew to be decent and upstanding. Though what I said was very largely true; government, business, the military were all riddled with dishonesty and everywhere one turned there was graft and bribery, cheating and petty crime.

Scipion took my face between his hands, and looked at me with genuine tenderness. "We've known each other such a long time, Yeyette," he said, using my old girlhood name. "I would hate to see you go down that road."

But of course I did not heed Scipion's words. I put on the pleasure-seeking, indolent life into which Paul led me as easily as I had once slipped into the loose-fitting, body-draping gowns of Martinique. Growing more and more heedless of responsibility, and leaving the oversight of the children to Euphemia and the other servants, I slept until noon each day, had a late breakfast and then devoted my afternoons to pleasure. Paul visited me at five each evening, we spent several lazy hours in bed, dined late and then whiled away the long, wine-sodden night in Paul's private grotto in the garden of his mansion.

Night after night I danced there in the grotto, in the nude, behind a gauze curtain, while Paul and his wealthy men friends watched. My dance was only one of many attractions: hermaphrodites, men of prodigious size and even more prodigious virility deflowering young girls, raconteurs who told ribald stories. Young men and women of exceptional beauty were hired to decorate the grotto and provide diversion; long before the night was over all the clothes had come off and an orgy had begun.

I slept in the grotto on many an inebriated evening, and wakened, bleary-eyed and hung over, to face the unwelcome noon. The louche admiration of the men flattered my vanity, for I was by then past thirty, and proud that my voluptuous figure was still attractive. It amused Barras to watch other men make love to me, and I was complaisant. Some of the things that went on in the grotto were distasteful to me, and I soon discovered that Scipion had been right about Paul: he did take both men and women into his bed, and he did mix pleasure and pain in ways I found perverse and repulsive. But I was always free to leave if I did not like what was going on. Paul had other mistresses to turn to, and a harem of beautiful boys.

It was a season of excess, of daring, of hardly knowing right from wrong, up from down. We danced, drank, indulged. We had lived for so long under the shadow of the Red Lady that we hardly remembered what normal life was like. We were survivors—for the moment at least. How long our continued survival would last, we could not have said.

26

THE TRUTH WAS, I suppose, that I had been thinking about marriage.

The life I was leading was excessive, and I knew it. Besides, I was getting on in years. It was not seemly for me to parade myself naked behind gauze curtains, or to be one of Paul's mistresses but not the principal one.

I liked the money and things Paul gave me—especially the money—but I had learned the importance of being able to support myself. While spending many hours there in Paul's grotto each night I had done more than dance; I had made the acquaintance of other rich men: bankers, financiers, men of business. And inspired by Paul's great success, I had gone into the provisioning business myself in a small way, supplying goods to the army. I was no Paul Barras, of course, I was under no illusions about that. But I learned from him, and I was beginning to make a success of my newfound trade.

I used my network of contacts to find out, as best I could, what each of the regiments needed, and then used my wits (and more contacts) to locate the goods, and sell them at high prices to the colonels and supply officers. I had capable, ambitious young men—some of them my admirers—working alongside me. I was always on the watch for more such young men.

There was a rather odd-looking, dark little officer who I often saw

with Barras. He was small, almost puny, with a melancholy expression on
his round young face and fierce, angry-looking eyes. Although his clothes
were well made he looked ill at ease in them, and he carried himself
badly; that he felt awkward and self-conscious in the company of older,
more worldly people was very evident.

It amused me to watch him as he stood near Barras, trying in vain to
look nonchalant. He bit his nails. He took a snuffbox from his waistband
and extracted pinches of snuff, only to spill a good deal of it on the costly
carpet before he could manage to inhale it. He scratched his wrists and
his neck so frequently that I wondered if he had the itch. Unlike most
of the other young men around Barras—the ones who were attracted
to women, I mean—this odd little officer did not approach any of the
women to talk to or flirt with. I wondered why.

One evening I approached him, partly from curiosity but mostly in
hopes that he might be a good source of information about his regiment
and its needs.

I smiled—careful not to show my teeth, as they had grown very
brown and I had lost several of them, the result of eating too much sugar.
I gave him my hand to kiss.

"General Buonaparte, at your service," he said, and abruptly bent over
and brushed his lips against my knuckles. He spoke with a very thick
Italian accent. He did not look at me. He reeked of cologne.

"And do you know who I am?"

"Everyone of consequence does. You are the former Vicomtesse de
Beauharnais. You are said to be one of the most desirable women in
Paris, despite your age."

"I don't know whether to thank you or slap you."

His features remained impassive. "I merely repeat what is being said."

He suddenly reached up to scratch his neck.

"Filthy town, Toulon," he muttered under his breath.

"What did you say?"

"Toulon. It's a filthy place. I was stationed there. Everyone in the
barracks came down with scabies."

"I believe there are pills you can take to relieve it. I know a very good
Polish physician who—"

"Never mind!" He cut me off rudely. "I abhor all medicines and all
doctors. I find that barley-water, or strong lemonade, or if necessary
leeches, will cure any ailment. And a strong will, of course."

"Is that so? And what about a broken leg?"

He shrugged. "Broken bones, battle wounds—for those we call in the butchers—I mean the surgeons." He smiled then, and it was as if the skies cleared and the sun broke through. His smile was full of merriment and charm. I thought, how could anyone resist it?

Suddenly he reached up to open the high collar of his velvet jacket, with a motion so violent that he tore off one of the gold buttons. He scratched his throat, and as he did so I saw that he was wearing an amulet, suspended from a gold chain.

"A good luck charm, general?"

"All soldiers are superstitious."

"Perhaps you would like your fortune told. I read the cards."

"I'll save you the trouble. My fortune—" he began, his grey-blue eyes taking on a faraway look, his voice changing in tone, and becoming lower. "My fortune is to rival Charlemagne. To ride into battle among Turkish warriors, and capture Constantinople. To conquer India, with a million men and a hundred thousand elephants."

He talked on, as if to himself, forgetting me entirely in his reverie. Eventually his attention returned to the room, and to me. I asked if his regiment was in need of eggs, or canvas for tents, or horse-collars.

He seemed to find my question amusing.

"Eggs? You are asking me if I or my men need eggs?"

"Among other things."

"If we need eggs, we go to the farmers."

"The farmers sell to me—or my contacts. I sell to the army."

"You mean you cheat the army. I'm sorry to hear that such an attractive woman has such a venal heart."

"There is nothing venal about making an honest profit, general. Or about helping to feed the armies of the Republic."

"Rubbish! You profiteers, you and Barras and all your kind, make fortunes while we officers and our families starve."

"You appear to be prosperous enough," I retorted, looking at the expensive gold embroidery on his tight-fitting red velvet waistcoat.

"Any prosperity I enjoy is quite recent, I assure you. For years I was a struggling junior officer, hardly able to afford a decent pair of boots, much less to send money to my widowed mother and my sisters and brothers."

He went on, telling me of his relatives and his hopes for them, of his courageous and beautiful mother, of his late father who died too young, of his own army service during the Revolution. We moved out onto the terrace as he talked, the night being warm.

"I proved myself at Toulon. My batteries held off the English fleet. They made me a brigadier-general at twenty-four." Even in the moonlight I could see the flush of pleasure that saying these words gave him.

"And now?" I asked at length. "What now?"

"I am planning an invasion of Italy. To begin at the first thaw, at the end of winter." His words became clipped, brusque. In imagination he was already on the battlefield, sending orders to his troops. I found the chameleonlike quality of his mind and emotions fascinating.

We talked for some time there on the terrace, in the summer evening. As time passed I felt there was something stirring between us. An intimacy that was not quite friendship, nor infatuation. A closeness for which I had no name.

Yet at the same time I felt on guard, as I never did with Scipion, or even with Paul. This young general, with his thick accent and blunt words, his vehement opinions and charming smile, both compelled and frightened me. I had never met anyone like him.

"Barras was wrong about you," he said to me before we parted. "He told me you were hard. But you're not. You're soft. Quite gentle really. I suspect you have a kind heart—despite your acquisitive nature."

"I hope we meet again soon, general," was all I said in response. But I was thinking that young General Buonaparte, though unformed, was indeed hard, hard at the core. Will, drive, ambition flowed through his veins and his mind never stopped churning. He lacked polish, but possessed something of far greater value: pride. Not hauteur, like Alexandre, or self-satisfaction, like a dozen other men I could name, or a naked confidence in his own power like Paul. But pride in who he was and what he had it in him to do. In this we were alike, for by the time I met the young general I too felt proud of who I had become and how far my talents had taken me. I was ready to go further, if given the chance.

27

BUT OF COURSE LIFE INTERVENED, and the unexpected happened.

I was in the newly redecorated gold-and-rose sitting room of my house on the rue Chantereine, being served tea and cake by one of the maids when another maid came in to tell me that a gentleman was calling.

In walked Donovan.

It had been a long time since I last saw him, working as my father's overseer at Les Trois-Ilets and commanding one of the local militias. He seemed taller and more lean, his jaw more set, his mouth firm. His mouth! I could still remember the feel of it on mine, his warm, full lips, his warm breath, the way he filled my senses until I reeled, overcome.

Seeing him, I felt an echo of those long-ago, faroff encounters. I felt a tingle along my skin, a jolt up my spine. He came up to me where I sat on the long sofa beside the fireplace. He bent down and kissed me, not on the cheek but on the mouth. There was possession in that kiss.

He sat beside me, opening his coat.

"It's good to see you." My words were trite, but sincerely meant. With him near me, my body responded, not only with desire, but with a sense of safety. I relaxed.

Then he reached for my hand, and I sensed at once that something was wrong. He was comforting me. Why?

"Rose, I am in Paris for two reasons, one sad, one, I hope, happy." He paused, and looked directly into my eyes.

"Rose, I am so very sorry to have to tell you that your father has died. I am here to try to settle his estate. He owes a great deal to moneylenders and bankers. Les Trois-Ilets has been seized by his creditors. I am trying to save something out of the estate for your mother and aunt."

"I've been sending money to Martinique, quite a lot—"

"I know you have, Rose."

"But I've heard nothing from anyone in my family for a long time." My tears overflowed, and Donovan held me in his strong arms until I managed to recover myself.

"I'm so sorry, Rose. So very sorry," he murmured as he stroked my hair. "It was difficult for letters to cross the ocean. We were blockaded, and then even after the blockade was lifted, few ships called at Fort-Royal. I could not get word to you." He paused, then went on.

"Your father was good to me. He took me in and gave me a home, when I had none. I miss him."

We consoled one another for a time, then he spoke again.

"Martinique has been in turmoil for years. The countryside was in chaos, Fort-Royal was held for many months by rebels. No one knew whom to trust. It was too much for your father. He died cursing his life."

"Where are mother and Aunt Rosette now?" I asked presently.

"They live with your cousins at an estate near the Morne des Larmes. When I left they were in good health. They send their love. They want you to come home. It is what I want too."

He kissed me then, a lover's kiss, and I was aware of the deep, fierce hunger of my body for his, a hunger that had gone unsatisfied for so very long. When he touched me the craving intensified, the long unslaked appetite was unleashed. We were a banquet for each other, a banquet for all the senses. We took our fill, devouring, gorging, until, surfeited with desire and the assuaging of desire, we lay back on the silken pillows of my high carved bed, replete and joyful.

I felt made of air, my sorrows and burdens lifted, my entire body light and free. I lay there, content simply to be lying next to him, our bodies so close they seemed to form one body.

It was all I could do, when the time came, to say goodbye to him, even though he promised to see me again very soon.

In fact, we saw each other nearly every day, now that Donovan was in Paris. I invited him to my house. I saw him in the park when I drove my phaeton there in the afternoons. We went shopping together, I for soft silken underclothes, he for hats and gloves and a set of fine duelling pistols.

And always, with the most delicious abandon, we made love. He could not banish my mourning, but he eased it, and I was grateful.

"Come with me to Martinique, Rose," he said as I lay in his arms. "Things are improving there. The plantations are beginning to produce cane again, and the Americans are buying it. I have bought a plantation of my own. I call it Bonne Fortune. I have a hundred Africans working on it, and I plan to hire more."

"Who is looking after it for you?"

"I have a good overseer." He smiled at the thought, having once been an overseer himself. "And Jules-sans-nez is there." He stroked my cheek as he talked on. I closed my eyes. "Come with me," he said again. "Bring the children. Leave this place of debauchery and crime, this topsy-turvy Paris. You will have complete freedom at Bonne Fortune. And we will have each other."

"It would not be—a permanent arrangement, I assume," I said after a time. "No promises, no vows."

"I am not the sort that makes promises."

I knew that he would say that, of course I knew. He was not offering me marriage. He could not. Only rapture, for as long as it lasted.

It was becoming more and more clear to me that my life was in transition. I knew that Paul was tiring of me, and he seemed to go out of his way to bring me together with General Buonaparte. He seated me next to the general at dinner parties, and spoke well of him to me when we were alone together, which was less and less often.

"You know, Rose, you could do far worse than marry that little Corsican, Buonaparte. I happen to know he admires you."

I dismissed the suggestion as outlandish, but it worried me. It was one more hint that Paul wanted me out of his life. Yet I was dependent on the bank drafts that he sent me. My income as a provisioner was far less than what I needed to run my household and pay my bills.

About a month after Donovan came to Paris, I gave a dinner party at my house. Paul was not there, but Donovan was—and indeed he was far and away the most handsome man present. The occasion was Eugene's leaving to return to military school. He was fourteen years old and one of the most promising boys in his class, a dutiful, serious boy, always extremely polite and loving to me. He had a natural patrician air that reminded me of Alexandre, but he had none of Alexandre's snobbery or hauteur. Nor was he an intellectual—thank goodness! The military life had always appealed to him, and it thrilled him that I was becoming acquainted with General Buonaparte, the hero of Toulon. (For in fact the general had done more at Toulon than contract scabies; he had performed brilliantly as an artillery officer, gaining a major victory.) At Eugene's pleading I invited the general to my dinner party.

Donovan was among the first to arrive and was happily greeted by the children. He brought marzipan for Coco, a very grown-up necklace of pink coral for Hortense (his special favorite) and a long, wicked-looking cane knife for Eugene.

"It takes an edge as sharp as any saber," Donovan told Eugene. "On Martinique we use it for everything: cutting cane, clearing brush—and of course for self-defense." He swung the wide blade through the air, making a swishing sound. "They won't teach you about the cane knife in military school. But if you should ever go into battle, you'll find it useful."

"If! If I go into battle! You mean when I go into battle! My father always said, son, you must defend the Republic against her enemies. I will fight for France! I will win glory for her!"

I shuddered when I heard Eugene's words. I feared for him.

"Fighting is not the best way to win," Donovan was saying. "I know. I was a soldier once. I have led men into combat. The very best way to win is to appear so strong, so formidable in defense, that the enemy will not dare to attack."

Eugene looked dubious.

"What if the enemy is overconfident, and attacks anyway?"

"Then you must wait—and at the last moment, defend yourself."

"Wait? Wait? What's this I hear?" It was the piercing, insistent voice of General Buonaparte, who shrugged off his cape as he entered the salon, a large leather case in his arms.

"Who is telling the brave Eugene to wait and not to fight? No—you must always advance. Take the battle to the enemy. Conquer him by your audacity!"

He advanced himself as he spoke, striding into the room with vigor, carrying his leather case up to Eugene and laying it on a table near him.

Eugene straightened himself and saluted, grinning. I could not help noting that Eugene, though only fourteen, was already as tall as the general.

"Here is a little something to take with you to military school. A memento."

Eugene discarded the cane knife and opened the case. Inside was a gleaming sword, the hilt chased in silver and bronze, the blade in perfect condition, without any chipping along the edge, as if it had never been used.

Eugene's eyes gleamed. He ran his hand along the flat of the flawless blade.

"General," I said, "this is my friend from Martinique, Monsieur Donovan de Gautier." The two men nodded to one another, the contrast between them very marked. Donovan was much taller and better looking. I made introductions among the other guests, who were beginning to arrive.

Among them was Fanny de Beauharnais, who when introduced to Donovan, gave him a wide smile of approval. (I had confided to her all that went on between us—or almost all.) When presented to General Buonaparte, however, she visibly drew back in evident scorn.

"The hero of Toulon," she said, her tone icy. "The man who jumps when that despicable Paul Barras snaps his fingers."

"And you, I believe, are Fanny de Beauharnais, the woman who dresses badly and writes execrable verse."

"At least I don't murder innocent people."

"No, you only murder the French language."

"You're a fine one to talk about murdering the French language, when you can barely speak it!"

"But when I do speak it, my words have value."

"Please, general, Fanny"—I said, intervening, "let us remember that this is a party for Eugene, and be civil to one another."

"Forgive me, my dear madame," General Buonaparte said, taking my hand and kissing it. "I was provoked."

Fanny opened her mouth to speak but took note of my imploring glance and thought better of it.

"Of course, my dear. We will overlook the insults of annoying little men."

Much to my relief, the focus shifted to the magnificent sword, which General Buonaparte was lifting from its case.

"This belonged to your father," he said quietly to Eugene. "I rescued it from among his effects, confiscated when he was arrested. The despicable Paul Barras, as someone just called him, was a great help to me in obtaining it. I present it to you with Monsieur Barras's compliments and my own. Your father served the Republic well."

And then, in a gesture that brought tears to every eye in the room, the general knelt and presented the sword to Eugene.

A hush fell as Eugene, fighting for composure himself, received the beautiful sword and kissed its hilt.

High drama indeed! I saw that Donovan too was moved, and that he joined enthusiastically when the guests burst into sustained applause. I went to Eugene and kissed him, and presently we all went in to dine.

There must have been at least twenty guests at my long dining-table that evening, but General Buonaparte was easily the most vocal of them all, dominating the room with his amusing, knowledgeable talk. He did not insult Fanny again, and she restrained herself from taunting him. I had seated her next to Donovan and was glad to see that they got on well together.

The general held forth on a subject he knew extremely well: artillery. He talked of siege guns and howitzers, shells and shot.

"Gunners are no ordinary soldiers, I can assure you," he concluded. "Oh no, gunners are artists! They must be masters of strategy, mathematics, mechanics, the very art of war itself! Come with me to Italy, Eugene, and I'll make a gunner of you. You're old enough now to be a powder monkey. Then you'll become a loader, and then a sponger, and finally a gun captain. That's a fine, proud thing to be, a gun captain. Twenty-four crewmen under you, ten drivers, a dozen horses, carpenters to repair the gun carriage—and all of them taking orders from you."

Eugene beamed. "I'll bring along my father's sword. And my cane knife," he added with a smile to Donovan.

"You'll go back to school," I said firmly. "No more talk of going to war."

"Ah, but there will be talk, madame," the general retorted. "The British are still trying to keep their foothold in Brittany, and the Austrians are on the move against us. We cannot wait to go on the offensive. We must advance! We must go on the attack! We must show the enemies of the Republic that the hour of our victory is at hand!"

28

THE PARISIANS, in that summer of 1795, were restless and rebellious. Even on the night of my dinner party for Eugene, we could hear the disturbing sounds of people grouping together in the street, shouting for an end to high food prices and even (I could hardly believe it) for the return of the king. The king was long dead, of course; what they really wanted was to feel that they had some influence, and could make things better for themselves by taking action to force change.

They were fed up with being ignored by the new unscrupulous politicians and wealthy exploiters who had come to power. Paul Barras was among the worst of these exploiters, I knew. I was not proud of my association with him. But what else could I have done? How else could I have lived, in those dangerous and turbulent days, without his money and his support?

On into the fall of that year the unrest all around us grew, until on one terrible night we began hearing alarm bells ringing and drums beating all across the city. No one could sleep. We were far too much on edge for that. We knew, of course, that there were extremists who wanted to overthrow the government yet again and who were prepared to take up arms and destroy the Tuileries Palace where our current officials met. For months there had been rumors of another widespread uprising. On that night it began.

We locked all the doors and barred the windows, and prepared for the worst.

All was confusion on that awful night, but as Paul told me later, he was determined not to let the rabble of Paris destroy what had taken six long years of revolution to create—namely, a true republic, imperfect but capable of improvement. The mob, he said, was determined to dig the Revolution's grave. They had to be stopped.

And who better to stop them than the hero of Toulon, General Buonaparte?

Barras sent for him and told him to disperse the immense crowd that was threatening the Tuileries Palace. There was a storm that night and rain was falling in torrents. The streets were full of sticky black mud. The rioters were sure that they would meet with no resistance, whatever they did. They thought the soldiers could not fire their muskets in all the rain.

But General Buonaparte, Paul told me afterwards, acted with remarkable cleverness and dispatch. He ordered forty big guns brought into the city and positioned around the palace. When the mob launched its assault, he ordered his gunners to fire.

No one expected such a merciless assault. The killing was dreadful, bodies all over the streets, blood everywhere.

"It was all over in a few minutes," Paul told me. "Buonaparte did exactly what was needed. He saved us. He saved the Revolution."

The hero of Toulon became the hero of Paris. Promoted to major general, his salary tripled and his importance immeasurably increased. Everyone praised Buonaparte—everyone but the hundreds of men and women killed by his murderous cannonade, and their relatives and friends. But they were of no account. They belonged to the past. Buonaparte was the future.

And he was mine—if I wanted him.

Flowers began arriving daily at my house on the rue Chantereine. Huge bunches of roses, lilies, exotic hothouse flowers that lived only a day. There were always love notes with the flowers.

"I am consumed with you. I long for the sight of your sweet face."

"I cannot wait until tonight. Would that you were here beside me as I write this, so that I could kiss your rosebud lips!"

"I am enchanted with you. Never free me from this enchantment, I beg of you!"

He had a fertile pen, did General Buonaparte. He was well read for a military officer. He knew how to write a graceful love letter.

But when we met privately, as we began to do at around this time, he was as inept, as unsure as a besotted schoolboy. His attempts at lovemaking were clumsy. He mauled me, he fell on me like a starving man falling on a plate of roast chicken. He had no finesse, no sense of the erotic. Not that any of this would have mattered, had I returned his infatuation. But I did not. I could not. And in any case, I was involved with Donovan, who continued to try to persuade me to pack my things and return with him to the Windward Isles.

One afternoon a card was left for me, along with a huge basket of hothouse flowers and herbs—lavender, thyme, anemones, carnations.

"My dearest," the card read, "I must see you tonight on a matter of the greatest urgency. Be prepared for my visit at nine o'clock."

It was nearly eleven when he arrived. Most of the servants had gone to bed and I was on the point of going to bed myself, thinking that the general had been unexpectedly delayed by some urgent business. Then I heard a carriage and the insistent clicking of boot-heels on the flagstones at the front entrance to my house. I knew at once who it was.

He fairly shouted my name as he was admitted, and ran in to my salon.

"Rose! Rose! It has happened! I am officially entrusted with the invasion of Italy! Rejoice with me!"

He looked, on that night, as I had never before seen him look: he seemed transformed, completely taken out of himself. Had he been a priest or monk, I would have said that he had glimpsed the Beatific Vision. His eyes were bright, his brow unlined and serene.

We embraced and I congratulated him warmly on his success—saying nothing of his lateness, or the inconvenience to me.

"I have you to thank, Rose, for giving me the confidence to make my plan of campaign and present it to the Directors." We had a new government at that time, headed by five Directors, chief among them Paul Barras. "You listened to me and encouraged me, and gave me hope when I was almost in despair."

"I was glad to do what I could to help you, general," I said, suppressing a yawn. He was right, of course. During the past several months I had spent a good deal of time patiently hearing him expound his plans to lead an army into Italy, and reassuring him when he was in a low mood, as he often was.

He sat down beside me and took my hand in his. I could not help noticing that his hands, as always, were cold and clammy, the nails bitten down to the quick.

"I had already made up my mind to discuss an important matter with you, Rose, even before I learned that the Directors have approved my Italian campaign. It is this. I need a wife."

He looked at me intently, waiting for me to say something.

"Oh," I said at length.

"I need a wife, Rose. I need the respectability of a wife, children. Family."

"Yes. I see."

"And she must be French, not Corsican. My mother has chosen a Corsican bride for me, and I will disappoint her, but that cannot be helped. No, my wife must be French, because I myself must seem French. I am changing the spelling of my name from Nabuleone Buonaparte to Napoleon Bonaparte. I am gallicizing myself.

"And while we are speaking of names, dear Rose, it pleases me to call you by your second name. You were christened Rose-Joseph, I believe you told me?"

"Yes."

"I prefer Josephine. It suits you so much better than plain Rose. I shall call you Josephine from now on."

"And what if I prefer my own name Rose?"

"You may think of yourself however you like, but your public name will be Josephine."

I started to refuse, but had second thoughts. Rose was a rather plain name, and in truth I had always thought of myself as Yeyette. Josephine had an elegant ring to it, more in keeping with the rather elegant woman I had become. I could still be Yeyette to my family, after all. I did not demur.

In that moment, I later realized, I capitulated to the general. What he wanted for me began to govern my life, though I did not yet perceive it. My very identity became his to command.

He talked on, ticking off one qualification after another for the wife he needed. She had to have noble blood, superb social connections, she had to be an able hostess, she could not be taller than he was.

"And of course she must be rich, like you, my Josephine."

There was an awkward silence. I confess I had led General Bonaparte (I must spell his name in the French way from here on) to believe that I was rich. It was not difficult. As I have said, all creoles were assumed to be wealthy, and my pride demanded that I maintain the illusion of wealth. Not great wealth, of course, but substantial wealth, comparable to that of the most prosperous of the Grands Blancs of Martinique or the successful merchants of Paris.

I said nothing.

A puckish smile broke over the general's features. I thought, he can certainly be charming.

"You know what I am trying to say, my dearest Josephine. I am proposing marriage to you. I am offering to let you share my future."

I got up then, and moved to stand by the fireplace. So this was where his businesslike catalog of wifely attributes had been leading. This very unromantic train of logic. This was his idea of a proposal!

I was more amused than offended by the oddity of it all, so like him. He was an original. But of course the idea was absurd.

"If you need a wife, then by all means you must find one. I know many eligible women, not all of them rich by any means, but closer to your age and capable of aiding you socially."

"I do not want anyone but you."

"It is impossible." I wanted to add, "It is impossible, because of Donovan," but I did not.

"Why? Nothing is impossible, if two people of strong will desire it. You are not pledged to anyone else." It was a statement of fact, not a question.

"No. Not exactly."

"Barras tells me that you are not. Surely you can't be waiting for Barras to propose to you?" He grinned. "We both know that your connection with him has been on the wane for some time. He has been quite candid with me about it. Besides, he never loved you, and I do."

He came over to me and took me in his arms, his ardor so intense that he trembled.

"Tell me you love me a little, my beautiful, my one and only Josephine. Make the happiness of this day complete."

"I will have to think about it," was all I said. I was too weary to argue with him, and in truth I did not want to spoil his day of triumph. I could not accept him, yet I could not bring myself to crush his hopes. He was so ingenuous, so boyish. I could not help liking him.

"It is after midnight, and I am sleepy. You must let me rest."

I saw the disappointment that crossed his eager face, and almost regretted having caused it.

"Until tomorrow then, my lovely one." He kissed me again, then turned and was gone. The room felt empty without him.

29

THE BANK DRAFTS FROM PAUL BARRAS were coming less often, and his visits to me were infrequent. I made efforts to increase my income from army contracts, and did my best to exploit my connection with General Bonaparte whose troops were gearing up for the coming Italian campaign.

But the truth was, that in order to maintain the large house and staff of servants that I had then, plus keep my children in costly schools, it was necessary to find another source of support. I would either have to marry, or take another rich lover, or—and I thought about this more and more often—return with Donovan to Martinique.

The pull of my attachment to Donovan was strong, and I longed for the islands, always my home. I dreamed of returning to the old Martinique, the way it was in my girlhood, with Donovan beside me. But I was more and more convinced that like General Bonaparte, I needed to marry. I wanted permanence. I wanted a respected stepfather for my children. Eugene, in particular, needed a strong man in his life. Hortense, I knew, disliked the general, especially his way of coming up to her and pulling on her ears until she cried out in pain. He laughed when he did it, which made her dislike him even more. But Hortense, being a girl, was not my primary concern: Eugene was. Bonaparte had offered to take Eugene to Italy with him, and I thought, if he will promise to keep Eugene away from the worst of the fighting, then maybe I should let him go. He was so very eager to begin his military career, and he idolized the general.

Besides, I was beginning to see that there was more to Bonaparte than an unpolished, precocious artillery officer and young commander of men. He had a quality that drew people to him—that drew me to him. He could be ruthless, and he had massacred many innocent Parisians at Paul Barras's request. Yet I also saw him, in that cold winter of 1795, giving out wholesome loaves of army bread to starving, shivering Parisians in the rue Sainte-Nicole and I know for a fact that he kept a list of families in need (many of them Corsicans) and made certain they were helped with food and fuel until spring came.

Besides, he was a rising star.

Everyone said so, and I listened to what was being said. I listened—and in the end I decided to accept his proposal of marriage.

I did not do so blindly, nor dishonestly, or so I believed. I summoned the general to my house and spoke frankly to him.

"I cannot pretend that my feelings for you are as strong as yours for me," I began, when the general had seated himself before the fire in my salon. I paced as I spoke, and was uncomfortably aware of how stilted and formal my words were, like the language in one of the cheap novels Euphemia liked to read. "However, on mature reflection, I have decided to accept your proposal of marriage."

Before I could say another word he jumped up from his chair and ran to embrace me, kissing my face again and again and saying "Josephine! Josephine! Oh my darling, my adorable Josephine!"

I gently pushed him away and went on with what I needed to say, making him sit down again and hear me out.

"I want you to know that I am not rich, and I cannot bring you any sort of dowry."

"Oh, I know that. I've already been to see your bankers, I know exactly how much money you have. And I know that Barras will stop sending you checks once we are married."

"I should also tell you that I have slept with many men."

"Everyone in Paris knows that."

"And that I have had another proposal."

It was true in a way. Donovan did want me to live with him, presumably for a long time. Just not with a ring and a promise made before a priest. In any case, I felt powerful telling the general that he had a rival.

My words had a strong effect. Once again Bonaparte jumped up from his chair, but now his face was set sternly in anger.

"Who is he?"

"I prefer not to say. I intend to refuse him."

"I must know who he is."

I was silent.

"I cannot fight an invisible enemy!" he cried out, taking a step toward me. I was frightened. I kept my voice as low and controlled as I could.

"There is no need to fight. As I said, I intend to refuse him."

I watched as his anger gave way to exasperation, then a look of sour contempt, then defeat, then melancholy. How changeable the man could be!

"Don't let us clash on the happiest day of our lives," he said at length. "As long as you promise to be mine . . ."

"Yes. I will marry you," I said again.

He was tender and full of endearments; I was kind. He went out and bought me masses of flowers, and brought me a ring that had belonged to his grandmother—a ring with a tiny stone in a very plain old-fashioned setting. I put it on my little finger as it was too small for my ring finger.

"I don't wonder it doesn't fit your ring finger," he said, caressing my hand between both of his and kissing it. "My Corsican grandmother was a very little woman, barely taller than a child. Her family was very poor and she told me that as a girl she never had enough to eat. But she was strong, and very brave. They say she killed a wolf with a knife when it attacked one of her lambs."

He smiled. "We Corsicans are savages."

"I know."

And then he fell upon me and devoured me, and I did my best to enjoy it.

Bonaparte spoke often and at length about his destiny, how he was fated to achieve great things, on a vast scale; now I was linking my destiny to his. In my more reflective moments I thought of Orgulon, and what he had told me about my future. Was I making the choice that Orgulon would approve? I thought so.

The day of the army's departure for Italy was approaching, and Bonaparte spent every waking hour getting his men ready and reading messages from his informants in the Italian states. When with me he often lapsed into a preoccupied state, pacing the floor and muttering to himself in Italian.

He wanted us to be married before he left on campaign. He wanted everything settled between us.

I arranged for our wedding to be held in the fashionable church of St-Sermin and drew up a long guest list. I ordered a bridal gown from Madame Despaux and an immense cake from the patisserie Terlay, which at that time made the best pastry in the capital. Planning was well advanced when I received a note from Bonaparte.

Josephine, soul of my life, meet me at seven o'clock tonight at the city hall in the rue d'Antin. Bring witnesses.

With the note was a gift, a medallion engraved with the words "To Destiny."

Alas! All my elaborate arrangements had to be abandoned. There was to be no fashionable wedding, no gifts, no envy from the other women as I walked down the aisle in my Madame Despaux gown.

I was crushed. I wept on Euphemia's capacious bosom and she patted my head consolingly. After an hour I pulled myself together and sent hurried messages to my friend Therese Tallien and her husband, to Paul Barras (I felt it only right that he be present, to give me away) and to my financial adviser Jerome Calmelet, who had stood loyally by me throughout the ups and downs of my years in Paris. I told them to be at the city hall at seven, and thanked them for their willingness to be my witnesses.

I did not take Hortense with me that night, at her request. Nor did I send a message to Aunt Edmée or Fanny de Beauharnais. I knew that Fanny disliked Bonaparte and was certain that Aunt Edmée would be disappointed in my choice of husband. To her, high birth and wealth were what mattered in a husband; I felt sure she would be ashamed of me, marrying a Corsican from an obscure family. And a man whose idea of grooming was to douse himself with strong cologne to obscure the odor of scabies.

I looked at myself in the mirror as Euphemia helped me dress. There were shallow lines at the corners of my mouth and eyes, and the skin of my neck and bosom was no longer dewy but slightly dry and veined, its tone more ivory than snow white. I looked quite pleasant, however, with a perpetual smile and a benign tolerance in my glance. My eyes were bright and charmingly uptilted, giving me a gamine, girlish look that belied my thirty-two years. I would not be thirty-three until June, I reminded myself. I still had three months to be thirty-two.

Euphemia fastened a red, white and blue sash around the waist of my white gown and handed me my husband's gift, the engraved medallion on its gold chain. I slipped it over my head.

"May it bring you good fortune, my sister," she said, using the family term she never allowed herself to utter. And then, for good measure, she slipped into the pocket of my gown a protective charm. "Just to keep the evil spirits at bay," she murmured, and we exchanged a knowing smile.

3 0

SO, MADAME BONAPARTE, I hope you are content with your new role. I see that you are much in demand." Paul Barras spoke in wry tones, a mocking grin on his face, looking around him at the crowd that had gathered in my boudoir. They were there that morning as usual, the petitioners, the people wanting favors, or hoping to obtain my help in gaining some political post for themselves or a relative.

"Thanks to my husband's importance, yes."

"But your husband is far away."

"He left two days after our wedding, as you well know."

Paul took out his snuffbox and extracted a pinch of the yellowish powder, expertly putting it up his nose, sniffing, and sneezing.

"How sad for the bride," he went on, "to have no honeymoon. You must be lonely. The grotto is not the same without you." He gave me a significant look, and I remembered, very vividly, the dimly lit large room in which I had spent so many pleasure-filled, indolent nights.

"I have plenty of company, when I want it."

"I wonder if your new husband knows about your chief companion, the intriguing gentleman from Martinique."

I felt my face flush, but answered as nonchalantly as I could.

"Monsieur de Gautier is a business partner. And yes, Bonaparte knows him. They have met."

Donovan had delayed his return to Martinique and we had joined forces in the provisioning business, which was more lucrative than ever. I was dismayed that Barras's spies knew of my relationship with Donovan—both business and personal.

"Don't worry," Barras was saying. "I won't tell Bonaparte about you and this Monsieur de Gautier. It's just between us. After all, I don't want anything to distract Bonaparte from the victories he is winning."

My husband had been achieving astounding military success in Italy, his victories in battle much talked of that spring.

"We are in daily communication," I said enigmatically, making Barras laugh.

"You mean *he* is in daily communication. I know what passes through the post office and the military mail pouches. He writes to you, but you never write to him."

He was right. Bonaparte wrote me frequently, sometimes three or four times a day. But I hate writing letters. I did not write back.

"Besides, I know you, Yeyette. You are too lazy to put in the effort to write a letter!" He reached into his pocket and brought out a carved ivory box.

"Look inside," he said, handing it to me.

I opened it. It contained assignats of high denomination, a good deal of money. Quickly I snapped it shut.

"Now then, in return for my silence over this matter of Monsieur de Gautier. I shall expect you in the grotto tonight—and for many nights to come. In your usual place, behind the gauze curtain! I will be watching for you."

With a laugh he reached out to pat me on the behind. I turned away and began speaking to someone else, but my attempt at indifference could not erase the impact of his familiarity. It galled me to realize that Paul Barras still owned me, as he owned Bonaparte and virtually everyone else of importance at that time.

I caught sight of my image in a mirror. There I was, Madame Bonaparte in name, but still the Vicomtesse de Beauharnais beneath my newfound status, in a gown cut too low for respectability, flashing rings on every finger and with the gleam of avarice in my dark blue eyes—the eyes, I continued to remind myself, of a woman no longer young.

Despite this realization, I had to acknowledge that in outward ways, my life had changed. Everywhere I went I was greeted with loud acclaim as the wife of the man of the hour, Bonaparte. When I drove out in my phaeton I was applauded. At the theater, everyone stood when I entered my box—just as once, before the Revolution, they had stood to honor the king and queen. Shouts of "Madame Bonaparte!" reached my ears when I went into the street and even the dressmakers' assistants who fitted my gowns managed to murmur their approval of my husband though their mouths were full of pins.

I confess that I liked being the wife of a Someone, even though I was uncomfortable knowing that my every move was scrutinized, my every word repeated and evaluated. And I realized, for I am not a fool, that all the extra compliments that came my way were nothing more than flattery, they were not sincerely meant.

When I cut my hair and wore it in soft curls around my face, and all the fashionable women cut theirs in imitation of me, and when all the shopkeepers fawned on me and offered to extend me credit, or when everyone crowded around me the moment I entered a ballroom, I felt a rush of pleasure. I took much satisfaction from moving into Bonaparte's large, solid, stone-fronted house in the rue des Capucines and calling for his handsome carriage (my phaeton being used less now) whenever I wanted to go out. It gave me great satisfaction to be able to send more money to my mother and Aunt Rosette in Martinique. I bought Aunt Edmée a beautiful rope of pearls when, having become a widow, she married the aged marquis in a small ceremony at Fontainebleau. I even went to the dentist and had the look of my remaining teeth improved, though I still kept my mouth shut when I smiled.

By the time Bonaparte had been away in Italy two months his letters to me had become frantic.

"You are the soul of my life," he wrote. "I cannot live without you. I cannot eat or sleep for worry. I fear I will end my life if you do not come and be with me."

I sent word to him through one of his officers that I was ill and could not come. But that message only made him more upset and desperate. In the end, with great reluctance, I agreed to join him, on condition that I be allowed to bring along my business partner and my maid. Bonaparte was so eager to have me with him that he raised no objection.

"Only come quickly, soul of my life!" he wrote to me. "Make haste, make haste, on wings of love!"

When I said that I wanted to bring along my business partner of course I meant Donovan, and I intended to bring Euphemia as well, though she absolutely refused to go with me.

"If you think I'm going to let those nasty Austrians shoot me, Yeyette, you're moonstruck," she announced when I told her about the trip. "I'm staying right here."

By chance a girl came to me just then, hoping to be employed in my household. She had a letter from one of Bonaparte's friends, Laure Permon, recommending her. I agreed to take her on as my maid, and told her we would soon be leaving for Milan.

She seemed to be a quiet, efficient young woman, reserved and well-mannered, nondescript in appearance. Her name was Clodia. I did not inquire very deeply into her background because I was involved in getting ready to leave and also because I am a trusting person—too trusting. I was to find out later that she was not what she seemed. In a few days Donovan, Clodia and I got into the heavy, lumbering traveling coach Bonaparte sent us and started off for the south.

I was unprepared for the rigors of the long journey. I had no idea how far away Italy was, or how very steep and dangerous the mountains were that separated Italy from France.

We had mountains in Martinique of course, high volcanic peaks that rose above the beaches and forest and towered over the land. I knew at first hand how high and rugged one of those peaks was, Morne Ganthéaume, where the Sacred Crossroads were. But those peaks were nothing like the Alps, which rose up in an impenetrable snow-covered barrier before us, a chilly wasteland of ice and cruel cold winds.

As soon as I saw the first jagged peaks I wanted to turn back. I had had more than my fill of traveling already, riding in the rattling, bouncing coach along dusty roads, my bones aching from being constantly shaken and jounced, my throat dry and my head pounding with pain.

"I'm not going any further," I announced to Donovan and the sullen Clodia, who, I could tell, hated coach traveling as much as I did.

"We'll stop for the night," Donovan said, shouting up to the coachman to halt at the next large and prosperous-looking inn. "You'll feel stronger in the morning."

But in the morning the mountains only looked steeper and more forbidding, and my head pounded so furiously that Clodia had to prepare a draught for me to dull the pain. As we began our ascent into the foothills the coach horses tired quickly and we had to get out and walk to lighten the load. I had brought no walking shoes and so wore out my thin slippers on the rocky hill roads, which became more narrow as we climbed.

Soon we reached a point where the coach could go no further. We hired mules at a way-station at the edge of a beautiful green valley and all our baggage was transferred onto the backs of the patient, surefooted beasts. I had never before ridden a mule. I was accustomed to horses, which, I soon discovered, had a very different gait.

Donovan handed pistols to me and to Clodia.

"The mountains are full of brigands," he told me. "Don't hesitate to use these."

I knew how to shoot a pistol. My father had taught me when I was a girl in Martinique, for Les Trois-Ilets where we lived was in an isolated rural area and the only protection we had was what we provided for ourselves, since the militias took days to gather and arm themselves and the nearest soldiers were in Fort-Royal many miles away.

On the Alpine trails, however, pistols proved to be useless because of the near constant mists and fog and the icy wind at the summits. It was impossible to keep the powder dry and I doubt whether my pistol would have fired, had I used it.

In any case, the danger in those mountains lay along the paths themselves more than in the menace of marauding thieves. I held my breath as my mule picked its way daintily along a path only inches wide. On one side of the narrow path lay a sheer rock wall, on the other was a sharp drop, thousands of feet down. I could not look, I had to shut my eyes and hold onto the saddle for dear life, letting out a small scream every time my mount stumbled over a loose rock or slipped when the going became wet from the relentless rain-laden winds.

Though wrapped in blankets, I was frozen. I longed for heat, shelter, a crackling fire. My clothes were soaked and my hair plastered to my face under the sodden fur hat I wore. At night we slept on the bare floors of tiny wayside huts, the hardy muleteers sleeping in the open air. Each morning I awoke sore and stiff, demanding to know how much further it was until we were out of the mountain passes. I cursed Bonaparte for putting me through this hardship and wanted desperately for it to be over. But at the same time I knew that once we reached Italy my days and nights with Donovan would have to end, and I clung to him, taking solace from our closeness as I always did and wishing, at times, that I had gone to Martinique with him instead of marrying Bonaparte.

On that subject Donovan said little.

"Whether you are married or not matters nothing to us," he told me. "What we are together is far stronger than any marriage vow."

It was the truth, and I knew it.

When at last we came down out of the mountains and, after another week of travel, arrived at the Serbelloni Palace in Milan where Bonaparte had his headquarters, I was in awe. My friends and I admired Greek and Roman designs above all others, and sought to imitate them in our dress and the décor of our houses. Here at the graceful, rose-colored palace was true classical architecture come to life: the simple, noble columns and pediments, the polished marble walls and floors within, the fine bronze statues and paintings, all in a setting of blooming gardens and sparkling fountains.

Bonaparte was away with his troops, preparing for yet another clash with the Austrians, but I made myself at home in the palace, fawned over by the staff and formally greeted by the local dignitaries and cheering crowds. Bonaparte was a hero to the Milanese: therefore I was a heroine, and they tired me out demanding audiences, holding banquets in my honor and making elaborate formal presentations to me. They gave me lengths of lace and jewels, bolts of silk and antique busts, casks of wine and flavorful pastries and cheeses.

Donovan found lodgings for himself in the city and began doing business there. I glimpsed him at many of the public events held in my honor, standing at the back of crowds or sitting at distant banquet tables, far away from me yet with his eyes on me, a half smile on his lips.

Bonaparte rode into the palace courtyard at a gallop one midmorning on his splendid white warhorse, shouting for the grooms and jumping down from the saddle to come looking for me. I was watching for him from a balcony, and went to quiet him as he ran up the marble steps, shouting my name.

"Josephine! My sweet incomparable Josephine!"

His embrace was suffocating—and endless. Even after he had kissed me a hundred times and spent hours with me in the old-fashioned canopied bed in his suite of rooms he could not stop grabbing me, feeling my breasts and hugging me to him. The servants and the officers of his entourage were embarrassed, I was embarrassed. Bonaparte was acting like a lovesick schoolboy, not like the conqueror of Italy.

"Please, my love, let me go. Let me breathe!" Gently I pulled away from him, releasing myself from his clutching hands. His face fell, then turned petulant, then surly. He threw up his hands and stalked off, only to return to my side, contrite and affectionate, half an hour later.

"Josephine, mi dolce amor, I could not stay away. If only you knew how I have suffered, all these months, without you."

He looked so pitiful that I almost laughed.

"You really are amusing, my little Punchinello," I said, making light of his exaggerated words.

"You mock me, yet my sufferings are very real."

"As were mine, in going over those fearsome Alps."

He scoffed. "What are the Alps? A children's mule-ride. A saddle-romp. While I have gone for months with no sleep, leading my men into deadly battle, worried to death about their lack of coats and boots and musketballs and gun-carts. Working through the night on papers and dispatches. Visiting the bedsides of the dying. Calming disputes, preventing my men from looting, raping. Can you imagine what pain it gives me to have to shoot my own men, men who love me and who have followed me faithfully for months, because they are looting?

"These were men I myself stole for, stripping boots and jackets off dead Austrian officers. Taking chickens and geese from farmyards so that they could fill their starving bellies. These were men I loved!"

I wiped his tears and did what I could to comfort him. How could I not offer comfort and solace to a man who wore a large portrait of me on a chain around his neck, and showed it off proudly to his major-generals?

He gave a ball at the palace to celebrate my arrival and I dressed carefully as I knew I would be the center of attention. In Paris I was a leader of fashion and I wanted to be in that position in Milan as well. I wore a gown designed by Leroy, still one of the most sought-after dressmakers in Paris. The gown was of a fine Indian muslin, so fine that my flesh-colored tights could be seen through its soft loose folds and also my lack of a chemise. My muslin tunic had no sleeves; my arms were bare and I wore no gloves. Instead of jewelry I had garlands of flowers around my head and neck. I was Juno, Ceres, Helen of Troy brought to life.

A loud collective gasp greeted me when I entered the ballroom—yet it was not, as I had expected, a gasp of wonder. It was a gasp of shock.

Women stared at my legs, men at my near-naked bosom. A few of the older matrons pointedly left the ballroom, and did not return. Others covered their faces with their fans and retreated to the opposite end of the room from where I made my entrance. Following the gasp there was an awkward, prolonged silence.

Then Bonaparte signaled the orchestra to play, and they began the "Minuet Milanaise" while I took my place beside him on a raised dais covered in burgundy velvet.

I sensed that something was terribly wrong but could not imagine what. I was always admired. Why did I see no admiration in the faces of those highborn Italians gathered at the Serbelloni Palace? Was I too plump? Or a trifle too thin? (The Italian ladies were very generously built.) Were they envious, too overcome by the classical loveliness of my gown to react?

The answer came in the Milanese newspapers the following day. Reading them, Bonaparte was outraged.

"General Bonaparte gave a ball for his bride, the former Rose Beauharnais, courtesan in all but name and a living inspiration to lechery," he read aloud as we ate our midday meal.

"This Rose Beauharnais, who now calls herself Josephine Bonaparte, revealed far too much of herself for decency when she arrived at the ball wearing a transparent nightgown in the antique style with flowery garlands like those of a bacchante. Bare arms and hands made her nakedness complete."

Bonaparte got up from the table and began walking rapidly around the enormous dining room, still reading.

"We urge all decent ladies to avoid occasions where this immoral woman will be present, and to keep their daughters from following her extremely undesirable example."

He looked up from his reading and threw the paper into the fire. "How dare they!" he cried. "How dare they criticize my wife!"

"How dare they criticize Leroy," I said wryly, adding, "when they are so dowdy themselves?"

"This newspaper will be silenced," Bonaparte announced. "The editor will be thrown in jail."

But it was not enough to stifle the newspapers. The clergy of Milan condemned me from their pulpits, calling me a strumpet and a whore, a tool of the devil and a demon sent to corrupt the morals of all God-fearing Italians.

Bonaparte, who had no particular regard for priests, shrugged off these attacks when they were reported to him, as he had shrugged off the gossip that reached him from Paris about me and Barras, saying he would send a message to the pope who would make certain they were stopped. Apparently the pope had less power—or less inclination to silence his clergy—than Bonaparte supposed, for the priests' condemnation of me went on throughout my stay in Italy, until I began to feel like an interloper.

It did not matter how many balls or banquets were held in my honor, or how many tributes were paid to the heroine of the hour. I was still shunned by the pious, and looked at with suspicion by everyone else. I saw the condemnation in the eyes of the women, the dread (combined, to be sure, with lechery) in the eyes of the men. I knew that I had been weighed in the balance and found wanting. What I didn't realize was that a far harsher and more wounding judgment was yet to come.

31

THE FOLLOWING SUMMER Bonaparte rented a villa near Milan and it was there, one afternoon, that I met my Corsican mother-in-law Letizia for the first time.

She came striding across the broad green lawn toward me, a frightening figure all in black, walking with vigor and speed though she had a slight limp and leaned on a wooden cane with an ebony handle. She looked like something out of a children's picture book, a witch or demon, for the black widow's cap she wore with its long black veil erased her humanity and made her appear to be a vengeful spirit emerging from the depths of hell.

I was lounging in a garden chair, a light silk wrap around my shoulders, drowsing in the warm sun amid blooming carnations and forsythia, lilacs and rose bushes. I heard her loud, strident voice from some distance away.

"Where is that woman! That shameful woman my Nabulio thinks he married! Where is she?"

I sat up and pulled my silken wrap more tightly around me as she approached.

"Is it you?" she demanded as she came closer. "Are you the one?"

"Good afternoon, Madame Buonaparte," I said, extending my hand, being careful to pronounce her name in the Italian fashion rather than using the French form Bonaparte now preferred.

"Stand up, woman! You're in the presence of your elder!" she commanded, throwing back her veil to reveal a thin, sharp-featured face with blazing black eyes, thick dark eyebrows and a mouth like Bonaparte's, small and firmly set. Her complexion, unimproved by rouge, was yellowish and lined, though she was by no means elderly; her energy and vigor belied her forty-nine years.

She did not take my hand.

"You are a bad woman! You try to trick my Nabulio! You say, 'I have baby.' You trick him!"

She shook her fist at me, a veined and knotted fist that protruded from the tight-fitting sleeve of her black gown.

"But you wait! You are wrong! You will see. You are wrong!"

She did not wait for me to respond, but turned and stalked off the way she had come, poking her cane into the carefully manicured lawn as if she meant to wound it.

That evening at supper the entire Buonaparte family gathered, each family member in turn greeted happily by my husband and then presented to me.

"You have already met mama," Nabulio said, wagging his finger at Letizia playfully. "Mama told me that she said angry things to you. That's all over now. I want you to love each other, care for each other. Mama, you will be the grandmother of our children and grandmamas are always loving, not angry."

At Bonaparte's further urging Letizia held out her hand to me, and I grasped it. Her skin was rough and very dry, the nails neglected. She did not grasp my hand in return, nor did she smile. Instead she gave the barest dignified nod.

"My brother Joseph," Bonaparte said, indicating a tall, handsome man of about thirty, who gave me a curt bow but, like his mother, did not smile. I looked questioningly at Bonaparte, who understood at once why.

"He's an attorney," Bonaparte said with a grin. "He never smiles."

"He does, however, look after your best interests," Joseph retorted. "And he has noted some irregularities in your wife's business activities— and business partners." Joseph raised one dark eyebrow quizzically.

"Say what you mean, Giuseppe."

"I will speak plainly—when we are alone."

I felt a chill. What irregularities? And what did Joseph Buonaparte know about Donovan and me?

Bonaparte glared at his brother, but said nothing further. At length he resumed his introductions.

"Unfortunately my brother Lucien is not here. He disgraced himself rather badly, and cannot be included in the family circle just now."

"He married a whore," Letizia said. "We hate whores."

Bonaparte presented me to a fat, dumpy girl with small, malevolent-looking eyes. She glowered at me, then curtseyed awkwardly, her weight making her clumsy.

"Elisa," Bonaparte said, then hurried on to a good-looking young man, attractively pale and slim, with a touching vulnerability in his expression.

"Louis. Our intellectual. Our artist."

"Oh," I responded as Louis, with surprising grace, took my outstretched hand and kissed it. At last, I thought. A civilized Buonaparte.

"And this is our Paulette," Bonaparte announced with pride, presenting a beautiful girl of about seventeen, who dropped a deep curtsey and then, when her brother's back was turned, stuck out her tongue at me and whispered "We hate whores."

Yet you look like one, I thought, observing the girl's deep décolletage, tastelessly extravagant gown and cheap sparkling necklace. She was saucy, brazen and challenging in the way she stood, breasts outthrust, a hand on one wide hip.

"What was that?" Bonaparte turned again toward Paulette, who had resumed her pleasant demeanor.

"Nothing, brother."

"My two gems," he was saying. "My beloved Josephine and my precious Paulette. Are they not lovely?" He waited for sounds of agreement from his family, but hearing none, went on.

"I want you two to be the best of friends. Paulette has many admirers and needs the guidance of an experienced older woman of the world."

"And as we all know, this Josephine of yours has belonged to the whole world."

Bonaparte came close to slapping his sister for her insulting remark, but stopped himself.

"Control your tongue, Paulette," he said in a menacing undertone. "I will have order in my family."

"You are not on the battlefield now, brother," put in the fat sister Elisa. "We are not your soldiers, to be ordered around."

"That's enough Elisa." It was Letizia's reprimand that silenced the girl.

There were two more siblings to be introduced, a girl of about fifteen and a boy a few years younger—Hortense's age, I thought.

"My dearest Josephine, may I present my sister Caroline and my brother Jerome."

Caroline curtseyed and Jerome bowed. Both looked at me with much curiosity.

"Is it true, Madame Josephine, that you come from a place where dead people walk at night?" It was Jerome's high, solemn voice.

"So they say. I have never seen one."

"I hope I never do."

"Gesù!" cried Letizia and crossed herself rapidly.

Bonaparte bent down and put his arm around his youngest brother. "Jerome, you must never speak of spirits in front of our mother. You know better."

"Our mother sees her dead babies," Caroline guilelessly whispered to me. "She had five dead babies. She sees them in her dreams."

"Shall we dine?" Bonaparte's hearty invitation put an end to the disturbing talk of ghosts. The meal was lavish, twelve courses and a delicious succession of local wines. The hired chef catered expertly to Bonaparte's palate, remembering to include an entrée of the small squids that were his favorite and for dessert, fresh cherries to be dipped in chocolate or brandy.

It was an exceedingly tense and uncomfortable meal, despite the abundance and excellence of the food, and after it ended Bonaparte and Joseph were closeted in isolation for more than two hours in the room Bonaparte had chosen for his study. When at last he emerged, and sought me out, he was pale. I thought, has he discovered that Donovan and I are lovers? Will he divorce me?

"What do you know of the Bodin Company?" he asked me.

"Only the name. My partner Monsieur de Gautier has mentioned it."

"My brother tells me that this Bodin Company has been defrauding my regiments, providing lame, sick horses instead of sound mounts to the cavalry and spoiled flour to the regimental bakers and inferior ramrods for the cavalry pistols, so brittle they crack and break the first time they are used. I was told they sell us port wine that is nothing but cheap red wine mixed with sawdust plus a few almonds and raisins for flavoring."

"This is the first I've heard of these wicked things, I assure you."

"No doubt you have been taken in by the assurances of others."

"I trust those I work with."

"You have been led astray. It's time you stopped dabbling in business affairs. You should be devoting yourself to domestic matters—and, of course, to your public role as my wife. The newspapers continue to denounce you. You must alter your mode of dress."

"I will look into it." Clearly Bonaparte's conversation with his humorless brother had upset him. He clutched his stomach, as he always did when in distress.

"Let me get you some oil of wintergreen," I offered. I kept a bottle of the potent green liquid near at hand. I poured some into a glass. Bonaparte drank it, then collapsed on the sofa beside me, putting his head on my lap. I knew what he needed. I began to rub his temples, humming a soothing African song Euphemia had sung to me as a child. In a few moments Bonaparte, his eyes closed, began to look more peaceful. His lips turned upward in a smile.

"I miss Hortense," I said after a time. Eugene I saw now and then, as he was serving as Bonaparte's aide-de-camp in Italy, to his unutterable delight. I was so proud of him! But Hortense was in school near Paris, and I had not seen her in a long time.

"When do you think we can go home?"

Bonaparte sighed, nestling farther down into my lap. "My home is on the battlefield," he said. "With my men."

I knew that the way to handle my husband was not to argue with him or confront him but to soothe him, gentle him as one would a restless horse, until he was calm. Then, sometimes, it was possible to persuade him to do something I wanted—though those times seemed to come less and less often now.

"In Corsica," he began in a conversational tone, "our family had vineyards and orchards, groves of chestnuts and olives. My grandmother kept goats. She was a great woman, my grandmother. She used to say that if she was ever in trouble, all she had to do was call out and two hundred relatives would be there in minutes to help her.

"Family! Family is everything," he said, looking up at me.

"I know. That is why I want to go back to Paris, to be with Hortense and Aunt Edmée and the marquis."

"You have all the family you need here. But you must find a way to ingratiate yourself with them. Talk to them. Entertain them. Sing and drink a cup of wine and laugh with them. We Corsicans love that."

I made efforts to approach the prickly, hostile Buonapartes, especially the gentlemanly Louis. But all I got were sour looks and chilly words. Louis politely avoided me. Paulette referred to me, very loudly, as "the old woman" and Elisa swore at me in Corsican.

One night at supper Bonaparte stood and raised his glass. "I have happy news," he said, beaming. "This afternoon my beloved Paulette became engaged to General Victor Leclercq, with my blessing, and I have given Elisa's hand to an upstanding Corsican patriot, Felix Bacciochi. I want the joy of a double wedding, to be held here at the villa. Dear Josephine, as my hostess you will have the pleasure of making the wedding arrangements."

The family burst into applause, and Paulette and Elisa were hugged and cheered and teased and toasted again and again.

I clapped with the others, and tried to feel pleasure at the thought of my two sisters-in-law making happy marriages. But my heart sank. How was I to undertake all that would be necessary to prepare for this grand event, with only the small villa staff of servants to help me? Already I felt the weight of the Buonapartes' criticism, for I knew that nothing I did could possibly please them.

My head began to pound. I felt ill, and soon retired to bed. I did not get up at all the following day. I did not want to face my in-laws. But early the next morning Bonaparte threw open the door of our bedroom, pulled back the curtains with a noisy scraping of their wooden rings across the poles, and shouted, "No more of this laziness! You're not in Martinique now! Time to be up and productive!"

The sudden glare of the sun coming through the windows hurt my eyes and made my lingering headache worse—as my husband knew well, for I was often troubled with headaches and he was accustomed to how sensitive to light and noise they made me. He himself rose early, often before dawn, and refused to acknowledge or tolerate any illness in himself. It was one of many ways in which we differed: he was dynamic and restlessly energetic, while I was calm and dreamy and moved through my days at a leisurely pace.

"Please, Bonaparte, the light is hurting me! Please, make it dark again. Let me rest!"

But he was already throwing back the bedclothes and grasping my arm, pulling me out of bed. My maid, the perpetually sullen, silent Clodia, brought me a morning robe and had the big iron hip-bath brought in. I asked her for a powder of willow-bark for my head.

"Paulette and Elisa are waiting. They want to know why you haven't done anything about the wedding."

"Didn't you tell them I wasn't well?"

"In our family, illness does not interfere with obligations."

Clodia brought me the packet of willow-bark powder and mixed it in some wine. I drank it thirstily, praying for relief from my throbbing head. I needed Euphemia. She always had a charm or an herbal concoction to heal me, and unlike Clodia, Euphemia was sympathetic.

I managed to bathe and dress and, after eating a bowl of fruit, asked Clodia to admit Paulette and Elisa to my sitting-room.

They came in, looking piqued and aggrieved.

"This is the gown I want," Paulette announced imperiously, holding out a sheet of paper with a crudely drawn green gown. "And I want it right away."

"I want a gown covered in gold and pearls," said Elisa. "A big, fancy one, with a headdress to match. You have to get it for me. My brother says so."

"Wouldn't your mother want you to wear white wedding gowns?" I asked. Letizia was a traditionalist, that was quite evident.

"This is our wedding," Paulette snapped. "We will wear what we like."

I felt trapped. If I did as the brides asked, Letizia would surely condemn me for abandoning custom and defying the church—for in church weddings, brides always wore white gowns. Yet if I disappointed Paulette and Elisa they would be certain to hate me forever.

Bonaparte had left for his military camp, which was some ten miles from the villa. I could not turn to him to solve my dilemma. With some trepidation I decided to seek out Letizia. Just possibly, I thought, if I appealed to her for help she might look favorably on me.

I found her in the huge kitchen of the villa, sitting among the servants, chatting away to them in Italian. She sat in a rocking chair, moving it back and forth on its wide rockers with her small black-booted feet.

She was knitting, her needles flying, an immense ball of black wool unrolling from a basket on the floor. I approached her shyly, hesitantly, feeling awkward.

"Madame Buonaparte," I began, then murmured, "Letizia." She looked up at me, with a look that made me self-conscious and uncomfortable. "Madame Buonaparte, what's that you are knitting?"

She smiled, a cold smile. "Your shroud," was all she said.

32

MUCH TO MY SURPRISE AND DELIGHT, Euphemia came to join me at about this time. I had been writing to her often, urging her to make the journey to Italy and reassuring her that much of the fighting was over and that she would not be in any danger from cannonfire or marauding soldiers if she came. I was so glad to see her that I burst into tears.

We sat together in the garden and she told me all her news. She handed me a portrait miniature of Hortense, who looked so grown up I almost didn't recognize her.

"She's a young lady now. Almost pretty. She misses you such a lot. She has an admirer. He's English, I'm sorry to say. Young Lord Falke. Very dashing."

"And Coco? How is she?"

"Into everything. A strong little thing. She turns cartwheels like you used to do. Hortense is teaching her her letters."

"As you once taught me, Euphemia." The memory of Euphemia, then a young girl herself, teaching me my alphabet reminded me that my beloved half-sister was getting on in years. I thought of her as eternal, as someone who had always been there and always would be, but as I looked at her now, I could not help but realize that of course she was aging, her tightly curling hair in its neat bun turning grey, her shrewd yet kindly eyes ringed with lines. She moved more slowly than I remembered, and her large, capable brown hands with their pink palms were losing their plumpness and becoming gnarled, the finger joints swollen.

Having Euphemia with me at the villa made the surly coldness and hostility of the Buonapartes even more evident, and stiffened my resistance toward them. My husband's youngest sister and brother, Caroline and Jerome, I could tolerate but the others irked and angered me more and more. Louis, who I thought of as the civilized Buonaparte, cornered me one morning as I was leaving my bedroom and slipped his arm around my waist.

Startled, I whirled out of his grasp. He laughed. "Come now, sister-in-law," he said in a honeyed tone I had never before heard him use, "you won't deny me a kiss. From what I hear you've never denied anyone." He reached toward me and I eluded him. At that moment he was repellent.

"Wait till I tell my husband about this!" I said through clenched teeth.

Louis shrugged. "He won't mind. We've shared many a servant girl, Nabulio and I."

"I am no servant girl!"

Louis curled his lip disdainfully. "No. You're a slut. Everyone says so."

I slapped him and went downstairs where the Three Graces—or so I had begun to refer to Letizia, Paulette and Elisa—were waiting for me. Letizia sat in her rocking chair, knitting, and glanced up at me with a frown. Elisa glared at me, her double chins shaking, and muttered something under her breath. Paulette, I saw, had gone into my wardrobe and taken my favorite gown, a gossamer-thin ball gown made of fine peach-colored Milanese silk, and put it on. She had arranged her hair like mine, with curls framing her face, and fresh flowers entwined among the curls and when I entered the room she walked toward me, swaying her hips in an exaggerated fashion, her lips pursed coquettishly, a little lapdog like mine in her arms.

"Oh, Bonaparte," she cooed, batting her eyelashes, "can't you just please let me go back to bed? I have the most awful headache—I may never get out of bed again!" It was a grotesquely acute caricature of me, startlingly recognizable and very cruel. Paulette was clever—and she knew how to wound.

Elisa laughed until she choked, and even Letizia let out a surreptitious snort of amusement. I watched impassively, my face stony, until Paulette tripped on the hem of the gown—which was too long for her by many inches—and fell, ripping the precious silk and upsetting a table that held a small antique statue of Aphrodite, one of Bonaparte's favorite acquisitions. The statue shattered. Clodia appeared, broom and dustpan in hand, and began to sweep up the translucent white fragments. Paulette, uninjured by her fall, picked herself up and resumed her impersonation. She had hardly opened her mouth to speak when I interrupted her.

"If you say another word I'll tell Bonaparte you've broken his favorite statue. Then I'll tell him that you've ruined my ball gown that was a gift from the city of Milan, and that the city fathers and all the members of the silk guild will be offended when I fail to wear the gown next week at the reception they are giving me."

Paulette's defiant posture began to crumple under the weight of my words, but she silently mouthed "old lady."

"And then there is the matter of your wedding. What would the bridegroom say, I wonder, if he knew you had been meeting Corporal Trenet in the garden late at night?"

"What?" Letizia, startled, sat up in her chair and stared at her beautiful young daughter.

"How did you know that?" Paulette demanded of me.

"Gesù!" cried Letizia and crossed herself, her knitting needles falling to the marble floor with a clatter.

"All the servants know. Including my Euphemia."

"That black devil!" Letizia spat out. "Only witches have black devils for servants!"

"Witch! Hag! Whore!" Elisa shouted every epithet she could think of at me, but ran out of words when I took from my pocket a silver watch fob and dangled it before her.

"But that's Felix's!" she cried out in surprise, leaving her string of epithets incomplete. "I gave it to him. You thief! You stole it!" She reached out a fat hand to grab the heavy silver object but I pulled it back, out of her grasp.

"His manservant brought it to me, along with this note." I took a folded sheet of paper from my pocket, on which a letter was written in large, somewhat uneven handwriting. It was signed, in large letters, "FELIX." I unfolded the paper and held it up. Elisa made a sound that was somewhere between a sigh and a groan.

Paulette began laughing.

"Shall I read the note?"

"No!" was Letizia's command.

Elisa's face was very red. She looked to be on the verge of tears. Paulette giggled.

"My dearest lady beautiful Josephine," it began, "when I see you the moon begins to hide and the sun goes behind the cloud and the stars snuff themselves. It is you, bright light lady, who make them ashamed. I, Felix Bacciochi, must hold you in my arms. It is your wish also I believe. Most dear lady, tell me of your heart."

FELIX

The clumsy love letter from Elisa's fiancé was so touchingly sincere that it was almost endearing, except that fat, loutish Felix who stank of garlic and doused his sparse hair in olive oil, was himself repellent.

"What do you think of your Felix now?" Paulette said. "We all know Nabulio had to buy him for you. He never loved you."

"He did! He does!" Elisa insisted, stamping her foot. But her voice broke.

"Enough!" Letizia stood, gathered her knitting, and limped out of the room without looking at me. Elisa and Paulette followed.

I had triumphed—for the moment. But I still had the responsibility of arranging the double wedding of Paulette and General Leclercq and Elisa and the faithless Felix Bacciochi. Bonaparte insisted that it be a very grand event, with hundreds of guests, a sumptuous banquet and a noisy artillery salute plus fireworks to round out the evening.

Fortunately I had Euphemia to help me with the preparations. But Euphemia, shunned and despised by the Buonapartes as a "black devil," and indignant over their constant ill treatment of me, saw the upcoming celebrations as a way of evening the score against my spiteful inlaws.

"You must put the spirits on your side," she told me. "The spirits will take revenge."

In one corner of my dressing room she built an altar to the Ibo Red Goddess and spent time each day in front of it, asking the goddess's aid.

"Big storm coming," I heard her say under her breath. "Big storm on the wedding eve, sure as anything." The guests were invited to come to the villa for a banquet on the night before the wedding, then to stay overnight with us and attend the ceremony the following morning.

Euphemia and I went together into the nearest town and visited the marketplace. Euphemia sought out the vegetable vendors.

"Do you remember the big yams we used to grow at Les Trois-Ilets, the kind that made your whole body itch if you ate them raw? They must have yams like that here in Italy."

We searched the stalls until we found what Euphemia was looking for, large healthy-looking yams with thick skins. We brought some back with us and stored them in the cellar.

The wedding day approached.

The guests were invited, the villa chapel decorated with greenery from the garden and bunches of pink and yellow and deep red roses. Ten cannon were drawn up the hill to the villa from the military camp by laboring oxen and put in place in the courtyard to fire the salute to the newlyweds. A team of fireworks technicians was hired to put on a dazzling display. The bridal gowns were sewn and fitted (white gowns, to the brides' dismay; as I suspected, Letizia insisted on white).

General Leclercq had a new dress uniform and the unhappy Felix Bacciochi, frightened to death of his brother-in-law-to-be, was measured by a tailor from Milan for a new suit of fashionable cut that would, it was hoped, diminish the appearance of his protruding belly and stout legs.

As Euphemia had predicted, when the wedding eve came, the weather turned cloudy and rain began to fall. A hailstorm churned the road to the villa to a muddy quagmire, and the guests, in their finest gowns, coats and trousers, arrived wet and disgruntled, the women's feathered headdresses damp and their skirts mud-spattered, their satin slippers hopelessly ruined.

The banquet tables, which had been laid in the garden under canvas tents, had to be moved indoors in great haste, with many a broken dish and smashed goblet as casualties of the move. Delayed by the worsening storm, the guests were late in arriving and it was after midnight when the first course was served.

Everyone ate hungrily, especially the Buonapartes. Euphemia made certain that Paulette, Elisa and Letizia all were served generous portions of raw yam, flavored with spices and garnished with goat cheese, a Corsican delicacy.

It was nearly four o'clock in the morning when the banquet ended and the guests made their weary, tipsy way to the rooms prepared for them. But they got little sleep, for shortly after dawn the peace of the villa was shattered by loud screaming.

"My arms! My arms! My legs! My face! Oh God, my face!"

It was Paulette's shrill voice, bewailing the bright red welt-like marks that had appeared all over her body. Soon Elisa joined in with shrieks and wails and before long everyone in the villa—wedding guests, servants, even the grooms and gardeners—knew that the brides-to-be had broken out in hives.

Paulette and Elisa, beside themselves with panic and humiliation, and tormented by severe itching that no amount of scratching could assuage, refused to put on their wedding gowns and locked themselves in Paulette's room. Bonaparte, using tactics that had made him famous in Paris, turned the villa's heavy furnishings into battering rams and broke down his sister's door, while I and others watched in amazed horror.

"Dress yourselves at once," he ordered his sisters in the sternest tone. Paulette threw up the sash of one window and climbed out on the stone window ledge. Elisa clambered after her, but was too stout to reach the ledge. Bonaparte grabbed Elisa and thrust her into the arms of a bewildered Felix, whose efforts to soothe her met with more screams and shrieked curses.

"Paulette!" Bonaparte continued, "unless you dress yourself immediately I shall order Corporal Trenet's execution."

At the mention of her lover's name Paulette turned, trembling, and began to wail. Her lovely face, now swollen, red and blotchy with hives, was the picture of misery.

Bonaparte took a step toward the open doorway.

"Yes, yes, all right," she sobbed, and screamed angrily for her maid.

"I shall expect to see you and Elisa in the chapel in an hour."

We all dispersed to our rooms, well aware that we too would be expected in the chapel very soon to witness the wedding mass.

Try as we might, Euphemia and I could not entirely suppress our laughter as, exactly one hour later, we watched the wretched brides walking down the aisle of the chapel, their faces hidden behind thick veils, scratching themselves continuously. Letizia, in her pew, also scratched and fidgeted. Outside, rain poured down and there was an occasional clap of thunder.

"It is the Red Goddess," Euphemia whispered. "She is announcing herself."

As soon as the mass ended, Paulette and Elisa ran to their rooms and would not speak to anyone, not even their new husbands. Bonaparte threw up his hands and swore, but left them alone.

The guests went home. The fireworks were forgotten, the wedding gifts abandoned in heaped piles in a locked chamber of the villa. And the ten cannon, whose gunners stood ready to fire, were left to sink further into the mud of the courtyard, under the pouring rain, until Bonaparte remembered to call off the salute.

33

BONAPARTE WAS DREAMING OF EGYPT—and I was dreaming of Donovan.

My husband's great Italian adventure was over, we left the villa and returned to Paris where I was joyfully reunited with Hortense and Coco. Our lives had changed, and would never be the same again, for Bonaparte had risen greatly in stature and popular esteem and his ambitions were soaring. He wanted to conquer the world, beginning with Egypt.

I, on the other hand, was suffering, and I found relief only in Donovan's arms. I craved relief from the burden of my unhappy marriage, and freedom from my hostile in-laws. I disliked my public role as Bonaparte's wife, and wanted only the quiet and privacy of a life lived outside the public gaze.

I felt as though I were living two lives: one as Madame Bonaparte, and one as my authentic self. As Madame Bonaparte I was gracious, hospitable, dignified—but false. As Donovan's lover I was open, genuine, passionate—in short, my real self. I was Yeyette, creole of Martinique. I was who I was meant to be.

Donovan always seemed to know how and where to find me, how to elude the watchdogs Bonaparte put around me and slip through the network of his spies. While we were in Italy, he had come often to the villa. On many a night when Bonaparte was away, with his troops, I listened for the faint scratching at my window that told me Donovan was on my balcony. I got up and opened the window, catching my breath when he took me in his arms.

We lay together in the bed I shared with Bonaparte, an immense featherbed of the kind the Italians call a *matrimoniale*, a marriage-bed. (I enjoyed the irony of it, lying with my lover in the bed I was supposed to share with my husband.) Together we sank deep into the soft downy warmth, our breaths one breath, clinging to each other, becoming one flesh. I lost myself in him, letting his strength and his ardor take all my worries from me. In his comforting embrace my fears fled and all my tension eased. I was myself again. I was deeply content.

In those stolen, heavenly hours together I felt no awareness of past or future, only a rich, full present. I sighed, savoring each moment, wishing with all my heart that every hour of my life could be as blissful as the one I now enjoyed. I existed: that was enough.

Despite Bonaparte's insistence that I give up the provisioning business and devote myself to family I continued to cultivate my contacts in the army. As Bonaparte's wife I was in a better position than ever to stay on good terms with the supply officers who bought foodstuffs and clothing for their men, and Donovan, from his rented rooms in Milan, and afterwards in Paris, was my partner in each of these transactions. Our business dealings gave us an excuse to meet, though we often spent more time together than any purely business arrangements justified.

Late one afternoon as I emerged from Donovan's lodgings in the rue Angereau I came face to face with my brother-in-law Joseph.

"Meeting your lover again?" he said with a smirk.

"I don't know what you mean."

"Of course you do. We are not fools, you and I. Only my brother is a fool, for refusing to believe the truth about you. Your lover is Monsieur de Gautier, and these are his lodgings."

"I hope you are not inventing lies about me, Joseph," I said evenly. "I would hate to have to force Bonaparte to choose between us. You know how much he loves me."

"I know you have him in thrall. You have some sort of dark power over him that keeps him from realizing what a she-wolf you really are."

"Let's not insult each other, Joseph. Besides, we both know that insults are the only weapons you possess against me. If you had proof that I am an unfaithful wife to Bonaparte, you would assuredly produce it. But there is no proof, as your suspicions are unfounded."

I began to move past Joseph, intending to walk to the nearby inn where my carriage was waiting.

"I have all the proof I need. I have the word of your maid, Clodia."

Joseph's words made me pause. I felt my cheeks grow hot, and knew that they were turning red, betraying my distress. What did Clodia know? I had always been careful to remove every evidence of Donovan's presence in my bedchamber. There were no messages or notes from him that she could have seen, no gifts, not even flowers. Donovan came and went in my life like a shadow, leaving no trace behind.

"If Clodia says she has seen me with another man, then she is lying," I said, keeping my voice as firm as I could. "If you are bribing her to lie, Bonaparte will find out and you will lose his trust."

He smiled. (It was a first! A smile on Joseph's somber face!) "I think we both know, Josephine Beauharnais, who is about to lose his trust." At his most hateful, Joseph always called me by my first husband's name. Along with the rest of his family, he continued to deny that my marriage to Bonaparte was legal, because it was a civil marriage and not blessed by the church.

"I am Madame Bonaparte, and I am not going to listen to any more of your slander." I turned and walked away. Behind me, I could hear Joseph's mirthless laugh.

As soon as I saw Donovan again I told him what Joseph had said about my maid. He said nothing, but merely pursed his lips and frowned.

"Has she seen us, do you think?"

He shook his head. "No. Unless she was concealed in the bedroom." He looked thoughtful.

"She has always been secretive. She makes no noise when she walks. She is a spy for Joseph. And she has never liked me, I can feel her coldness."

"All good reasons to dismiss her. Why haven't you?"

I shook my head ruefully. "I can't bear to let servants go. It seems cruel."

"You must send her away. Immediately."

I nodded. Yet I procrastinated. Telling a servant to go was so distasteful, almost painful. I asked Bonaparte to do it for me.

I entered his study with trepidation. He disliked being interrupted. He sat at his large desk of polished walnut, half a dozen maps spread out before him, books piled high at his elbow. He was deep in thought, his mouth pursed, his forehead creased. His intensity filled the room. Eventually he became aware of my presence. Immediately his appearance changed, with the quicksilver suddenness I had so often observed in him. He smiled, his eyes limpid, and held out his hand to me.

I crossed to him and took his outstretched hand.

"Bonaparte, I have a favor to ask."

"Yes, my beloved?"

"I need you to dismiss my maid, Clodia." He lifted his eyebrows in mild surprise.

"Oh? And why is that, my lovely girl?"

I was prepared for his question.

"She has been stealing from me."

"I see. Do you want me to talk to her?"

"No. I just want her gone."

The finality in my voice made him curious.

"Has she been aggravating you in some other way?" he asked, his interest aroused.

I hesitated. "She has been—taunting me. About our having no children." It was untrue, of course. But I knew it was a sensitive subject with Bonaparte. As soon as I spoke the words his expression turned grim.

"It seems our failure to have children together is the topic of the day. I never stop hearing about it from my relatives."

The Buonapartes had scattered, Letizia and Elisa and Felix living in Naples, Paulette and General Leclercq in Marseille, Louis with his regiment in some provincial town, I wasn't sure which, and only my nemesis Joseph in Paris, near us.

"My mother writes me constantly—she goes to a notary to do it for her, as she never really learned to write properly—and nags me about your barrenness. She can't quite decide whether it is a result of your promiscuity or God's wrath because we were never married in a church."

He looked amused, yet it was a wry amusement that told me he too regretted our childless state. In fact I would have borne Bonaparte a child, even more than one, for I have always loved children. But the more unhappy I became in our marriage, the more relieved I was that there were no babies to complicate our lives. If we had had a child or two, Letizia would surely have disapproved of me as a mother, and would have tried her best to take my children away from me and raise them herself.

"Perhaps Letizia has been influencing Clodia."

"Probably."

"Please Bonaparte, relieve me of this unpleasantness and dismiss Clodia."

"Very well." He turned back to his maps and books, and I prepared to leave. Then I heard him say, "No, wait."

He was frowning. "Clodia is a Corsican girl. I think she's a relative, the daughter of one of my mother's cousins, Adele Permon."

My heart sank. Bonaparte would never dismiss a relative. I felt sure of that.

"Perhaps she could work in the kitchens?"

"That would be a demotion. An insult to the family."

Once again, as so often in my marriage, I felt trapped. Joseph was threatening to reveal, through Clodia, that I was an unfaithful wife. Yet Bonaparte was bound to protect Clodia and keep her near me, where she could spy on me and betray me. What was I to do?

I did the only thing I could.

I went to Donovan, and told him that our secret life together, if not our business partnership, might have to end.

34

EGYPT! IT WAS ALL I HEARD ABOUT, all anyone seemed to talk about. Bonaparte was leaving soon for the land of the pharaohs, and I would be blessedly free of him for many months.

I could not wait for him to go, for all the two hundred ships to be loaded and all the fifty thousand soldiers to be outfitted and made ready for the grand campaign. Donovan and I were kept busy buying tons of hay and oats from farmers as far away as Creil and Rozoy, not their best grains of course, or their freshest, but what they had been hoarding and were willing to sell if the price was high enough. We then sold this food to the supply officers for as high a price as we could get—for in business, that is what one does, surely, maximize one's profits—and we made a good deal of money in a very short time.

We not only bought and resold hay and oats, but olive oil and brandy, chickens and ducks, empty casks and barrels, canvas for sails and rope for hawsers, leather for saddles and anything else of value we could acquire, to pass along to the troops at high prices. We were avid for gain, we thought of little else in the final weeks before the army was due to depart. I had made money before, as the partner of the late Baron Rossignol, but with Donovan I was on my way to becoming truly rich.

Wealth, I was discovering, was a protean thing; my concept of it changed as I became more affluent. I had once thought the Grand Blancs of Martinique wealthy, until I encountered the rich of Paris. Then I redefined wealth yet again when I encountered the political fortune of Paul Barras and his banker and financier friends. Donovan and I, I realized, had become far better off than my Uncle Robert in Martinique, at least as affluent as my former stepfather the Marquis de Beauharnais. Had we been able to continue along our path of wealth-building for another year we would have begun to eclipse some of the wealthy Parisian merchants whose fine houses and beautiful furnishings I had long coveted.

As it was, I was able to pay for a grand renovation of Bonaparte's mansion on the rue Chantereine (now renamed, in his honor, the rue des Victoires)—or at least to begin to pay for it. The house was redone in the classical style, which was then much in vogue. In imitation of the villas of Greece and Rome, the walls were painted in deep reds and dark blues, with white Doric columns and white trim. The furniture I had made to order, the designs drawn from models brought from Rome by Bonaparte. Antique statues, some life-size, were placed in the foyer and in the stairwells, their nearly translucent white marble gleaming softly beneath lamps of burnished brass.

All was going well, I thought, except for my nagging fear, which I shared with Donovan, that Clodia, urged on or bribed by Joseph, would tell Bonaparte what she knew of my adultery. Bonaparte would not hear of having her dismissed; she was family, hence she could do no wrong. She would be in my household for life.

Donovan said little on the subject of Clodia, but I could tell by the firm set of his jaw that he took it very seriously indeed. He would not hear of our ending our secret liaison, and he certainly saw no reason for us to cease to work together.

"Nothing must interfere with the operations of our business," he said. "Not now, at this crucial time." Having known what it was to live with deprivation, he was eager to attain wealth—as eager as I. He planned to pay off all the debt on his plantation in Martinique and buy a second property, even larger and grander than the first. Clodia's inconvenient revelations could interfere with these plans. Our fantastic prosperity could disappear overnight.

"Things may turn out better than you imagine," he said. "Your fears may be exaggerated."

Then, about ten days before Bonaparte was to depart for Marseille, to launch his Egyptian campaign, Clodia disappeared.

One evening she was there, helping me undress after a dinner party held in Bonaparte's honor; the next morning she was gone.

At first I thought she must be ill, and keeping to her room, a tiny cupboard of a room in the attic where all the women servants slept. But when I sent Euphemia to look for her she came back and said the little room was empty.

I felt a stab of unease. I knew well that servants often left their posts suddenly, without warning and without giving notice. Sometimes they returned within a few days, sometimes they left for good. But for Clodia to disappear, thin, dark, small Clodia with her taciturn ways and furtive manner, seemed sinister. I could not help wondering whether Donovan had found a way to get rid of her.

"Perhaps she's gone back home to Corsica," was the view most often expressed by the other servants. "Perhaps she has had a letter from her sister, telling her that her mother is ill and she needs to return home," one of the grooms suggested. "Perhaps she has a lover, and she ran off with him," was another view—but I knew that to be very unlikely. Clodia had never been known to keep company with a man.

By the time she had been gone two days it was assumed that she would not be back, and I chose another girl to take her place as my maid. But my suspicions nagged at me. Had Donovan done the unthinkable and spirited her away? I didn't dare ask him directly, for fear I would dislike the answer he gave.

I was nervous. I felt a vague pounding in my skull. I jumped when my new maid came quietly up behind me and said, "Mistress, the general wishes to see you."

I was trembling when I entered Bonaparte's study, and my fear increased when I saw that Joseph was already there, his hawklike face dark with anger. Bonaparte, on the other hand, was a figure of farce, though his demeanor was serious. He had taken to wearing a turban, which his new Turkish manservant wound around his head each morning and secured with a diamond stickpin. With the turban he wore a long jeweled coat of russet velvet, black silk trousers and gold slippers with uptilted toes that curled toward the ceiling. In this garb, he liked to say, he was ready to take on the hosts of the Ottoman Empire, the rulers of Egypt.

As soon as Bonaparte spoke I knew that he was angry.

"Are you selling inferior grains to the Sarre regiment, Josephine?"

"The Sarre regiment? I am not sure what was sold to them, if anything."

The Sarre was Alexandre's former regiment. Of course I knew that Donovan and I were providing them with horse fodder, and that it was of inferior grade.

"I inspected that regiment this morning. It's a wonder their horses are still alive."

"Our suppliers may have tricked us, and substituted bad quality foodstuffs for the good ones we thought we were buying."

"Nonsense!" was Bonaparte's sharp reply. "The guilt is yours, and yours alone.

"This cannot continue," he went on, pacing the room in his golden slippers with their curled-up toes. "I told you to cease your business endeavors yet you defy me. You weaken my army by poisoning their horses with rotten grain. According to Joseph, you dishonor your marriage vows—and you have even gone so far as to eliminate the witness to your amours, our relative Clodia, the maid you asked me to dismiss."

"I did not eliminate her," I said quickly. "I do not know what happened to her." And I began to cry.

Tears always moved Bonaparte. I could count on that.

Joseph took a step toward me. "You killed her—or your lover did."

I shook my head, not looking at him, my tears continuing to flow.

"See here, brother, we don't know for certain where the girl is or what happened to her." Bonaparte, uneasy, was defending me. I knew I was safe.

"It's as plain as day. You are letting yourself be blinded by this lying, whoring woman."

"You can say what you like when we're alone, Joseph, but I won't have Josephine insulted in her presence." He put his arm around me, and I buried my face in his shoulder.

Joseph swore, long and loudly and explosively, in Italian. "Can't you see how she is manipulating you?" he shouted, reverting to French. "Using you, deceiving you . . ." He sputtered, having run out of words.

I felt sure that, for the time being at least, I had won.

Or had I?

Bonaparte waved his brother out of the room, Joseph slamming the door with a vengeful loud bang that shook the walls.

When we were alone, Bonaparte began slowly to divest himself of the fantastic costume he was wearing. He removed the diamond stickpin from his turban and unwound the yards and yards of ivory linen. When the last of the cloth was unwound, and lying in a heap on the red and gold carpet, he shook out his shoulder-length brown hair and then proceeded to discard the jeweled coat, silk trousers and, last of all, the fantastic gold slippers. He stood before me in his underclothes, a small, quite ordinary-looking man with piercing eyes that now, to my surprise, twinkled with amusement.

He came up to me and pinched my cheek, so hard I cried out.

"I don't care about the girl," he said. "But I do not forgive you for poisoning the horses. See to it that top-grade oats and hay are sent to the Sarre regiment immediately. If you don't, I'll know. As to your friend, the handsome Monsieur de Gautier, I think it would be good for you to be away from him for awhile. Egypt, from what I understand, is quite lovely in the early spring. I'd like you to come with me on my campaign."

"Oh no, Bonaparte! I would miss Hortense too much, and Coco, and Euphemia, and besides, travel is too hard on me. My headaches, you know."

"I hear they have very fine Arab physicians in Cairo. And healthful springs by the old temples to the gods."

"Please, Bonaparte!"

"Pack your things. We leave in five days for the Land of the Pharaohs."

35

WITH A HEAVY HEART I embraced Hortense and kissed little Coco goodbye and joined Euphemia in the great lumbering carriage that was to carry us to Toulon, where the army and navy were assembling. Eugene rode alongside us, a seasoned veteran of the fighting in Italy and, at seventeen, already a stalwart young officer. He could not wait for the exciting campaign to begin. He told me that he would make me proud of him and I assured him I could not possibly be more proud, not if I lived to be a hundred years old. He smiled at me, lovingly but slightly patronizingly. My day was past, his smile told me, while his was just dawning.

Bonaparte did not travel with us in our coach, but he was not far away. We were part of the long line of vehicles, horsemen and footsoldiers that were under his command, all making our way along the crowded high road toward the south.

All the roads had deteriorated in the years since the outbreak of the Revolution. In the old days of the monarchy the nobles had been responsible for making certain their villagers kept the roads clear of fallen trees and filled the deepest ruts and removed stones and other obstacles. But there were no nobles any more, and the revolutionary governments—we had had so many of them!—were too busy making laws and executing traitors and defending France from outside attack to pay attention to the humble work of keeping the highways passable.

Every few miles, it seemed, we had to stop while a makeshift bridge was thrown together over a swollen stream, or a team of oxen was hitched to a broken carriage to drag it out of the way. The constant delays were exasperating, as was the pace at which we rode, for even when the roads were at their best the long snakelike caravan crawled forward at less than ten miles a day, and when it rained our progress was much slower.

After a week of grueling days on the road I sent Eugene with a message to my husband. I asked if he would join me for supper. I was traveling with our chef from the Paris household and he prepared excellent meals for us when we stopped each night.

It did not surprise me when Bonaparte, having been invited to dine at eight o'clock, came riding up to our makeshift wayside lodging at ten. He threw off his waistcoat, opened the top of his shirt and, sitting down at the table, began to pull off his tight boots.

I stood behind him and began massaging his temples. Immediately I felt his shoulders relax. In another moment he sighed, and announced that he was ravenously hungry, not having eaten all day.

The chef brought in the first course of our supper, a fragrant, tempting soup, with crunchy fresh-baked bread. Bonaparte ate with gusto.

"Thank heaven you are with me on this campaign," he said at length. "I need you. You bring me luck." He smiled his winning smile.

"I know you think so."

"Ever since we met I've gone from success to success." He reached one hand down the front of his shirt and brought out a small miniature attached to a silver chain. It was my smiling face.

"You once wore an amulet, as I recall."

"You are my amulet now."

"Euphemia would say, you believe in putting the spirits on your side."

"I believe in luck."

I did not tell him that he made his own luck, by his sheer ability, his force and cleverness, and his remarkable capacity to lead and inspire his men. But then, if he lost faith in the power of amulets and miniatures, who was to say whether his ability might falter?

I let a long comfortable silence pass before I spoke again. At length I said, "When we reach Egypt, you will conquer Cairo, or Alexandria, or some other important place, and then set up a camp and consolidate and organize your men, isn't that right? As you did in Milan, on the Italian campaign?"

"If all goes well, yes."

"In a few days we will be near the spa at Plombières. The baths there are renowned for making childless women fertile. I could take the waters and visit old friends—you know how the Parisians love to go to the spa in summer. Then, once you are established, you can send for me and I can join you for your victory celebration."

"What friends?" His eyes had narrowed at my mention of visiting old friends.

"Fanny de Beauharnais, Georgette DeLongpré, Agnes Crébillon and her daughters—"

"And Monsieur de Gautier?"

"I doubt very much that he would be there."

"Or our friend Barras?"

"Hardly. There is no decadence at the spa. Only refinement—or the pretense of refinement." We both laughed.

"Very well. I'll send my brother to look after you—and perhaps Paulette as well."

"As you wish." I knew better than to protest at having to endure the presence of the hostile Buonapartes at Plombières. I would make the best of the situation. At least I would have a respite from the tedium of travel.

I said my goodbyes to Bonaparte and Eugene at Dijon and told my driver to take the road eastward. After two days we turned upward into the mountains.

The air became fresh and cool as we ascended from the hot plains into the pine-scented hills. Once we were on our own, and no longer part of the long military train of riders and carriages, we were able to go much faster and the tedium of the journey fell away. The road to the spa led past quaint villages and along the banks of green streams, under the shade of great old trees and through mountain passes where boulders of immense size stood sentinel as our carriage rumbled by.

I had often heard friends speak of Plombières but was unprepared for the charm of the small town, its promenade lined with glowing lanterns and overflowing flowerboxes, its old-fashioned cottages, each with its own scented garden, its inviting shops, elegant assembly rooms and tea rooms adjacent to the towering neo-classical entrance to the baths.

I was received with much fanfare and presented with a two-story cottage overlooking the promenade. A band came to play under my window and when I went out on the balcony to listen, I saw that a crowd had gathered to clap and cheer. There were the usual shouts of "Vive Bonaparte!" and "Vive Madame Bonaparte!" and I waved and bowed.

As I had hoped, a number of my friends and acquaintances from Paris were visiting the spa town. At a crowded tea-dance I encountered Henri and Bernard, the men Fanny de Beauharnais called the Inseparables, both greying, wearing identical skin-tight brown trousers, flowered waistcoats and pale blue silk shirts. They greeted me effusively.

"So pleased to see you," said Henri with a gracious little bow. (Bowing, which had disappeared along with noble titles during the Revolution, had begun to return as part of a change in manners.)

"We are honored to have Madame Bonaparte among us," said Bernard, who also bowed.

I smiled. "Thank you both. You remember me when I first came to Paris as a raw creole from Martinique, a thin girl with a nasty husband."

They guffawed. "Even then you were beautiful. In your honor we have written a poem." They proceeded to recite it in unison:

> *"Madame Bonaparte la bonne*
> *Madame Bonaparte la belle*
> *All our hearts you have won*
> *And our loyalties as well!"*

"We are in search of a musician to set our little verses to music," Henri said in a confiding voice. "We thought we had found one, but he disappointed us."

Bernard nodded sadly.

"Thank you for the kind tribute," I said. "And tell me, is Fanny here in Plombières? Is she coming?"

"Fanny arrived weeks ago. She holds her salon at her cottage every Thursday night. She wants to see you."

I presented myself at Fanny's quaint rented cottage on the following Thursday night. No sooner had I crossed the threshold than a cheer arose from the small crowd within. Fanny, her hair dyed a brilliant red and her aging face clownishly overpainted with powder and rouge, emerged from out of the crowd, leaning on a mahogany cane.

"My dear Rose," she said, embracing me with her free hand and looking down at me fondly. Her gaze seemed unfocused, her expression slightly vague. I thought, she is slowing down. Her eyesight is failing. But her mind was still sharp and her opinions caustic.

"So you married that dreadful man," she said to me under her breath. "Why on earth would you do that, especially when that other one, that handsome Donovan, was so much more appealing?"

"We'll speak of it later," I told her. "You must come to my villa for tea."

She led me into her music room and introduced me to her current protégés. Much to my embarrassment, they fawned over me, praising me extravagantly, complimenting my dress, my simple hairstyle—I had had Euphemia pin one perfect white rose in my hair—my string of pearls and the gold brooch I wore on the shoulder of my gown.

The days were long past when my dress caused murmurs among the straitlaced nobles of Milan. I no longer dressed like a daringly stylish Parisian, in gowns of semi-transparent fabrics that clung to my breasts and teasingly revealed my calves and thighs. Under relentless pressure from Bonaparte I had changed my style, adopting the purer, more chaste designs taken from the simple garb depicted in classical statues. These days I looked much more like a Greek goddess and less like a flamboyant, wealthy courtesan sitting in the balcony of a Paris theater. I had left behind that other, more daring self, and had remade myself into the elegant wife of a greatly admired French general, a general whose degree of public popularity was rising with every fresh military undertaking.

With a stab of regret I realized that the people in Fanny's salon were welcoming me and flattering me for one reason alone: they were seeking my patronage. The patronage of Rose Tascher, creole of Martinique, who as a girl had once told fortunes for a few francs in Fanny's drawing room in Paris. About a thousand years ago, or so it seemed.

What would these people think, I wondered, if I offered to tell fortunes now? I decided to find out.

"Some of you remember when I was among you, in Fanny's salon, many years ago." I saw some heads nodding. "I told fortunes then. I can still tell fortunes. What if, just for fun, I told my husband's fortune?"

There was a gasp of shock, and then a shiver of titillation.

I saw a gleam of eager interest dawn on the faces nearest me. "Bring her the cards!" someone shouted.

"I have my own cards," I said. "I always carry them."

Sitting at a nearby table, I drew a deck of tarot cards from the pocket of my gown and shuffled them, thinking all the while of Bonaparte and his army. When I felt I had shuffled adequately and concentrated long enough, I began to lay out the cards, face up, across the polished wood surface.

First to appear was the Fool. Ah, I thought, so Bonaparte is a fool for undertaking this venture into Egypt. Then came the card of the Lovers, with its intertwined male and female figures. As soon as I saw it I realized its meaning: Bonaparte will take a lover while he is in Egypt. I felt a pang, for until now I believed that he had been faithful to me. I knew I had no right to expect fidelity, as I had a lover of my own. Yet the thought of my husband with another woman was surprisingly hurtful to me. I drew out the next card. It was the war chariot, the symbol of the military campaign. Yet right behind it came the seven of wands, which some call the card of strife, and the Hanged Man, the card of reversals of fortune. The meaning was plain: Bonaparte would be defeated.

I felt a chill of unease and fear. But I didn't dare reveal to the group watching me that their hero Bonaparte was about to fail in his grand endeavor. I had no doubt that I was reading the cards correctly, and that they were accurate—for the tarot never lies. Yet it would not do to tell what I knew.

I composed myself, with some difficulty, and made up a tale which I hoped would gratify the onlookers.

"The Fool represents each of us on our life's journey; this card stands for Bonaparte at the present point in his life. It does not mean that he is foolish, merely that, like all humans, he is helpless as a fool when confronted by the strong hand of destiny."

A chorus of nods and audible sighs of agreement greeted my words.

"Yes, he is a man of destiny," I heard someone say.

I went on. "This card with the man and woman represents our marriage, in which we are happily joined," I said, pointing to the Lovers. "This one is Bonaparte's war chariot, and the next shows the swords of his men. This final one"—I pointed to the card of the Hanged Man—"represents the fate of the enemy at the hands of the victorious French army. The enemy will be hanged!"

A cheer broke from every throat. I had told them what they wanted to hear. Their faith in Bonaparte was intact. They looked forward to a future full of victories. But I knew the truth: that my daring, brilliant husband was on his way to ruin.

36

I REGRETTED HAVING TOLD BONAPARTE'S FORTUNE. Now I knew things about his future that I did not want to know. And I was terribly worried about my brave, eager Eugene, so desirous of proving himself in battle. Now I knew that the battles he would fight in Egypt would be losing battles, and that his danger would be greater than I had imagined.

I kept this knowledge to myself, tempted though I was to share it with someone I trusted. I did not even tell Euphemia, though for all I knew she was aware of Bonaparte's future herself, from her own readings of the cards. Like me, she kept a tarot deck nearby at all times, and often laid out the cards, frowning and muttering to herself. But she had other means of divination at hand, rituals and prayers and small fetishes she wore and spoke to, and she used those just as often.

Euphemia was ill at ease in Plombières. She disliked the crisp, cool mountain air and the frosty air of superiority some of the well-to-do visitors affected. As I have said, manners and social rules were changing; the equality so vaunted by the Revolution was giving way to gradations of rank, as in the days of the monarchy. Social snobbery was returning, and social climbing. And it was not entirely a bad thing, because the Revolution had swept away politeness and civility and replaced them with a blunt, brutish coarseness that led to barbarity. Surely civility is better than barbarity, even if it brings snobbishness in its wake.

I pondered these things as I sat out on the balcony of my rented cottage, and watched the evening promenade along the edge of the park. Couples strolled companionably arm in arm, older people were driven slowly along in open carriages, exchanging greetings with those they passed. The pace was sedate, the atmosphere cordial. I gathered my shawl around my shoulders as evening settled in, bringing cooler air with it. Even then I lingered, watching the lamplighter illumine the street lamps and enjoying the scent of night-blooming flowers rising up from the garden below.

My summer idyll was brief, however. I had not been in Plombières many weeks before I learned that my reading of Bonaparte's fortune had been correct. Who should appear in the spa town but Scipion du Roure, fresh from a naval battle just off the coast of Cairo, wounded in the arm and leg and as deaf as an old man!

He was taking the waters to help heal his battle wounds, and I went to visit him at his rented cottage.

I found him sitting in an armchair, with silken cushions around him on all sides, his injured arm heavily bandaged and one leg immobilized and wrapped in linen and gauze. He looked very ill, his face had a bilious yellow-green cast and he had lost all the plumpness in his cheeks. Two orderlies stood by.

Scipion looked up when I came in, and tried to reach out to me with his good arm, but his eyes were hooded and so full of pain and bitterness that I hardly recognized him. I was much dismayed.

"Don't move, dear friend. Stay as you are. Let me come to you." My eyes filling with tears, I went to his side and leaned down to embrace him. He winced at my touch, making me realize how much pain he was in.

I sat beside him and held his hand. When he spoke, his voice was a shout.

"I can't hear much," he boomed out. "Ever since the explosion my hearing is terrible."

I managed to convey to him that if he would lower his voice, I would try to raise mine, though I am naturally very soft-spoken.

"What explosion?" I asked loudly, putting my lips close to his ear.

"*L'Orient*. She exploded."

"The flagship of the fleet."

"Yes. I was third in command." His face darkened. "We were anchored in the shoals off Cairo, taking in supplies. Half our men were on shore.

The English cowards attacked us!" He closed his fists and gritted his teeth. "They attacked, when we were helpless, lying at anchor! Bastards! Cowards!" He was trembling.

I waited for him to go on. "They fired at us broadside. There was nothing we could do, they were too fast and we had too few men." His voice dropped. "It must have been near midnight when we caught fire. We tried to keep the fire from reaching the powder stores, but it spread too quickly. The whole ship went up—' He lifted his arms, and the effort made him cry out in pain. "The noise was terrible! I was thrown into the water. I couldn't hear anything. Someone helped me up onto a spar. That's all I remember."

"And the battle—" I began.

"Was lost. Only three of our ships were still afloat by dawn. I was lucky to get home to France. Bonaparte and his army are trapped in Cairo now. The English control the harbor."

The news was very bad, far worse than I expected. It was bad enough to have lost a major naval battle, but for the army to be caught in an enemy country with no escape was infinitely worse.

"Ah, but I know Bonaparte," Scipion was saying. "He is wily. He will find a way to conquer Egypt." Scipion did not despair.

I did my best to smile reassuringly.

News of the disaster at Aboukir Bay spread swiftly through the spa community at Plombières and overnight the mood at receptions and dinners turned somber. Conversation stalled. People who were normally outgoing became indrawn, uncommunicative. Everyone felt the need for companionship, yet no one wanted to speak of the terrible news. Scipion was lionized and received much sympathy, along with many gifts of hot soup and brandy-filled chocolates. But no one wanted to bring up the loss of the French ships, or the growing fear that nothing was going well in Egypt for the French.

Summer turned to fall, and many of the guests at the spa left for Paris. I lingered, for Bonaparte had told me to wait at Plombières until he sent for me. I was content there. the last thing I wanted was to resume my place in Paris society at a time when my husband was losing a campaign. Everywhere I went I was overshadowed by his reputation, his good or ill fortune. At Plombières I could at least enjoy a certain amount of solitude.

In the evenings I played vingt-et-un with a small circle of friends, among them Scipion who, as the weeks passed, began to heal and was even able to walk along the promenade provided he used a cane and leaned on the arm of his companion. Gradually his hearing came back, and when I talked with him I no longer had to speak close to his ear in my loudest voice.

The cold weather, shorter days and leafless trees did nothing to lighten my mood. I never received any letters from Bonaparte, and I sensed that something was wrong between us. The English blockade alone could not account for my hearing nothing from him, for others in Plombières were receiving letters from husbands and sons in the army and I assumed Bonaparte was communicating with the government in Paris. Why was he not writing to me?

The answer came when, toward the beginning of November, I received a letter from Eugene.

"My dearest maman," he wrote, "what a grand time we are having here in Cairo. General Bonaparte is welcomed by everyone here with great acclaim, and enjoys his title as 'Sultan Kebir.' (We had an uprising but quickly snuffed it out.) We have been to the great pyramid and I climbed nearly to the top. We plan to dig wells in the desert and channel the Nile so more land can be irrigated. Soon all Egypt will be like France, with a free and educated public and no more superstition.

"You would laugh to see Bonaparte riding a camel. He has created an entire regiment of camels. It might also interest you to know that my half-brother Alexandre, the son of my father and Laure de Girardin, is an officer in the Consular Guard. He looks more like my father than I do (he is much slimmer than I am), and acts more like him too. Laure is in America, married to a planter. Alexandre says she has gotten very fat."

I read on, though the light in the room was failing, and as I read I realized why I had received no letters from Bonaparte.

"You may hear some gossip about the general," Eugene wrote, "so I am writing to tell you what is really going on. Here in Egypt it is the custom for the rich sheikhs to offer their daughters and the sons of their slaves to visiting dignitaries. A young girl named Zenab was given to General Bonaparte, after he had turned down the boys and rejected most of the girls as too rank in odor. Zenab is called 'the General's Egyptian.' Actually he doesn't see her very often, and doesn't really like her, no matter what you may hear.

"There is another woman, though, called 'Cleopatra' or 'Bellilotte.'

She is a cook's bastard. The general met her at the Tivoli Egyptien, a new ballroom in Cairo. Her real name is Pauline Fourès and she is the wife of a young officer, Lieutenant Fourès. The only reason the general seduced her was that he heard you and Monsieur de Gautier are lovers. Always before he would not believe it but now he does."

I put the letter down. I would read the rest later. I felt as if a darkness had descended around me. Bonaparte, at last, had discerned the truth and was disillusioned. How would he treat me now? He was a man who always took revenge on those who injured him.

What revenge would he take against me?

37

SCIPION WAS RECOVERING SO WELL that he was able to be up and around
for most of the day and went for walks each evening. From time to time
we went for carriage rides in the woods surrounding Plombières, and he
got out of the carriage and took his exercise along the forest paths. I
walked beside him to steady him, offering him my arm when he faltered,
and as we went along we chatted, to keep each other company.

Winter was upon us, it had not snowed as yet but the only green in the
forest was the dark green of pine needles and the landscape, like the sky
over our heads, was mostly a dull grey. We wrapped ourselves up in thick
woolen cloaks and I wore a snug woolen cap—quite becoming, Scipion
said drily, meaning the opposite—that kept my ears warm. Our rides and
walks in the chill air were invigorating, and very enjoyable; sometimes
we stayed out for half a day.

We shared a lot during those excursions, our memories of Martinique
and of people we had both known, our experiences under the Revolution
in its earliest years, when Scipion was serving under new masters in the
Caribbean and I was the guest of Citizen Robespierre in the Carmelite
prison, our happiness in our children, and our feelings about our
marriages.

His marriage to his ever smiling, ever charming wife Julie gave him
much satisfaction, and he felt that he had chosen well. Yet he confessed

that he bore a constant sorrow. He had not been able to foresee that childbearing would tax Julie's body and permanently weaken her. She was only thirty-one but looked ten years older, he said, and with each passing year she declined in energy and strength. He feared for her, and looked forward to his own recovery so that he could rejoin her in Paris.

"And what of you, Madame Bonaparte?" he asked teasingly. "What is it like to be the wife of the greatest of generals?"

"I am happiest when away from him," I confessed in my turn. "I know now that I should have gone to Martinique with Donovan instead of marrying Bonaparte. Eugene writes that Bonaparte is angry with me and has taken a mistress in Egypt."

"The one they call Cleopatra, or the one they called the Harem Girl? Or is there some other one that I haven't heard about?"

"The men in the ranks always know everything, don't they?"

Scipion nodded. "Yes, and it always filters up to those of us higher up."

"So my humiliation is public knowledge."

"If you will forgive me, so are your own indiscretions, past and present."

My smile was wry. "It isn't possible to enjoy a private life, is it?"

"Not for someone as prominent as you are, Rose."

"And yet I still have old friends who are fond of me."

"Very fond. Very fond indeed."

One afternoon we returned from one of our longer excusions and I offered Scipion a mug of hot spiced wine at my cottage. We went inside and took off our warm outer garments. I asked the cook to prepare the drink and then went out onto the balcony overlooking the park. Scipion was making his way slowly toward the balcony from an adjacent room.

Suddenly I felt a lurch, and a sickening jolt. The structure gave way under my feet. I reached for the metal railing—but it was no longer there. I screamed as I fell—and then was aware of nothing more.

When I awoke I was aware only of pain. Agonizing pain in my back, my legs, my neck and head. Oh God, I remember thinking, please let me die.

BUT I DID NOT DIE, I lived with pain. Euphemia hovered over me, anointing me with foul-smelling salves, making me drink odious but healing liquids made from herbs—the same liquids she had made me drink as a child whenever I was ill. I remembered the smells from my childhood and took an odd comfort from them, as I took comfort from Euphemia's constant presence and soothing words. She hung a fetish around my neck and Scipion, when he came to visit me each day, hung a small gold cross there too.

"The doctor says you are very lucky to be alive, Rose," I heard him say one day. "You and I are survivors, that much is certain."

"Bonaparte always says I bring him luck," I answered, the sound of my voice weak in my ears—and saw that Scipion was startled.

"You're talking! Do you know how long it has been since you talked to me?"

"How long?"

"Almost ten days. We all thought you were dying. The doctor called it 'sleep death.' He told us to prepare for your funeral."

"I hope he was wrong." I did my best to smile. At the sight of my smile Scipion's eyes filled with tears.

"My dear girl, oh my dear," he said, taking my hand in both of his and kissing it. "I can only imagine what General Bonaparte would be feeling at this moment, if he could be here with you. We sent a message to him, describing the terrible accident, how the balcony collapsed and you fell to the pavement. But I doubt the message will reach him. The coast is blocked. Not even the messages from the government in Paris can get through to him."

I thought of Bonaparte, in Cairo, with his mistress, the cook's daughter, the one all the soldiers and sailors were gossiping about. Would he be glad, if he heard of my accident? Was he so angry with me that he would welcome my death? Or was I merely indulging in morbid thoughts because I was in such pain?

Then I thought of Donovan. If only I could see him! But there was a small black cloud of suspicion hanging over Donovan. What had happened to Clodia? What had Donovan done with her? Or to her? I did not like to think about this, and tried to put it out of my mind.

One day I opened my eyes after a long nap and saw Hortense sitting beside my bed. With her was a tall, blond, blue-eyed boy in a guardsman's uniform.

"Oh, maman! My sweetest maman!" Hortense cried as she bent to embrace and kiss me. "I came as soon as I got Monsieur du Roure's letter. I have been so worried about you!" It was many minutes before we were able to converse, we were both so overcome with emotion. I noticed that the blond young man sat quietly, very self-possessed yet with a sympathetic smile on his handsome face.

"Maman, this is Lord Falke. Lieutenant Falke, I should say. Of the Ardennes regiment. His father is English but his mother is French and he is loyal to France, having been raised here."

The lieutenant came to my bedside and, with a light and gentle touch, lifted my hand to his lips. The gesture was so kindly and graciously done that it moved me. "It is my very great honor to be presented to Madame Bonaparte," he said. "I see now that all Hortense has told me about you does not do you justice."

"You flatter me shamelessly, lieutenant. And I thank you for it. As you see, I am not myself these days."

"Hortense and I hope that you will be much better once you have been treated by the physicians we brought with us from Paris, Dr. Morel and Dr. Hezancourt. With your permission we would like to bring them in to examine you."

I nodded. Apart from Euphemia's constant treatments, I had had no real medical care since my accident. Plombières was full of "spa doctors," as they were called, men who treated wealthy aging women by submerging them in tubs of churning hot water or used "galvanic energy" to stimulate their tired overlarded limbs. There were no first-quality physicians in the town, and most of the doctors in neighboring towns had been coerced into serving in the army.

The two bearded, middle-aged men Lord Falke ushered into the room took immediate charge of me and before long Euphemia and her medicines were banished. Dr. Morel, the senior of the two physicians, was a broad-shouldered, muscular man of about forty, well dressed and with a sober expression. His colleague Dr. Hezancourt was younger, perhaps thirty or thirty-five, blond and slight and with kind eyes.

"Can you sit up?" Dr. Hezancourt asked me.

"No. My back hurts too much."

"Can you lift your arms?" asked Dr. Morel.

The two men exchanged glances.

"Have you been bled?"

"No."

A basin was brought in and my wrist, suspended over the basin, was cut with a razor. Drop by bright red drop my life blood flowed into the bowl.

Dr. Morel drew a glass jar out of his bag. I knew what it contained:

leeches, hideous black bloodsucking creatures that made me shudder. I looked away as the ugly wriggling things were lifted out and placed on my wrists. I felt no pain, only revulsion. We had had leeches in abundance in Martinique. It was impossible to walk through the rain forest and not be attacked by them. They burrowed under the wet fallen leaves, they attached themselves to horses' legs and, unless one was careful, to human legs as well. I remembered the many visits doctors had made to Les Trois-Ilets to treat my very ill sister Catherine. Each time they came they brought their jars of leeches. Poor Catherine, who had always been pale, turned a ghastly white after the horrid things drank her blood.

The leeches did their work on me, again and again, yet I remained as painfully immobile as ever. Dr. Morel then instructed my cook to boil a large quantity of potatoes in a pot and when the mixture had turned to mush, he wrapped it in toweling and made bandages for my poor arms and back. The heat felt good, but though the experiment was performed a number of times, the potato therapy did not improve me.

Nor did I improve when a sheep was slaughtered and gutted and its fleece wrapped around my painful back. Scipion, Euphemia, Hortense and Lieutenant Falke dined on mutton for days, and I had more than my fill of mutton stew.

Finally in January, after achieving no cure, the two physicians returned to Paris, amid an effusion of bows and excuses, and I was left once again to Euphemia's care. Though it caused me much discomfort I was able to sit for short periods of time, and Hortense helped me to recover a skill I had long lost—embroidery. The sisters at my convent school in Martinique had taught me the chain stitch and the stitch called "à la reine" but I had long since lost any skill with the needle I once had. Together we created a fire screen with intertwined bees (for Bonaparte) and roses, my favorite flower.

Hortense and Andrew (the Christian name of her admirer Lord Falke) played cards with me, vingt-et-un and a new game that everyone in Paris was playing. They enlivened the long winter evenings with talk of the goings-on in the capital: the triumphs of Mademoiselle Chameroi, the finest dancer at the Opéra, the great success of Monsieur Biennois's new shop in the rue Saint-Honoré, at the sign of the Violet Monkey, where the elite went to buy their ivory traveling-cases fitted with silver shaving-pots and moustache combs inlaid with mother of pearl. They brought news of Paul Barras, who still held on to power though he was increasingly disliked, of the social prominence of the Buonapartes and of a disturbing increase in crime.

"Right before we left to come here," Andrew said, "everyone was talking about the Gardel Gang. There are forty gang members, it is said, all former soldiers I'm sorry to say. They carry sabers and roam the streets looking for victims, then cut off their heads."

"They stab people too, and cut off fingers and noses and leave them as trophies," Hortense added in a breathless tone.

"How gruesome!"

"And then there are the 'Hot Foot' bandits who steal and run away so fast no one can catch them."

"It sounds as though Paris is overrun with crime," I remarked. "Thank goodness Plombières is a quiet, law-abiding place."

Hortense and Andrew looked at one another, but said nothing.

"What is it?" I could not help but note the significant silence, and the quick exchange of glances.

"Nothing for you to be concerned about, Madame Bonaparte."

"I want to know. What are you two keeping from me?"

"Truly, there is no need for you to upset yourself, maman."

"You are upsetting me now. I demand that you tell me this thing, whatever it is."

Both young people looked uncomfortable. At length Andrew spoke. "We did not want to tell you this for fear of worsening your condition. A shock can bring on a relapse." He looked at me, and seeing how resolute I was, went on.

"One of the gardeners in the park saw something on the day your balcony collapsed. Two men came to work on it. He assumed you had hired them, or your friend Monsieur du Roure had. But later on he saw a stranger paying them, and it looked as though he was paying them awfully well for making a simple repair."

"Yes? Tell me the rest."

"Monsieur du Roure and I have discovered who the stranger was. The gardener described him for us. We have gone to every landlady in Plombières and asked whether a man of that description was staying in her lodgings around the time your accident took place. Madame d'Aigrefeuille said yes, and showed us the name written in her registry."

I leaned forward, though the pain almost made me cry out.

"It was Joseph Buonaparte."

38

I FELL ASLEEP, and dreamed.

In my dream I was drowning, thrashing and flailing under water, trying desperately to breathe. I choked. I knew I was about to die.

Then suddenly I felt myself lifted up by unseen hands and carried across seas, mountains, beaches, green forests. I am dead, I thought. I am dead, and I am being taken to heaven.

Yet it was not in heaven that the unseen hands deposited me, but on Morne Ganthéaume, at the Sacred Crossroads. It was night. I saw, by torchlight, the large clearing where I had first seen Orgulon, the great quimboiseur. The clearing was deserted, save for the stump of a large tree. On the stump sat Orgulon, smoking his pipe.

The light was dim, but I could make out his red cloak and the red feathers in his sparse grey hair, and his necklace of shark's teeth.

He looked at me, out of his one good eye.

After a time he removed the pipe from his mouth and spoke.

"Once again the fer-de-lance has come for you. To kill you. Beware of that fer-de-lance! You have been bitten, but you will not die. I will not let you die. You must be saved. You have a purpose. Find it, and live!"

"Orgulon!" I called his name, but my voice was weak. The torchlight faded, the Sacred Crossroads dimmed, then disappeared.

I heard Hortense calling me.

"Maman, maman, wake up! You are having a nightmare!"

"Orgulon!" I said once again, and opened my eyes. I was in my bedroom in the rented house in Plombières, and Hortense was sitting beside me, looking down at me anxiously.

I felt groggy, but calmer than I had been in all the months of my illness.

"Don't worry," I whispered. "I am going to be all right. The snake came for me, but I am stronger than he is."

To myself I added, I am going to find my purpose, and live.

39

RIGHT AWAY I BEGAN TO FEEL BETTER. The pains in my back, arms and legs grew more bearable, and I was able to move my arms enough to feed myself. Everyone said how much more color I had in my cheeks and I had Euphemia dress my hair with more attention to style and put a different silken dressing gown around me each day.

It was as if a curse had been lifted, not only from my aching body but from my mind as well. I began to look forward to being healthy again, to being able to move without agony. I worried, however, that the accident might have left me unable to have more children. I knew that Bonaparte wanted a family, and I imagined that my body might be overtaxed, or permanently weakened, by all that I had been through.

I had, to be sure, a much larger worry. It seemed overwhelmingly certain that my hostile brother-in-law Joseph had hired assassins to bring about my accident. Therefore he wanted me dead—and would go on making attempts on my life, unless he was stopped. I began keeping a pistol near me at all times, and took some comfort from knowing that Scipion too was armed.

"I have arranged for our travel back to Paris, Rose," Scipion told me one day. "I think you are well enough. I've written to the Ministry of Marine and they say they can use me in their offices in the capital, even though I am not fit to go back to sea."

We left soon afterwards, Scipion escorting me and Hortense and

Euphemia in our large traveling carriage with four armed outriders. Lord Falke went south to Naples, hoping to cross to Egypt, despite the British blockade, to join Bonaparte's army.

Though it meant a longer and much rougher journey, we avoided the main roads and large towns on our way northward toward the capital. I knew it would fatigue me to receive long and tedious official greetings at every town we passed through and I did not want the pity of those who would see me in a wheeled chair (for I could not walk far as yet unaided).

Also we had been hearing ongoing rumors that the campaign in Egypt was going badly for the French—something I expected, but did not know for certain. There was no word of new victories, only of Bonaparte's marching his men into the Syrian desert, with what result we did not know. I was eager to get to Paris so that I could once again be close to the best sources of information—the bankers and financiers in Paul Barras's circle. It was a measure of how well I was healing that I wanted to be well informed. In the meantime, the last thing I wanted was to be pressed for news by townspeople and villagers, most of whom did not know where Egypt was, much less what its conquest might mean for France. (Or what Bonaparte's failure there might mean.)

I could not help but wonder whether I would see Donovan in Paris. I had had no word of him in many months. We had agreed, before I left for Plombières, that it would be best if we did not try to communicate with each other, because of Bonaparte's suspicions. After my accident I asked Fanny to write to Donovan at his lodgings in Paris and tell him what had happened to me, but she said she had received no reply.

There was no question of our going on with our provisioning business; the company we had worked through, the Bodin Company, went bankrupt and Monsieur Bodin himself was in jail for fraud. I hoped that my personal fortune was still safe in the bank but I couldn't be certain. Despite my protestations to Bonaparte and others, my dealings had in fact been dishonest, at least some of the time; the dishonesty had not been mine, others had committed it, but I knew of it and did not protest. Still, I reasoned, this was the way those with army contracts always did business. It was expected. Someone would be certain to profit, why not Donovan and me? After all, I had always been a good businesswoman.

Once we were settled in Paris in the rue des Victoires, I sent Euphemia to inquire discreetly after Donovan. When she came back from her errand I could tell at once by the look on her face that she was bringing bad news.

"He's gone. He's been gone a long time. It was either that or go to jail, his neighbors said."

"Did he go back to Martinique?"

"Most likely. He left this note for you."

I unfolded the large sheet of paper and read it, slowly.

"My dear," it began,

I leave today for my plantation Bonne Fortune and I hope that you will come and join me there. It is not safe for you in France—for either of us. Your husband is a remarkable man but he is malevolent. I do not trust him and neither should you. You are forever in my arms,

Donovan de Gautier

Where was I to turn? What was I to do? I was the wife of an extremely prominent man, yet in Paris, that was, for the moment, a liability. For the government was in turmoil, its leaders caught up in petty squabbling and Parisians angrily dissatisfied with their rulership. Little or nothing had been heard from my husband for many months. My money, I soon discovered, had been seized when the Bodin Company declared bankruptcy. I was supposed to have an allowance supplied to me by Joseph Buonaparte, my enemy, but I did not dare go to him and demand payment. Food was scarce in Paris, and even going to the market was unsafe, for thieves roamed the streets and crime had gotten much worse.

I remembered a lovely country house Bonaparte and I had visited, a riverside mansion surrounded by vineyards and wheat fields called Malmaison. I had wanted to buy it, but Bonaparte had said no, it was too costly. Perhaps, I thought, in this time of turmoil and scarcity the price of the house might have come down?

In a country house I would be safe, not only from the thieves of Paris but from my Buonaparte enemies. I could stay there in peace, surrounded by trusted servants, behind the thick old walls and ornate metal gates, until Bonaparte came back from Egypt.

There was one man who might lend me the money to make my country dream a reality. With Euphemia's help I put on the most fashionable of my gowns, fastened an embroidered white cap over my hair and did my best to look like a woman who had not undergone a terrible physical ordeal. Thus arrayed, and feeling an upsurge of hope, I set off to visit Paul Barras.

40

MY EUGENE CAME BACK TO ME one morning as I was pruning roses in my new garden at Malmaison. He was not in uniform, and at first, as he approached, I did not recognize him as his body had thickened during his year-long stay in Egypt and he wore his soft, broad-brimmed black hat pulled low over his forehead.

His smile was still warm and youthful, however, and when I saw who it was approaching I cried out for joy and hugged him very tight.

"My dearest, dearest boy, how glad I am that you are safe!"

"We've both been through the wars, have we not, maman? You with your terrible accident and I, I fear, with this permanent souvenir from Syria."

He took off his hat and I saw that the entire left side of his head was wrapped in bandages.

"Eugene!" was all I could manage to say, my surprise and horror were so great.

"I didn't write you about my wound because I didn't want to worry you. At first they gave me up for dead—"

"As they did me, in Plombières," I put in.

"—and later, they thought I might never see again, but they were wrong. I have a little trouble remembering things, and my ears ring sometimes, but otherwise I am very fit."

"How did it happen? Tell me everything."

We sat on a bench and Eugene recounted his perilous months in Bonaparte's army.

"We were never able to control much of the country. We took Cairo, as I wrote you, but the people there rebelled and every time we left the city we were always under attack from the Bedouins and the peasants. Bonaparte was savage. He cut off more heads in a week than the revolutionaries in Paris did in a year. And he didn't seem troubled by it. I know, I was there with him most of the time, in his tent, sitting beside him as he wrote out his dispatches, even helping him shave and dress himself. He made me ride alongside his carriage when he went out with his mistress, the one I wrote you about, the one he calls Bellilotte."

"That was cruel."

"I was enraged at first. Then I realized he wasn't trying to hurt me, he was trying to punish you by hurting me."

"We need not say any more about that. We both know him well."

"I'm very sorry, maman. I never meant to be disloyal to you. I thought of leaving my post, but—"

"But if you had done that, your army career would have been over. I quite understand."

He shook his head. "I was angry about it all. But there were much worse things to be angry about."

He got to his feet and paced back and forth, his hands behind his back, looking down at the grass. I thought I detected an occasional unsteadiness in his gait, and I wondered if it was the result of his head wound.

"So many of our men died. They got syphilis, or the Egyptian eye disease, which drove them mad, or the plague. It swept them away like the Nile sweeps away boats at flood tide. And all General Bonaparte could think about was how he was going to conquer India once he had taken Egypt and Turkey."

He paused, shaking his head, then continued.

"We marched all the way to Jaffa. We took the Turkish garrison there. The general said we couldn't take any prisoners, we had no food for them. So we slaughtered them, thousands of helpless soldiers, most of them too old to fight. And not only the soldiers"—his words caught in his throat, and for a minute or two he could not continue—"but their wives and children. So many children! Oh, maman, if you could have seen them, the poor little things clinging on to their fathers' legs, cut down without mercy—"

I crossed myself and murmured a prayer.

"It was ghastly. I felt sick and weak, but the general only taunted me.

"'Be a man, Eugene!' he said. 'Be a soldier!' He laughed in that way he has, a snide laugh, and he pinched my cheek, too hard. I swear, at that moment I could have killed him, I hated him so much."

He sat down again, beside me on the stone bench.

"We set siege to Acre then, just like the crusading knights did centuries ago. I was careless. I got too close to the walls. I was hit. Bonaparte had me put aboard an Arab dhow, and sent to Cyprus. There were very good physicians there. I rested for a month, then found a Portuguese merchant vessel to take me to Marseille. I landed two weeks ago."

"I hope you will stay here with me for awhile. We will get you the best physicians in Paris."

Eugene agreed to stay on with me in Malmaison, and grew stronger by the day. Through a courier he maintained close contact with events in the ministries in Paris—for he was still Bonaparte's aide-de-camp, even though thousands of miles away—and we were both aware that the power of the five Directors was in decline.

I felt stronger, having all my family around me again, Hortense and Coco, Euphemia and now Eugene. I isolated myself at Malmaison, doing my best to ignore the gossip that reached me, the nasty things my in-laws were saying about me and the inevitable rumors that Bonaparte would soon divorce me.

That he had a pretty young mistress in Egypt had become common knowledge in the capital. I still had many friends and was a sentimental favorite of the Parisians, having been one of them for so many years and having been a victim of the Terror who was miraculously saved from death through a stroke of good fortune. However, Parisians are notoriously fickle and feel a frisson of excitement when a new love threatens to upset an established marriage. I knew that if I went out in society, there would be a thousand questions about my marriage. I would feel tense and uneasy, even among those I knew best.

I also knew that, if I visited the capital, I might, if I were very unlucky, meet my nemesis Joseph Buonaparte, who had a country house not far from the capital. He was never out of my thoughts in those worrisome days, the fear of him nagged at me terribly. Would he try again to bring about my death?

I kept watch from my window each night, unable to go to sleep for many hours as I imagined assassins creeping across the garden toward the house, coming to kill me. I kept my loaded pistol under my pillow and slept with my newest companion, a big Russian wolfhound I called Mitka, by my side.

41

"HE IS COMING! He is coming!" Word of Bonaparte's sudden, unannounced return from Egypt swept up from the coast and there was rejoicing from one end of France to the other.

No one seemed to care that little, if anything, had been achieved in Egypt or Syria. (Bonaparte had claimed much but done little.) Or that while he was away on the other side of the Mediterranean, his conquests in Italy had been reconquered by the Austrians. All that mattered was that the hero Bonaparte, the savior of France, was returning, and that he would sweep all difficulties away.

We heard that he was at Lyon, then Montluçon, then Orléans. He would soon be among us.

I dreaded his return, and braced myself for quarrels and confrontations. I did not expect Bonaparte to appear the way he did, on my doorstep, with no warning.

His gaudy gilded carriage, ornamented by sphinxes and with golden pyramids at each corner of the roof, swept into the forecourt of Malmaison, causing much excitement among my servants, who rushed out to greet the general and applaud him.

He alighted from the carriage, looking somewhat bilious, I thought, even dissolute. His skin, which had grown darker and more leathery in the Egyptian sun, had a yellowish cast Joseph stepped down out of the carriage next, making me shiver and reach for Eugene's arm, and then out stepped a buxom blond woman in a preposterous, ill-fitting purple gown and hat.

"The cook's daughter," I murmured to Eugene, as we stood in the vestibule, watching the scene in the courtyard through the open door. Soon Euphemia came to join us, leading Coco, and finally Hortense came to stand beside her brother. Thus arrayed, we waited for Bonaparte to enter the house.

But he did not. Instead he stood on the gravel of the forecourt, speaking in a loud voice to Joseph.

"I leave it to you to sell this overpriced extravagance of my wife's," he said in a loud voice. "Find a reputable land agent and get what you can for it. I am sure she paid far too much."

"Whatever she paid, I doubt it was cash," Joseph replied drily. "It is said she has returned to her rich boyfriend Barras. He gave her the money to buy the estate."

"She is still my wife. She cannot acquire property without my permission. As for Barras—" He did not finish his sentence. His tone was dismissive.

Joseph spat. "All Paris hates Barras. He can't last. The Parisians are behind you, Nabulio. You, as always, are the man of the hour!"

"Never mind Barras and my wife. She is no more to me than the dirt under my feet. I will divorce her and marry this beautiful girl"—he put his arm around his mistress's plump waist and hugged her to him. "She won't deceive me, will you Bellilotte? She will be a faithful and loving wife to me. She is not a whore like the other one." He squeezed the blond woman until she squealed, making him laugh.

"Go in and look around," he said to her, giving her a little push toward the house. "See if there is anything inside you want."

She ambled toward the entrance. She had no grace. There was a sort of wobble in her walk. People said, of my walk, that I did not walk at all: I floated.

As we watched, she came through the doorway with a swish of her awful purple skirts. She looked up and down the marble columns in the foyer (they were not real marble, of course, but she couldn't have known that) and the beautiful tiled floor, the fresh flowers from the greenhouse—and then she looked at the five of us.

She scrutinized me, her eyes resting shamelessly on my full bosom.

She barely glanced at Hortense (who, I must confess, was not a pretty girl, though her character was very fine). She ignored Eugene, whom she had known in Egypt for almost a year. Instead her eyes rested on Coco, who was a precociously pretty child with my father's small, almost womanish, delicate features. She had her mother's lithe, slender body, her ripe coppery skin, and her beautiful black eyes and luxuriant curling black hair which Euphemia tamed each morning and tied back off her face. Coco was an irrepressible, exuberant child, energetic and active. She resisted all attempts to dampen her spirits and turn her into the sort of meek, inert, doll-like lump of walking obedience most wellborn parents desired their daughters to be.

"So this is your love-child," Bellilotte said. Her voice was high and brash.

"Coco is my stepsister. And I do not recall inviting you into my house."

She continued to regard me coolly. "He said you were a haughty bitch." She swept past us and on into the dining room, where Eugene, courteously but firmly, attempted to take her arm and lead her back outside.

"Don't try it, boy. You heard what your father said. He wants me to look around. Don't make me scream for him."

Just then Euphemia trod on Bellilotte's gown, making it impossible for her to move without tearing the fabric.

"Get your black foot off my gown!"

Euphemia reached into the bodice of her own silk gown and pulled out her favorite idol, the Ibo Red Goddess. She swung the small carved image on its chain in front of Bellilotte's alarmed face.

"Have you ever seen one of these?" she asked.

Bellilotte, her light blue eyes wide, nodded her head slowly.

"It can bring rain, cure fevers, make men fall in and out of love—all sorts of things."

"I—I have seen idols before. When my husband and I—I mean my former husband and I—were in Bengal, when we were first married—"

"Why, this little statue can destroy a woman's beauty in a few moments. Hives, warts, wrinkles, pockmarks: the Red Goddess can bring them all. Ah, what harm they can do to a lovely complexion!" She raised the fetish higher, and swung it back and forth with greater vigor.

Bellilotte instinctively put her hand to her dewy cheek, as if to ward off the hives and warts and other disfigurements.

"Bright eyes can grow dim, lovely hair can fall out," Euphemia said, as if chanting, her voice singsong in its rhythms. "Rank odors can arise from her womanly parts, odors no man would ever want to come near—"

Without waiting to hear more, Bellilotte began to run, her gown tearing as she took her first steps, for Euphemia kept her foot firmly clamped on the hem of her skirt. In her torn gown, her eyes wide with fear, the girl ran to Bonaparte in the courtyard, who showed his annoyance.

"Out so soon?"

"That black woman threatened me."

"How?"

"She said she would make warts on my face."

Bonaparte laughed. "Pay no attention. Get into the carriage and wait for me there."

Pouting, Bellilotte obeyed, taking her time climbing gracelessly into the carriage, trailing shreds of purple cloth. Once inside, she stared out the carriage window watching all that was going on.

My arm on Eugene's, I now walked out into the courtyard at a stately pace. My knees trembled, for Joseph stood there, beside his brother, glancing up to watch my approach and talking to Bonaparte all the while.

When I reached Bonaparte I stopped and addressed him.

"I bought this house with my own money," I said, as slowly and clearly as I could. "It is mine."

Bonaparte whirled to face me. "May I remind you, madame, that you are still my wife. The wife of General Bonaparte, no less. Everything you own is his. And you have no money of your own, as you well know."

"I have what I borrowed from Barras."

He snorted. "Borrowed? On what terms?"

I had no answer. I had accepted the money Barras offered me, taken from his overflowing safe. I had assured him that I could repay him, knowing, all the while, that he would expect no repayment, then or ever. Knowing that he was so rich he needed none.

Bonaparte rudely turned his back on me and resumed his conversation with Joseph.

"It will amuse me to sell this costly place and use the profit to drive Barras out of office."

So that was why Bonaparte wanted my lovely Malmaison. To pay for his planned takeover of France. Eugene had kept me informed of the secret meetings and intrigues being carried out toward this end. I was well aware that my husband, responding to the loud, overwhelming outcry of support he received on his arrival in France, intended to become its sole ruler—and very soon. Given this grand plan, I realized that his visit to Malmaison and his conversation with me must seem unimportant indeed.

"I forbid you to use my house for your selfish ends."

I don't know where I found the courage to say this—perhaps from the feel of my son's strong, sturdy left arm, perhaps from my hatred of Joseph, and my anger at what he had tried to do to me, perhaps from my contempt for the blowsy Bellilotte. Or perhaps because I had grown stronger since my struggle for life in Plombières and in the long months of my recovery.

Bonaparte turned slowly back toward me. His eyes had narrowed.

"Do you imagine, madame, that you can do anything at all without my permission?"

Childishly, I kicked dust on his dark blue trousers. I heard snickers of laughter.

"Take your mother back into the house, Eugene, before I am forced to discipline her in front of the servants."

Quietly Eugene responded. "I think, general, that she has a right to be here."

"Perhaps you did not understand me Eugene. I do not blame you for any of your mother's many wrongs. Nor for her infidelity, or for the shame she has brought on me and my family, or for the way she has disgraced herself and you, or for the dishonor she has brought on the people of France as my wife. It is not your fault that she is unworthy to be the consort of a head of state. I cannot forgive her—but I can and do forgive you for your loyalty to her. I will always look on you as my son. I will keep you near me. You have earned my favor."

I was never prouder of Eugene than I was in that moment.

"General," he said, "I cannot serve you if you desert and insult my mother. I must take care of her. I hereby decline any offer of continued service you make to me. I will now say my farewell, and resign my post."

He gently lifted my arm off his and, taking a step toward Bonaparte, drew from his scabbard the sword Bonaparte had presented to him years earlier, Alexandre de Beauharnais's sword. The blade gleamed in the sunlight, but even in the brief instant it was exposed to the light I could tell that it had grown dull, that its once flawless surface was nicked and scratched and that the hilt had rusted. It was no longer the blade of a boy, but of a warrior, a battle-scarred length of grey metal, a blade that, I felt sure, had taken many lives.

Eugene knelt and offered the sword to Bonaparte.

And then the general's stern face began to soften, his narrowed eyes began to widen and fill with tears. He opened his arms to Eugene, and to me, and without thought we ran into his embrace.

"Oh, all is forgiven. Only love, only love," he murmured in a broken voice, kissing us again and again. He reached for Hortense, and Coco, and finally Euphemia. Forgetting everyone else, oblivious to all but our feelings of unity and affection, we hugged and kissed one another again and again.

Bonaparte picked me up and carried me into my great round bedroom, ignoring the squawks of the furious Bellilotte, and there we made love, again and again, his ardor seemingly greater than ever. My relief was beyond description. I yielded happily to his embraces and gave him the peace of heart and body that he craved. We were one again. We did not come out of the bedroom for three whole days.

42

"MONSIEUR," I called out to the workman standing on a ladder high above my head. He didn't hear me.

"Monsieur!" I called out again, more loudly.

"Pardon me, milady." He made an awkward attempt to bow, standing on his ladder. "Please tell me what you desire."

He began to descend the ladder.

"Oh no, please. Don't bother to come down. I just wanted to ask you about the chandelier. About all the candles."

We stood in the grand dining hall of the Tuileries Palace, a vast room whose dimensions I could not even begin to guess. A room larger, perhaps, than all of Les Trois-Ilets put together.

Tall columns of veined pink marble topped with gilded Corinthian capitals framed high rounded windows. The elaborately carved moldings were painted in silver and gold filigree. Lifesize nude statues filled niches above which were golden coats of arms supported by winged cupids. On the painted ceilings goddesses of plenty and harvest gods disported themselves amid cornucopias overflowing with fruits, nuts and candies. A smiling Bacchus reclined in inebriated satiety above my head. All around me, where I stood on the shining parquet floor, stretched long tables laid with crisp white linen and crystal, shining silver epergnes and vases of sweet-smelling flowers from the greenhouses.

Though I could still hardly believe it, I was mistress of the Tuileries Palace now. My immensely popular husband, through a series of political maneuvers, had succeeded in making himself the most powerful man in France. We moved into the palace and were attempting to revive the grand state kept there by the king and queen before their executions.

It was all very strange to me—very strange and very uncomfortable. I am a planter's daughter from Martinique, not royalty. To be sure, I had observed the late queen from a distance, when I was a girl staying with my Aunt Edmée in Fontainebleau. But I had never attended a royal levee or ball. I was not familiar with court etiquette. I had many titled friends and acquaintances who were at home in the palace, and from being among them I had acquired, over the years, a certain elegance (so people said) and an ability to put others at ease as a hostess. Still, I felt very much a novice in my role as mistress of the Tuileries Palace. I had a great deal to learn. I planned to begin learning from the servants who, after all, were the ones who made the palace run smoothly.

"Please tell me your name monsieur."

"I am Christian de Reverard, milady."

"Then, Christian, kindly tell me how it is that the candles are all lit at the same time when the guests come in for supper. It always seems to happen as if by magic."

The man smiled. "It is quite ingenious, milady. You see, each candle is connected to one other by a small string. I am attaching the strings now. The strings cannot be seen from the floor, where you are standing, but if you were to come up here next to me, on a ladder, you could see them quite clearly."

I peered up toward the beautiful ceiling high above me, where the goddesses and gods were in their wispy costumes. I could not see any strings among the candles.

"At a signal, when the procession begins and you and the First Consul lead in your guests and the musicians begin to play, lit candles are touched to the strings at each end of the room. It only takes a few seconds for the fire to leap from candle to candle, until all are lit."

"And how many candles are there?"

"Goodness, I have no idea. Only the Grand Master of the Candles knows that."

"May I ask, Christian, how you learned all this?"

"I was a groom at Versailles, milady, from the time I was nine years old."

"My father was a groom there too. I wonder if you knew him. Joseph Tascher de la Pagerie."

"There were many of us, milady. Hundreds. I cannot remember all their names."

"No, of course not. Thank you so much, Christian. I will not forget you."

"I am honored to be of service, milady. May I resume tying the strings now?"

"Of course."

It was time to dress for the ball we were giving that evening. We had much to celebrate. For the first time in many years, France was at peace. A treaty had been signed with England and both countries agreed to end their fighting. The worst excesses of the Revolution were long over. Many of the titled lords and ladies who had fled during those dark years were returning, and the priests also, and Bonaparte was on his way, people said, to restoring Catholicism in France—something the revolutionaries would never have believed possible.

To be sure, some people were saying that bad times were returning. That soon we would need another Revolution to get rid of Bonaparte. And it was true, he ruled quite firmly. More firmly than King Louis had. He did not like anyone to criticize him. Many newspapers had been forced to cease publication because they printed critical articles about him and some plays that attacked the government were banned.

Still, I did not think things were as bad as they had been before the Revolution, when everyone was going bankrupt and there was no bread and the king and queen did not seem to care.

No, things were not as bad. France was prosperous once again, and people had faith in Bonaparte. He was still so young—only in his early thirties—and he had done so much in his short lifetime.

I, on the other hand, was nearing forty, and there was no disguising that unfortunate fact.

I was getting to look old. I was old. My husband told me so constantly, even in front of others.

What he said was quite true. My teeth were black stumps, the stumps of an old woman. I couldn't bring myself to wear the wooden teeth others of my age wore. My husband kept telling me that General Washington, one of his heroes, wore wooden teeth and I should too, but I couldn't bear the thought, and the pain (I know there would have been pain, a great deal of it), the awful pain of having the stumps drawn would have been unbearable. So I just kept my mouth shut, and hid my black stumps behind my fan when I talked, and did not open my lips when I smiled.

My hair was dyed, as it had started to turn grey. I wore thick white makeup to disguise the red blotches in my complexion. I wore too much rouge, Bonaparte said. But I had to wear it. I no longer had any youthful color in my cheeks. And at times—yes, I confess it—I wore gowns that were too revealing, gowns that might looked well on me once but that were much too young for me now. I had a weakness for trying to look girlish, like the pretty girl I had been in Martinique.

The truth was, I could not bear to think of myself as other than a girl. Becoming an older woman, even a handsome older woman, frightened me. I had not the gift for that, as some women did.

So I did everything I could to keep old age away. I slept with a slab of raw meat on my face to freshen my complexion. I wiped thick unguents on my stinking gums to sweeten my breath. I doused my body in perfume. I stayed out of bright sunlight and let the soft glow of candles flatter my face and neck.

I did my best.

It was not good enough.

On the night of our celebration ball, I dressed in a gown I hoped Bonaparte would like. It was of soft sheer ivory muslin, and it clung in a flattering way to my bosom and hips. The white lace bodice was subtly revealing yet chaste—a good compromise, I thought, between what was then fashionable and what was appropriate for the mistress of the Tuileries. Over it I planned to wear a cashmere shawl in the stylish color of Fly's Bottom but at the last minute I changed my mind. I had an inspiration.

That season, to celebrate the peace between England and France, the best dressmakers were featuring something called an English spenser, a very short, military-style jacket with brass buttons that stopped above the waist and gave a very smart appearance. I had ordered several of these, in blue, grey and green. I asked my maid to bring me the blue one and put it on over the muslin gown, adding a jaunty heron feather in my curly hair.

I was nearly ready. Looking at my reflection in the pier glass I seemed pale. I picked up my pot of rouge and added yet another layer to my wan cheeks.

No, I thought. He will say I'm wearing too much. Quickly I wiped the rouge away. But then I appeared grey, my skin lacking in warmth and life. I put on some more rouge, hoping I had struck a balance, avoiding unsightly aging without looking artificially youthful. It was so difficult to get it right!

Sighing, I put the pot of rouge down and went boldly into Bonaparte's dressing room.

His turbaned bodyguard Roustan, tall and muscular and dressed only in garish red Turkish trousers, glared at me. I hated Roustan, and he knew it.

"Sir, I am ready." Bonaparte insisted that everyone call him "Sir," now that he was the head of government. I thought this affectation absurd.

He was dressing in front of a large triple mirror, two valets assisting him. He paused long enough to turn to gaze at me. Instantly his eyes darkened. I knew that look.

"Take off that British-looking thing." He turned back to the mirror and focused once again on his toilette.

"If you mean my jacket, it is called a spenser, and it is very fashionable."

"Take it off at once."

I sighed and removed the spenser. I knew there was no use arguing with him.

He ignored me while he finished dressing, and allowed himself to be inspected by the valets, who at length nodded, indicating that no more improvements could be made.

The valets stood back against the wall, squeezing themselves into as small a space as possible.

Bonaparte, who had never been vain about his looks, scrutinized his appearance in the tall mirrors. I thought I detected the briefest, and slightest, of smiles cross his thin lips. Vanity, I thought. He has vanity in him after all.

He turned back toward me.

"Disgusting. No one wants to look at an old woman's tits."

"But sir—"

His stare was like ice.

I turned to go, then looked back, over my shoulder.

"I am much admired," was all I could think of to say. A feeble rejoinder, and I knew it.

"You are much flattered. And take off that ridiculous rouge! You look like a streetwalker. Which you almost are," I heard him mutter under his breath as he turned toward the nearby desk and sat down, pulling a pile of papers toward him.

"I must sign these dispatches," he said curtly. "You have ten minutes to dress yourself properly."

"I would rather throw myself off the roof."

"That would please us both, but I doubt if your children would be very happy. Now go away and do as you are told."

I hesitated, standing first on one foot, then the other. I was working up my courage to refuse his command.

He had picked up his pen and, having dipped it in the large crystal inkpot, was wiping it on a cloth. He knew that I was still standing there. He sighed. Without looking at me he lifted the heavy inkpot and hurled it in my direction.

It struck me in the stomach, making me cry out. Roustan and the two valets, who had witnessed all, made no move to aid me. Black ink flowed down my spotless white muslin gown and onto my new silver slippers. Soon the thick red and gold Turkish carpet under my feet was stained and ruined. Methodically Bonaparte went on signing the papers on his desk, blotting each as he signed it and setting it aside.

I turned and ran, my slippers squelching under me, my eyes blinded with tears. I ran down the endless corridors, past the long benches where the grooms waited to be called to service, past the apartments where my attendants (ladies in waiting in all but name) were standing in small groups, ready to go in to the ball. Past Hortense's rooms which were next to mine. Past the servants who guarded my door.

Wailing like a child, I ran into Euphemia's open arms.

43

AS SOON AS HORTENSE and I entered Foncier's, and she began walking listlessly from one polished glass case to another, glancing dejectedly at the sparkling rings and pins and necklaces inside, I knew something was very wrong.

Her engagement had been announced, we had been shopping for her trousseau for weeks and her apartment adjacent to mine in the Tuileries Palace was heaped with boxes of silken petticoats and gossamer-thin morning gowns, veils of English point lace and lengths of Turkish velvet and Indian muslin, magnificent necklaces of coral and pearls, plus all the gloves, stockings, muffs, cloaks, bonnets and soft cashmere shawls any girl could imagine having. Now she was in her favorite jeweler's, Foncier's, choosing a pair of earrings to wear at her engagement ball that night, and she looked more down-at-the-mouth than ever.

I went to her and kissed her on the cheek.

"What is it, my dearest girl?"

"Oh, maman—" She turned her head away, trying to hide her tears.

I nodded and smiled to Monsieur Foncier, who was watching our every move about the interior of his shop.

"How can I be of service, madame?"

"We will take these earrings," I said, indicating a beautiful pair of matching yellow diamonds. "Please have them sent to the palace."

"Of course madame. And may I add my very best wishes to the bride-to-be."

I hurried out of the shop with Hortense in tow. Once we were in our carriage Hortense gave in to her sorrow and wept into her cream linen handkerchief, with its embroidered initial *B,* for Buonaparte.

"Oh, maman, I am so miserable! I thought I could make myself accept him, perhaps even be happy with him. But I can't! I just can't!"

I tapped on the roof of the carriage and the driver cracked his whip. With a lurch we were on our way, back to the palace.

"It's Andrew, isn't it," I said as we passed along the roadway.

She nodded. "He wrote to me. He is in Lyon, with his regiment. He says he will never marry, if he cannot marry me. He wishes me happiness. But I can't have any happiness without him. I know that now."

Several months earlier, Hortense had agreed, with surprising alacrity as I thought, to marry Bonaparte's brother Louis. Bonaparte had not approved of her sentimental friendship with the fair young Anglo-Frenchman Andrew Falke. Instead he wanted a dynastic marriage for Hortense, one that would ensure that she would have a child, or preferably several children, who would bear the blood of the Bonapartes and of the Beauharnais.

"Since it is now clear that you and I will never have a child, Hortense must have one for us," my husband told me bluntly. We, his family, were the country's First Family. We were not royalty, yet we lived as though we were. We reigned—or rather, he reigned, and we obeyed him, as all his other subjects did. And, as he pointed out, a First Family needed a younger generation to carry on its name and inherit its power.

Hence the plan to marry Louis Bonaparte to Hortense. Only now Hortense was yielding to the weight of her sorrow.

"I have only seen Louis once, maman, on the night he proposed to me. But I know that there is something wrong with him. Why does he shut himself away in that chateau far from Paris? Why does he never come to see me or even write me? Why is his skin so dark and puffy and full of sores?"

"You will see him tonight, at the ball."

Louis Bonaparte had become an enigma. Once a handsome boy, outwardly mannerly, who had distinguished himself fighting at his brother's side in Italy, he had become a fleshy, sensuous man whose large troubled eyes darted here and there unnaturally. I had reason to know what lay beneath his courtly exterior; I remembered how he had fondled me and insulted me at the villa in Italy. But I hoped he had outgrown such boyish callowness.

Louis had not gone to war with Bonaparte in Egypt. Instead, Letizia and Joseph had decided to send him on a long tour of Sweden, Norway, the German lands, and finally Italy. When he returned from his many months abroad, he complained of severe pains in his joints and kept himself away from family gatherings, living like a recluse at the estate Bonaparte bought for him.

"Do you know what he told me he does, maman?" Hortense asked me. "He writes stories. Stories about women who turn into demons. He says all women are really demons, no matter how sweet they seem to be."

"I wasn't aware Louis was an author." I wondered whether Fanny knew of his books. So many people scribbled in those days, the bookstalls of Paris were full of slim volumes of stories about ordinary men and women who encountered otherworldly perils and monstrous enemies. There was a craze for the fantastic, not only in books but in paintings and the theater.

"Aren't you fond of him at all?"

She shook her head slowly.

"Andrew is the only man I have ever loved. I only agreed to marry Louis because I thought the general—I mean the consul—would be kinder to you if I married his brother. I hate the way he treats you."

I said nothing, merely patted her hand. The last thing I wanted was to have Hortense know how I suffered under my husband's increasing unkindness. I write "unkindness," out of habit; I should write, "cruelty."

"And that awful woman! That Belliotte! A tavern slut! How can you tolerate his bringing her here, to the palace?"

I shrugged. "He rules here. I am merely part of the decoration."

"Maman!"

"I do my best to tolerate what cannot be helped. Some men," I went on, unsure of how much I ought to say to Hortense, who had been largely shielded from the sordid aspects of sex, "find low women particularly exciting. Their own highborn wives seem dull by comparison."

"I hope Louis is not like that."

"You and Louis have only one obligation to each other, and to France. You need to give the nation a baby boy. Two baby boys would be even better."

"I understand that."

"If it is any consolation to you, I imagine that once you have your sons, Bonaparte would allow you to live apart from Louis."

"But not with Andrew!" Once again her tears gushed forth.

"Andrew will have a family of his own, and for the same reasons. He is heir to a fortune, a title, social position. He is a link between generations of Falkes."

We went on in silence, the carriage bouncing and rattling.

"When I was your age, Hortense, I was in love with Scipion du Roure, as I have often told you. More than anything in the world I wanted to be his wife. And he was in love with me too—in that strong, infatuated way only young people can know. But both Scipion and I understood, young as we were, that we would have to marry others. Others chosen for us by our elders."

"And it turned out badly for you, mother."

"Never say that. I have you and Eugene. I am very happy that marrying your father brought you to me. And Scipion is happy too. I have met his wife Julie many times. She is delightful, and we are friends. She has made him an excellent wife."

"But he doesn't really love her, does he? Not the way I love Andrew."

"No. And both Scipion and Julie have had other loves. And, of course, now she is very ill. She hasn't recovered from giving birth to her youngest child. It was a difficult birth, Scipion told me, an incompetent accoucheur."

Hortense was quiet. When she spoke her voice was very low.

"I dread all that, you know. Giving birth. Having babies. So many women die. So many babies die."

"We must get Euphemia to make you a fetish. I wore a powerful fetish on the night you were born."

"I think a good midwife will make more of a difference."

"You will have both. And don't forget. I was a midwife once. I helped to bring little Coco into the world."

"Coco, whose mother died."

What could one say? Hortense was right. Poor Selene had died, of exhaustion and fear and pain. I had been able to save one of Selene's twins, but not the mother.

Suddenly a terrible image flashed through my own tired, overstressed mind, an image of Hortense dying as Selene had died, following the birth of a child. What if her life were to be sacrificed for the sake of the dynasty my husband hoped to found? The thought angered me—yet made me feel guilty as well. If I had been able to have Bonaparte's child, then Hortense would not need to marry Louis Bonaparte. Perhaps she could have married her beloved Andrew, though Bonaparte would surely have tried to prevent that.

My thoughts were going in too many directions. I felt dizzy, and reached for the velvet rope that hung from the window, to steady myself. I forced myself to focus on the present moment, the swaying carriage, the shouting in the street outside our windows, and Hortense's taut, pale little face, the face of a girl about to do something she dreaded, for my sake.

44

IF HORTENSE THOUGHT that by marrying Bonaparte's brother Louis she would be sparing me mistreatment at the hands of my angry, resentful husband, she was wrong.

In fact, his punishing behavior toward me increased in the months following Hortense's marriage.

"Where do you think you're going, little fool?" he would call out to me across a crowded assembly room, when he saw that I was leaving the gathering early. "You'll stay till the end of the evening, like everyone else."

"Don't bother telling her anything," he would say with a laugh to anyone who tried to talk to me seriously. "She wouldn't understand. You know the old saying, 'Not much between the ears.'"

He made cruel references to my being an old hag, to my being sterile, even to my relationship to Barras, which was long over. When we were alone he called me slut and whore and told me again and again how everyone at his court wanted him to get a new wife, a young and pretty one.

"And I'm searching. Oh yes, I'm searching. I can feel it. I'm going into heat," he would say, and then he would send for Bellilotte or some lewd actress or coarse woman from a brothel and shut himself in our bedroom with her for the rest of the night.

That was only the beginning. After each of these encounters he would force me to listen while he described every detail of the woman's body, the size and form of the cleft between her thighs, the shape of her breasts, the curve of her hips, the smoothness or roughness of her skin, even the pimples on her private parts. Then he would tell me, sparing no detail, what course their lovemaking took, what noises she made, how he gave her pleasure and what she did to him in return.

"See!" he would exclaim, throwing aside his jacket and shirt, "here is where she bit me with her sharp little teeth when she was in ecstasy. Ah, she was a rare one!"

I held my ears but he pulled my hands roughly away, and sometimes bound them behind my back while he shouted about the pleasures he took, pleasures of every variety, some quite disgusting.

I begged him to stop, but he went on and on, goading me until I stood up to him and spat out ugly accusations and insults.

"It's a wonder, given all your prowess with these delicious women, that there aren't dozens of little Bonapartes running around. Tell me, how do you account for that?"

It infuriated him to be reminded that he had never—so far as he knew—impregnated a woman. Had he had a bastard child he would have boasted of it night and day.

"Could it be that the great Bonaparte is incapable of fathering a child? That it is not I who am at fault, but you?"

Whenever I said this Bonaparte shouted and swore and, quite often, lifted up chairs and tables, heavy metal candelabra and delicate firescreens and flung them against the walls. When this happened I fled, and he shouted after me that he would divorce me.

But then, late at night, when I had barricaded myself into Euphemia's room (I always went there for safety, for Euphemia kept a big sharp cane knife under her mattress), I would hear a scratching at the door. I knew that sound. I would open the door and see my husband standing there, looking pale and dejected, a blanket wrapped around him.

"I'm ill," was all he had to say. I always let him in, clutching his stomach. He lay with his head in my lap and I rubbed his chest and belly while he groaned, eyes closed, and complained, "No doctors! No medicine! No doctors! No medicine!"

I gave him oil of wintergreen to drink and eventually, after much rubbing of his stomach, I felt his tight muscles relax.

Where is your fat Bellilotte now, I wanted to ask. Where are all your other pert little tavern maids and dirty serving girls? I'm the one you come to for consolation when you really need it. But then, I'm also the one you slap and strike and shout at.

We went on this way, with Bonaparte behaving quite cruelly to me yet, in his weakest moments, clinging to me, while Hortense prepared to give birth to her first child.

Ugly gossip said that it was Bonaparte's child that Hortense was carrying, and not Louis's. I lived under this humiliating cloud (though knowing very well the gossip was untrue) throughout the long months of her pregnancy, until at last, in the late fall of 1802, she gave birth to my grandson Napoleon-Louis-Charles.

The tiny, red-faced baby boy squirming in his gilded crib was the heir to the Bonaparte succession. The hope of France, as my husband called him. He kissed Hortense and gave her a jeweled necklace with diamonds as large as pigeon's eggs, a necklace that had once belonged to Queen Marie Antoinette.

At the baptism, I was not given a prominent place. I stood at the back of the massed dignitaries, behind all the Buonaparte relations, behind the court officials and the marshals of the army and admirals in their gold braid and shining medals. I was expendable.

I was expendable as far as the succession went—but I still had my uses.

In a hundred ways, each day, I played my role as the First Consul's wife with skill and grace—or so I was often told. When members of the vast palace staff came to me with questions (how many guests would be attending the supper in the Gallery of Diana? Should the ice blue Sèvres china be used, or the burgundy with violet rims? Ought the fountain to flow with claret wine or another variety? Would the First Consul be requiring cherries beside his bed as usual, or should another fruit be substituted, since cherries often upset his stomach?), I invariably answered them in as practical a way as I could, using mostly common sense.

Not only were there questions from the chamberlain and cooks to be answered, but I had to decide delicate issues of precedence (who was to walk into the dining room, and in what order) and dress (I decided on black coats and trousers for the men in preference to blue coats and scarlet vests at some point, I can't remember exactly when). I had to decide on the nature of the many repairs the palace needed, and to order the painting of walls defaced by revolutionary graffiti. Some of the hundreds of rooms had to be simply locked up, and ignored; they bore the stains and ugly scars of revolutionary violence, and it would have been far too costly to repair them all.

Bonaparte expected me to bring back the elegance and manners of the old court, and so I taught the younger ladies to curtsey in the low, floor-sweeping manner used before the Revolution. I brought back the old dances, the felt-topped tables in the Salon des Jeux, even the low chairs called voyeuses, designed for spectators to straddle while observing the games of piquet and backgammon we played in that salon. Everything was as authentic as I could make it, given my usual laziness (yes, I admit it) and my limited knowledge of the old court. I had heard that Queen Marie Antoinette had gossamer-thin silken hangings in her boudoir, and so I ordered some just like them to adorn the walls. When one of the older chambermaids discovered, in a chest in the attic, a beautiful, much used quilt of velvet and taffeta and declared that this quilt had once covered the queen's immense canopied bed, I had it carefully cleaned and put on my bed, though when I pointed it out to Bonaparte he called it an old rag and laughed at me for using it.

There is one thing I have always been very good at; I remember people's names. At our many soirees, teas and receptions I was able to introduce people of varied backgrounds to one another (for we had a wide variety of people at the consular court) without stumbling over their names or titles, and I often found myself at the center of a very miscellaneous cluster of people—for example, a venerable duchess from prerevolutionary days, an aging debauchee from Paul Barras's circle, a brilliant young military officer with skintight breeches and a gleaming sword, and a titled Englishwoman of the kind Bonaparte called "cold and hideous," who recalled visiting Voltaire at his estate at Ferney and admiring the long, swanlike necks of his chambermaids.

I was at home in many sorts of company, for my experience of life had been uniquely varied. Thus I was able to listen patiently while an elderly general described his battles against the Turks, laugh at a joke about a choleric gourmand who died from eating too many strawberries, look properly offended (though I was not) when a rumor was spread about a titled nobleman who made love to his own valets and nod knowingly when someone remarked that the King of Denmark was often to be found visiting brothels.

Hour after hour, I stood, elegantly attired (or so I believed, Bonaparte's sour views to the contrary), listening politely to gossip, flattery, trivial remarks and the occasional veiled insult—and did not let my serene, benevolent smile fade.

I dined on pigs' heads and oysters, roast oxen stuffed with chicken, course after course of delicacies, always aware that my husband was far away, at the other end of the immensely long table, flirting and pawing the women he chose to sit near him.

I was useful, I was decorous, I knew how to be a good hostess. Many people thought (or so they said) that I looked lovely—at least from a distance. Bonaparte no longer slept in my bedroom, except on very rare occasions, though he did come and scratch at my door when his stomach pains were strong. He no longer wanted me, but to an extent he needed me. Or perhaps he simply had not yet found the courage to discard me.

"See here," he said to me one morning after summoning me to his study, "I am being put in an awkward position. I am about to be elevated to the rank of Emperor of the French. At some point in the future I will have to marry a princess, someone of royal blood so that together we can produce a child to rule Europe. I do mean to rule Europe, surely you are aware of that."

"Everyone is aware of that, sir."

"I cannot yet bring myself to put you aside. God knows why—but I cannot. As long as you are obedient, and keep your distance from me, and accept the fact of our separation and my complete freedom, I am prepared to make you my empress. But it is only temporary. When the right time comes, you must give up your position and accept a divorce. Is that understood?"

"I do not understand. Why don't you simply divorce me now"—I could not help weeping as I said these words—"and find an empress later?"

He reached for me and clutched me to him. "Because I cannot. I cannot. Not yet. Do not force me. Accept this bargain, and let me move on toward my destiny."

I crumpled, I wept, but at last I agreed. For however long it lasted, and however distasteful it might prove, I was willing to become Empress of the French.

45

OH WHAT A FUSS THEY MADE, those dreadful sisters-in-law of mine! How they tried to destroy my great day, the day of my coronation.

For weeks beforehand they set siege to Bonaparte, one after the other coming in and haranguing him (I could hear them at it), shouting at him that he must not let his disgraceful, unfaithful wife stand beside him at the sacred ceremony and receive the holy oil from the pope himself!

Why, it was tantamount to washing away all my sins, or so they said.

Beautiful Paulette, now haughtier than ever because she had become the wife of an Italian prince (her first husband General Leclercq having died), fat Elisa, who was herself a princess of some little place in Italy and unbearable Caroline, who gave herself airs as the wife of General Murat (who was unfaithful to her) and who refused even to look at me, she was so full of disdain and disgust.

And also there was Joseph's wife Julie, from a rather humble family somewhere in the south of France, who was not a nasty person like the others but who was influenced by Joseph to insist on my being excluded from the ceremony.

It was all so needlessly dramatic, and they were so malevolent to me! The only blessing was that my awful mother-in-law Letizia was not there. She stayed in Rome, away from it all, having told Bonaparte just how angry she was with him for not divorcing me years ago. To Letizia,

Bonaparte's political advancement was unimportant. What mattered was that he did not have a real family, with children of his own, and an obedient, subservient wife. A Corsican wife Letizia chose for him.

At least she stayed out of our way on coronation day, though she did come to Paris soon afterwards and made her usual trouble.

My coronation gown was beautiful. (A costume designer dressed us all, just as if we were characters in a play.) It was of white satin sparkling all over with gold and silver embroidery and diamonds. Tiny sprigs of lace stood up from the sleeves and neckline, creating a fairylike effect. Over the gown I wore a thick mantle of purple velvet, lined with ermine, that must have weighed a hundred pounds or more. The mantle had a long heavy train and when Paulette and the others were ordered to carry my train they exploded in fury.

Wasn't it shameful enough, Elisa told the grand chamberlain who was in charge of arranging the ceremony, that they had to walk behind me, they who were all respectable faithful wives, having to defer to a royal slut who everyone knew used to dance naked in all the drawing rooms of Paris. (Stories of my wild behavior during the days of the Directory were becoming more and more exaggerated with each passing year.)

They could not be expected to debase themselves by actually bearing my train, my sisters-in-law said. No, they would not, and that was that.

The chamberlain told the Master of Ceremonies, the Comte de Ségur, who told Bonaparte, who got angry and shouted at his sisters and Julie. They gave in, and from then on held up my train in a vengeful way, maliciously tugging at it and pulling me off balance. They took out their anger on me at every opportunity, stepping on my feet, Paulette actually shoving me, at the rehearsals, glaring at me venomously and calling me "old hag." They could hardly have been more childish, or more hateful. Bonaparte was particularly annoyed because just then, about a week before the coronation, he had acquired a new mistress and was spending his nights in her company.

I knew the signs: he yawned all day long, rushed through all his paperwork and wore twice as much Dumarsay cologne as usual. His apartments reeked of musk, I could not cross the threshold of his study without choking and coughing.

But this was not just any affair: he had seduced Eugene's beautiful blond fiancée, Elizabeth de Vaudey, leaving Eugene brokenhearted and dishonored.

I tried to tell Eugene that this was a blow directed at me, not at Eugene, that Bonaparte often did what he could to hurt me through hurting my children, knowing how much I loved them. But Eugene was inconsolable—and disillusioned, for he had always been loyal to Bonaparte and he knew, as indeed we all did, that Bonaparte loved him like a son.

It was a cold, cold day, coronation day, the trees heavy with thick white frost and a light snow falling outside Notre Dame, where a carefully chosen crowd waited, shivering, for the immense orchestra to play and the grand ceremony to begin. It was the first week of December, the chestnut vendors were warming their hands over their stoves outside the cathedral and there was a rim of ice at the edges of the Seine.

When we got down from our carriage and went inside the entire congregation stood and began to clap, music swelling toward the vast ceiling of the ancient church. I smelled incense, woodsmoke and the heavy scent of Julie's smelling salts (she had been feeling faint) as I took the arm of the handsome young valet appointed to escort me and began to walk down the center aisle, my slippers sinking deeply into the new purple carpeting.

I walked with difficulty, clinging to my escort's arm for support, for the unseen four women behind me, holding up my train, were constantly pulling me back. They had been instructed to walk in unison, but of course they did not; Elisa's clumsy tread was out of step with Julie's light brisk lope and Paulette, her attention on herself, went along at a pace all her own, as she had at the rehearsals, enjoying the attention her beauty attracted and dismissive of the task she had been assigned.

My husband was very regal in his suit of heavy white satin embroidered in gold and with a long gold fringe. He wore a wreath of laurel leaves that gave him an antique air, and when he moved he glittered with a thousand jewels. He looked sleepy, I thought, and kept yawning conspicuously throughout the high mass. I picked out Elizabeth de Vaudey among the onlookers, and Eugene—seated some distance from Elizabeth, looking somber—and Hortense, swathed in black wool against the extreme cold. She was about to give birth to her second child, indeed I wondered whether, with all the excitement and heightened solemnity of the coronation, she might go into labor right there in the church.

Louis was not beside her. His mysterious illness had worsened, and I was told (for I did not see him, no one but Hortense did, and his physicians, and one other) that his skin had erupted into a mass of ugly stinking boils, even the skin inside his nose. He walked like a drunken man, I heard, he had no control of his balance and had to use two canes to get from his bedroom to his sitting room. It was said that his physicians treated him with arsenic and bismuth—the traditional medicines for what we called the "English disease," the terrible sickness French soldiers catch from English whores.

I was amazed that he was able to father children, given his condition. He kept Hortense completely away from me at their palace in Holland (Bonaparte had made Louis King of Holland) and did not even let her write me letters, so I knew very little of her life with him. Euphemia did manage to find out, however, through Hortense's serving women, that Louis had told Hortense immediately after the marriage ceremony that he was in love with another woman and that this woman, a commoner, was living at the palace and was allowed into his presence frequently.

I had much to be sad about on that coronation day, though I did my best to rise above it and also to ignore the freezing cold in the great cathedral. I noticed that Bonaparte was very pale throughout the three hours or so we were in church and wondered whether his stomach was hurting him, as it often did on solemn occasions. In his impatience he prodded the cardinal who stood at the pope's right hand with his scepter, making the old man move faster as he prepared the holy oil for our anointing.

We knelt and the oil was poured on our heads and hands. The two ornate pearl and diamond crowns laid before the high altar were blessed and then, in a sudden departure from the rehearsed order of the ceremony, Bonaparte got up and lifted the larger of the two crowns and, very slowly and with the greatest drama, lowered the crown onto his own head.

The meaning of the gesture was not lost on the observers, or on the participants in the ceremony. Pope Pius VII had come all the way from Rome to place the crown on Bonaparte's head, just as, a thousand years earlier, the pope had come from Rome to crown the great Charlemagne. Now Bonaparte was telling the world that he had no need of the Holy Father—that he was emperor in his own right and by his own power, not by the grace of God and the church.

It was a very daring gesture, and a sacrilegious one. I felt ashamed, though by this point I was so very tired that all my feelings were dulled. I watched as Bonaparte picked up the smaller crown, my crown, and placed that too on his own head, then took it off and put it on me, over my diamond diadem, taking it on and off several times and adjusting it as if he were a milliner bringing a new hat to the palace for me to try.

More sacrilege, I thought.

Finally the climax of the ceremony arrived. Bonaparte and I began the long climb up the several dozen steps to where two golden thrones awaited us on a high dais at one end of the church. Here was where I needed my train-bearers, for the steps were steep and the ermine-lined velvet mantle felt like lead. A hush fell as we began our ascent—a symbolic ascent to power, to a transcendent height above the ranks of ordinary mortals. There were no sounds but the shuffling of feet and the occasional cough from the frozen congregation.

The reek of Julie's smelling salts was strong in my nostrils as I began the climb, but it soon grew faint, and as it did so, I felt the mantle grow heavy. I glanced back—and saw that none of my sisters-in-law was holding my train. They stood motionless at the foot of the wooden staircase, staring straight ahead of them. They did not lift a hand to help me. No one did.

Bonaparte, his own train-bearers lifting his heavy purple mantle, had already begun to climb toward his throne and was too far above me for me to call out to him.

I saw then with a terrible clarity that I was utterly and completely alone, and that unless I took off the heavy mantle I would be unable to ascend to my throne.

Then, all at once, I felt the heavy weight taken from my shoulders and I heard a voice say, "Follow your husband, madam. I am right behind you." Where had I heard that voice before? Confused but grateful, I took a step up, and then another, and realized with such relief that I almost felt weak at the knees that someone had come to my rescue.

It was not until I reached the top of the dais and took my place beside Bonaparte on my golden throne that I saw who my rescuer was. It was Christian de Reverard, the candle-lighter from the ballroom at the Tuileries, in his most elegant livery of blue and gold. He smiled at me and bent to adjust my mantle so that it draped around my feet, and I smiled back.

Then with a burst of trumpets and a thunder of kettledrums the orchestra began to play an anthem of triumph, and the crowd in the cathedral shouted "Vivat imperator in aeternam! May the Emperor live forever!"

Standing to receive the acclaim, I held on to the side of the chair as wave after wave of sound passed over and around me, echoes reverberating throughout the vast room, a baptism of sound for the beginning of my husband's imperial reign. He was now Napoleon I, and I, Rose Tascher of Martinique, was Empress Josephine, blushing, smiling, dizzy on my great height, and weeping from sheer relief.

46

THERE WAS A LEGLESS MAN who waited for the emperor outside the palace door nearly every day, wearing a tattered regimental jacket and torn stained trousers. He was shabby, woefully dirty, lost and obviously greatly in want.

Bonaparte had become accustomed to seeing him, and looked for him each day, disturbed when he was not there.

"Here, old father, have a drink on me," Bonaparte would say to the man, handing him a coin or two. Or, "Here, father, get yourself warm. Find yourself a room."

I always smiled at the man, for the sight of him tugged at me as it evidently did at Bonaparte, and when he saw my smile he usually nodded and touched his dirty black hat out of respect.

He was there outside the main entrance to the Tuileries, he was there in Milan, when Bonaparte had himself crowned King of Italy, and again in Mainz after the wars started again and the newly formed Grande Armée won victories over the Austrians. He was outside the walls of Vienna when Bonaparte's carriage passed by and in Paris again for the celebrating of Bonaparte's great victory over the Prussians at Jena.

Some days I did not see him, for in those earliest months after I was crowned empress I was often confined to my bed with the terrible headaches that seemed to get worse with each passing year. Traveling made my headaches more severe, and Bonaparte insisted that we travel constantly together, saying he did not trust me to be faithful if he left me on my own at my beloved home of Malmaison.

My physicians dosed me with calomel and tried to raise blisters on the back of my neck to relieve my pain. But they could not remove the true cause of my headaches: the fear I felt. Fear of Bonaparte's towering anger. Fear of poison. (Letizia came back from Rome with an Italian apothecary in tow, and everybody knew that apothecaries were renowned for their deadly poisons.) Fear that Joseph would once again try to arrange my death. And fear that the day was coming closer when Bonaparte would tell me I had to agree to a divorce—and with it, to want and loss.

Meanwhile there was the legless man, our shadow, the very embodiment of want and loss, for he was evidently penniless and could not move. There he was each day, and each day Bonaparte greeted him kindly and I smiled at him, and then we moved on.

Until one day he was not there.

Bonaparte noticed his absence, raised his eyebrows and then walked on past the usual crowd of waiting onlookers and stepped into his carriage. I followed—now that Bonaparte was emperor, I was required to walk some twenty paces behind him—and looked in vain for the legless man.

I found myself brooding on his absence, and wishing I had an explanation for it. I sent Christian—who following my coronation had become a sort of general factotum for me, always at my side to help me when others failed to—to the palace gates to look for the shabby veteran, to see whether he was waiting there and to give him a coin. But Christian came back shaking his head, and I went to bed feeling oddly worried and dejected.

For two days I continued to worry and fret, hoping that the poor man had come to no harm. On the third day, in the evening, as I sat alone at my embroidery frame near the windows in my small boudoir, I heard a voice from outside say, "Yeyette."

I turned toward the sound.

I knew that voice—knew it almost better than my own.

He leaned back against the stone wall just beyond my window, his arms folded, his gaze intense even across the distance that separated us. By the light of the torch fixed into the wall I could see that he was wearing the same tattered regimental jacket and torn stained trousers that I had seen on him every day, and he held the same dirty black hat in his hands, but his legs were sound and his face was no longer the pitiable face of an old veteran but the face of love.

"Donovan!"

I opened the windows and ran out onto the terrace, heedless of the cold, forgetting, in my delight, to look for the spies Bonaparte paid to keep watch on me. In an instant I was in his arms, my mouth on his, that tasted of wine and spices. I felt my body fold into his as it always had, his strong arms around me, his dear, warm, unshaven cheek against mine.

"Donovan, has it been you, all this time?"

He laughed. "Of course!"

"And you are not really hurt?"

"Not a scratch. Although I did get trampled once or twice by all the people waiting to see you and your famous husband."

"Quick! Before we are seen!" I pulled him inside my boudoir and shut the windows, closing the velvet curtains. I led him into the first of the three small rooms adjacent to mine that Hortense had lived in before her marriage to Louis, rooms still kept for her use though Louis never allowed her to come to the palace any more. We sat in the darkened sitting room, holding each other, talking softly.

"No one will find us here," I said, thrilled, excited at the prospect of hiding, like a child playing a game. I had not felt so alive in years.

"Won't there be a hue and cry?"

"Yes! Oh yes!" I was gleeful. "But they would never think to look here!"

He stroked my arm as we talked. His fingers were soft, warm, almost weightless. I reached up to touch his face. The face I had longed for, day after day, night after night, for so many years.

Just to hear him breathing and talking, to feel his fingers touch my arm in the dark, was a pleasure beyond description.

"You are all I believe in any more," I said, and then we kissed, and lay together on the broad sofa, our lovemaking all the more urgent because we could hear footsteps just beyond the wall, and voices calling out. The servants were asking one another where I had gone. I nestled into his arms, secure in the dark, aware that I had not felt secure in a very long time.

In Donovan's strong arms I was no longer empress, I was a treasured woman, ageless, vibrantly alive, whole and rich in feeling. The heavy garments of responsibility fell away and I was clothed in the fresh light clothes of a loved woman, beautiful and youthful and unencumbered.

Later, when Donovan had gone and I had returned to my boudoir I stood before my pier glass, astonished to see, not my usual careworn face and round, motherly body but a glowing girl, my face radiant, my skin shining, my body slender and lithe. I was all warmth and life, like a garden newly bathed in dew, the thirsty plants turning their leaves to the moistening rain. I shut my eyes and imagined myself back in Martinique, in the rain forest, the broad-leaved trees bursting into fulgent life all around me. The rich smell of the fallen leaves, the moist earth, the jungle flowers pressed in on me, and I felt as if I had been born anew.

47

MY MIGRAINES WERE GONE. My physicians were astounded, my servants, especially those who had witnessed my acute suffering for so many years, were frankly amazed. Only Euphemia, looking into my shining eyes and observing the changes in mood and appearance that had come over me, guessed the truth.

"So he's back, is he?" she said in an undertone.

"Yes, but you must keep his return a secret," I whispered, looking around to see who might be listening. "No one must know."

She smiled. "That face of yours is going to tell the world."

Several hours later Euphemia came to me again.

"Where is he staying?"

"Anywhere a legless man can take shelter I guess."

"You keep promising me a cottage of my own, at Malmaison," she said, "now that I am getting old."

Euphemia did not know how old she was, as her mother never told her the year of her birth, but we reckoned that she had to be close to sixty—and her wrinkled cheeks and pouchy eyes were proof of her advancing years.

"Maybe it is time to make good on your promise. He can stay with me."

It was a very good idea. Bonaparte rarely went to Malmaison and when he did he only visited the house and the grounds adjacent to it, not the extensive gardens and fields of wheat and vines, or the folds where I kept my Merino sheep, or the pig farm (Bonaparte hated pigs) or even the ponds where my black swans floated serenely amid the lily pads.

I told Bonaparte that I was going to build a small village, like the one Marie Antoinette had built at Versailles, and that I intended to house aging servants there.

"Good," he said, waving his hand dismissively, barely looking up from the papers spread out on his desk. "That will keep you busy."

What he meant was, that will keep you from harassing me about my mistresses.

With the chief architect from the Tuileries I laid out a plan for a hamlet of twelve cottages, to be built in a wooded setting around a pond. There would be a chapel, a stable, a blacksmithy and a small shop. Work began at once and within a month the first of the cottages, an ample brick dwelling with four bedrooms and a sizable gardener's shed, was nearly complete. Euphemia moved in—and Donovan quietly moved in at the same time, occupying a comfortable bedroom designed specially for him with a hidden trapdoor leading to the outside.

As one by one the other new villagers began to occupy their cottages, they were told that Euphemia had agreed to shelter a poor helpless veteran of the wars. They were sympathetic—and surprisingly incurious. They went their own way, and they let Donovan go his.

Bonaparte was preoccupied with his current venture: defeating the new coalition of enemies that had risen against France.

The forces of Prussia, Austria and Russia had joined forces to defeat us along with our old enemy Britain. It was a mighty set of foes—but then, as Bonaparte never tired of saying, it was his destiny to confront and destroy all the enemies of France.

"I shall take over all Europe," he announced. "It is in my stars. But you, Josephine, shall stay here and build your little village. I cannot take you with me where I must go this time. I will need to move too quickly. You would only slow me down, with your headaches and your complaints.

"Think of it," he continued, rubbing his plump soft small hands together, his left cheek twitching with a nervous tic. "Berlin, Warsaw, Vienna, even London—all under French rule—and soon. There is no force great enough to stop us. France is invincible. I am invincible."

I hardly heard his words. I was thinking of Donovan, and of how we would be able to be together, day after day, night after night, at Malmaison.

"This news agrees with you, I see," Bonaparte said, looking intently at me for the first time. "You are looking very well. Not so old."

"Thank you sire. It must be because I am looking forward to hearing of your great victories."

So Bonaparte went off to war, and I began spending most of my time at Malmaison, with Donovan.

We were discreet, and Euphemia, who had long been urging me to leave France and return to Martinique to live with Donovan, protected us. That I often spent time at Euphemia's cottage aroused no suspicion, for everyone knew how much I loved her and that we had been inseparable all my life. That Euphemia's veteran houseguest went to the main house on the estate—my mansion—aroused no suspicion either, for it was well known that he lived from my largesse (I saw to it that this story was spread) and I often entertained impoverished soldiers and sailors, mothers without husbands or male protectors, and various unfortunates from the nearby town of Rueil. I was viewed as a local benefactress. I was called "the Good Josephine"—a name that often made me laugh, when I considered my reputation and some of the events in my past.

Donovan and I spent long hours together, loving, holding one another, sharing meals—and talking, telling one another all that we had been doing and thinking since he left Paris so many years earlier.

"I often think what a terrible mistake I made, marrying Bonaparte instead of going back to Martinique with you," I told him. "I regret it every day." I told him of Bonaparte's cruelties, and of the odd tie that still bound us, despite all the turmoil in our marriage. "Sometimes he tells me he needs me. I am his good luck charm, he says. I am the only one who can give him solace when he is sick or troubled. I know that in a perverse way he loves me—even though he wants to hurt me.

"And he adores Eugene. He has adopted him, formally. My Eugene is now Eugene-Napoleon of France, a prince of the empire."

"I remember how Eugene worshipped the general when he was a boy," Donovan said with an indulgent smile.

"Eugene needed a father. Bonaparte filled that need."

"And you, Yeyette, needed a husband. And you knew I could not offer you marriage."

I hung my head. "Yes," I said quietly.

"You were right to make the choice you made. How could you know what Bonaparte was really like? He did not know himself. He has changed as he gains more and more power."

"How I hate it all! Being his wife, putting up with his mistresses, walking twenty paces behind him—"

"Being Empress of France."

"You know that matters nothing to me!"

"You enjoy being mistress of Malmaison. Had you come with me to Martinique, you would have been mistress of nothing at all."

He got up from the sofa where we had been sitting and walked to the fireplace. The hearth glowed bright, from time to time a burning branch split with a crack, sending a shower of glowing orange sparks upward. His face toward the fire, his back toward me, Donovan went on.

"When I got back I found my plantation in the hands of slave rebels. All the cane was burned, the house was destroyed. I had nothing. I was adrift, lost. I hid in the forest. There were outlaws there, black and white together. I joined them for a time."

He paused. When he went on his voice was strained, I could tell that what he was telling me was painful for him.

"The English came, their fleet anchored in the harbor of Fort-Royal. They were in charge, they were unopposed—but they had too few men to control the interior of the island. No one was really in charge. It had been like that for so long! I was foolish to imagine that my little plantation could survive amid all the chaos.

"Bonne Fortune! What an ironic name!" His laugh was bitter.

"There was an English officer, a Captain Jack Mowat, who approached me one night outside a tavern. I hadn't eaten in three days. I must have looked like something he'd hung from his yard arm."

"'Come on in and feed yourself,' he said. His French was poor but I understood well enough. He seemed kind. I was in no position to refuse what he offered. After I finished eating and drinking he put a bag of coins on the table between us."

"'How would you like to work for me?' he said.

"I was startled, but said nothing.

"'We can use a man like you in Paris. There is a ship in the harbor that can take you to LeHavre tonight.'"

"He wanted you to spy for the British."

"Yes."

"To turn against your country, your own people."

"No."

Donovan spun around and faced me, and came over to sit beside me once again.

"I have never told you about myself, about my origins."

"No."

"I was not born in Martinique," he said, taking my hand in both of his. "I was born in Ireland, in Dundreary. My name at my birth was Donovan Brown."

"Like my grandmother Catherine Brown! So we are—"

"Distant cousins, perhaps."

"I have only the faintest memories of Ireland. I never had a father. My mother died when I was very small and a man—he said he was my uncle, but I have no idea who he really was—took me aboard a ship. He called himself Jean de Gautier. So I became Donovan de Gautier. I think I must have been about four years old.

"He took me with him. It seemed we traveled the seas forever. I don't know what he was—a pirate, a merchant, maybe both. He kept me alive, for my mother's sake I think. There were battles. My uncle died, not of wounds but disease. We were becalmed. It was unbearably hot. He couldn't survive. I brought him water to drink—endless cups of water, but he just got weaker and weaker.

"Most everyone on the ship died. It was terrible. The smell—oh, the smell . . . I still have nightmares about it. Then a French ship came and rescued the few of us who were still alive.

"I still remember the captain's voice booming out across our deck.

" 'Come aboard! We are here to save you! Come aboard!' "

I shook my head in disbelief. "What a harrowing story!" I cried. "What an ordeal!"

"The French ship brought us to Martinique and left us there. I have been on my own ever since."

"And you still have no idea who you really are."

"I am Donovan Brown."

"Do you think Jean de Gautier was really your father?"

"I don't know. We didn't look alike. His eyes were very blue, like my mother's. Mine are brown."

"So when I first saw you, you were an orphan, living on your own. I used to try to guess who you were. You wore the clothes of a Grand

Blanc, but they were old, worn out clothes. And you did not look like the child of a Grand Blanc family."

"I belonged nowhere. I lived on the streets of Fort-Royal. I waited outside the bakeries and at the end of the day the bakers' wives would sometimes give me rolls. I fought vultures and wild dogs for scraps of meat. I learned to hold horses for a few coins. I ran with a pack of boys, mostly quatroons and octoroons. I learned French, a little Ibo and a little Carib. I remembered some Gaelic, but never used it. I always felt as though I belonged among the Grands Blancs. I wanted to be a soldier, a swordsman. I practiced against the other boys, with sticks, there in the street."

"Why did you come to Les Trois-Ilets?"

"I saw your grandmother in a shop one day. I heard her talking to some English people. Her accent was the accent I remembered from my childhood. She reminded me of my mother, and my lost home. I heard that she lived at Les Trois-Ilets. So I went there—and then I saw you."

It was by far the longest speech I had ever heard Donovan make. It explained a great deal.

"My dear grandmother! She was always so outspoken, so very tart!"

"You are like her in that way."

I smiled. "I hope so—a little.

"But tell me, why are you revealing all this to me now?"

Instead of answering he folded me in his arms and kissed me, long and lovingly.

"Because I must leave you, dearest Yeyette. And soon. And I may never see you again."

4 8

HE LEFT A FEW DAYS LATER. As he prepared to go, gathering his things with the help of Christian, he told me the reason for his haste, and revealed the plan in which he hoped to play a vital part.

"What I tell you both now is known to very few. You must not repeat it."

"Of course not," Christian and I said, speaking as one.

"You will be protected by the simple fact that no one will suspect you. The sweet, vague, kindhearted empress and her faithful manservant: no one would imagine you might carry important information of use to the enemies of France."

"It is because I am a good Frenchman that I assist you," said Christian staunchly. "I am a supporter of the true king, Louis XVIII, in his court in Warsaw, and not of this false, self-made Emperor Napoleon, who has no royal blood yet believes that he owns the earth!"

"There are many who feel as you do, Christian. King Louis will one day rule, I am certain of it."

The old king, Louis XVI, had left a son behind when he was executed but the boy had died in prison. His rights passed to his uncle Stanislaus, who called himself Louis XVIII.

I had never taken any interest in politics. I had observed the ebb and flow of power, to be sure, and had even helped to turn its direction one way or another, but power itself never captured my interest.

That kings should rule over others seemed to me natural and right. After all, there had been kings in France for hundreds of years. They were a race set apart, born to govern others. But now, in our day, for the first time, the power of kings had been questioned, and challenged, and ultimately set aside. Now, it seemed, the strongest man, or the richest, or the most frightening, was thought to be the one who ought to rule.

My husband Bonaparte had simply taken power. Stolen it. Or so it seemed to me, as I began to think about the subject seriously for the first time. The more I thought, the more I realized that everything about Bonaparte was false: his titles, his claims to sovereignty, the ceremonies he invented to impress the public. He was a sham. And I was a sham as well. I was part of his façade.

His military victories were not false, to be sure; they were genuine enough. But his authority to lead armies was not legitimate. It was based on theft—the theft of the true royal authority from King Louis XVI, an authority now possessed by King Louis XVIII.

I knew that my thinking on this subject was very simple, yet I felt there was truth in it. And if Donovan was prepared to fight for the cause of the monarchy, then I ought to be too.

I listened closely to all that Donovan told me on our last night together. We sat before the fire, drinking wine, allowing ourselves to be lulled into drowsy relaxation. We fed each other Donovan's favorite chocolates, the kind called "Venus's Nipples." No one disturbed us, through the long night hours.

"I will remember this night," Donovan said as I laid my head on his chest. "The warmth, the comfort, the feel of you beside me. I will carry it all with me into the nights to come."

"Where will you be?"

"Portugal. Then, if we succeed, probably Spain."

"And if you do not succeed?"

"Then you will hear nothing further. You will know that I am— beyond reach."

He rubbed my cheek gently with his knuckles.

"We must stop him, you know. It must be done, before he swallows up everything we value. He will never stop on his own. He will never be satisfied."

"Have you heard that he has been sending his political enemies to the Seychelles Islands? At court they are calling this purge the 'Little Terror.' It is a repeat of the Great Terror, the one under Robespierre that I remember so well."

"Then if I disappear, and you hear no news from Portugal, you can send someone to the Seychelles Islands to find me."

He got up to put a log on the fire and sat down again.

"I have heard him say he means to conquer the world," I remarked.

"It is not just a boast. The latest information I have from Captain Mowat is that right now Bonaparte is plotting to divide Asia between himself and the Russian tsar Alexander. They have drawn up maps showing how they mean to divide the continent. They have signed treaties and agreements."

"The Chinese may balk at being ruled by a Corsican," I said with a smile. "They have their own emperor, if I am not mistaken."

"And don't forget India. The general would have his hands full defeating the British there. It all reminds me," Donovan went on, "of an old poem I heard recited once, about love, and sitting and finding rubies beside the Ganges, and wooing that goes on forever—if only there were world enough and time."

I hugged him.

"Only now it is fighting that seems to go on forever," I said at length.

"Not forever. As a matter of fact, there are a number of French generals who are conspiring against Bonaparte even as we speak."

"Which generals?"

"It is better that you not know any names. But they are active. They are working secretly to undermine Bonaparte's authority with the soldiers. They call him tyrant. They refer to him as 'The Sultan.' Even members of his own family are listening to the dissidents."

"What?"

Donovan nodded. "Including your old enemy Joseph."

"I can't believe it."

"It is true. They say Bonaparte is looking for a way to reassure Joseph and retain his loyalty."

I had been pondering politics; now I was confronted with one of its murkier aspects: the problem of assuring loyalty.

"Bonaparte retains his position through fear. But with family, fear is not the strongest motivator. There has to be a bond of blood, a bond so deep nothing can destroy it."

"I always thought the Buonapartes were inseparable, that they would stand together, no matter what."

"Joseph can be lured away. He is envious of his younger brother's success and this envy leads to rivalry and malice."

Our long beautiful night together gave way at last to the earliest pink light of dawn. Donovan dressed quickly in his disguise, slipping into the shabby clothes and black hat of the legless veteran, spreading a thin layer of grey ash on his face to make himself look older and unhealthy and pulling his hair down across his forehead to make it look unkempt.

Christian arrived to help him onto the small wheeled platform that was his usual way of getting around, and to lift his bags. A cart waited at the edge of the wood to carry him to Dieppe where arrangements had been made for him to cross by fishing boat to England. From there he would join the expedition to Portugal.

We embraced fervently one last time. I kissed his ash-covered cheek.

"If only you could stay!" I could not prevent myself from saying.

"I have never been good at anything but being a soldier, Yeyette. That is what I have to offer. I offer it gladly—only with a divided heart, for part of me stays here, with you."

"And part of me goes with you, my own dearest Donovan."

He trundled off in the murky dawn light, along the path that led around the lake and into the thick stand of trees, an unobtrusive, pitiable figure in his worn uniform, just another casualty of the wars, a legless veteran doing his best to sustain life in perilous times.

49

MY BELOVED OLDEST GRANDSON CARLO lay on the little bed I prepared for him at Malmaison, a bed fit for a royal child with gilded eagles at its head and foot. Sweat poured from his fair hair down his forehead and into his eyes, and his sweet face was flushed red with fever, yet he smiled at me when I bathed his forehead with a wet cloth and smoothed back his wet hair.

He had been very ill for nearly a week. As soon as I got Hortense's message from The Hague saying Carlo was ill I ordered the swiftest, lightest carriage from the imperial stables and rushed to Holland to get her and the boy. Her husband Louis had been behaving very oddly, Hortense said, and she needed to get herself and Carlo away from him as soon as possible.

Louis, she told me, had taken to shutting himself in a dark room for days on end to work on his forever unfinished stories, refusing to see a doctor about his own worsening sickness and forbidding any doctor to visit his ailing son. Her contempt for him was evident in her words. She described her husband as a walking pustule, covered in weeping sores, unsteady on his painful legs, his vision growing weak and his temper becoming ever more menacing. Most striking of all, she said, was his complete and unswerving attention to his stories. Nothing else mattered, she told me, not his health or the health of their son, not his kingdom, certainly not his marriage. All he wanted was to seek solitude, to be left alone to write.

Carlo began coughing, and couldn't seem to stop. Hortense and I helped him to sit up. We patted his back, spoke soothingly to him, gave him tea with honey to drink—knowing, all the time, that nothing was helping him and that he was getting worse. Each time he coughed he spat up blood, and with it, a thick greenish fluid that stank horribly.

I sent for the physician who had helped me after my terrible fall in Plombières, Dr. Morel. His manner was comforting, though I remembered very well how ineffectual his methods had been when I was in such agony after my fall. He looked considerably older than he had in Plombières, stouter and more red in the face.

"Your Royal Highnesses," he said when he arrived at Malmaison, bowing to each of us in turn, then going immediately to little Carlo's bedside.

"Has the boy been bled?" he asked, honorifics forgotten in the intensity of his concern for his small patient.

"Yes," Hortense answered. "I opened a vein myself as soon as he felt hot to the touch. I knew he had fever."

Hortense showed the physician the recent opening she had made in the crook of Carlo's scarred little arm.

"This vein has been opened before," he said, scrutinizing the injury. "Many times before."

"Carlo has often been ill. His father does not allow any physicians in the palace. So I bleed Carlo myself. It is my belief," she added, "that Carlo and his brother are often ill because they are near my husband, who grows more and more ill all the time."

The doctor looked up at Hortense. "What is the nature of his illness?"

Hortense looked over at me, but I had no advice to offer her. No one in the Buonaparte family had ever admitted that Louis had the English disease, but it was obvious to everyone. The stigma attached to that disease was very great, the shame to the family enormous.

"It is the disease no one wishes to name," Hortense said bravely.

"Ah. I understand. I have treated many patients with this unnamed disease. Tell me, does your husband find it hard to maintain his balance when he walks?"

"Yes."

"And does he have a severe rash, with infected blisters?"

"Yes."

He nodded knowingly. "I suppose his sight is growing dim, and his temper very difficult?"

"Your conjectures are accurate, doctor."

He put his hand on Carlo's hot forehead. "How long has he had this fever?"

"About nine days."

"Is he able to take any nourishment?"

Hortense shook her head, and began to cry quietly.

"Your Royal Highness, if it is any comfort to you, I do not believe your son has his father's disease. That disease is confined to women of easy virtue and the men who visit them. It is incurable. Your husband will not live to be old."

"Doctor! Must you be so blunt? You see how upset my daughter is."

"Your Imperial Majesty, when dealing with disease it is always best to speak the truth. Not to disguise it behind lies, or make it more palatable by using false terms. The truth is the truth."

I was afraid that the doctor would blurt out the truth about Carlo: that he would not live. I felt certain of it, as certain as if I had told his fortune.

My sorrow at this prospect was great, yet nowhere near as great as Hortense's. Carlo was her favorite, her firstborn. I thought how terrible would be my pain if I lost Eugene. My dear Eugene, who had only recently married and presented me with a grandchild and namesake, little Josephine. I wore a lock of her baby hair near my heart.

But I was wrong about what Dr. Morel would say. After examining Carlo thoroughly, he drew a small packet from his bag and gave it to Hortense, telling her to mix the contents with watered wine and pour it slowly, drop by drop, into Carlo's mouth.

"It has a sweet taste, he will not reject it. But do not give it to him too quickly, or his stomach may not absorb it all.

"I will return in the morning," he said and then, with a bow, left us.

We stayed by Carlo's bed, now sitting together watching over him, now resting on sofas. Euphemia and Coco joined us, and kept vigil while we rested.

Coco had grown into a lovely girl, with skin only slightly darker than Euphemia's. She was maturing swiftly, her limbs lengthening, her face losing its childish plumpness. Though I had told her who her parents were she did not know the story in any detail, how my father's liaison with Selene had upset the household in Martinique and how Selene had died during the slave rebellion. I told her only that our father had loved Selene and that she had been a beautiful woman. There seemed no need to add how disruptive Selene's sultriness had been, or how manipulative she herself had been. Coco was not like her mother in that way, she was a more thoughtful, unselfish girl and it was like her to be concerned about Carlo, the cousin she loved.

Dr. Morel returned in the morning as promised. He examined Carlo while Hortense and I sat nearby, waiting anxiously for his conclusions, watching his every move, scanning his face in an effort to read his grave expression.

When he finished he came and joined us. He looked resigned, and Hortense gripped my hand apprehensively.

"Dear ladies, I am going to speak to you now, not as physicians usually speak to royal persons, but as someone who has a high enough regard for you both to give you my honest views.

"The boy is gravely ill." Hortense stifled a sob. "There are efforts we can make, if you choose, with leeches and cupping and further bleeding, but if this boy were my son or grandson I would treat him with kindness and simply let him sleep his way quietly out of this world."

Tears spilled from my eyes as he went on. "I do not honestly believe that he can be brought back to health, only that he can be made to live a few more tortured days, in pain, his mind increasingly disordered. In the end it will not even comfort him that you are near. We will pray that God grants him health. But I recommend that we do nothing further ourselves to prolong his weak life."

Hortense released my hand and ran from the room.

"I am going to leave these opiates with you," the doctor said, taking several packets from his bag. "They will help him sleep. You know where to reach me if you should need my help again."

I managed to mumble my thanks as the doctor left but my heart was leaden with sorrow. I went to find Hortense and attempted to comfort her.

It is hard for me now to remember all that happened in the next few days. I know that I made an effort to eat, and bathe, and to reply when the servants came to me for their daily instructions. I thought of sending for Louis but Hortense insisted that he would not come. With the help of

Christian I managed to compose a dignified bulletin to appear in the court circular, announcing that Louis-Napoleon-Charles, grandson and namesake of the emperor, was in failing health. A swift rider was sent east to Warsaw, where Bonaparte was holding court, to inform him of the impending tragedy. But I knew that the message would not reach him in time.

In the end there was nothing we could do but sit by Carlo's bedside, watching as his life ebbed. We sang to him, lullabies and children's songs, and Euphemia repeated prayers in the Ibo tongue. Coco diligently gave Carlo the soothing drug Dr. Morel had left with us, and felt his forehead from time to time, and changed his linen. I admired her devotion, and could not help noticing that she began coughing and that beads of perspiration were forming on her forehead and running down her cheeks.

By the time Carlo's funeral was held, Coco was burning with fever, and once again I summoned Dr. Morel.

In those cruel days I suffered twice, once when my dear grandson was taken from me and again when Coco, the child I had brought into the world so many years before, followed him to the grave. Carlo was taken back to his father's kingdom for burial, but Coco, my half-sister, who had never had a real name or a real home other than with me, I buried in the chapel at Malmaison, beneath a small stone monument that read simply "Beloved Child of the Islands."

50

I WAS ON THE WAY OUT. The time had come. I could tell by the way I was treated by the courtiers, the way my principal lady of honor, the haughty former Duchesse de La Rochefoucauld, elderly and contemptuous, showed her disdain for me with every swish of her heavy silk skirts, every scornful glance from under her sparse eyebrows. As though she were the real empress and I was only an imposter!

She was much older than I, and we remembered each other from the days—so long ago now!—when I was a new bride just arrived from Martinique and Alexandre spent a great deal of time with her husband. I was then a gawky provincial, who spoke French with a thick creole accent and had no education; I was awkward in society though it did not take me long to find my place within it.

The former duchess, belonging to the old aristocracy and of much higher birth than I, looked down on me and was offended that I should be elevated to the rank of empress. Like everyone else at court, she knew that soon Bonaparte would divorce me and marry a princess, a woman of royal blood; I was no longer deserving of respect or honor.

The duchess, and her haughty attitude, set the tone for all my ladies. They regarded me with disdain. They were lax in serving me, and attending on me. With Bonaparte away from court, in Poland and later in

Spain and Austria, there was no one to reprimand the wayward servants and officials of my household.

I was badly served and subjected to much unkindness, surrounded by people who despised me and could not wait to have me gone.

At that time, given the extreme anxiety I felt, I even feared that I might be poisoned, so that Bonaparte as a widower could choose a royal bride. I had never, even for a minute, forgotten Joseph's plot to kill me. (How could I forget it, when I still had chronic pain in my back and legs from my terrible fall?) Nothing would be easier than to slip some arsenic or other poison into my food. Italians were very good at that, everyone said. There would be no suspicion—at least not overtly expressed. To openly suggest that the empress had been poisoned would be treason, and no one wanted to be accused of treason, for the emperor was still sending traitors to the Seychelles Islands and they were never heard from again.

Two Polish noblewomen visiting Paris brought back news from Warsaw—news of my husband's liaison with a pretty blond eighteen-year-old named Marie Walewska.

"But is she royal?" I wanted to know. "Does she have royal blood?"

"No," I was told. "She is a noblewoman, but she has no royal blood."

Ah, I thought. Then I am safe. He won't marry her.

"But they say he is very much in love with her, Your Imperial Highness," the younger and prettier of the two Polish women said with a venomous smile. "And, as we have heard, it is his plan to take a new wife. One who can give him children."

"Children are a gift from God," I said, as icily as I could. "And how many do you have?"

"I—that is, well, at present—"

"She has had only miscarriages, Your Imperial Highness," the older noblewoman admitted, "but is still young enough to bear living children."

"If she hurries," I said, looking her up and down as if to assess her age, and assessing it unfavorably.

It was the sort of conversation I found myself in too often these days, an exchange of insults. I found such conversations more tedious than wounding, yet the longer Bonaparte stayed in Warsaw, and the more people gossiped about his liaison with the pretty young countess, the more tense I became.

"She has a husband, to be sure," the former Duchesse de La Rochefoucauld announced to the ladies of my suite, who were eager for every nuance of information about Madame Walewska, "but he is very old, over seventy. And she is obtaining a separation from him."

"Oh?" I said. "Why only a separation? Why not a divorce?"

"Divorce is not permitted in Catholic Poland," was the arch reply.

"But in France it is allowed, even though we too are Catholic." There was a murmuring among my ladies—the inevitable response to any mention of divorce.

The former duchess turned slightly toward me, with a swish of her skirts.

"As Your Imperial Majesty is aware, the rights of the church are a matter on which His Holiness and our emperor have worked out a compromise."

"Like the compromise between the adulteress Madame Walewska and her conscience," I snapped.

A titter ran through the room, and several of my ladies hid their mouths behind their fans.

"Adultery may not be the most suitable topic for discussion," the former duchess said acidly. "May I suggest another?"

"By all means, madame. What shall it be? Loyalty, perhaps? Kindliness? Avoidance of hurtful gossip?"

But the subject of Bonaparte's liaisons could not be suppressed, as it was bound to affect the entire imperial court when, one day, he found the woman he intended to marry and bade farewell to me. When that day came, and it could not be far off, my household would be dissolved and the new empress would choose who would serve her. Appointments would be lost and gained, status changed. In the meanwhile the news from Poland would be eagerly exchanged and endlessly discussed.

But I, in the privacy of my interior apartments, had a secret no one knew: I had my letters from Donovan.

They arrived in the most unlikely of guises. Sometimes there would be a silk lamé gown delivered from a dressmaker, with an underskirt that had a hidden pocket filled with sheets of writing. Sometimes a basket of melons would arrive at the palace for me and in the lining of the basket I would find a note. My Russian wolfhound Mitka wore a wide collar with a pouch for carrying small packages; from time to time I found a letter inside the pouch. I never knew when I might receive a message, but they came frequently, and with each new message I felt a fresh surge of hope.

"My own Yeyette," Donovan wrote,

I am with you in my every thought. Never doubt this. We are in Portugal near the seacoast. Our commander Lord Wellesley is a stalwart man. I am with the Highland Light Infantry but will go in disguise into Spain very soon. Burn this note! And pray for your Donovan.

Not long afterwards another message informed me that he had made his way into Spain.

You would be very surprised if you saw me Yeyette. I am now in disguise as an Irish priest hiding in a mountain village. The Spaniards shelter me. They hate the Great Satan (as they call Bonaparte) and want to see him defeated. They hate the French. It is said Bonaparte is coming to Madrid. You are in my heart.

Soon all the talk at court was of Spain. Bonaparte left Warsaw, and Marie Walewska, and marched to Madrid where his army conquered the city and then attacked the invading British. I could hardly sleep at night, I was so worried about Donovan. I did not know the name of his village, or even what province he was in. His messages began to come less frequently. He wrote of taking part in ambushes and raids, of having to steal food to survive, of midnight assaults and dangerous clashes with French squadrons. As winter closed in, I received the shortest note yet, scrawled in a trembling hand:

Dearest Yeyette, your image is forever before me. I am so cold and there is nothing to eat. I need you. Donovan.

I was always careful to burn the messages I received but this one I could not bear to destroy. I felt that it might be the last letter I ever received from Donovan. With dread I folded it up into a tiny square and put it inside the charm Euphemia made me wear around my neck for protection. I vowed never to take it off.

Not long afterwards Christian came to me in a much agitated state. I was presiding over a ceremony at court but managed to excuse myself on the pretext of feeling unwell. As I left the room I felt many pairs of eyes on me, wondering, speculating.

"What is it, Christian?" I asked when we were alone. "Is it Hortense?" Hortense was recovering from childbirth, having had another son, whom she named Charles-Louis-Napoleon.

"No, Your Imperial Majesty, it is news from Spain. Dire news." He looked quickly around to assure himself that we were not being observed, and even pulled back a nearby curtain to see if anyone was behind it. There was no one.

"There has been a terrible battle at a place called La Coruña. Bonaparte sent in all his men to attack the British, who had been starving and dying all winter. The British fought bravely, but they had no bullets left. They stood where they were, hacking at the French with their bayonets. Many died. The rest went to the seacoast and had to be rescued. It must have been a sight to see, all those hungry soldiers being rowed out to meet the warships on fishing boats, dinghies, smugglers' trawlers, anything that would float."

He shook his head, as if in disbelief at the imagined sight he was describing.

"And Donovan?" My voice was choked, I could barely speak.

"I don't know. I have heard nothing. But there is no reason to despair. He may not have been with the army. His task was to sabotage the French, and to gather information. Not to fight. He is a clever man. A survivor."

"In his last message to me he said that he was starving."

"I don't know, Your Imperial Majesty. I simply don't know. We must hope for better news soon. In the meantime, the opposition to Bonaparte is growing. Even within the army, and here at court. They say Bonaparte is having to divide his army, that he is being forced to fight in too many places at once. He is leaving Spain to fight the Austrians. Once he leaves, the British will invade again."

I returned to the salon where the ceremony was in progress. I leaned on Christian's arm. I felt shaky, uncertain of my footing.

"Courage, empress," I heard Christian mutter. "Be brave. Fight with your bayonet."

I smiled. But after the ceremony ended, and the last of the guests and courtiers had bowed and curtseyed their way out of the salon, I felt a great emptiness inside. Though the ceremony had been a long one, and I had eaten nothing for many hours, I had no appetite. I felt listless, numb. As if all my thoughts and feelings had been purged.

As I made my way back to my apartments, passing along the maze of corridors in the great sprawling palace, I came upon a message scrawled on a peeling wall in stark black paint. I reeled in shock. It read: EMPRESS OF NOTHING.

51

I WORE WHITE TO MY DIVORCE. It was a pretty dress, in very fine muslin, several layers of it, with a gathered bodice, low cut, that flattered my bosom and puffed sleeves in the newest style. I wore a veil, not unlike a wedding veil. My gown had a train, with a wide row of lace and ruffles, but this time, unlike my coronation, there was no question of any Buonapartes carrying my train, or refusing to carry it. I was on my own.

Most of the Buonapartes were present, there in the candlelit throne room, for the divorce ceremony. They stood there gloating, their long campaign to get rid of me over at last. Paulette, very beautiful in her maturity, yet so ugly and spiteful inside, Caroline, sleek and smug, hateful Elisa, who I knew to be in conflict with Bonaparte over her title and her lands, always greedy for more, and Louis, his pustulant face all but hidden under a slouch velvet hat with a very wide downturned brim, seated because he could no longer stand for more than a minute on his unsteady legs.

Joseph was not present, he was in Madrid attempting to restore order to his strife-torn kingdom, and my awful mother-in-law Letizia was not present either, thankfully. It would have made me very angry and upset indeed to see her there among her children, steely-eyed, hostile, knitting with her black yarn and crossing herself and muttering "Gesù!" every time my name was mentioned.

My good, dear Eugene was there, but as Bonaparte's deputy, not as my comforter or supporter. He stood beside the emperor, who was now, of course, his adoptive father, and waited to be of service. He was Prince Eugene now, I reminded myself, a married man and a father (his wife Augusta, of whom I was fond, was a Bavarian princess), a wounded, decorated war hero and among Bonaparte's most valued commanders. He had grown into a fine man, a man any mother would be proud of. Yet on this day he was trembling visibly, his hands shaking as he handed Bonaparte the divorce documents, his entire body quivering with such agitation that I thought he might have an apoplectic fit.

He was torn; his loyalty to Bonaparte was very strong, his honor as an officer unimpeachable. He would do his duty, obey his orders. Yet his love and loyalty to me knew no bounds—and today he was being commanded to assist in the painful process of making me a divorced woman.

Shame, sorrow, pity, and a lasting stigma: that was divorce. From this day on I would be a discarded, disgraced woman, and Eugene was about to collaborate in any disgrace. It was no wonder he was trembling.

I stood before a table where the official papers severing me legally from my husband were spread out. Bonaparte sat behind the table, in a thronelike chair. It was a civil divorce, to be sure, not a religious annulment. Six months earlier the pope had excommunicated Bonaparte and once again the imperial throne and the Vatican were at odds. But the important thing was, once these papers were signed, Bonaparte would be legally free to marry again. As would I

I would be free to marry! Why did the thought bring me no joy, only apprehension? Was it because the only man I would think of marrying, Donovan, was not the kind who would ever tie himself legally to one woman? Or was it because, having been wed to two men already, one of whom, Alexandre, was practically married to another woman already and the other, Bonaparte, had treated me with exceptional cruelty for years, I was frightened by the thought of ever being a bride again?

I did not know. All I knew was that, at long last, the dreaded day had come, the day I would once again be Yeyette Tascher from Martinique, former viscountess, former empress, former mistress of the Tuileries, former wife of the most powerful man in Europe, Napoleon Bonaparte.

I stood quietly, listening to the opening remarks made by a court official. I tried to remain composed, but felt faint. I could hear Paulette snickering, and Elisa sniffing. I swayed slightly, and reached for Christian's arm to steady me. I saw Eugene start to come toward me, but shook my head ever so slightly and smiled, to indicate that I was all right. The look on my son's face, a look of deep anguish and concern, wrenched my heart.

The moment came when I had to read the speech Bonaparte had written for me.

"With the permission of my dear husband," I read, "I proudly offer him the greatest proof of devotion ever given to a husband—"

I could not go on, my tears were flowing too fast. I handed the paper I had been reading from to Christian, who read the rest of it in a strong, clear voice.

It was a touching ceremony, dignified and elevated in tone. Yet everyone present knew the stark reality behind the solemn words, the truth about our fissured marriage. The many mistresses my husband had had, his liaisons with actresses and dancers, titled ladies and courtesans. His long love affair with Marie Walewska, who had recently borne him a son. The quarrels. The stubborn silences. The tearful reconciliations. The passion thwarted, the love cankered and soured and turned to hate.

And yet, despite the freight of emotion in that candlelit room as the ceremony concluded, there was a residue of affection. Bonaparte rose and came toward me, and kissed me on the cheek. "I will always be your friend," he murmured.

My friend! My nemesis, more likely. I had no doubt that, whatever tender sentiments he may have expressed, he would quite ruthlessly do me injury whenever it suited him. And if he should find out about my renewed liaison with Donovan, what then? I did not allow myself to imagine the consequences. For even though I was no longer his wife, I had no doubt that he still counted me among his possessions, part of his vast empire of lands, goods and chattel.

I set off for Malmaison, my own place, my fortress, my refuge. I was glad to be leaving Marie Antoinette's former apartments, with their host of memories, and the haunting presence of the late queen. I realized, as I left, that I had been living under her shadow for many years and I was stepping out from under that dark penumbra.

When I reached Malmaison, and drove up through the front gate, I was much moved to see that all the servants and tenants from the estate farms had assembled in the broad courtyard to wait for me. There were hundreds of them, the grooms and valets in their velvet livery, the maids in their long blue gowns and white aprons, the herdsmen in their muddy trousers and their jackets, the farmers and gardeners, even the laborers who were building a new wing on the house came down from the scaffolding to stand quietly, hands folded, in respectful attendance as I reached the main door of the house.

They did not clap or cheer, as the crowds at the Tuileries had always done. But their silence was eloquent. And as I alighted from the carriage and began to pass among them, reaching out to touch as many hands as I could and saying "Thank you, my good people," I heard many a voice call out, "Welcome home, Good Josephine."

52

WE HAD BEEN HEARING for several years about The Austrian archduchess Marie Louise.

She was very young, a child really, barely out of the schoolroom. But she was said to be tall for her age (she was only seventeen when Bonaparte divorced me), and haughty, as would be expected in a great-niece of the former queen Marie Antoinette, and she played the piano fairly well and knew how to sketch and draw.

To be sure, she was gawky and ungraceful, and quite plain, with pop eyes and the family curse, the ugly Hapsburg lip; everyone agreed that in my prime, I would have outshone her as the sun outshone the stars. But then, I have no royal blood, and Marie Louise was an emperor's daughter.

I didn't really know what to believe about her. Unkind people, people who wanted to wound me, remarked on her lovely complexion and shapely arms and hands and said that she had a good intelligence and the kindest eyes in the world; more tactful friends confided to me that her cheeks were far too red and her body far too fat for a girl of seventeen. At twenty-five, they whispered, she would look like a hefty Austrian barmaid, not an empress.

But on one point all were agreed: Marie Louise would very probably give Bonaparte the thing he wanted most, a son. The Hapsburgs were fertile. Marie Louise's mother had had thirteen children, her great-grandmother had had twenty-six sons and daughters. She herself could surely be counted on to produce an heir to the imperial throne.

Hortense, who to her chagrin had been appointed as lady-in-waiting to the future empress, told me quite a lot about her not long after she arrived in Paris.

"She is afraid to meet you," Hortense confided to me after she had been in attendance on Marie Louise for a few days. "She thinks you are beautiful, and she has no illusions about her own looks. She is only of average prettiness."

"Maybe she only says that because you are my daughter."

"No, I think she is being candid. At first I thought she might be trying to flatter you through me, but now I don't think so. She is really quite innocent and trusting."

"Lord help her at Bonaparte's court, with all the intrigue and spying and rivalries that go on!"

"She fears all that as well. She didn't really want to marry Bonaparte, but she agreed to in order to please her father. She adores her father. She told me that when she heard that Marie Walewska had had Bonaparte's child she ran from the room and went to the chapel and begged her confessor to free her from having to marry him. She said she cried all night."

"Poor child."

"She asked me a lot of questions. She wanted to know if Bonaparte would cut off her head if she displeased him. Imagine!"

"Tell her he won't cut off her head, he'll just divorce her."

"She wanted to know if Bonaparte is musical, and whether he likes to dance."

I had to laugh at that, since Bonaparte cannot carry a tune and hates to dance, though he does try on occasion.

"She asked me, are there any museums in Paris? And would Bonaparte be offended if her wedding gown had English point lace instead of Brussels point. I said I thought she ought to avoid anything English."

"I must say she sounds like a nice, sensible girl."

"I think so. She deserves a better fate than being married to Bonaparte. But then," Hortense added ruefully, "at least she isn't going to marry a husband with the English disease."

The wedding was at the Louvre, and as Hortense told me afterwards, Marie Louise's beautiful white satin wedding gown had not a scrap of English point lace. Eugene was a prominent member of the wedding party, as was Hortense, but I was given strict orders to stay away. Not that I would have wanted to attend! I had no desire to confront my young rival—for that is how the courtiers regarded her—or to be a spectator at my husband's second wedding.

As it turned out, I did well to avoid the ceremony, for it had a disastrous aftermath.

A grand ball was held in honor of the newlyweds at a lavishly decorated ballroom rented for the occasion. Everyone of importance in Parisian society was present, besides all the court officials, prominent diplomats, surviving members of the old aristocracy and, of course, the Buonapartes— even pregnant Caroline.

The ball began well. In honor of his bride, Bonaparte attempted to dance every dance (he had taken a few lessons) and his attempts were rewarded with polite applause, and shy smiles from Marie Louise. The grand room filled quickly, there was too little space for all the invited guests, and many others had managed to find their way in uninvited. Bodies were packed together. The heat in the room rose measurably. The dancing grew more lively.

And then a woman screamed.

Smoke began pouring from walls and doorways. Curtains caught fire, and went up in bursts of flame. Gowns were set burning, and then there was pandemonium as panicked women collided, their wide skirts igniting each other. Shouts and screams rose from hundreds of choking throats as the room filled with smoke and it was discovered that all but one of the exits was blocked by flames.

Bonaparte ungallantly took out his sword and hacked his way to the only open doorway, dragging his terrified bride behind him. Others were trapped, and trampled. Many burned to death. Many others were horribly disfigured. All the Buonapartes escaped, even the elderly Letizia, but Caroline suffered a painful miscarriage—and blamed Marie Louise.

"You've brought a curse on us all," Caroline shouted at her new sister-in-law as she was lifted into the imperial coach clutching her stomach.

I heard about the whole ghastly episode the following day, from none other than Bonaparte, who rode to Malmaison in a great hurry and in the greatest distress. I could tell, from the way he instantly jumped down from his lathered horse, that his business with me was urgent, but I wondered, what could bring him here, all the way from Paris, and on the morning after his wedding night.

"They are out to get me, all of them," he shouted as he burst into my sitting room unannounced, his clothing disheveled and his sparse hair in disarray. "This is their doing, the plotters and counter-plotters. The ones who want me dead."

"What is their doing? What are you talking about?" I asked him.

"The fire, the fire."

I looked at him blankly.

"The fire in the grand ballroom last night. Haven't you heard?"

I shook my head.

"Arsonists. Plotters. They set the fire. The building burned to the ground. Dozens of people died. Caroline was taken suddenly ill, and has lost her baby."

"How terrible!"

"They meant to trap me inside and kill me. They very nearly succeeded."

"But who?" I asked, feigning ignorance though I knew full well who the principal plotters were likely to have been.

"I'll find out. I'll kill them all. I swear it!"

He paced back and forth, glaring down at the floor, swearing in the Corsican dialect.

"And that girl! That big, soft, dull girl they had me marry! She hasn't a brain in her head, always going on about her father this and her father that. Do you know, she actually told me she had never seen a naked man? She blushed red as a sunset when I took off my nightshirt.

" 'Have you never seen a stallion?' I asked her.

" 'No, sir.'

" 'Or a bull?'

" 'No, sir.'

" 'What, not even a male dog mounting a bitch in heat?'

" 'I was only allowed to see female animals, sir. Never males.'

"Can you imagine! The ignorance, the stupidity—"

"They were keeping her pure," I ventured.

"They were keeping her moronic. When I think of my dear, devoted Walewska, who was ready to marry me if I asked her, who bore my son, who never asked anything of me, always was loyal and put up with all my rages and really loved me . . ."

"I thought Madame Walewska had a husband already."

"There was a separation. I could have gotten an annulment." He dismissed my demur with a wave of his hand.

"Oh, Josephine, I chose the wrong one!" And with a sigh of genuine remorse he flung himself on my sofa, his hands over his belly.

It was my cue. I sat down and took his head into my lap, rubbing his temples and murmuring soothingly that all would be well. Evidently divorce had not severed at least one old ritual that still bound us.

"You won't desert me, will you Josephine?"

I wanted to say, it was you who deserted me, but held my tongue.

"I am Your Imperial Highness's loyal servant," I said.

"You were always my good luck charm. Last night I began to fear my luck had run out. There's a curse on the Hapsburgs. I know it now. I can feel it. Why didn't anyone tell me? But you, my Josephine, will send me luck. You will read your cards, cast your spells, pray to your powers on my behalf, won't you? Even now?"

There was pleading in his eyes. I felt his fear. He needed to believe he had not lost me. He needed the reassurance I had always provided, the reassurance only I could provide.

I saw then that I still had power over him, and that in time, that power might be used to break his dark hold over his empire.

"I am yours to command, Your Imperial Highness," I said dutifully, but in my heart I knew that along with the arsonists, the plotters and counter-plotters, there was now the force of Bonaparte's own need weighing on his mind, a heavy aching need that tugged at him and threatened to hinder all his grand designs.

53

TO MY INDESCRIBABLE JOY, I received a letter from Donovan in the spring of the year 1811, just as the imperial court was holding its breath and waiting for the new empress Marie Louise to give birth.

A tall, strong French cuirassier came to me at Malmaison, looking very impressive, like a Roman soldier in the time of the Caesars, in his steel plumed helmet and embossed steel breastplate.

He saluted me, and then reached solemnly into the short scabbard strapped to his waist and pulled out his sword. Wordlessly he handed me the murderous-looking weapon, with its razor-sharp blade, and I took it, gingerly, by the curved handle, afraid of cutting myself. As I took it I saw, enclosed within the elaborate handle, a rolled-up scrap of paper. I looked up at the cuirassier but he did not meet my gaze. His face remained impassive.

Was it a trap? Or was he a member of that ever larger group of French officers who sought to overthrow Bonaparte? I was so terribly eager to read the note—for I was sure the paper must be a message from Donovan—that I took a chance and trusted the tall steel-helmeted man before me.

"Thank you," I said gravely, handing back the sword but keeping the note. "Will you take some refreshment?"

Food and wine were brought. I had the valet escort the officer to the dining room. As soon as he was gone I tore open the letter.

"Dearest Yeyette," Donovan wrote, "how I wish you were beside me! What frolic we would have! The man who carries this will tell you his true identity and has news of me. Trust him."

As I read on, overjoyed that Donovan was alive, my fingers went to the pendant charm I wore around my neck, enclosing the last note I had received from him, in which he said he was freezing and starving. I had been true to the vow I made on the day that note arrived: I had never taken it off.

> *I cannot tell you where I am but the bearer of this note will tell all. Our fight against the Great Satan goes well. We prepare for new battles. Oh my Yeyette, I have found at last the cause for which I was born, the realm to which I belong. At last I have stepped out of the shadows into the light. Pray for me my dearest. Until I am in your arms, I am ever yours.*

Moved by the inspiration in Donovan's message, I could not help but weep. He was alive, he was full of hope and felt uplifted by his labors. I reread the brief note several times, then went in search of the cuirassier. He had taken off his helmet and breastplate and was eating, rapidly and very hungrily, what lay on the plate in front of him: a roast chicken, some pâté, strawberries from the greenhouse and a loaf of fine white bread.

He stopped eating abruptly as soon as he saw me and stood up, standing smartly to attention. I saw then that he was a handsome, redheaded young man, well built and strong, with wary blue eyes. He fairly glowed with youth; looking at him, I felt old.

"Please, finish your meal," I urged him. "We are not at all formal here at Malmaison."

"Thank you, madame," he said and sat down again. At a reassuring nod from me he resumed eating hungrily.

"I suppose you have come a long way, and without much food," I said. "I appreciate the sacrifice you have made. The writer of the note says that I am to trust you. Who is it that I am to trust?"

He stood once again. "Sergeant Edward Costello, 95th Rifles," he said.

An Englishman! "Ah! So you are not a cuirassier after all."

For the first time he smiled. "No. It is merely a useful costume while I am here." He sat down again.

"Please tell me about Donovan."

He took a swallow of his wine, then put down his fork. "We fought together in Portugal and Spain."

"I received word of the terrible battle at La Coruña."

"It was a defeat, but we survived it. Or I should say, some of us did." He looked down at the plate in front of him, with its chicken bones and strawberry leaves. "We were driven out of Portugal by the French, but we came back. Donovan and I led bands of villagers in raids against the invaders. We burned provision wagons, stole horses, ambushed stragglers. In the good weather, in the growing season, we went about our work. In the winter we froze with the peasants in their huts and waited for spring."

"And Donovan? Tell me about him."

"Ah, there's a brave man! He taught me to fight. Never lose your daring," he said to me. "Daring is everything. He said he had learned that from General Bonaparte.

"He often talked about you," the cuirassier went on after a pause. "He said you had the softest eyes in the world." He smiled again. "Now I see why."

I sighed. "These poor old tired eyes have been bothering me a lot. They sting and burn, and the drops the doctor gives me to soothe them don't seem to help. Ah, the long list of my ailments! My ears ring and buzz, my eyes sting and I have a humor in my head that won't go away. How my head hurts sometimes! I am getting to be an old woman."

The cuirassier shook his head. "No. Never that."

Edward moved into Donovan's rooms in Euphemia's cottage and the villagers were told that he was an officer recovering from a slight wound. They paid little attention to him, caught up as they were just then by news from the Tuileries, where Empress Marie Louise had just given birth to a son.

At last, Bonaparte had a son of his own, a royal boy, with the blood of kings in his veins and the French imperial crown as his inheritance. He was given the grand title King of Rome, and I heard that an architect had been commissioned to design a palace for him, a palace larger than Versailles, more impressive than the largest royal residence ever built.

The Duchesse de La Rochefoucauld lost no time in coming to Malmaison to tell me all the news from court. She had seen the newborn lying in his golden cradle, she said, and he was rosy and plump and perfect in every way. She called him the "son of France," and told me in detail how Bonaparte boasted of his size and strength, and how Marie Louise blushed at all the compliments being paid to her.

I was not rude to the duchess, but I hardly listened to anything she said, as my thoughts were elsewhere. I was thinking of Donovan, and feeling for the thousandth time the joy of knowing that he was alive, and longing for the day when we would be together once again, and I could tell him all that was in my heart.

54

"YEYETTE! YEYETTE! Wake up, Yeyette!"

It was Euphemia, her voice cracked and hoarse, her urgent shouting triggering a spasm of coughing.

I sat up in bed. It was still dark, but the birds had begun a sleepy chirping outside my window.

"What is it? Is it Hortense? Is it one of the children?"

Still coughing, Euphemia shook her head. "Put on your dressing gown. Come quickly," she gasped. She went to my wardrobe and brought out a gown, moving with surprising agility for her seventy-odd years. She handed the garment to me and helped me wrap it around my waist. Then she led me downstairs and out into the courtyard where a wagon was waiting.

"Tell me where we are going!" I demanded after Euphemia had fairly pushed me up and into the wagon and made me sit down on the rough bench behind the driver.

"You will see. He has come. The great one has come."

It was all she would say, as the wagon rattled along, headed in the direction of the cottages around the lake where Euphemia lived. I saw that she was tense and pale, but also full of a strange excitement. I had never seen her in this state before.

Dawn was breaking as we reached the lake, and I saw at once, through the morning mist, that a tent had been erected beside the water. As we came closer I made out the figure of a very old, very dark man with red feathers in his straggling grey hair and wearing a dirty red cloak. He was seated on a tree stump. Around him were three African men in loincloths but with ragged jackets covering their chests and arms.

It was Orgulon.

The wagon stopped and I got down, hardly able to believe what I was seeing. The ancient quimboiseur, who had looked as old as time itself when I saw him in my girlhood, now appeared almost skeletal, with little flesh on his bony legs and a skull-like face. His skin was greyish-black, his withered hands bent, the fingers curled under, like the claws of a chicken. Yet when I approached him, and he turned his wrinkled face toward me, I saw that the look he gave me with his one good eye was still powerful, and I shivered slightly under his gaze.

A fire had been lit in one corner of the tent, and there was a strong odor of incense in the air. A drift of smoke reached me as I knelt down on the damp grass beside the old man.

He fixed me with his one-eyed gaze. Presently he spoke, his voice faint and raspy.

"The time has come," he said. "The fer-de-lance will strike. You must kill it."

"How?"

"Frighten it. Then kill it. And the demon that sent it."

"How will I know the demon?"

"You married him. Now you must destroy him."

I cannot describe the feelings the old quimboiseur's words evoked in me, a shattering, numbing blend of awe, dread, and a curious exaltation.

Once long ago Orgulon had saved my life, and told me I was being spared for a purpose. Now he had come all the way from Martinique, an arduous journey of many months, to announce to me that my purpose was at hand.

I did not doubt his oracular words.

"His way lies eastward. Follow him. I will send you a light to see by."

He sighed then, and his head slumped forward on his chest. The men who stood by, in attendance on him, gently eased him onto a mat and drew a blanket over his shrunken body.

I did not linger, but returned to the house along with a trembling Euphemia.

"He spoke to you. He knew you."

"He remembered me from all those years ago, when I went up Morne Granthéaume in search of him."

"You were lucky he didn't shrivel up your heart in your body."

"Of course not. He believes I have something important to do. He wants me to live so that I can carry out my important task."

"What task?"

I looked at Euphemia. Her eyes were wide with fear and uncertainty.

"To kill the fer-de-lance."

Orgulon lived just long enough to deliver his message to me. When Euphemia and I returned to the lakeside cottages later that afternoon, his attendants were wrapping his body in strips of bark tied with red cloth.

"Where will they bury him?" I asked Euphemia.

"The grave of a quimboiseur is always hidden. The body dies, but the spirit walks at night. It goes in search of the gods of the underworld—and finds them at the sacred crossroads, the place where the living meet the dead."

"But that was on Martinique, far away."

Euphemia shook her head. "There are many sacred crossroads in this world, wherever the gods are revered."

As we stood by, Orgulon's attendants completed their task. Leaving their tent in place and their fire burning, they hoisted the old man's body on their shoulders and noiselessly walked off into the forest, oblivious of us and of the cottagers who had come out onto the grass to watch what was happening.

"Good Josephine," one of the cottagers called out to me, "who were those men? What were they doing here?"

"Old friends of mine from Martinique," I told them, leaving them unsatisfied but reluctant, since I was their social superior and benefactor, to ask more questions.

It was dusk, the blue hour. A cool wind stirred the leaves in the trees around the lake, and I pulled my shawl more tightly around my shoulders.

Suddenly the darkening sky seemed to grow lighter. A curious radiance flooded from the western horizon, then gathered itself, moment by moment, into a glowing ball with a long trailing tail, all agleam.

I had never seen anything like it. Gradually, as we watched, night fell, but along with the stars there glowed in the sky this radiant bright orb with its shining train.

"I will send you a light to see by," Orgulon had told me, and here it was, light abundant, his gift and his legacy. I stood in awe, wondering at the light, hoping it would not fade, seeing in it a sign that I could indeed carry out the task Orgulon had given me. I stood for a long time, until Euphemia tugged at my sleeve and insisted that we leave, reminding me that I had had no supper and that she, for one, was getting cold.

I let her lead me back to the house, our way lit by the glow above us. Orgulon's light. I shone within, exulting in all that I had seen and heard that day, sure that my life had taken a new and wondrous turning.

55

"IT IS A COMET, OF COURSE," Bonaparte snapped as he looked up from his desk, lifting his pen from the paper in front of him. I had come to the Tuileries to receive my allowance, the money he had agreed to give me each year when he divorced me. I knew that he was about to leave once again on campaign, having raised a vast army that included not only Frenchmen but Germans, Poles, Dutch and Italians. It was said to be the largest armed force ever assembled. I wanted to make certain I received my allowance before he left.

After keeping me waiting for more than an hour, Bonaparte had finally had me admitted to his study and wordlessly handed me a bank draft. I thanked him but did not leave right away, despite his glare of impatience. I lingered, fascinated. Since receiving Orgulon's message I saw my former husband in a new light, as the demon who must be destroyed.

There he sat, in his gilded chair, on a deep padded cushion. I knew why he needed the thick cushion—because he was increasingly troubled with hemorrhoids that gave him much pain. On the wall behind him was an immense portrait of himself as a young man, long locks flowing, sword in hand, fending off a horde of enemies against a dramatic landscape.

Does he really imagine that he still looks like that, I wondered.

Doesn't he realize how fat he has become, how his stomach sticks out from under his vest? How he slumps, and glowers, and has become as white and pale as a mushroom?

"Why are you still here? Can't you see how busy I am? I've answered your question about the light you've been seeing in the sky. It is a well known celestial phenomenon. A comet. Shall I spell the word for you? Fools believe comets foretell disaster. I know better. This one foretells my victory over the Russians."

"But France is in fact in the midst of disaster," I argued. "Look at all the people who are out of work, and all the banks that are failing. The newspapers are full of stories about riots and strikes and shortages of food. Why, I've got beggars by the score coming to my door at Malmaison."

It was true. Even at Malmaison, my oasis of peace and safety, the quakes and tremblings of the Paris financial markets could be felt—and their human wreckage encountered. Even I, who did not usually read newspapers or interest myself in the ups and downs of others' investments—unless of course I was likely to profit from them—could not ignore the stories I was hearing, stories of bands of starving men and women roaming the streets like packs of hungry wolves, stories of suicides, of people turned out of their houses and camping by the roadside in shelters made of old lumber and stones and bricks. My cooks served soup to the poor wretches who came to my door, and I sent food into the nearby village of Rueil to relieve the want there.

Standing where I was, in Bonaparte's private study, and seeing the inescapable change in him since he divorced me and married Marie Louise, it was hard to escape the conclusion that his marriage had brought him—and France—bad luck. And the comet symbolized it.

"They think I will stop when I have conquered Russia, you know," Bonaparte said, his mood suddenly shifting, his irritability retreating before a wave of reverie.

"They are wrong. The road to Moscow leads on, over frozen wastes and steppes, and tall high mountains, to the fabled land of India. Do you remember when I went to Egypt?"

"Of course, Your Imperial Majesty."

"That was meant to be the start of a longer journey. I thought I would conquer the land of the pharaohs with ease, and then lay siege to Constantinople, and then go on to India, and complete my conquest of the world. That dream has not died."

As he spoke he picked up an exquisitely carved porcelain figure of a young man from the desktop in front of him. He ran his hands over the smooth porcelain absentmindedly.

"Then I was a young commander, with much promise but no fortune. Now I am a rich man, even though my people are in distress. What better use of my wealth than to conquer the rest of the world? Besides, it is the only task left that is great enough to challenge my genius."

With a snap he severed one of the porcelain figure's legs and discarded it carelessly on the desk.

"I am writing to Tsar Alexander about this, to caution him. He has declared war on France. But he cannot declare war on my destiny!"

He is mad, I thought. He has taken leave of his senses.

"I am reminding the emperor that the course of human events is inevitable and that most men are mere pygmies. A few of us are giants. I am one of those few. The day of the giants has come."

With a snap the remaining leg of the porcelain figure came off.

"And what of the women?"

He shrugged. "Less than pygmies. Flies. Gnats." He swatted an imaginary insect. "You will see," he went on. "The world will see. I will wage a holy war against the Slav barbarians, and then conquer the Hindu heathens! I will civilize the globe!"

Waving his arms wildly, he flung the truncated porcelain boy into the fireplace where it smashed. "Now, leave me in peace. I must make my preparations. Soon the spring will be here and there will be grass enough for the horses, and the grand campaign can begin!"

MY FORTY-NINTH BIRTHDAY WAS APPROACHING, and I could not deny that my step had grown slower and my eyesight weaker. I was no longer spry, in fact my knees hurt when I walked around the lake where my black swans floated and I groaned a little each time I got up from a soft cushiony chair. I was not old yet, but I soon would be. How, I wondered, could I find the strength to follow Bonaparte eastward until I encountered the fer-de-lance and destroyed it?

Full of confusion, but concerned to find answers, I sought help from the one man who had always in the past come to my aid: my old friend Scipion du Roure.

I sent Scipion a letter telling him I needed to talk to him urgently and waited for a response. He sent word back that he would come to Malmaison as quickly as he could and in fact he made the journey from his home in Caen in record time.

I was watching for his carriage from my balcony. When it arrived I felt my spirits lift. I had not seen Scipion in several years—not since my divorce in fact. I knew that he had become a widower and was no longer an active naval commander. He had retired to Normandy, where he was still near the sea but within a few days' journey from the capital.

With some difficulty Scipion alighted from his carriage and began to make his way toward the house, using a cane to support his bad leg, the old war wound from the naval battle off the coast of Cairo evidently plaguing him. I hurried downstairs to greet him and lead him into my private sitting room, where we could talk confidentially.

After hugging each other warmly and exchanging news of family and mutual friends, we began to talk in earnest. I opened my heart to Scipion.

"You may find what I am about to tell you somewhat fantastic," I began, "but I urge you not to dismiss it, or to look on it as the product of a disordered mind. And remember, I am a child of Martinique, where sorcerers wield much power."

"I would never dismiss anything that is important to you, Yeyette. And I remember Martinique and its distinctive culture well." His grey eyes, hooded now and surrounded by wrinkles, looked at me steadily, expectantly.

"Well then, I recently had an important visitor . . ." I described my encounter with the dying Orgulon and his message, and told Scipion what I thought it meant. I needed to find the dreaded fer-de-lance, I said, and kill it—and also destroy the demon that sent it. I needed to follow Bonaparte eastward, led by the new white light in the sky. When I finished I sat back and waited to hear what my old friend had to say in response.

He sat in thoughtful silence for a time, then looked over at me.

"What you say is quite fantastic, Yeyette, even preposterous. I cannot embrace it with my mind—but my intuition tells me that you sincerely believe what the old man told you. And as it happens, I believe that there is much evil being loosed in the world, far too much violence and havoc. Our emperor is at the center of it all.

"As you know, Yeyette, I have a son, Jean-Georges, who is an officer in the Rouen Dragoons. He is preparing to join the campaign. I have urged him not to go. In doing so I have abandoned all my old loyalties, my naval oath, even, one might say, my loyalty to France. But the life of my son is more important to me than any of these things, and I do not want to see that life squandered by a maniac who wears the name of emperor!"

I had never seen Scipion speak so vehemently. The words were wrenched from him, he was both angry and anguished.

"My son Eugene is with the army as well, as you know. Bonaparte has put him in command of many men. I do not want his life thrown away either."

"Then let us work together to save our sons. I will help you, Yeyette. You intend to travel eastward. Very well. I can arrange passage for you by ship as far as Riga—the northern seas will be clear of ice in a few weeks—and from there I can direct you to contacts in Smolensk and towns nearby. Russia is vast, but I will do what I can to ease your way. I will give you names of people you can turn to if you need them. I will forewarn each one. Of course, you will need land transport, horses, money—"

"I have ordered a traveling coach," I said, interrupting him. "I have the funds Bonaparte allots me, and I intend to sell two of my diamond parures to raise extra funds."

"Better not to carry much money with you. Carry letters of reference and arrange for bank drafts instead."

"When I was empress none of that was necessary," I remarked ruefully.

"But you are not empress any longer. You must be prudent, and careful. Ah, Yeyette, how brave you are!" Scipion smiled and patted my hand. "Think what your Aunt Rosette would say, if she could see you now and find out what you are doing."

I thought of Aunt Rosette as she had been in my childhood, always wearing her threadbare green gown with the crimson rosettes, their color faded to a dull pink.

"She would faint—if she were still living. She and my mother are both in their graves in the church at Les Trois-Îlets."

"I'm sorry Yeyette."

"They lived very comfortably in their old age, on the money I was able to send them. The slave rebellion left the plantation in ruins but mama and Aunt Rosette moved to Fort-Royal and were happy there, once all the turmoil died down."

"No doubt they thought of themselves as royalty, with you becoming empress."

"I'm glad mother died before I was divorced and disgraced."

Scipion and I talked on, through the afternoon and all through dinner. He stayed for several days, helping me plan for the shipboard portion of my trip and advising me about how to prepare for the land portion. He talked with Christian and my tall, strong pseudo-cuirassier Edward Costello, both of whom insisted on going with me on my journey.

Scipion went home to Normandy for a few days, then on to Le Havre to arrange our sea passage, and finally returned to Malmaison to accompany us to the port.

It was a great deal for him to undertake, on such short notice and with a need for secrecy. On his return to Malmaison he looked tired. One evening after dinner I insisted that he try to forget all that was on his mind and stroll with me through the gardens. Though he had to walk haltingly, leaning on his cane, he seemed to enjoy the brief respite from all that preoccupied him. June had come, and many of the flowering plants were in bloom.

"Is that jasmine I smell?" he asked as we passed a bush with a mass of white flowers.

"Yes. I've always loved it."

"You wore jasmine in your hair on the night I first met you, at the ball in Fort-Royal. Do you remember?"

"Did I?" I was being deceitful, for of course I remembered, just as I remembered the pale yellow gown I wore on that night and the new yellow slippers that went with it. I remembered everything, that Aunt Rosette had been taken ill and had to go and lie down, leaving me unchaperoned, that I had agreed to meet Scipion in secret on the beach, and that he had kissed me under a mango tree.

"The scent stayed with me for days afterwards," he said. "You were the most enchanting girl."

I smiled. "All girls are enchanting at fifteen."

"You were exceptional. Do you remember what I called you that night?"

"Bird of Paradise."

We paused in our walking, breathing in the warm scented night air, recalling the sweetness of our past tryst. Frogs croaked, and somewhere in the distance birds were twittering.

"Dear Yeyette," he began afresh, reaching for my hand. "When you return from your journey—"

"If I return," I interjected.

"When you return, please tell me that we might talk of our future. We are both free now, we could marry."

"Scipion, please, I cannot think of anything now but the task before me."

"Then promise me that you will not reject the thought completely."

"You know that I have always been fond of you. Very fond." I squeezed his hand, then released it.

"Is there someone else?"

I paused, then admitted the truth. "Yes. But he has pledged himself to fight Bonaparte, and I have no idea where he is or how much danger he is in."

"How terrible for you, my dear."

We did not speak of Scipion's suggestion again, but I saw the sadness in his eyes as he said goodnight to me that night, and the resigned look on his face when, our final preparations complete, our party climbed into the coach for the journey to LeHavre. I knew then that Scipion had come to Malmaison, not just because I had asked him to, but because he had been thinking of me with love, and intending to ask me to share his life.

56

I WAS PROUD OF MYSELF for the first three days at sea. Though our vessel, the schooner *Gallimaufry*, rose and dipped alarmingly as she made her way through the rough waters of the English Channel I did not get sick. I stood at the rail and watched the horizon, grasping at the nearest ropes to keep my balance, looking forward to evening when the comet became visible and shed its bright light among the stars.

On the fourth day, however, a storm blew down from the north and I had to stay below in my cabin, on my uncomfortable small bed, clutching my stomach and swallowing the bitter medicine Euphemia insisted that I drink. I was glad, then, that I had relented and let her come with Christian and Edward and me, despite her age and infirmities. At first I had said no when she wanted to come with us, but she argued and argued, and in the end convinced me that I had to have a maid.

"How can a lady travel without a maid? Especially a lady that was an empress?" Her indignation was strong, even if her logic was weak.

"I am traveling as plain Madame d'Arberg, Euphemia, not as a former empress, and I have Christian and Edward to look after me."

She swore in her mother's language. "I'd like to see Christian and Edward arrange your hair, or wash your underclothes, or mix your orangeflower water when you get frightened."

"I can do for myself."

She howled with laughter—at which I took offense, but then relented. She was right, of course. I needed a maid, and there was no time to find and train another one. Besides, Euphemia was my beloved guardian, my very dear sister, even, as I came to realize the older I got, my surrogate mother. Had I left her behind I would have missed her terribly.

Scipion had arranged passage for us aboard the French schooner which was bound for Riga carrying a cargo of provisions for the army, to be unloaded at the port, then shipped by wagon overland to storage depots at Minsk and Smolensk. We passengers were mere extra cargo, unimportant and largely ignored by the crew as they went about hoisting and striking sail, polishing their weapons and guns and cleaning the vessel, and above all, keeping watch for English ships.

"Can you swim?" Edward asked me on the day we boarded the *Gallimaufry.*

"Of course. I was raised in the Windward Isles. We swam every day."

"Good. If we come under attack, rip off your skirts and petticoats and jump into the water. Swim hard for land. A ship of this kind never goes far offshore, so you can probably save yourself."

Strong swimmer though I was, the thought was not comforting. The Channel waters were freezing cold, and the waves were high enough to obscure the coastline. I prayed that we would not come under attack.

The plan I had worked out, with Scipion's help, called for us to travel by sea up the French coast and through the Dutch islands to Amsterdam, then to continue on via Hamburg and Gdansk to faroff Riga, where we, like the rest of the ship's cargo, would go ashore and travel overland in hopes of encountering Bonaparte and his army somewhere west of Moscow.

Day by day I traced our progress, borrowing the captain's sketchily drawn charts of the coastline. Strong winds drove us backwards at times, and frothy seas washed over our decks. As Edward had told me, the ship hugged the shore, but clouds often hid it, and though it was midsummer we had many days of rain.

We called in at Amsterdam and found the port full of news about Bonaparte's campaign. He was said to be in Poland, on his way to visit his old love Marie Walewska. The army would rest in temporary camps near Warsaw, as many of the men were ill with fever.

We sailed on northward around the Danish peninsula, encountering a foreign ship, a privateer, that chased us for half a day before retreating into the mists of the Kattegat. I shivered night and day now, for we had entered the frigid Baltic and felt the chill of the far northern summer. Deep fogs swathed the barren coast and the sea looked grey and oily as we made our way along, inching ahead as it seemed to me.

At Hamburg we went ashore again and learned that the French had crossed the Niemen River into Russia, and were pursuing the Russian forces.

We were all finding the voyage tedious. The ship stank from the filthy bilge-water, there was no more fresh food (for we dared not go ashore in enemy ports to replenish our stores) and we rose each morning to the dull sameness of a stale routine.

Finally, after many weeks, we reached Riga, where French gunboats protected the schooner's passage into the harbor. At last we were able to stand on dry land, our legs so unaccustomed to its rock-solid feel that we swayed as we walked.

Riga was full of conflicting stories about the grand French army. Some said a great battle had been fought and the French were in retreat, others that there had been no battle but the Russians were refusing to defend their land. It was rumored that French deserters were being rounded up and shot by the thousands. One persistent rumor was that Bonaparte was dead, eaten by wolves as he ran in panic through the forest. It was a very dramatic story—if hardly credible—and we heard it again and again as we disembarked and prepared for the next stage of our journey.

We were in Latvian territory now, and the dark-skinned, round-faced Latvians, dressed in their jackets of furs and skins, tall fur caps pulled down over their foreheads, stared at us, curious to know who we were and where we came from. They muttered to one another in their own tongue, pointing at Euphemia and looking up at the exceptionally tall Edward in his cuirassier's armor in some awe. I was dressed as a respectable French townswoman, Christian as my servant. To a Parisian observer the four of us, traveling together, would seem a conventional group: the well-to-do older lady, her maid, her servant and a soldier escort, brought along for protection. But to the inhabitants of Riga, where women never traveled without their husbands, fathers or sons, and where well-to-do women had dozens of servants, not just two, our party seemed very odd.

We were relieved when, our carriage loaded and our bags secured on top behind the coachman, we set out along the only road that led out of Riga, the narrow highroad that ran eastward along the foreshore until it turned and rose into pine-covered foothills.

Springs creaking, axles groaning, our carriage rolled and bumped along the ill-maintained road, clouds of choking dust rising into the still air. I had been cold when at sea, but now I sweltered in the baking hot sunshine, and drank often from the water jug at my feet. It was a thirsty landscape, with yellowing grasses at the verges of the road and harvesters moving through fields of rye and barley, slashing at the crops with scythes. The black earth was fertile; in some fields oats grew thick and green, clearly a second crop that would not be harvested for another month or more.

We stopped to water the horses and replenish our own vessels. Near the well sat a prosperous-looking peasant in a vest made of skins, pounding a shoe on a last. Christian approached him and, by an exchange of signs, received permission to draw water. This accomplished, Christian again engaged the man in a wordless conversation.

"I was asking him about the soldiers," Christian told me when he returned to the carriage. "He says he hasn't seen them, but he believes they are five days' journey to the east of here."

We went on, hoping to find an inn before nightfall, but though we passed through several small villages there were no inns. Nor were we offered hospitality in any of the houses—indeed the villagers were nowhere to be seen. We slept in our carriage, uncomfortably, exhausted and hungry.

Scipion had given me names of people he knew or knew of, people who could help us. But they all lived in cities, and there were no cities in eastern Latvia.

"What we need is a guide," Edward announced. But how were we to find one?

We went on, hoping to discover a source of help. I began to lose heart and reproach myself for failing to make wiser plans. The sky darkened and wept with rain, a warm autumnal rain that soon became heavy. The thick dust of the road turned to mud. Our poor horses slogged on, slowly, barely able to lift their hooves from the sucking quagmire.

Hour after hour we inched ahead, until at dusk we heard a welcome shout from the coachman.

"I see a light ahead," he said. As we went closer we saw that the light was coming from the large window of a stone structure. We heard male voices singing. We drew into a muddy torchlit courtyard and at once bushy-bearded men in long black robes appeared, staring at our carriage. They called out to us.

"Monks!" Christian said. "We are saved."

Our hosts, for that is what they proved to be, were Latvian Orthodox brothers. They welcomed Christian, Edward and the coachman into the refectory where their own evening meal was in progress—and oh how good the food smelled!—but they made it clear that neither Euphemia nor I could be allowed into their all-male precincts. We were shown to a barn and food and blankets were brought to us. Gratefully we ate and made beds for ourselves by piling up hay. The barn was dry, the lowing of the animals soothing, and we went to sleep to the sound of the pelting rain.

57

WE LEARNED NOT TO EXPECT INNS where we could sleep, or bakeries where we could buy bread, or blacksmithies where our horses could be shod and our carriage repaired. But we found what we needed: hospitality from monks and, later, from Russian villagers who offered us bread and salt, fresh horses at infrequent posting stations, and, after our carriage broke down, a sturdy wagon large enough to hold us all and our baggage as well.

By the time we had been traveling for ten days we were bedraggled but road-hardened, accustomed to making our way through countryside where we knew no one and could understand little of what was being said around us.

We discovered that uttering the name "Bonaparte" was enough to make all those near us cringe and cross themselves (they crossed themselves backwards, I discovered).

"Franzki, Franzki," they repeated fearfully, with gestures that made it plain they wanted no Franzkis, or Frenchmen, among them. Yet they did not shun us or threaten us, and only once, in a village where it was evident that cottages had been burned and we were offered no food (for there was none, we soon realized) were we spat upon and cursed.

One morning after setting off quite early we began to hear, in the distance, a low rumbling sound. At first I thought it might be thunder but there was no lightning to be seen and unlike thunder, the sound was continuous, a perpetual grinding rumbling noise that did not go away or diminish. In fact, it seemed to become gradually louder.

I listened intently, and could soon make out, above the rumbling, a jangling noise and then rhythmic thuds. There were muffled shouts, and now and then the crack of a whip.

We had found the army.

Before long we were on the verge of the worst congestion of vehicles I had ever seen. Baggage wagons, carts, gun carriages clogged and blocked the narrow road, while soldiers on foot and on horseback did their best to drive their way through the mass of wheeled vehicles. Slowly, churning the road to muddy tracks and clumps, the clustered mass of men and objects moved forward, leaving in its wake broken wagons and collapsed horses, their legs flailing vainly in the air.

Our driver did his best to force our wagon through the tangle of vehicles, enduring the curses and threats of other drivers and the aggressive jockeying that nearly threatened to overturn us. We attracted no special attention, and were shown no courtesy. We had to fight for every foot of roadway. The profusion of legs, hooves and wheels parted when officers rode through, preceded by orderlies shouting "Make way! Make way for the general!" But such partings were rare, and we were not important enough to have a pathway made for us.

We had found the army—but we had not found Bonaparte. When we called out to passing officers, inquiring where the emperor was, they gave us only the vaguest of replies.

"He is up ahead," they said, or "He has gone on in advance."

When evening came the men built camp fires and cooked soup in large cauldrons, each man in turn dipping his wooden bowl in the steaming mixture until all was consumed. Brandy-bottles were passed around, stories of past campaigns told. Longstemmed pipes were extracted from boots and precious tobacco smoked. Then, as the stars came out and the great comet flared in the western sky, the soldiers lay down around their dying fires, pulling their dirty overcoats over themselves, and slept.

We slept too, Euphemia and I on a blanket under our wagon, Christian and Edward taking turns to keep watch near us. Our bellies were full, for we quickly discovered that the men in charge of the large leather-covered baggage-wagons were glad to sell us provisions.

We continued to travel with the army until, a few days after we initially joined their caravan, an incident occurred that affected me profoundly.

We came within sight of a village and immediately there was much shouting of orders, with men running here and there and horses being saddled. A detachment of cavalry was formed, and as we watched, they rode swiftly to the village and began setting fire to every house in it. They did not spare the barns; as they went up in flames we could hear the frightened cries of the animals trapped inside. We saw no villagers, at first, but when the horsemen returned from their destructive raid they drove several dozen men ahead of them, roped together at the waist, their hands bound behind them.

An officer barked orders and in response, a line of infantrymen formed. They began loading their muskets.

I watched in horror as the victims were executed, each man reduced to a heap of flesh and pooling blood. They were the enemy, I knew. They were Russians, and the Russian tsar had declared war on the French Empire. Yet they were men, like the men that had offered us bread and salt and shared their shelters with us only a few days earlier. They had wives and children, mothers and fathers.

"The Russian army does not spare the French, milady," Christian said to me, observing my distress. "It is war."

I saw three villages burned that day, and many more men executed, and by the afternoon I was heartsore and weary. Was this what I had been sent to do, to follow Bonaparte's army and watch villagers die?

A large wagon broke down on the road, bringing the procession of men and carts to a temporary halt. I got down out of our vehicle to stretch my legs, and decided to walk along a path that led up the side of a hill. Walking felt good to me, there was a breeze and the air was fresh, free of the dust of the road and smelling faintly of woodsmoke.

I reached the hilltop and sat down on the yellow grass, suddenly feeling the weight of my distress for the men who I had seen killed that day, and for all the others I knew must have died in the past—and would die soon.

Where are their families? I asked myself. What will they do now? How will they bear their deprivation, and their sorrow?

Knowing that no one could see me, I gave full vent to my tears, thinking of Eugene, and Scipion's son Jean-Georges, and all the other men and boys who were being led into danger for the sake of seeking glory and following the emperor, and all the Russian men and boys who would fight against them.

At length I dried my eyes and looked out toward the horizon, where the sun hung low, its golden rays slanting down across the rolling plain and lighting the road. The enormous caravan of marching men and lumbering wagons, jostling carts and rearing, struggling horses spread itself out in a long undulant line below me, the sunlight glinting off the metal of the guns, the slow movement of the line of men sinuous and vaguely sinister.

It was like a snake, I realized. Like a snake moving with slow and deadly precision toward its prey.

All at once I knew, with a clarity that could not be denied, that I was looking at the fer-de-lance. This, Bonaparte's army, was the deadly fer-de-lance I had been sent to destroy.

I stood then, overcome by the realization that I was looking at the terrible thing I had to kill.

But how? Frighten it, Orgulon had said.

Frighten the snake. Spread fear in the army. That was what I had to do. I stood where I was for a long time, doing my best to gather my thoughts. Then at last I descended the hill, filled anew with an urgent sense of purpose and hope, and confident that the help I needed would be at hand.

58

IT BEGAN ON THE HOT, dusty road to Ghbatsk. An Italian and a Bavarian got into a fight, and the Bavarian, who was bigger and stronger, called the Italian a coward, following which some Spaniards came to the Italian's defense and soon there was a brawl.

Officers intervened, and the melee was brought to a halt, temporarily, but the bad feeling lingered and more fighting broke out a few hours later.

"The Germans don't like the Italians very much," I remarked to Edward, who was riding next to me in the wagon.

The tall cuirassier agreed.

"What if we started a rumor that the Italians were hoarding all the best grain?"

"I think I can do that," he said, smiling, and headed off along the road.

I turned to Christian. "Is it true what they say, that the Russians have a million men under arms, and a thousand guns, while our own Grande Armée has only one-quarter that many?"

"I'll try to find out," said Christian, and got down out of the wagon to mingle with the nearest detachment of soldiers. "That's the sort of information every one of our men ought to have."

We spread rumors, we provoked violent arguments, we elicited anger and fear, jealousy and resentment. When after several days of heavy rain there was an outbreak of quinsy, with the men coughing and shivering and losing their strength, a new rumor was spread: that the Russians were poisoning our food stores in order to make the men sick.

Now there was panic, and more demoralized men became ill. Rain continued to fall in sheets, hard, slanting rain that soaked bedding, flour, firewood, weapons and the precious cartridges needed to fire them. The four of us, Edward, Christian, Euphemia and I, took refuge under the leaky canvas cover of our wagon and tried to get warm.

"I heard one of the Austrian officers say that Moscow is only about ten days' march from here," Edward told us. "Surely the Russians will offer battle any day now to prevent our army from entering the city."

"How can they fight in all this rain?" I wanted to know.

"Weather never stops slaughter," was Christian's reply. "I ought to know. I was with the émigré army at the siege of Thionville. You never saw such storms! But the massacres went on just the same."

"I didn't realize you had been a soldier, Christian. I thought you worked in the royal household from the time you were very young."

"You are forgetting, milady, that there was no royal household for many years. After they killed the king in '93 I went to Coblentz, to fight under his brother against the revolutionary armies."

I looked at my faithful servant with a newfound respect.

"Then you are right at home."

"Let us simply say that these circumstances are not unfamiliar to me."

Edward laughed. "Nor to me."

"Humph!" It was Euphemia, wet and wretched, expressing her distaste. "I am no soldier. I hate all this—this misery! I want a dry room and a hot fire and a dish of good Carib crabs and plantains!"

"I need you here, Euphemia. You insisted on coming. Remember why we came, and who sent us."

Despite the wet and cold, the sodden clothing and blankets, the fires that would not start and the deep, sucking mud that turned the road to quicksand, my own spirits were soaring. With the vital aid of Edward and Christian, I was succeeding in weakening the fer-de-lance. Every day more of the men were deserting, melting away into the countryside, abandoning their units. Stragglers, too ill or weak to march, sat by the side of the muddy road, in the rain, dejected and worn out. Each morning the corpses of those who had died the previous night were gathered and burned, their possessions quickly snatched up by the living.

In their efforts to stir up discord and fear of the Russians among the men, Edward and Christian found allies by the dozens, officers and soldiers alike who had no heart for the campaign and secretly resented Bonaparte and his aims. The leaven of dissatisfaction continued to spread, indeed to increase as the soldiers became convinced that there would be a battle before the army reached Moscow.

"Have you noticed," I remarked on the first clear evening, "that the comet has grown brighter?" All those within the sound of my voice looked up at the sky apprehensively.

"It is a bad sign, a sign that this is a year of misfortune. The brighter it grows, the greater the misfortune."

Whether because their fears affected their vision, or because, in their weary state, they were very suggestible, the men grew even more fearful and imagined that the great light in the sky was indeed becoming brighter.

"Perhaps it is a sign of the last days," some said. "The end of all things."

As expected, the Russians drew up their forces, at a place called Borodino, where three broad rivers ran together. The place was said to be heavily fortified, and the Russian army was said to be immense (though hardly a million strong, as our rumor had it) and determined to win at all costs.

On the night before the two armies were set to engage, Bonaparte rode out along the battle lines, exhorting the men and encouraging them. I was not present of course but Edward was, and he came to tell us afterwards what the emperor said and how it was received.

"Pay no attention to what you may have heard about the strength of the enemy!" Bonaparte shouted as he rode past the men. "We are invincible!"

"But what about the comet?" came a voice from the ranks.

"A sign of victory!"

"Or disaster," said a rash young soldier, who boldly challenged the emperor, stepping forward out of line as he spoke.

Instantly, Edward told us, the emperor's round face reddened and he brandished his whip, riding up to the boy and glaring down at him.

"What is your name, soldier?"

"Auguste Ibert, Your Imperial Highness."

"Auguste Ibert, you are a disgrace to France." He beckoned to the two guardsmen who rode near him as escort. "Execute this man," he said in an icy tone when they approached. Ibert was led away.

"I watched him go," Edward told us. "It was terrible. I have seen deserters shot before, and traitors, but I never sensed such outrage in the ranks. This execution almost led to a riot. The officers restrained their men, with great difficulty. Poor Ibert was tied to a stake within sight of us all and shot, and you could feel the men's horrified reaction. At that moment they hated their emperor—though they feared him even more."

At dawn on the following day the Grande Armée, shrunken in size and strength, with many of the men filled with misgivings, faced the Russian foe and began their attack.

We were several miles away to the west of the battle front, deep in a protected culvert, along with dozens of other supply wagons and powder wagons and carts and scores of noncombatants. I had no wish to observe the fighting, dramatic spectacle though I was sure it would be. I was worried about Eugene (who had no idea I had been traveling with the army; I was plain Madame d'Arberg, just another superannuated camp follower, and no one took any particular notice of me). I wanted Eugene to be safe, yet nothing mattered more to me than that our army, this improbable congeries of Frenchmen, Germans, Poles, Dutch and Germans from all corners of Europe, should lose its deadly venomous force and be defanged. And I wanted it to happen right away.

The thunderous noise of hundreds of guns, all pounding at once, the ground shaking under us with the terrible force of their repeated explosions, was enough to make me hold my palms over my ears and cringe in dread.

So this is what battle is like, I thought. This earsplitting, ceaseless noise that cuts through to my very bones and makes them shake. It went on for hours, the relentless pounding and shaking. The air filled with smoke, and the reek of powder.

And then the wounded began staggering in.

A dressing-station was hastily set up near where our wagon stood. Dazed, bleeding men entered the tents where surgeons in red-stained leather aprons waited to treat them. Some were calling out, frantically, for help. Others came in twos and threes, leaning on each other for support. The weakest crawled on hands and knees or dragged themselves over the dry grass toward the tents, their faces distorted, grimacing with pain.

Edward and Christian joined the stretcher-bearers and went out to the battlefield to bring in more men. Euphemia was put to work tearing cloth into strips for bandages and I went into the nearest tent to assist the surgeons.

Before long hundreds of injured men were stumbling in or being carried to the tents, filthy, sweat-soaked soldiers and officers, their once smart, clean uniforms grimed with blood and ash and the black smears of gunpowder. Many were brought in on stretchers, more dead than alive by the look of them, and laid before the open tent-flaps in untidy heaps. Some were delivered by being laid on top of long muskets that formed makeshift planks.

"Brandy! Bring me that brandy," the surgeon nearest to me shouted. I brought it and the surgeon poured some over the gory leg of an officer. The man screamed.

"He's lost too much blood. Hold him down."

Orderlies forced the wounded man's shoulders to the table on which he lay and pinned his arms to his sides. With others I held his uninjured leg down, so that the surgeon could treat the bleeding one. Swiftly the surgeon cut away reddened flesh and shattered bone, while the patient, his screams subsiding, fainted and lay still.

Hour after hour, as the earth beneath the tent grew red and the surgeon's apron became covered in fresh gore, the parade of hurt and dying men continued. The air reeked of ordure, flies swarmed over the living and the dead, the latter unceremoniously piled in mounds and covered in canvas for there was no one to bury them. The terrible carnage went on, the thunderous cannonade as well, until around midafternoon the guns stopped firing and we all paused to listen to the quiet.

It was not completely quiet, of course. There were still men groaning and crying out in pain, and we could hear in the distance the rattle of musketfire and the pounding of horses' hooves.

We had no real idea how the fighting was going, for the random reports that reached us contradicted one another. "We've captured the bastion," one voice shouted. "We're losing! The Russians are overrunning our lines!" another said. "The enemy is on the run!" we heard, but then we were told the Grande Armée was being beaten back and that Bonaparte was calling for the reserves.

Back and forth the messages went, all afternoon, leaving us uncertain of anything except that many, many men had been badly hurt, and that their suffering was heartrending.

At dusk I looked up and saw a tottering figure walking hesitantly toward the tent, one arm outstretched in mute appeal. His shirt and trousers were bloodstained, his face bruised and bloodied. He looked as if about to collapse.

I went out to help him, looked into his eyes and recognized Donovan.

With a cry I rushed to support him and, weeping with joy and dread, guided him in to where the surgeons were working.

"Help this man! Quickly!" I shouted, my voice hoarse and raw. "He must be saved!"

But Donovan was sinking to his knees, and I could not support his weight. With a choking sound he fell forward, his body inert, eyes shut, onto the reddened earth.

59

"NO! NO!" I cried out again and again, shaking my head in denial as orderlies lifted Donovan onto the surgeon's table and cut away his shirt to reveal his terrible wound.

"A shell," the surgeon remarked. "A shell must have exploded quite near him. There is much damage to the abdomen. It is a vital wound."

Fateful words, a vital wound. I had been hearing them all day, as the surgeon did his bloody work, and most of the men he had been speaking of had died.

Donovan's life was ebbing, and I knew it. Only a wisp of hope remained. He stank of powder, and breathed in hoarse gasps interrupted by spasms of coughing. When he coughed he brought up blood.

I handed the brandy to the surgeon and gritted my teeth when he poured it over Donovan's open wound, making him convulse and scream, his scream little more than a gurgle in his throat. I washed the blood from his face. His forehead and cheeks were scratched and scraped raw and there was a wound above his left temple.

"I had no idea you would be here," I murmured. "I didn't know you would be in danger."

"Do you know this man?" the surgeon asked me.

"Yes. He is Donovan Brown. I mean Donovan de Gautier."

"What is his regiment?"

I shook my head. "I don't know."

And of course I didn't. All I knew was that he was pledged to stopping Bonaparte, in any way possible. Today his purpose had brought him to this battlefield—and I, unwittingly, had weakened the army and very likely helped to cause his injury.

"I didn't know, my darling, I didn't realize you would be here," I whispered to him, my tears falling on his closed eyes as I bathed his face. "Please forgive me. I implore you."

The next few hours were among the most painful of my life. I wrestled within myself, now blaming myself for what had happened to Donovan, now arguing that he and I were acting toward the same end, and that he would have approved of everything I and my companions had been doing, had he known of it.

I could not bear to watch as the surgeon removed the fragments of the burst shell from his red gaping wound and cauterized the charred flesh around it with a hot iron. His belly was fearfully swollen, his face pale and thin—nearly as pale as the faces of the dead men piled like cordwood under the canvas behind the tent. I did not trust the surgeon to tell me honestly whether he expected Donovan to live. Besides, I didn't want a medical judgment—I wanted a miracle.

I held his cold hand and rubbed it between both of mine, looking down into his face. Was he asleep, or had he lost consciousness? I couldn't tell.

"He must be moved off the table so I can attend to others," the surgeon said. I looked around—and saw that Edward and Christian had entered the tent and stood quietly by.

"We'll put him in the wagon." Carefully my two companions laid Donovan on a stretcher and took him to our wagon, where I made a bed for him on the hard wooden slats under the canvas roof.

"He'll die if we don't get him indoors, near a warm fire," was Christian's observation. "I say we leave tonight, and try and find a town where we can take shelter and let him rest."

There seemed to be nothing else we could do. I wrapped Donovan as tightly as I could in what thick blankets and garments we had and lay down next to him, hoping to warm him with my body. We set off, through the detritus and confusions of the aftermath of battle, toward the northeast.

———

FOR FIVE DAYS, under a sky dark with low-lying clouds that wept chill rain, we made our way toward Moscow. At night we were offered shelter in the huts of peasants and craftsmen, ploughmen and village elders. Donovan's dreadful wound did not fester, thanks to Euphemia's healing herbs and poultices, and his lungs did not fill with thick fluid that might have choked him. We did our best to keep him warm and to dress his wound with fresh bandages.

Though he did not show any sign that he heard my words, I talked to him, telling him how swiftly he was healing and how he would soon be completely well. I told him of the outcome of the battle, how neither side had conceded defeat (for so we heard), and I recounted to him my own efforts to weaken the deadly, serpent-like French army and my resolve to do what I could to weaken Bonaparte as well.

I held his hand and talked to him, smoothing his dear brow and kissing his wounded forehead, assuring him that I would never leave him and that all would be well.

On the sixth day, toward midafternoon, we crested a low hill and came upon a remarkable sight. It was as if hundreds of huge colorful balls had been tossed down across a landscape, immense blue, red, yellow and gold balls, each set atop an imposing building. On closer view the balls proved to be the domes of churches, each with its glittering cross that caught fire from the sun's slanting rays.

I held my breath at the magnificence of the spectacle and Christian and Edward too marveled at the vast size and splendor of the Russian capital.

"How many people live here, do you think?" I asked Christian. "More than in Paris, surely."

He shook his head. "I have no idea," he said. "I have never seen any city as large as this."

"Or as empty." Euphemia's tone was quizzical, skeptical. "Where have all the people gone?"

As we drove down the hill and into the city it became more and more evident that the Muscovites had indeed departed. There were no carts or carriages, no marching soldiers, no religious processions, not even an open-air market with vegetable and flower-vendors, public letter writers and guards to keep the peace.

We passed mansions, churches, shops and squares: all empty, as if swept by a great wind that had blown everything and everyone away. Only in the poorest, oldest and shabbiest quarters, where the streets were narrow and many of the wooden houses decayed and nearly roofless, did we see a few people huddled in the shadows. Like the buildings they occupied, they were in decline, the women dressed in the cheap, dirty frills of prostitutes, the men roguish-looking and sinister.

After much searching we found our way to the Dorogomilov Bridge, where, according to instructions Scipion had given me before we left France, we expected to find the home of his friend Hagop Garabidian, an Armenian merchant long resident in the city.

Our wagon entered the wide courtyard of an imposing stone mansion and, much to our surprise, we found the courtyard full of people.

"Is this the house of the merchant Garabidian?" Christian called out in French to one of the men, who was carrying a heavy wooden box.

The man nodded, and inclined his head toward the front door of the house. Edward and Euphemia stayed with our wagon while Christian and I presented ourselves at the door, which was opened to us by the merchant himself, a nearly bald, energetic, ruddy-faced man of about fifty who ushered us into his bare salon. I told him that I was a friend of Scipion du Roure and at the mention of Scipion's name his face brightened. Yet he went on to explain that we had come at an unfortunate time, as he was just about to leave the city.

"We have all been ordered to evacuate as quickly as possible," he explained. "It is not safe for any citizen of Moscow to remain here as the French army is arriving and our military commanders have decided to retreat."

"Just as they did at Borodino," Christian commented.

"Yes. Is there not a French proverb about this course of action?" he asked with a twinkle in his eye. "Reculer pour mieux sauter? Step back in order to jump ahead further?"

"We have come from Borodino," I told our host. "We have an injured man with us who needs rest so that his wound can heal."

"Ah, then my house is yours, of course. I shall leave you the guest cottage. There is food in the cellar and firewood in the shed. The police have been confiscating all the food and fuel in the city in order to deny it to the French but they have been lax in scouring the suburbs."

Monsieur Garabidian showed us the large, spacious guest cottage and then left us to settle in, saying that he and his household would be gone by nightfall.

"I caution you, do not stay any longer than absolutely necessary," he said as he left us, brushing off our thanks with a wave of his plump beringed hand. "Moscow is a dangerous place. There is looting. Once the French come they will seize the city and cease to be disciplined men. They will become marauders."

We thanked him for the warning, and for the food and shelter.

Inside the cottage, we found that most of the furniture had been removed, but there was a table, and a number of soft pillows and a thick carpet that we spread before the hearth to make a bed for Donovan. In the cellar we found oil for lamps, meal and flour, beets and turnips, some wine and even a cask of vodka.

Edward looked around the large storage area thoughtfully. "If we must, we can take refuge here, in this cellar," he said. "Garabidian was right about the danger of looting and lawlessness. Such a fine, rich proud city, abandoned in such haste. It is an invitation to pillage. This house could be assaulted."

I shuddered at the memory of being in the cellar of Les Trois-Ilets on the night the plantation burned, how we were forced to take refuge there, until Euphemia showed us a way out. The thought was a chilling one; that night had been among the worst I ever spent.

The next morning the courtyard was deserted and we realized that the merchant and all his servants had gone. But at midday we heard the tramping of feet and the creak of carriage wheels, and knew that the remnant of the Grande Armée was beginning to arrive in the city.

All that afternoon and evening, as the noise of the incoming army continued, I felt frightened—far more frightened than I had been at Borodino. Euphemia felt the same fear.

"There is evil coming," was all she would say, but I could tell from her frown how troubled she was. Her premonitions were rarely wrong.

I could not sleep that night. I watched over Donovan, worried that Euphemia's prophetic words might concern his welfare. But he slept soundly enough, and his forehead was not hot with fever. It seemed to me that his beloved face, lit by the flickering hearth fire beside his makeshift bed, was becoming less pale with each passing day. I kissed his cheek and murmured that I loved him.

Weary of watching over him, I got up and went to the window, which looked out over the nearby bridge and ramparts. In the distance I could see patches of orange, glowing on the horizon.

Fire!

Immediately I called the others, and we all stood looking out across the city, our trepidation growing.

"It's the soldiers! They're probably making fires in the streets to warm themselves!"

"Why would they do that when there are so many vacant buildings? No, it's the cooking fires, or maybe just sparks from the flints."

"Or pipes they forgot to put out, that started fires by accident."

Everyone had an explanation, but we were all thinking the same, unthinkable thing: what if the Russian soldiers had set fire to the city after the last of the Muscovite citizens left, to ensure that the French could not benefit from its remaining stores of food and fuel? What if the fires were deliberately set?

We did not try to sleep but sat before the window, watching the widening patches of orange, dreading that before long they would merge into one continuous, all-consuming blaze and that we would have to flee for our lives. If indeed the Russians had started the fire, we wondered, weren't our French soldiers now attempting to put it out? Would they succeed?

I thought afterwards how lucky we were that Hagop Garabidian's house had not been in the crowded heart of Moscow, where the greatest concentration of old wooden houses were, and where the fire was at its most destructive, but in a spacious outlying part of the city, where the houses were of stone and there were no storehouses or arsenals to be targeted for destruction.

For the fire did indeed spread, growing wider and more all-encompassing day by day, until it engulfed most of the city. The mansion grounds where we were did not burn, though the air we breathed was full of black smoke and ash and the heat of the fire was so intense we all felt singed by it.

What I remember most was the smell. An overpoweringly strong, acrid smell that all but burned our nostrils and made us cough and drink water until our stomachs nearly burst. I have never smelled another odor like it. It was as if all the stale, decayed things of centuries were burning, along with rancid incense and the worst stinks from a gigantic kitchen full of charred meat. The stench stayed in our clothes and hair, the very taste of it lingered in my mouth even after the destructive fire had begun to die down and the once grand city of Moscow was little more than smoking embers, amid the soot-blackened domes of the stone churches.

Finally after nearly a week we noticed that the air began to clear and that at night the horizon was once again dark, with no orange flames shooting into the sky, only the steady bright light of the comet shining down over all.

I decided then that it was time to seek out Bonaparte.

60

BONAPARTE, WHEN I FOUND HIM, after many inquiries, was at an undamaged stone house near the towering fortress of the Kremlin. He was pale and distracted, a man near the end of his wits.

He was pacing back and forth behind a huge desk littered with papers. Aides and messengers came in and out of the room in a steady stream, bringing more papers and taking others away. On the desk was a goblet filled with a dark liquid—barleywater, I felt sure. It was Bonaparte's preferred remedy for hemorrhoids.

As he walked back and forth, his gait jerky and unsteady, he mumbled to himself, opening and closing his snuffbox reflexively and pausing briefly to inhale a pinch of the yellowish powder and sneeze violently into a much used purple handkerchief. As if oblivious to those around him, he hacked up phlegm, spat, and wiped his mouth with the back of one small plump hand.

"Your Imperial Highness," I began, addressing him with the formality he always demanded, but he cut me off.

"I suppose you have come about your boy."

He seemed unsurprised to see me, which in itself surprised and confused me. Did he have intelligence that I had been traveling with the army?

"Well, he isn't here just now. I sent him to Russia, you know."

Now I was thoroughly confused. "Yes," I said lamely.

"Don't worry. He's alive. I'm alive too, as you can see."

"I can tell you are in pain."

"You always could tell that."

A messenger brought him a paper and he read its few lines hurriedly, then took up a pen, dipped it in the inkpot and scratched a few words on the bottom of it, leaving dark blotches of ink on the paper and the desk before handing the paper back to the messenger.

He reached for the goblet of barleywater and drained it. Then, glowering, glaring down at the floor, he resumed his nervous, angry pacing.

"Why in the name of all the saints in heaven haven't they come to surrender?" he shouted. "They are finished. I finished them at Borodino. What are they waiting for?"

"I can't say, sire."

"That mincing Tsar Alexander, a pretty boy, a boy in a man's uniform. And that old whoremonger Kutuzov, with his one good eye and his icons—what in hell are they doing? Are their brains so addled they can't remember how to get back to Moscow?"

He stopped where he was and looked at me, a gleam in his eyes. He had had a revelation.

"They are afraid of me," he shouted. "That's it. They fear that I will annihilate them the moment they set foot in my city. It is my city now, this ruined Moscow. I will rebuild it. It will be more glorious than before."

He bawled out "Messenger!" and snatched up a paper from the desk. A boy in a guard's uniform appeared in answer to his summons. Bonaparte took up his pen and dipped it in the inkpot. But as he attempted to write, his hand shook violently and he could not form the words. Cursing, he made another attempt, dipping the pen in and out of the inkpot convulsively, making the ink fly out and spill. With a roar of frustration he flung the pen across the room and shouted at the guardsman.

"Write this down! To Tsar Alexander and his lackey Kutuzov, surrender or I shall annihilate you! The emperor of the world has spoken!"

The messenger hurriedly did as he was asked, then gave the paper to the emperor to sign. He spat on it.

"There. There is my signature!"

Knowing better than to challenge this bizarre response, the man folded the paper and left the room.

Bonaparte, his face contorted in a grimace of pain, poured more barleywater out of a pitcher and drank it.

"There are no decent physicians here," he remarked in a low tone. "Corvisart says he can do nothing more for me." Corvisart was his preferred physician, who traveled with him. "I sent him back to Smolensk, with your boy."

"Eugene is in Smolensk?"

"He left two days ago. I would have gone with him, but I must wait for the surrender."

Once again his tone changed abruptly. "It's cold in here. Bring more wood for the fire!" Servants scurried to obey, carrying in armloads of wood and heaping them on the hearth, which was already piled high with brightly burning logs. The room was uncomfortably hot, and now began growing hotter.

"I can't abide a cold room. Or a cold woman," he added in an aside, chuckling to himself. He took another pinch of snuff, hacked, spat, and wiped his spittle.

I noted that his pacing had slowed a bit. I stood quietly, afraid that if I sat, I might offend Bonaparte and trigger his anger. I wasn't sure what to do, what to say. I had not expected to find him in the state he was in, a frame of mind partly removed from reality, partly angrily engaged with it. My task, I reminded myself, was to destroy him. To put an end to his power.

I could start by undermining his confidence.

"It is being said that the Russians will not surrender. That they are preparing to offer battle in an area north of here."

It was an invention, of course, but I soon saw that it was effective. His small eyes grew keen with interest.

"No one is sure."

"I will crush them!"

"There are tales in the army that Kutuzov has a million men and a thousand cannon."

"Rubbish!" But I saw, for the briefest of moments, that his expression was fearful. "There are not a thousand cannon in all of Russia."

"He has ordered many new ones from the German armorers."

"I rule the German lands."

"You cannot control all your territories. Is it not true that your brother

Joseph has abandoned Madrid, leaving the country to be overrun by the British, and that there has been an attempt in Paris to take over your government?"

A shiver of dread passed through his restless body. I thought, he has not been sleeping. He is always at his most vulnerable then.

He shrugged, and the muscles of his cheek began to twitch involuntarily.

"Joseph is a coward. Always was. Even as a boy. I was younger but I could always beat him in a fight. He used to give up—and then drop rocks on my head during the night, when I was asleep. He was vicious."

"I know. He tried to kill me."

"I had nothing to do with that." He spoke hastily, defensively. "I told him to leave you alone." The twitching in his cheek was stronger and more frequent.

I hesitated, then became bolder.

"It doesn't matter now, because we are divorced. But I did have a lover during our marriage. Someone I adored, as I never loved you."

He gathered himself to lunge, but before he could move his face crumpled in pain, and his hands moved to his stomach.

"For God's sake, help me! Give me something, anything, to take this pain away!"

I went out into the corridor where aides and messengers stood waiting. I went up to one of them.

"I am the empress Josephine," I said. "Do you recognize me?"

"No, Your Imperial Highness."

I took a chance. I led the boy into the room where Bonaparte was now slumped into a chair, eyes shut, enduring a spasm of pain.

"Sir," I said, my voice low and cajoling, "please let me show this young man the miniature you wear."

I had a feeling he would be wearing my portrait, which had always been his good luck charm in battle. I was right. Preoccupied as he was with the sharp pain he was enduring, he made no resistance when I gently reached into his unbuttoned shirt—noticing, as I did so, that he was in dire need of a bath—and pulled out a chain. Hanging from it was a portrait of myself—from fifteen years earlier. I showed it to the boy.

Immediately he knelt and murmured, "Your Imperial Highness."

"Go quickly and find a physician. Tell him I sent you. Bring him back here with you as fast as you can. Tell him the emperor is in need of opiates. And hurry."

6 1

HALF-DRUGGED, IN CONSTANT PAIN, bloated on barleywater, Bonaparte dragged himself through his days in Moscow, keeping me beside him as his good luck charm.

I spent my days with him, and in the evening went home to Donovan and the others, safe in the cottage on Hagop Garabidian's estate. The long red wound in Donovan's belly began to knit itself together, and he opened his eyes and spoke a few words. Gradually he gained strength, and was able to sit up and talk, feed himself, and even, with the aid of a stout stick, to take a few faltering steps.

How I wished that I could spend my every waking hour with him! But Bonaparte, who had no idea Donovan was in Moscow, wanted me near him and relied on me to turn his bad luck into good. At times he was confused, and called me Marie Louise—or Marinska, his pet name for Marie Walewska—but he was in no doubt that I was the woman he wanted nearby. Sometimes he was quite lucid and knew precisely who I was.

"Josephine, my Josephine, where did I go wrong! How did I lose you! The minute I divorced you, my luck changed," he said ruefully one afternoon as he waited, fruitlessly, for a Russian delegation to appear.

"Do you know how many battles I have won, how many campaigns I have carried out to victory? Nearly fifty battles, that's how many. And a dozen campaigns or more—maybe two dozen. I leave it to the historians to keep count."

The numbers pleased him, but the fact remained that now, in the autumn of 1812, he sat in a ruined city, cheated of the satisfactions of victory, for neither Tsar Alexander nor his commander Kutuzov came to Moscow or sent replies to Bonaparte's imperious demands, and as the days grew shorter and the light paled over the ravaged city, Bonaparte sat in the dark and brooded.

"Sire, you have waited long enough for the Russian cowards to show themselves. Muster your men and lead them back to France, taking the laurels of Russia with you." It was General Berthier, Bonaparte's loyal, stalwart chief of staff who had been at his side on all his campaigns.

The emperor looked balefully at his general. "First they must acknowledge me."

"They are Asiatics, not Europeans. It is not their way." Clearly Berthier was exasperated. He looked over at me, signaling me to support him in his effort to rouse his master to action.

But I had other ideas.

"I will wait ten more days," Bonaparte replied gravely. "Perhaps their messengers are galloping toward Moscow even now, bearing the crown of the tsars as a gift for me."

"Surely, Marshal Berthier, you would not wish the emperor to return to Paris without some signal token of victory. Why, he ought to be given a coronation, right here in Moscow!"

Berthier, appalled, glared at me.

"But Your Imperial Highness," he sputtered, "a crown, a coronation— we could be here for weeks."

"Then we shall. Josephine agrees with me, don't you my dear?"

"Of course. Your judgment is always best."

"But Your Imperial Highness, there is no food left in Moscow!"

He was wrong about that. We had food, in Hagop Garabidian's cellar, though it was beginning to run out.

"There are food stores in Smolensk. Prince Eugene has been sent to look after them."

Berthier was adamant. "If we stay here any longer, we will not only starve—we will freeze. Already the men are making bonfires in the streets at night, burning furniture from the great houses to stay warm!

You cannot spend the winter here in Moscow. It is far, far colder than Paris at its worst."

But all Bonaparte would say was, "I cannot return to France without the crown of the tsars." He drank his barleywater and held out his wine glass to me, watching as I poured half a dozen precious drops of the liquid opiate into it, the remedy that gave him relief from his terrible stomach pains. Before long he was drowsing, and then he fell asleep.

Day by day Bonaparte's most trusted aides came to him to make the same argument as Berthier. They urged him to be sensible, to spare his men, to hurry back to France and then return in the following spring to consolidate his Russian victory. They urged, pleaded, cajoled, begged. They tried to remove me forcibly from his side, accusing me of treason.

But the emperor held onto my arm with a grip of iron, and would not let me be moved. "She is my good luck charm. Without her I am nothing," he repeated, and the fear in his eyes was unmistakable. When late at night he sank into a deep, drugged sleep Edward came to the mansion and escorted me home, his size and strength intimidating to those who had become my declared enemies.

I was determined to keep Bonaparte in Moscow until the first snow fell.

As Berthier and the others repeated endlessly, the army could not march far in freezing weather. Certainly not as far as Smolensk, nearly two hundred and fifty miles away.

Yet in his half-mad state Bonaparte continued to be opposed to leaving, and all I had to do was reinforce this reckless, heedless attitude in him until it was too late—too late for him to save what remained of his army from destruction, and himself from ruin.

For that is what I saw ahead: his ruin. The destruction of the demon that sent the fer-de-lance. All I had to do was stiffen his resolve, convince him that I was his protection against failure, and wait for the season to change.

THE FIRST SNOW of the fierce Russian winter fell with the gentleness of rose petals, the light, spinning flakes drifting through the chill air to land lightly on the frozen earth.

Within hours the air was a white veil, thick with sparkling, starlike shapes that piled into mounds and drifts, obscuring houses, trees, wagons, people. The raw whiteness became a shroud, then a choking, suffocating blanket of cold that tore at the skin and made the lungs hurt and the throat ache with pain.

Overnight the snow turned to ice, gleaming like crystal and with the sharp edges of broken glass, ice that made boots and hooves slip and glide, ice that broke into pointed shards and formed itself into long, heavy spears that fell from roofs onto people and animals below.

With the snow came wind, a frigid, whirling wind that numbed cheeks, hands, feet and made it impossible to see one's way, wind that tore through bone and blotted out all sound.

Into the snow and wind walked the Grande Armée, on the day Bonaparte finally decided to abandon Moscow.

"I am leaving," Bonaparte announced on that morning, standing at the window of his study and watching the snow pile into drifts in the courtyard below. "Perhaps the tsar and his generals are waiting for us at Smolensk." He turned to me.

"There is only room in the carriage for myself and Berthier. You will have to find your way back as best you can."

I left him and returned to the cottage by the Dorogomilov bridge where I found Edward and Euphemia wrapped in their warmest garments and Donovan, wrapped warmly and leaning heavily on his stick, helping them to load our wagon with the remaining food from the cellar. Before long Christian arrived, followed by two Asiatic-looking men laden with piles of furs.

"Would you believe there is still a marketplace in this godforsaken city?" he called out to us. "Look! I have found us fur coats and hats, and boots lined with sealskin. The kind the men who live in the frozen lands wear."

"This is the frozen land, as far as I can tell," Euphemia said. "I'll take one of those coats."

"I had to give them one of your diamond necklaces in exchange," Christian whispered to me, indicating the men with the garments. "But it was worth the sacrifice. These furs may save our lives."

We bundled ourselves in the warm thick skins and pulled the outlandish hats down around our ears. Then, wrapping our poor horse in a blanket and fastening one of my wool scarves around his mouth, we set off to join the long procession of marching men, cavalry, carts, and wagons that was making its way out of the city toward the south.

62

I WAS SO COLD.

It was all I could think of, how cold I was.

Despite the fur coat, hat and boots Christian had bought for me, and the many layers of skirts and petticoats that I had put on, I could not stop shivering, and my teeth chattered constantly. I nestled down beside Donovan, but found no warmth there; he was as cold as I was.

We attempted to follow the wagon in front of us, but it was very hard to see what was ahead, so thick was the falling snow and so blinding the whiteness all around. We felt very much alone, enveloped in the swarming snowflakes that turned everything we could discern to indistinct mounds of white.

On and on we went, hour after hour, desperately cold and, eventually, quite hungry. But when the light failed and we stopped for the night, our bellies growling, the pitiful fire we managed to start kept sputtering, nearly going out. Edward gathered damp tree branches from under the snow and, by lining the wagon with them, kept us from turning to icicles. We hovered inside the cave of branches, our breaths steaming, our teeth still chattering. We did not freeze.

But a fire, we discovered, can freeze if the air is cold enough, and ours provided barely enough warmth to melt our teapot full of snow. At least we had some half-brewed tea, which tasted very good and kept our stomachs from growling for a short time.

Our turnips and beets were frozen, our flour had melded itself into frigid clumps and had Edward not found some dead birds, their small bodies still faintly warm, we would have had to go to sleep hungry. We skinned and half-boiled the birds, ate them ravenously, and lay down to sleep.

In the morning all was as it had been the day before: an all-enveloping whiteness, snow clouds that obscured the sun and fierce cold. We started ahead, but had not gone far before we began to see soldiers on the road—not living soldiers, but frozen ones, lying along the roadway, half covered in the newly fallen snow. Some looked as if they had fallen asleep, their faces peaceful, others stared open-eyed, open-mouthed into a vacant emptiness.

They were beyond help. We crossed ourselves hurriedly and went on, trying not to think, soon we will be like them, dead by the roadside.

"Damn Bonaparte!" I shouted. "I hope he dies too!" But I knew he was in a warm carriage, not an open wagon like ours, with every luxury, even his favorite silk-lined boots, boots he wore in order to protect the beautiful soft feet he was so proud of. And even as I cursed him, I realized, I had played an important part in keeping him in Moscow. I had played on his overweening pride, his jealousy, his physical weaknesses, to prevent him from leaving. And now I was looking at the result.

Yet as I stared at the frozen soldiers, I imagined I could hear what Orgulon would say—what Euphemia did say—that the evil Bonaparte had loosed upon the world must be destroyed, and that we were witnessing its destruction. It was a lesser evil, brought about to prevent a greater one.

I buried my face in Donovan's comforting shoulder and cried.

Fighting the cold, rubbing my arms again and again in an effort to bring some warmth back into them, tensing my muscles against the onslaughts of the merciless wind, I felt myself grow very tired. I was numb in mind and body both. I looked at my companions, ice-covered, frostbitten, and felt oddly detached from them. I could not feel the care and concern I normally felt. I was too sunken in my own wretchedness.

We spoke little to one another. It was all we could do to carry out our necessary tasks. We had no energy to spare in looking out for anyone but ourselves. I felt a dreadful aloneness. I could not even bring myself to pray, beyond repeating the words, Our Father, Our Father, again and again, until they were an all but meaningless buzz in my ears, a small sound pitted against the vast silence.

Then there came a day of sun, and thaw.

Not all the snow melted, of course, there were only droplets that melted, and then small rivulets at our feet, and, by midday, streams that appeared from nowhere at the verges of the emerging muddy roadway.

The pale, weak sun felt warm and I lifted my face to its rays.

We were able to make a real, hot fire for the first time in days. Euphemia concocted a broth from our flour and vegetables and we had a meal of sorts, though we burned our mouths on the hot soup, we were so eager to drink it. We laughed—how long had it been since we had laughed! We smiled at each other. Donovan and I embraced, lovingly.

Then we heard the hoofbeats.

From a distance came riders, not riders in the blue jackets of cuirassiers or the grey-blue greatcoats of lancers, but the brown skins and furs of Cossacks!

"Get back!" Donovan called out, indicating that Euphemia and I should get behind the men, who were drawing their muskets. Euphemia obeyed him at once.

"I can fire that," I said confidently, taking up one of the guns. "My father taught me when I was a girl."

"Here." Donovan handed me the cane knife he always carried. "Use this if you have to."

There were four riders, far more fleet, despite the snow and mud of the road, than our plodding horsedrawn wagon. Donovan and Edward wounded two of the men, who veered away, but that left two others, who continued to bear down on us, whipping their big, strong-looking horses, yelling at the top of their lungs, long curved sabers drawn.

I began throwing things out of the wagon, the carpets we had been sleeping on, our bronze teapot and cooking pot, our few personal possessions and last of all, my precious jewelry box.

The box landed on a patch of ice and the priceless rubies, emeralds and sapphires spilled out, sparkling in the wintry sunlight as if lit from within by tiny fires.

Forgetting us, the men reined in their horses and, jumping quickly down, began to scoop up the gems.

Christian shot one of the men in the chest and Edward and Donovan ran toward the other, falling on him and shouting. There was a scuffle, more shouting, and the Cossack went down under the blows from the butt of Edward's musket.

"Gather everything, quickly, before the others return." We did as Donovan said and had the presence of mind to search the two Cossacks and the saddlebags of their horses. We found no food, but gold coins and half a dozen men's wedding rings, presumably taken from previous victims. We resumed our way forward, muskets reloaded and ourselves vigilant. I kept my jewelry box near at hand.

We saw no more Cossacks that day, but we did see horrid sights: our own cold and desperate men, plundering the bodies of their frozen comrades, and even taking food from the arms of the dying. Women, camp followers, abandoned by the roadside, sitting in desolate clusters. Broken drums, discarded breastplates, regimental banners dropped into the snow and never retrieved. Crows feasting on bodies of fallen men and horses. In the distance, at night, we heard the mournful howling of wolves.

When I peered into the desolate whiteness during our long, hungry days my eyes burned. I blinked again and again but the burning persisted. The buzzing in my ears continued as well, and my poor black stumps of teeth throbbed. I felt a thousand tiny daggers being thrust into my gums, and a thousand more being thrust into my temples, whenever my headaches struck. Euphemia, who had her own aches and torments, rubbed my head and sang to me, but between the cold and my empty belly I was at times so miserable I wanted nothing more than to give up the struggle to live.

There came a day when we had no food, nothing to give our poor thin horse and the very air seemed made of ice. This is over, I thought. This is the end. We cannot go on.

My eyelids drooped. I was shivering uncontrollably. I tried to think but my mind was awhirl in confusion. Dizzy, I lay down and sank toward sleep.

Whether it was a dream or an apparition, or whether I opened my eyes and saw what I thought I saw I will never know. Before me were men in torn blue uniforms, their bleeding feet wrapped in thin cloths, the blood seeping out and staining the cloths red, their faces wrapped in ice-stiffened beards, their hands empty. They shuffled past me with heads bowed, following one another in an endless procession, defenseless against the blowing snow.

I saw them, or thought I did, and with a twitch and jerk of my muscles I opened my mouth to scream.

But then I felt Donovan shaking me, telling me to wake up, and I thought, I don't want to leave him. I felt his touch, and my eyes opened, and I tried with all my force to stay awake.

63

THE SLEIGHS WERE COVERED IN BELLS that jangled noisily. They came swiftly toward us, gliding with ease on their sharp runners over the snow and ice on the road, the horses' hooves swathed in thick felt to prevent them from slipping.

We counted three, then four, and finally six sleighs altogether, the last of them to reach us stopping so that those riding in them could hand out baskets and packages to the soldiers. Incredibly, we were given cheese and salt fish, coarse hard bread and brandy and hay for our horse.

"Provisions from Prince Eugene, by order of His Imperial Highness the Emperor!" shouted the occupants of the sleighs as they handed out their bounty.

We did our best to shout our joy, though our voices were hoarse, our throats scratched raw.

"Prince Eugene!" I called out to the man nearest me. "Is he with you?"

"No, madame, he is in Smolensk."

"I am his mother. We are in need of his help."

My words were greeted by an astonished silence. Then, all at once, the men in the sleigh jumped down and reached out to me, Donovan, Christian and the others, inviting us all to join them, offering us space to sit and spreading soft warm fur rugs over us and handing us the first fully cooked food we had eaten in many days, our cheese and salt fish and coarse bread given out to others.

Many of the starving soldiers of the Grande Armée were fed that day as well, though their number had dwindled a great deal and some, too ill to eat, had to be abandoned by the roadside. Eugene had sent as much food as he could from the storehouses at Smolensk, our new companions told us, but the storehouses had been raided by the Russians and much of the food he had expected to find there was gone, along with all the live animals and reserve supplies of materiél.

We were taken to Smolensk and the journey went quickly, as there were fresh post horses every fifteen miles (how very different from the stretch of road we had traveled in such cold and weariness!) and the sleigh seemed to fly rather than skim and bounce over the frozen ground. Once there, Eugene had us lodged in the palace he was using as his headquarters.

He embraced me joyfully and I wept on his strong shoulder. We talked for hours, about the campaign, about Bonaparte and his erratic behavior, and his stubbornness in refusing to leave Moscow until it was too late to avoid the snow and ice. I said nothing to Eugene about my own private mission, of course; I let him think that I had come east in search of Donovan. That made sense to him, and I let the matter rest.

"We have a long journey yet before us," he said at length, suddenly grim, and looking far older than his thirty-one years. "The army cannot hope to reach France for six weeks at least, and I pray we find the supplies we need in Minsk, as there are none left here.

"I'm sending you and your party southward," he went on, addressing me, "to Milan, where my family is, by way of Kiev and Budapest. You will have all the provisions you need and, of course, a full military escort. Augusta and the children will be very glad to receive you in Milan, and you can stay as long as you like."

"Thank you, dear Eugene. I only wish you could come with us."

"My men need me," was all he would say—and all he needed to say, for I could tell how strong was the bond between my son and the men he led. My pride in him was great, though all I had to do was look at him to feel a pang of guilt. I had helped to destroy that which meant so much to him. He belonged to Bonaparte almost as much as he belonged to me. The fate of the Grande Armée was bound to wound him, and that could not be helped.

Three weeks later we were in Milan, where the air was balmy—at least it felt balmy to me—and the gardens were still green. I was able to spend Christmas with my grandchildren, and I patronized all the toymakers in Milan, or so it seemed, in buying dolls and toy soldiers, miniature horses on wheels and stuffed dogs and bears, not to mention the trunks of small gowns I ordered for my little namesake Josephine and her sister Eugénie, suits of purple velvet for Eugene's only son Auguste, and a layette trimmed in gold lace for the baby Amélie, just a few months old.

The children embraced me and kissed me, they sat on my lap and fed me bonbons, they took my hands and pulled me out into the garden to play blind-man's-bluff. I ran across the brittle grass and chased them, and they shrieked with laughter and went to hide in the summer-house. We played tag in the wintry afternoon light, and Augusta, my loving daughter-in-law, chided me gently for tiring myself out.

For in truth I was panting, and my chest hurt from a cough I could not seem to recover from. I told myself the cough would go away in time, and tried to ignore the look of concern in Augusta's kind eyes. When Hortense arrived from St.-Leu with her boys the temptation to overstrain myself with the children grew greater. Donovan joined in, teaching the handsome Napoleon-Louis, who was nine years old and very rambunctious, to box and daring me to ride with him and the boy though the January winds were cold and I had to put on my Russian furs to keep warm.

I was foolish, I admit. But oh how I needed family around me just then, after all that I had been through. They seemed very precious to me, those new Bonapartes with their open faces and small open hands, reaching for grandma. They would not know want, or fear. No revolution would come to darken their lives or threaten them. They would always live amid prosperity and affection, or so I fervently hoped as I hugged them to me, knowing full well that I could not predict their futures, no matter how often I told their fortunes.

We lingered in Milan for months, doing our best to ignore the war alarums that reached us from Austria and the German lands. Edward left us to return to his regiment, but Christian stayed, at my request, as I had grown quite dependent on him and we were fond of one another. Donovan and I were closer than we had ever been, walking arm in arm in the afternoons like an old married couple, family life flowing around us like a balm. I taught Josephine and Eugénie to embroider, and in the spring I planted ferns and palms and sugar cane in the gardens of the palace, telling the children about how I had grown up in the midst of high cane fields that always smelled sweet. We played card games and shopped for fine Milanese silks, and I did my best to fill my days with enjoyable pastimes, ignoring the weariness that nagged at me and the dark thoughts that sometimes pushed their way up through even the happiest of hours.

Euphemia watched me closely, and read the changes in my expression and mood.

"Is it your ears again, or your teeth?" she said, handing me a goblet of orangeflower water, my sovereign remedy.

I had to smile. I could not keep anything from her.

"Both," I said. My ears buzzed dreadfully at times, as though all the cannon from the Russian battlefields were going off inside my head. And when that happened, my poor stumps of teeth felt the vibration from the buzz in my ears and began to ache.

"If only we were back home I would get some nightingales' tongues and crush them into a powder and feed them to you in a mango root on the night of the full moon. Then you would get better."

"And what of your sore knees, Euphemia? What would you do for them?"

"Walk more. Sit in the sun. Visit the quimboiseurs in the marketplace."

Neither of us spoke Orgulon's name, but we often alluded to him, and remembered him.

One clear evening, just at dusk, I took the children out into the garden to show them the night sky. I wanted them to see Orgulon's comet, the great light he had sent to guide me and protect me. But when I looked up into the vastness of the darkening sky I saw only the faint glow of sunset light, and the first bright stars. The great comet had faded, and was no more.

64

THE MILANESE WERE GETTING RESTLESS; our enclave of peace and security was about to be taken away.

We were living in Eugene's palace, and Eugene was Viceroy of Italy, the representative of French power, of Bonaparte's power. But Bonaparte's power was crumbling. One by one the realms he had conquered were breaking free, and the Milanese too wanted their freedom.

I knew the signs of rebellion all too well: the bells clanging furiously at all hours of the night, the angry crowds massing in the streets, the additional guards being brought in to protect the palace. Austrian troops were threatening to invade from the north and would soon be swarming into the lands Eugene governed—though Eugene himself was absent. He was still far away, somewhere in the German territories or in France, we didn't know for sure. Wherever he was, he was at Bonaparte's side, as always, leading the French troops into battle, and ultimately losing, for it was clear that Bonaparte's regime was very nearly at an end.

Soon we would have to leave Milan, but where were we to go? I sent Hortense and her boys back to St.-Leu, and Augusta and her children went south, to a villa near Naples, out of the way of the rioting and fighting.

A messenger arrived at the palace, Prince Tchernichev, sent to me by

Tsar Alexander. Christian ushered him into the room where I was waiting for him and left us together.

The prince wore the white uniform and green-plumed hat of an officer in the imperial guard. A tall, regal man with silver-blond hair, he had the air of one who had spent all his life in beautifully appointed drawing rooms, his every wish gratified by respectful servants. He spoke French with the practiced ease all Russian aristocrats seemed to command. I received him seated on a sofa, dressed in many yards of pale pink silk, artfully arranged, my dyed hair in a youthful upswept style, my mouth closed to hide my painful stumps of teeth.

The prince came up to me, bowed, and kissed my hand.

"Your Imperial Highness, I have been sent by my tsar on a matter of the utmost urgency."

"Yes, go on."

"The armies of Tsar Alexander have overrun the Confederation of the Rhine and will soon invade France. Our Austrian allies will be in Milan within a few days. You must leave at once. Once the Milanese are liberated, they will not spare the palace—or anyone in it."

Try as I might to remain poised, I felt a shiver of fear at these words. I remembered only too well the massacres in Paris during the Revolution, the bloodstained walls of the Tuileries Palace when Bonaparte and I moved in.

"His Imperial Majesty the tsar has asked me to offer you, in his name and at his invitation, the Goncharow Palace in St. Petersburg. You may stay there as long as you like, as his guest. A full staff of servants and all needed furnishings will be supplied, and His Imperial Majesty will be offering you a substantial pension."

He bowed once again, and I allowed his words to hang in the air, unanswered. We needed a refuge—but to return to Russia! I could not imagine it.

"His Majesty is very kind, and very generous. I will consider his offer."

"I urge you, before deciding, to keep in mind what you would face should you decide to leave Milan for France. In France there is nothing but chaos and want. All the banks are failing. People are desperate to leave. There are food shortages, riots, lawlessness on every side. The new king, when he comes to power, will not command the loyalty of his subjects without the support of Russian soldiers. For some time to come, France will be a Russian country!"

"I believe Emperor Napoleon has not yet been dethroned."

"He soon will be. When that day comes, you do not want to be in France, but in Russia."

I thanked the prince and went up to my suite of rooms, and out onto the stone terrace that overlooked the lake. I thought of my old house at Malmaison, and wondered who was caring for the lake there, and what had happened to my black swans and my lovely blue water lilies. My eyes filled with tears, and I realized that I was grieving, not only for the swans and the water lilies and my beautiful home, but for all the days and nights that I had spent there, sometimes in hope, often in dread.

No more, no more! I cried out inside. Give me peace now, peace and safety and hope. But where is it to be found? Where is the one place on earth that I can retreat to, where the world cannot find me and force me to live, not as I choose, but as others dictate?

I went to find Donovan. He was packing his trunk, preparing for a journey. For a moment I felt fear: was he leaving me again, on one of his secret errands? But his smile and quick kiss reassured me.

"What did the Russian have to say?"

"He offered me a palace in St. Petersburg, with servants and a pension."

"And what did you say?"

"I said I would consider it—but I was only being polite. I could never go back to Russia. Not after all that happened there. I nearly lost you there."

He stopped what he was doing and took both my hands in his, looking into my eyes.

"Yeyette, why don't we go back to Martinique? We can put all this behind us, all this turmoil, all our sad memories. I want to leave behind all that is dark and doomed. I still own my plantation there, Bonne Fortune. Before I left I put Jules-sans-nez in charge, with a good crew of freed slaves. I told him that if he could sell enough cane at a high enough price to make a profit, I would give him half the land. Let's go and see if he's succeeded."

I felt a glow at his words. Martinique! My old home! I grinned. "Euphemia would be delighted," I said.

"And you, my love? Would it delight you, my empress?" I fell into his arms, overjoyed and relieved. "Yes, yes," I said again and again, my voice so choked that I coughed, and for a time, could not stop coughing, so that Euphemia had to give me the strong syrup that made me sleepy.

I went to my room to lie down, asking Donovan to convey my regrets to Prince Tchernichev and his imperial master and to say that I felt I must decline their generous offer. He sat on the bed beside me.

"It is settled then," Donovan said, suddenly brisk in his tone. "We'll leave tomorrow for Genoa. I know I can find an English ship captain there who will take us to Lisbon, and from Lisbon we can probably go on to Bristol, and from there to Martinique."

"Donovan," I said sleepily, "before we go, I would like to visit Malmaison one last time."

"Are you sure? It is so far out of our way."

"I want to see my black swans again," I told him, my voice trailing off as I drowsed.

"Very well, if you must. I will write to Clodia, and tell her to get the house ready for us."

His words roused me.

"Clodia! My scheming, talebearing little maid from years ago?"

"The same. I sent her to Martinique to get her out of the way, as she was causing so much trouble for us. I made her my housekeeper at Bonne Fortune. She has been quite happy there. She married and has a family of her own now."

"And all this time I thought you had her killed!"

Donovan shook his head in wonderment. "What you must think of me! How could you imagine that?"

"She disappeared. When Bonaparte made people disappear, it always meant they were dead. I got used to expecting that. Forgive me."

"It was my fault. I should have told you."

I wanted, at that moment, to remark that life is full of mysteries, but I was too tired. I let my eyelids droop and heard the soft tread of Donovan's boots on the tile floor as he quietly left the room.

65

WE HAVE COME BACK TO MALMAISON, and I am to meet the king in twelve days.

Twelve days in which to have my new pink crepe gown made, and learn the etiquette of the new court, and find better medicine for this terrible cough which goes on and on and gives me sharp pains in my chest and throat.

We had not intended to stay so long here in Malmaison, but Donovan's old wound has been plaguing him again and I have been overwhelmed with guests and uninvited visitors eager to gape at the former empress and I confess that I am overtired at times by all that has happened in recent months.

The Russians have taken over Paris, as Prince Tchernichev told me they would, and Bonaparte has been forced to abdicate and the new king, Louis XVIII, has come to the throne.

All Paris is agape at the spectacle of a new court and a new monarch— even though the monarch is not very regal. I have seen him from a distance, and he is very fat, and pompous, and quite ridiculous. He limps from gout and they say his toenails are so long he has to have special shoes made.

What will I say to him, when we meet? My voice is soft and scratchy and he is said to be hard of hearing, as he is nearly sixty years old.

If we get along I may invite him to my fete, to celebrate my birthday next month. (That is, if we have not yet left for Martinique.) I will be fifty-one years old, as Euphemia never ceases to remind me. She says I am trying to do too much, but in truth I am enjoying myself, despite the weariness that overtakes me from time to time. There are so many people to see, old friends like Fanny de Beauharnais, who has proclaimed herself Louis XVIII's most loyal subject, and Juliette Récamier and the Prince de Salm, and old enemies like Bellilotte, once Bonaparte's mistress, who has become my friend, and Laure de Girardin, my first husband's mistress, on whom I conferred a pension years ago and is grateful to me, and the haughty Duchesse de La Rochefoucauld, who now curtseys to me on her ancient bony knees and pretends that she always served me with a good grace. Poor Marie Louise is long gone from Paris; she left with her son and returned to her family in Austria. They say that she was relieved to go.

I confess that I am basking in all the attention, even though the most energetic of my guests wear me out with their longwinded talk and their demands that I use my influence with the new king to acquire court appointments for them. I am being used, of course; that was to be expected.

I am eager to go to Martinique, yet I want to linger here at Malmaison, at least until I have met the king. I imagine that he will offer me a place at his court, some sort of position created just for me. I am not a relative of the royal family but I was once empress, after all, and that is no mean thing. (My husband's name is never mentioned, needless to say. But then, he was a usurper, pure and simple, whereas I am a French aristocrat by birth, and my father served at the court of the new king's grandfather Louis XV.)

Scipion has come to stay here at Malmaison, and he has promised to escort me to the Tuileries to meet the king. He arrived nearly a week ago, after Eugene sent for him. Eugene is worried about me. He frowns when he looks at me and says I am much too thin and my face is too red. He tries to convince me to eat more but I am not hungry, I am too excited about all that is going on.

Eugene is just a worrier, my doctors agree with me about that. Though I do notice that I am not sleeping well and that my nerves are so on edge that the least sound unnerves me. At times I imagine that I hear soldiers tramping into the courtyard, and then I sit up in bed and cry out, and Euphemia comes and soothes me.

Soldiers! The very thought frightens me. I wonder, will this new king Louis lead France into war again, and will we ever be free of the fear of battle? We will never be free of soldiers, of that I am sure, not even on Martinique. But as they say on that beloved, green island, we are all in the hands of fate, and now, as I wait for my fate to take a new turning, I look ahead with eagerness to the bright future.

EPILOGUE BY SCIPION DU ROURE

I FEEL IT IS MY SAD TASK to take up Yeyette's tale and tell the end of her story. Euphemia knew her longer and better than I did, but she is too lost in grief to put down any words, and Donovan, poor, broken man, is beside himself with sorrow.

Like a bright candle, my Yeyette burned herself out. In her last weeks she was quite dazzling, attending balls where Tsar Alexander honored her and danced with her, taking tea with the King of Prussia, entertaining guests at Malmaison, reading and answering letters sent to her each day from people who asked for her help. From a distance she looked like a quite young woman. It was only when one came close that the lines on her face and the shadows in her tired eyes showed her age. She moved with the grace of a younger woman, only she could not seem to stop moving. She would not pause, or rest, and she was in too much of a hurry.

We all tried to convince her to rest, and all three of the doctors Hortense brought from Paris ordered her to eat more and to drink sleeping draughts. But it was no use. I saw that. I knew her well. She lost the languor she had always possessed, and when I saw that that quality in her was gone, I knew that she could not last long.

She had so hoped to meet the king, but two days before we were to go together to the Tuileries palace she began sneezing and her cough grew much worse. Her poor body itched from a terrible rash (she called it, for some reason, "the revenge of the Bonapartes" and laughed about it) and within hours she was struggling for breath.

We all gathered around her bedside, Hortense and Eugene, Euphemia, Donovan and I, and her devoted servant Christian. There were many others who wanted to see her, but we kept them away, even the tsar, though we allowed his physician to examine her.

She embraced us warmly at the end, but could not speak. I saw that she was trying to, and imagined that the word she was trying to say was "love."

Among the papers she left behind in her final days was one I shall never forget. She wrote, "Part of me has always walked through this world as a stranger, bearing a gift I have never understood. I pass through, my tasks accomplished. I leave behind a whiff of mystery, a sweet scent that comes from a far place. Remember me."

A NOTE TO THE READER

Like my previous novels, *The Hidden Diary of Marie Antoinette* and *The Last Wife of Henry VIII*, *The Secret Life of Josephine* is a historical entertainment, not a historical novel. In it I tell Josephine's story in her own words and through her own lens of perception—fictionally imagined, and fictionally embellished. Readers eager to know more about the historical Josephine will find her life described in my biography of her.

The historical Josephine never went to Russia, never had a lover named Donovan, never (so far as is recorded) delivered a baby in the midst of a slave rebellion. But she was a very venal army contractor, and she did suffer terribly from migraines. And she did have many lovers, among them a younger man named Hippolyte Charles to whom she was lastingly attached.

Having written many biographies and histories, and several pseudonymous novels, I have turned very happily to historical entertainments as a way of blending fact and whimsy. Many thanks to my kind readers who have responded to this somewhat frothy mix with enthusiasm.

ML

ERICKSON Erickson, Carolly,
1943-

The secret life of
Josephine.

DATE			